"Engrossing!" —*Publishers Weekly*

"Gritty!" —*RT Book Reviews*

**Praise for the Goodreads-nominated
and *Romantic Times* award-winning
Elemental Assassin series**

BLACK WIDOW

"Everything that I adore about this series is right here and more so in *Black Widow*. There's expertly crafted fights, banter, and suspense that continued to keep me on the edge of my seat. I can't recommend this book enough and love being on the roller-coaster ride that is Gin Blanco's life."

—*All Things Urban Fantasy*

"*Black Widow* is crazy good and Gin Blanco is still one of the best-written heroines in urban fantasy. I was riveted from beginning to end."

—*Fiction Vixen*

POISON PROMISE

"An extraordinary series . . . One of the most intriguing heroines in the genre."

—*RT Book Reviews* (Top Pick!)

"A knockout . . . Lots of vividly depicted battles, a high body-count, and high-octane escapes worthy of a James Bond movie keep the pages turning."

—*Booklist*

"A quick-moving plot and characters that jump off the page . . . Estep finely balances a confident tough-edged personality with an inner life filled with doubts and emotions, making Gin a surprisingly down-to-earth heroine whom readers will root for."

TH

"By virtue of her enorm
series fresh and unputdow

"Made me fall in love with Gin all over again."

—*All Things Urban Fantasy*

HEART OF VENOM

"Amazing . . . Estep is one of those rare authors who excels at both action set pieces and layered character development."

—*RT Book Reviews* (Top Pick!)

"Action-packed with tons of character growth . . . One of the best books in the series, which says a lot because Estep's writing rarely, if ever, disappoints."

—*Fall Into Books*

DEADLY STING

"Classic Estep with breathtaking thrills, coolly executed fights, and a punch of humor, which all add up to unbeatable entertainment!"

—*RT Book Reviews* (Top Pick!)

"I've been hooked on this series from the first word of the first book. I can't get enough."

—*Fiction Vixen*

WIDOW'S WEB

"Estep has found the perfect recipe for combining kick-butt action and high-stakes danger with emotional resonance."

—*RT Book Reviews* (Top Pick!)

"Filled with such emotional and physical intensity that it leaves you happily exhausted by the end."

—*All Things Urban Fantasy*

BY A THREAD

"Filled with butt-kicking action, insidious danger, and a heroine with her own unique moral code, this thrilling story is top-notch. Brava!"

—*RT Book Reviews* (Top Pick!)

"Gin is stronger than ever, and this series shows no signs of losing steam."

—*Fiction Vixen*

SPIDER'S REVENGE

"Explosive . . . Hang on, this is one smackdown you won't want to miss!"   —*RT Book Reviews* (Top Pick!)

"A whirlwind of tension, intrigue, and mind-blowing action that leaves your heart pounding."   —*Smexy Books*

TANGLED THREADS

"Interesting story lines, alluring world, and fascinating characters. That is what I've come to expect from Estep's series."
—*Yummy Men and Kick Ass Chicks*

VENOM

"Estep has really hit her stride with this gritty and compelling series . . . Brisk pacing and knife-edged danger make this an exciting page-turner."   —*RT Book Reviews* (Top Pick!)

"Gin is a compelling and complicated character whose story is only made better by the lovable band of merry misfits she calls her family."   —*Fresh Fiction*

WEB OF LIES

"Hard-edged and compelling . . . Gin Blanco is a fascinatingly pragmatic character, whose intricate layers are just beginning to unravel."   —*RT Book Reviews*

SPIDER'S BITE

"The series [has] plenty of bite . . . Kudos to Estep for the knife-edged suspense!"   —*RT Book Reviews*

"Fast pace, clever dialogue, and an intriguing heroine."
—*Library Journal*

JENNIFER ESTEP

Spider's
TRAP

AN ELEMENTAL ASSASSIN BOOK

POCKET BOOKS

New York   London   Toronto   Sydney   New Delhi

Pocket Books
An Imprint of Simon & Schuster, Inc.
1230 Avenue of the Americas
New York, NY 10020

This book is a work of fiction. Any references to historical events, real people, or real places are used fictitiously. Other names, characters, places, and events are products of the author's imagination, and any resemblance to actual events or places or persons, living or dead, is entirely coincidental.

First Pocket Books paperback edition August 2015

POCKET and colophon are registered trademarks of Simon & Schuster, Inc.

For information about special discounts for bulk purchases, please contact Simon & Schuster Special Sales at 1-866-506-1949 or business@simonandschuster.com.

The Simon & Schuster Speakers Bureau can bring authors to your live event. For more information or to book an event, contact the Simon & Schuster Speakers Bureau at 1-866-248-3049 or visit our website at www.simonspeakers.com.

Manufactured in the United States of America

10 9 8 7 6 5 4 3 2 1

ISBN 978-1-5011-0517-3
ISBN 978-1-5011-0518-0 (ebook)

To my mom, my grandma, and Andre—
for your love, patience, and everything else
you've given me over the years

ACKNOWLEDGMENTS

Once again, my heartfelt thanks go out to all the folks who help turn my words into a book.

Thanks go to my agent, Annelise Robey, and my editors, Adam Wilson and Lauren McKenna, for all their helpful advice, support, and encouragement. Thanks also to Trey Bidinger.

Thanks to Tony Mauro for designing another terrific cover, and thanks to Louise Burke, Lisa Litwack, and everyone else at Pocket and Simon & Schuster for their work on the cover, the book, and the series.

And finally, a big thanks to all the readers. Knowing that folks read and enjoy my books is truly humbling, and I'm glad that you are all enjoying Gin and her adventures.

I appreciate you all more than you will ever know.

Happy reading!

❊ 1 ❊

"I really want to stab someone right now."

Silvio Sanchez, my personal assistant, glanced at me. "I would advise against that," he murmured. "It might send the wrong message."

"Yeah," Phillip Kincaid chimed in. "Namely that you've reverted back to your deadly assassin ways and are going to start killing people again instead of hearing them out like you're supposed to."

"I never really left those ways behind," I replied. "Considering that I could kill everyone here and sleep like a baby tonight."

Phillip snickered, while Silvio rolled his eyes.

The three of us were sitting at a conference table that had been dragged out onto the deck of the *Delta Queen*, the luxe riverboat casino that Phillip owned. Normally, slot machines, poker tables, and roulette wheels would have been set up on the deck in preparation for the night's gambling, but today the riverboat was serving as a meeting spot for some of Ashland's many underworld bosses.

Supposedly, this meeting was to be a peaceful mediation of a dispute between Dimitri Barkov and Luiz Ramos, two of the city's crime lords, who were disagreeing about who had the right to buy a series of coin laundries to, well, launder the money that they made from their gambling operations. Not that there was anything peaceful about the way Dimitri and Luiz had been standing nose-to-nose and screaming at each other for the last five minutes. Their respective guards stood behind them, fists clenched tightly and shooting dirty looks at each other, as though they would all love nothing more than to start brawling in the middle of the deck.

Now, *that* would be entertaining. I grinned. Maybe I should let them have at each other, gladiator-style. Winner take all. That would be one way to settle things.

Silvio nudged me with his elbow, as if he knew exactly what I was thinking. "Pay attention. You're supposed to be listening to the facts so you can be fair and impartial, remember?"

"I could be fair and impartial in stabbing them both."

He gave me a chiding look.

I sighed. "You always ruin my fun."

"That's my job," the vampire replied.

I palmed the silverstone knife hidden up my sleeve— the only weapon I'd brought on board—and flashed it at my friends under the table, out of sight of the bosses and their men.

"C'mon," I whispered. "Just let me stab one of them. Surely that will shut the other one up too."

Phillip snickered again, while Silvio let out a small, sad sigh. He wasn't crazy about my managerial style. Couldn't imagine why.

"I thought we agreed that you wouldn't bring any knives on board," Silvio murmured again. "So as not to send the wrong message."

"I left the other four in the car. So I'm only a fifth as deadly today. That's progress, right?" I waggled my eyebrows.

Silvio narrowed his gray eyes and held out his hand below the table. I reluctantly passed over the weapon, and he tucked it up his sleeve. I pouted a little, but he ignored me. He was getting good at that.

My friends turned their attention back to Dimitri and Luiz, who were still yelling and pointing their fingers at each other, each man trying to shout the other one down. But instead of listening to them, I glanced at the third boss who had shown up: Lorelei Parker.

Unlike Dimitri and Luiz, who were both dressed in business suits, Lorelei was sporting black stiletto boots, dark jeans, and a long-sleeved T-shirt, just like I was. The only real difference between us was that her leather jacket was a bright royal blue, and mine was a subdued midnight black. Her black hair was pulled back into a French braid, and her blue eyes were focused on her phone, since she was busy texting. The quick motions of her fingers made a silverstone rune ring glitter on her right hand—a rose wrapped in thorns dripping blood, all of it outlined in impressive diamonds.

Of the three bosses, Lorelei was the most intriguing, since she was a smuggler known far and wide for her ability to get anything for anyone at any time. Cash, guns, precious jewels, and pricey antiques were just a few of the things she was rumored to dabble in.

Only a single guard stood off to her side. Jack Corbin, her right-hand man. He too was dressed in boots, jeans, and a black leather jacket, but his blue eyes continuously scanned the deck and everyone and everything on it.

Corbin realized that I was watching him and tipped his head at me, before smoothing back his dark brown hair. Then he sidled a little closer to his boss, ready to protect her from everyone on deck, including me. I nodded back at him. My deceased mentor, Fletcher Lane, had a thick file on Corbin in his office, so I knew that he was far more dangerous than he appeared to be.

Then again, so was I.

Lorelei was here because she owned the coin laundries in question and was more than willing to sell them—to the highest bidder, of course. I didn't know if she'd approached Dimitri and Luiz about buying the front businesses or if they'd come to her, and I hadn't had the chance to ask any questions, since the gangsters had been screaming at each other the entire six minutes I'd been on the riverboat. Either way, the men just couldn't agree on who was getting what, and things had escalated to the point where Dimitri and Luiz were about to declare war on each other. That would mean shootings, stabbings, kneecappings, and lots of other messy crimes.

Don't get me wrong. As the Spider, I'd made plenty of bloody messes in my time. It was sort of my specialty.

But a few weeks ago, I'd taken down Madeline Magda Monroe, an acid elemental who'd declared herself the new queen of the Ashland underworld, following in the footsteps of her mother, Mab.

Just as I had killed her mother several months earlier, I took out Madeline with my Ice and Stone magic, and with no more Monroes left to grapple for control of the underworld, the other bosses had made me their de facto leader. At least until they started plotting how they could murder me and one of them could seize the throne they all coveted so very much.

I almost wished that one of them would succeed in putting me out of my misery.

Contrary to popular belief, being the head of the Ashland underworld was not a bed of roses. It wasn't even a bed of thorns. It was just a giant *headache*—like the one throbbing in my temples right now.

I'd thought I'd been a popular target over the summer, but now the bosses sought me out more than ever before. And they actually wanted to *talk* to me. *Incessantly*. About business deals and treaties and who was letting their gang members spray-paint rune graffiti in someone else's territory. As if I actually *cared* about any of those things. But as the big boss, it was apparently my job to listen. At least according to Silvio.

Lorelei was the one who'd requested this meeting, although she'd actually approached Phillip about settling the dispute instead of me. Apparently, Lorelei didn't want to acknowledge my new authority or involve me in her affairs. That, or she just hated me for some reason. Didn't much matter either way, since I cared as little about her as she did about me.

But Phillip was my friend, and he'd told me about the

get-together. So here I was, about to mediate my first big dispute as Gin Blanco, the Spider, new queen of the Ashland underworld. Yeah, me.

Still, I would have been perfectly happy to skip the polite nonsense of the meeting and let Dimitri and Luiz duke it out until one of them killed the other, but Silvio had pointed out that if I resolved their feud today, they wouldn't show up at my restaurant, the Pork Pit, tomorrow. Since I didn't want the criminals scaring my customers, I'd decided to be a good boss and put in an appearance.

Everyone had been sitting at the conference table when I walked on board with Silvio. But at the sight of me, Dimitri and Luiz had shot to their feet and started shouting accusations at each other, as if they thought that I would side with whoever yelled the loudest and the longest.

Now Dimitri was cursing at Luiz in Russian, and Luiz was returning the favor in Spanish. Since it didn't look like they were going to stop anytime soon, not even to take a breath, I tuned them out as best I could and stared out over the brass railing.

The Aneirin River flowed by the white riverboat, the swift current causing the vessel to sway ever so slightly. The November sun glinted off the surface of the blue-gray water, making it sparkle like a sheet of diamonds, while a faint breeze brought the smell of fish along with it. My nose wrinkled at the wet stench. A few crimson and burnt-orange leaves clung to the trees that lined the far side of the river, although the breeze would soon send them spiraling down to the ground—

Something flashed in the trees directly across from me.

I frowned, leaned to the side, and focused on that spot. Sure enough, a second later, a small gleam of light caught my eye, the sun reflecting off something hidden back in the trees—

Silvio nudged me with his elbow again, and I realized that Dimitri and Luiz had stopped shouting and were staring at me with expectant faces, their arms crossed over their chests. Behind them, their guards wore similarly hostile expressions.

"Well, Blanco?" Dimitri demanded in a low, gravelly voice. "What's your decision?"

"Yeah," Luiz chimed in, his tone much higher. "Who gets the laundries?"

I looked back and forth between the two of them. "Um . . ."

Dimitri frowned, and anger sparked in his dark brown eyes. "You weren't even listening to us!"

"Well, it was kind of hard to follow," I admitted. "Especially since I don't speak Russian, and my Spanish is rudimentary, at best."

Dimitri threw his hands up in the air and spewed out more Russian words, all of which sounded like curses.

Phillip leaned over. "I think he just insulted your mother."

I groaned, but I held my hands up, trying to placate the mobster. "Okay, okay. That's enough. Stop. Please."

Dimitri finished his cursing, but he still gave me a disgusted look. "I knew this would be a waste of time. I should have just killed Lorelei and taken the laundries. Just like I should have put a bullet in your head the night of Madeline's party and taken control of the underworld myself. Just like I should do right now."

Silence descended over the deck, and the only sound was the steady rush of the river flowing by the boat.

I laid my hands flat on the table, then slowly got to my feet. The scraping of my chair against the wood was as loud as a machine gun.

I stared at Dimitri. "That was exactly the wrong thing to say."

Everyone could hear the chill in my words and see the ice in my wintry-gray eyes.

Dimitri swallowed, knowing he'd made a mistake, but he wasn't about to back down in front of everyone, so he raised his chin and squared his shoulders. "I don't think so. There's only one of you. I have three men with me."

I smiled, but there was no warmth in my expression. "That's because you need guards. I don't. I never have. So if I were you, I'd start apologizing to me. Pronto."

Dimitri wet his lips. "Or else?"

I shrugged. "Or else your men will be dragging what's left of you off this boat, and Phillip will be sending me the cleaning bill."

Dimitri sucked in a breath, but anger stained his cheeks a bloody red. "Nobody threatens me."

"Oh, sugar," I drawled. "It's not a threat."

Dimitri kept staring at me, his breath puffing out of his open mouth like a bull about to charge. Beside me, Phillip and Silvio got to their feet and moved out of my way.

"Try to show a little restraint," Silvio whispered as he passed.

Restraint wasn't a popular word in my vocabulary, but I nodded, acknowledging his point. If I killed Dimitri and Luiz, it would just convince the other bosses that I wanted them all dead, and they would probably start trying to murder me again. I'd fought hard for my relative peace and quiet, and I wasn't going to throw it away on a couple of minor mobsters.

Even if I did feel like stabbing both of them. Violently. Viciously. Repeatedly.

Phillip and Silvio stepped over to where Lorelei Parker was still sitting at the far end of the table. Lorelei had quit texting and was staring at me, but she remained in her seat, with Jack Corbin standing by her side. The two of them weren't dumb enough to take me on, at least not face-to-face, but the same couldn't be said for the other bosses.

He wasn't brave enough to fight me on his own, so he turned to Luiz. "You help me with Blanco, and I'll let you have the coin laundries. All of them."

Luiz scoffed. "I want the laundries *and* that deli you own on Carver Street."

He sighed and nodded.

I rolled my eyes. A minute ago, they would have been happy to murder each other, and now they were going to work together to try to kill me. Well, at least Luiz had the good sense to try to squeeze everything he could out of the other gangster. Had to admire him for that. Even if he'd picked the wrong side.

Dimitri and Luiz shook hands, sealing their hasty deal, and then they both faced me, with their guards standing behind them, cracking their knuckles in anticipation of the beat-down they thought they were going to give me. Fools.

"Now what are you going to do?" Dimitri sneered. "Against all of us?"

"Me? I'm finally going to have some *fun*. I certainly deserve it, after listening to you two whine like a couple of kids fighting over the same ice-cream cone."

My insult was the last straw. Dimitri's cheeks burned even hotter, and he stabbed his finger at me.

"Get her!" he roared.

"Kill Blanco!" Luiz yelled.

The two bosses and their guards surged toward me, with Dimitri leaning over the table and reaching out with his hands, as though he wanted to strangle me to death.

I kicked my foot into the table leg, making the whole thing slam forward, right into the Russian's potbelly. He gasped and bent over double, causing his very bad, very obvious, very shaggy black toupee to almost slide off his head.

But I was already moving on to the next threat. Since I didn't have any knives, I leaned down, snatched up the chair I'd been sitting in, and slammed it into the head of the closest guard. He yelped and staggered away, clasping his hands over his bloody broken nose. He lurched past Silvio, who stuck out his foot and tripped him. The giant's head hit the top part of the railing, and the brass let out a loud, pealing note, ringing like a bell. The giant slumped to the deck unconscious. *Ding*. Down for the count already.

Silvio flashed me a thumbs-up. I grinned back, then turned to fight the next guard.

Phillip had made sure that no one boarded the riverboat armed, so I wasn't worried about getting shot. Even if someone had managed to sneak in a gun or a knife, I could always use my Stone magic to harden my skin and protect myself from any bullets or blades.

Using the same chair, I took out two more guards, opening up cuts and bruises on their faces, necks, and arms. By the time I got done with those giants, the plastic seat had cracked apart, so I ripped two of the metal legs off the chair and swung them around like batons.

Whack-whack-whack-whack.

I slammed the metal poles into every guard I could reach, cracking the chair legs into knees and throats and temples and groins. Moans and groans blasted out like foghorns across the deck, and more than a little blood arced through the air and spattered onto the glossy white wood and gleaming brass rails.

"Restraint!" Silvio called out after I jabbed the end of one of the poles into the face of the closest giant. "Restraint, please, Gin!"

"What?" I yelled back. "I'm not killing them . . . yet!"

At my words, the giant I'd been fighting froze, his fists drawn back to punch me. But he took my warning seriously; instead of hitting me, he whirled around and made a beeline for the gangplank on the other side of the boat. I let him go, since he was the last guard standing. The others were huddled on the deck, trying to find the strength to hoist themselves upright and will their eyes to stop spinning around in their heads.

"You!" Dimitri bellowed, having finally recovered his breath. He shoved his toupee back where it belonged. "I'm going to kill you if it's the last thing I do!"

With a loud roar, he charged at me. I dropped the

chair legs that I had used against the guards and simply squatted down. Then, when he was right on top of me, I surged up and tossed him back and over the side of the railing.

"Ahhh!" Dimitri screamed on the way down.

Splash!

Footsteps pounded on the deck, and I spotted Luiz rushing at me. So I squatted down again quickly, and then, when he was right on top of me, I pulled the same move and sent him overboard too.

Another loud scream, another satisfying *splash!*

I scanned the deck, but there were no more enemies to fight. So I looked at Lorelei Parker and Jack Corbin, who were in the same positions as before.

"You two don't want to join in the fun?" I drawled, picking up the metal chair legs and twirling them around in my hands. "I was just getting warmed up."

Lorelei let out a disgusted snort, while Corbin held up his hands and stepped back.

Faint cries sounded—"Help! Help! Help!"—and I strode over to the railing. Phillip and Silvio followed and stood on either side of me, and we all looked down.

Dimitri and Luiz were clinging to each other in the river, both of them thrashing around and trying to stay afloat by drowning each other. Dimitri had somehow held on to to his toupee, which he was now beating against Luiz's face. They both looked like the wet, slimy rats they were.

I grinned at Phillip. "You were absolutely right. Throwing people overboard is *tons* of fun. I feel better already."

"Told you so," Phillip said in a smug voice, his blue eyes bright with mischief and merriment.

Silvio sighed. "Don't encourage her."

More moans and groans came from the fallen giants on the deck. I tossed my metal poles aside, turned around, and leaned back against the railing. All the guards stopped and looked at me, wondering what I was going to do next.

"So," I called out, jerking my thumb over my shoulder. "Anyone else want to go for a swim?"

Strangely enough, no one took me up on my offer.

✴ 2 ✴

The guards staggered to their feet, shuffled over to the railing, threw down a couple of ropes and life rings, and fished their waterlogged bosses out of the river.

Silvio took hold of one end of the conference table that I'd kicked into Dimitri's stomach and scooted it back into place.

"What are you doing?"

The lean vampire pulled a silk handkerchief out of the pocket of his gray suit jacket and began wiping the splattered blood off the table. "The meeting's not over yet. You haven't decided who gets the coin laundries."

"Seriously?"

Silvio continued cleaning the table. "We can always reschedule it for another day . . ."

"Oh, no. Uh-uh. No way am I wasting any more time on these two schmucks."

He gave me a pointed look. "Now or later. Your choice."

"Fine," I grumbled. "Let's get this over with."

"There's no need to be all hasty," Phillip drawled, still leaning against the railing. "After all, Dimitri and Luiz need some time to dry off."

I looked over at the two gangsters, who were now sprawled faceup on the deck, panting and shivering from their forced swim, with water seeping out of their clothes and shoes and sluicing all over the wood. A few feet away, Dimitri's black toupee lay in a puddle all by itself.

I watched as Silvio righted each of the overturned chairs and slid them back under the table. Except, of course, for the one I'd used to take down all the guards. That demolished chair was a lost cause, just like this sham of a meeting.

"Besides," Phillip continued, "no underworld get-together is complete without violence and refreshments. We've already had one, so we might as well enjoy the other. So sit, relax, admire the view, have a drink. Trust me, alcohol always makes these shindigs much more tolerable."

"Sometimes I think that you and Finn were twins separated at birth."

Finnegan Lane was Fletcher's son and my foster brother. He'd wanted to come to the meeting to witness the fireworks between Dimitri and Luiz but had to wine and dine some rich new client instead, since he was an investment banker. Like Phillip, Finn thought that a stiff drink, a slick suit, and a smarmy smile could solve almost all of the world's problems and was determined to prove himself right.

Phillip sniffed and ran his hand over his golden hair, which was pulled back into its usual ponytail. "Nonsense. We could not possibly be twins, since I'm much more handsome than Lane could ever *dream* of being."

"Which is exactly what Finn would say, if he were talking about you."

Phillip grinned, then waved his hand and signaled one of his own guards.

The giant nodded back, turned, and opened a pair of double doors that led into the riverboat's interior. A minute later, a team of waiters wearing black pants and shirts topped with red satin tuxedo vests streamed through the doors. A gold pin glimmered on each vest—a dollar sign superimposed over an outline of the *Delta Queen*, Phillip's not-so-subtle rune for his riverboat casino and all the wads of cash it made him.

A female waiter brought me a new chair, while another moved around the table, taking drink orders from me, Phillip, Silvio, and Lorelei Parker and Jack Corbin, who were once again situated at the far end of the table. I requested a gin and tonic and told the waiter to keep them coming. He flashed me a sly smile, then headed over to take Dimitri's and Luiz's orders, since the bosses had finally hoisted themselves to their feet. A few other waiters hovered around the two men, wrapping blankets around their soggy shoulders, before passing out bandages and bags of ice to the guards I'd beaten down.

The waitstaff finished Silvio's wipe-down of the conference table and mopped up all the puddles of water. Once everything was pristine again, they disappeared back inside. Two of Phillip's guards rolled a wet bar out onto the deck, and a woman moved behind it and started mixing our drinks. The waitstaff reappeared, carrying silver platters piled high with food, which they deposited on the table.

Fresh fruits, gourmet cheeses, dainty desserts, even a tray of butter crackers shaped like miniature riverboats. My mouth watered, and my stomach rumbled.

"Nice spread, Philly," I said.

He saluted me with his glass of Scotch. "What can I say? Gustav does good work."

Gustav was the *Delta Queen*'s head chef. I'd never actually met him, but we had a bit of a competition going on when it came to our cooking, especially since Phillip came to the Pork Pit for lunch at least once a week. He ate at my restaurant because we were buddies, and he was best friends with Owen Grayson, my lover. But he also enjoyed my home cooking, which confounded Gustav to no end, according to Phillip. The classically trained chef didn't appreciate the culinary arts of barbecue and deep-fried Southern comfort food the way I did.

But I wasn't above eating someone else's food, especially Gustav's, which was truly delectable, so I grabbed one of the bite-size cheesecakes. The pumpkin filling was a thick, sweet burst of flavor in my mouth, while the graham-cracker crust had just the right amount of cinnamon crunch. The dark chocolate ganache drizzled on top added a perfect finishing note of decadent richness.

After I had downed several of those, I gobbled up some miniature apple and cherry pies, which were divine combinations of golden flaky crust, warm fruit filling, and airy dollops of vanilla whipped cream, all of it dusted with powdered sugar.

While the rest of us ate, Dimitri and Luiz dried off and trudged back over to the conference table. The Russian had taken the time to wring out his black toupee and plop the damp rat's nest back on top of his bald head, although it kept threatening to slide off with every move he made. Luiz stood shivering, his chin tucked into the blanket wrapped around his shoulders. He looked resigned.

Dimitri, however, still had some fire left in him, despite his chilly dunk in the river. The Russian threw off his blanket, slapped his hands down onto the table, and opened his mouth. But I fixed him with a stony stare and held up my index finger, and he bit back whatever threat he'd been about to deliver.

"This is what's going to happen next," I said. "I am going to sit here and enjoy this lovely spread that Phillip has so graciously provided. Then, if you're lucky, I will listen while you and Mr. Ramos calmly, rationally, and very *quietly* tell me why each of you thinks that he deserves the coin laundries. Are we clear?"

Dimitri opened his mouth again, but whatever he saw in my face made him swallow down his protests. "We're clear."

"Good. Let me enjoy another round, and then we'll begin."

Dimitri didn't like it, but he sat down across from me at the table, with Luiz taking the chair next to him. In between bites and booze, the two bosses alternately glared at each other and at me, shooting an angry glance at Phillip every once in a while for good measure.

At the opposite end of the table, Lorelei resumed texting, ignoring all the drama. She noticed me staring at her, scowled, and turned sideways in her seat to face the other way.

I didn't know why Lorelei was so disdainful of me. Sure, she'd sent some of her men to kill me, just like most of the other bosses had, and no doubt she was disappointed that I was still alive, despite her best efforts to the contrary. But we'd never had any direct conflicts or confrontations. Then again, if Lorelei Parker wanted to hate me, that was her problem. *Take a number, sugar, and get in line.* I had a long list of enemies, and one more didn't bother me in the slightest.

I polished off my gin and tonic and the last of the delicious desserts, and everyone pushed their nibbles aside. The waiters came around and freshened up everyone's drinks. When they had finished and moved away, I gestured at Dimitri, indicating that he could finally begin his spiel. Dimitri huffed at how long I'd made him wait, but he got to his feet, fluffed up his damp toupee, and began his long-winded rant about the coin laundries.

I tried to pay attention to him. Really, I did. But his speech quickly dissolved into a string of petulant pronouncements, claiming that he deserved the laundries just because he was Dimitri Barkov and he thought he was a badass. Yeah, even Luiz rolled his eyes at that, but he was smart enough to keep quiet. Or maybe Luiz thought that he could win the laundries simply by being the person who annoyed me less.

He might be right about that. I didn't see any other reason to give one man the businesses over the other.

But Dimitri plowed ahead full steam with his rant, oblivious to the fact that I wasn't listening to him. Neither was anyone else. Phillip was sipping his Scotch and watching a group of ducks swim across the river, while Silvio discreetly tapped away on his phone under the table, just like Lorelei. Even Dimitri's own guards looked far more interested in their food and drinks than in their boss's grandstanding.

Everyone's collective boredom, including my own, was probably the only reason I noticed the waiter.

He wore the same uniform all the other waitstaff did—black pants, black shirt, red tuxedo vest. But instead of coming out through the double doors like the rest of the staff had, he emerged from a walkway that wrapped around the side of the boat facing the river. Still, he might not have caught my eye at all if the sun hadn't reflected off the silver bucket he was carrying and flashed a bright spot in my eyes. I winced and blinked away the resulting stars.

The waiter placed the bucket on a serving stand next to the railing, about five feet away from where I was sitting at the end of the conference table. A bottle of champagne was nestled in a mound of ice inside the bucket.

The waiter left the bucket behind and fell in step with the others, grabbing the now-empty food platters and passing them off to other staff members, who whisked the trays across the deck, through the double doors, and out of sight. But he made no move to go back over and actually do anything with the champagne. Strange. You'd think that he would have opened the bottle first thing to start serving it while the other waiters replenished the food.

Another thought struck me. Nobody had ordered champagne when the first waiter had gone around, and everybody still had a full glass in hand, since our drinks had just been topped off. Now, Phillip could be playing the part of the gracious host and have asked that the bubbly be brought out in case anyone wanted it. But I'd never heard him give that order either.

Finn often told me that I was completely, utterly, insanely paranoid, but so many people had tried to kill me over the past several months that I thought my constant worry was more than warranted. I wasn't a superhero, but my Spider sense was definitely tingling right now.

I focused on the waiter, but he didn't do anything suspicious, and when the table was covered with food again, he took up a position by the railing, right next to the champagne bucket. He seemed as bored as everyone else, since Dimitri was still going strong with his speechifying, but something about the waiter wasn't quite right.

So I kept staring at him, trying to figure out what it was. He was average-looking, with sandy hair, brown eyes, and a medium build. Nothing about him really stood out at all. No distinguishing marks, no scars, no tattoos. He blended in perfectly with the other waiters, and he could have been a piece of furniture for all the attention he attracted.

All the traits of a perfect assassin.

I'd spent years being just as forgettable. Just another waiter, just another worker, just another bland, polite face in the crowd at some of the most lavish parties in Ashland. Sure, I might have actually been hired and served as a waiter, but what I'd really been doing was conducting reconnaissance on potential targets and scoping out security systems at some of the city's finest homes.

But if this guy was an assassin, and he was here to kill someone, then where was his weapon? I didn't see a gun outlined anywhere on his body. He could have a revolver or a knife tucked against the small of his back or strapped to his ankle, but it would be hard to get to a weapon in those spots, whip it out, and kill someone with it. Especially if I was his target. I could easily blast him with magic before he grabbed his gun or got close enough to stab me with a knife.

But the guy didn't make any moves toward me. He wasn't even looking at me. Instead, he stood by the railing, with one hand resting on the rim of the silver champagne bucket, and ogled Lorelei Parker, even though she was ignoring everyone and still texting.

"Gin?" Silvio whispered. "Is something wrong?"

He pointedly dropped his gaze to my lap. I looked down to find that my hands were clenched into fists so tight that I could feel my fingers pressing into the scars embedded in my palms—two small circles, each one surrounded by eight thin rays. A spider rune, the symbol for patience. My own personal mark, in more ways than one.

I relaxed my grip, then frowned. Because it wasn't my Spider sense tingling so much as it was the silverstone that made up my spider rune scars. The metal was itching and burning in a way that only meant one thing: someone here was using elemental magic.

I looked around the deck. Silvio had vetted everyone who was going to be here today, including Dimitri, Luiz, and their guards, and none of them had any kind of magic. Of course, someone could have been hiding their ability, but the vampire was nothing if not thorough. If anyone here had ever used magic out in public where other people could see it, Silvio would have found out about it.

One of Phillip's waiters or guards could be using magic, but I was familiar with them, given my frequent trips to the riverboat, and I didn't see anyone I didn't know from previous visits.

Except for the mystery waiter.

I studied him again, but his dark eyes didn't glow with magic, and no sparks of Fire or needles of Ice formed on his fingertips from where he might be reaching for some sort of elemental power.

So I focused on the feel of the magic itself. It wasn't the hot burn of Fire, the cold frost of Ice, or even the gusty breeze of Air. Instead, the power felt most similar to my own rock-hard Stone magic, although it wasn't exactly the same.

I scanned the deck again, but Dimitri was *still* talking, and everyone was as bored as before. My gaze latched back onto the waiter, and I finally realized what was wrong about him.

He wasn't wearing a gold riverboat rune pin on his vest like all the other waiters were.

Most folks in Ashland used some sort of rune to symbolize their businesses, their magic, or even their family ties. So did underworld figures like Phillip, but he and all the others kept a tight watch on their runes—whether they were fashioned into pins or rings or whatever—and especially on who was wearing them. Phillip and the other bosses wouldn't let just anyone sport their runes. No, in order to wear the symbol, you had to actually be part of the crew and loyal to the head honcho.

Black pants and a matching shirt would have been easy enough to get. So would a red tuxedo vest. But the gold riverboat rune pin was the one thing a would-be assassin wouldn't be able to pick up at the store the day he decided to impersonate a *Delta Queen* waiter, slip on board, and try to kill someone.

No, not someone. Me. The Spider.

"Stay here until I get back," I murmured to Silvio. "Don't let anyone leave."

"Back? Where are you—"

"I can't believe it!" Dimitri's loud voice cut him off. "You're not listening to me! Again!"

Dimitri threw his hands up into the air and started cursing at me in Russian again. Everyone else turned their attention to him, amused by his tirade, but I kept staring at the mystery waiter.

The man realized that I was looking at him, and he stared back, his eyes widening as he thought about what to do. He gave me a tight smile, then quickly looked away, focusing on Dimitri, even as he started shifting on his feet. He was trying to remain calm, but nervous beads of sweat slid down the side of his face, despite the cool November breeze. The waiter wouldn't be hovering so close and suddenly so tense at my watching him if I wasn't his intended target.

I surged up out of my seat, and he turned and ran.

He raced across the deck and onto the walkway that ran the length of the riverboat. I took the most direct route after him, leaping up into my chair and then on top of the table. I sprinted straight across the table, knocking off the remaining platters of food, turning over drinks, and generally making a mess. Surprised shouts rose up behind me, but I focused on jumping off the table and chasing after the waiter.

Guilty people always run. I should know. I'm almost always one of them.

But the fake waiter had a head start, and he was moving fast. He flung open a door and ran through a glassed-in viewing room that overlooked the river, then shoved through the opposite door and kept on booking it toward the back of the boat.

Luckily, he left the doors open for me, and I was able to make up a few precious seconds on him.

But it wasn't enough.

As I left the viewing room behind, the guy climbed up onto the brass railing at the very back of the riverboat, right next to the enormous white paddle wheel that loomed up over all six decks. Instead of looking back to see how close I was, he launched himself over the side in a perfect swan dive.

Splash!

The waiter cut through the surface of the water with all the grace of an Olympic high diver, and barely a ripple showed where he had landed in the river. Impressive. I skidded to a stop and leaned over the railing.

The guy surfaced and started swimming toward the

opposite shore as fast as he could. I started to hook my leg over the railing so I could dive in after him—

Crack!

Crack! Crack!

Crack!

Bullets *ping*ed off the railing, making me duck down behind the brass bars. I immediately reached for my Stone magic, using it to make my skin as hard as marble, even as I summoned up a cold, silvery ball of Ice magic in my right hand. I was one of the rare folks who were gifted in not one but two elements, and I was deadly in both of them. I peered through the gaps in the railing, searching for a target to blast with my Ice power.

But no more bullets zipped through the air toward me.

Five seconds passed, then ten, then twenty.

And still, no more gunfire.

At the thirty-second mark, I let go of my Ice power, although I still kept my skin impenetrable with my Stone magic in case the sniper was trying to lull me into a false sense of security. Then I straightened back up and looked out over the water.

By this point, the fake waiter had reached the shallows and was busy shoving through cattails. I cursed, because there was no way I could catch him now. So I waited, wondering if the sniper might show himself. Whoever had been firing at me was too smart for that, unfortunately.

But he wasn't too smart to peer at me through his binoculars again.

It was the same telltale flash of glass I'd noticed earlier on the main deck and one that I was all too familiar with, since I'd often used binoculars to spy on potential targets.

I frowned, wondering why the guy would be content just to stare at me when I was standing upright, giving him what looked like a clear, easy shot.

But the sun kept winking off the binocular lenses, and no more bullets zeroed in on me. Across the river, the fake waiter finally slogged out of the shallows and scrambled up onto the riverbank. A few seconds later, he vanished into the trees.

So why was the sniper still training his lenses on me? He should have been hightailing it out of here with his buddy, not sticking around to watch the aftermath.

Unless . . . this wasn't the aftermath he was waiting for.

I thought of the way the waiter had clutched the rim of the silver champagne bucket earlier. He might have escaped, but that bucket was still sitting there, right where he'd left it.

A horrible suspicion occurred to me. I'd wondered where the waiter's weapon was, but maybe he hadn't carried a weapon at all. Maybe he'd had something even more powerful and far more deadly, something that he'd purposefully left behind on the riverboat.

A bomb.

❄ 3 ❄

I turned and sprinted back the way I'd come, heading for the front of the boat.

Silvio and Phillip appeared at the far end of the walk-way, no doubt drawn by the sound of the gunshots and coming to help me, but it was too late for that.

It might be too late for all of us.

I waved at them. "Get back! Get everyone off the main deck! There's a bomb!"

Silvio must have heard me with his enhanced vampiric hearing, because he yanked on Phillip's arm, and they both whipped around and hurried back to the main deck, vanishing from my line of sight.

Screams and shouts rose up from that area, although they were too garbled to understand. All I could really hear was the heavy *thump-thump-thump-thump* of my boots on the deck and the roar of my own heart beating like a bass drum in my ears. I ran as fast as I could, but with every step, I worried that I was going to be too late to save my friends. Because that telltale flash of glass still gleamed in the woods across the river, and I expected the sniper to remotely trigger the bomb at any second.

That's what I would have done, anyway.

But the sniper must have had other ideas, because no explosion ripped through the air. No fire flashed, and no smoke boiled up into the sky. So I kept running. I didn't know why the bomb hadn't gone off yet, but I was going to use every extra second I got.

That was the only way we were going to survive this.

I raced back out onto the main deck to find that the meeting had dissolved into complete and utter chaos. Silvio and Phillip were yelling for everyone to get off the riverboat, with Phillip standing by the open double doors, trying to usher his staff to safety.

Across the deck, a logjam had formed at the top of the gangplank, with Dimitri, Luiz, and their respective guards scrambling to disembark first. Silvio was there too, shouting at them to go down the gangplank two at a time in an orderly fashion, but the thin vampire was no match for the giants, and he bounced off their tall, broad bodies like a tennis ball being whacked first one way, then back the other. No one was listening to him, and no one was getting off the boat.

Phillip ran over, grabbed hold of the closest giant, and flipped him over the railing and down into the river. Phillip's likely mix of giant and dwarven blood gave him more than enough strength to wade into the crowd, shove Dimitri, Luiz, and their men out of the way, and give Silvio some much-needed breathing room.

And create a perfect opening for Lorelei Parker to escape.

Lorelei was no match for the giants' strength, so she stuck her boot out, tripping one of them as he ran past her. The giant yelled and stumbled forward, knocking down two other men in front of him, like trees crashing together in the forest, and creating a clear path to safety. Lorelei leaped onto the fallen giant's back, hopscotched over the other two men, and made it to the gangplank as easy as you please. Even I had to admire her sneaky, effective technique. Corbin followed her down the gangplank, and the two of them disappeared from view.

I scanned the rest of the area. The conference table had been tipped over onto its side, with all the serving platters lying around it, the elegant displays of food littering the deck like garbage. Chairs had been overturned, glasses had shattered, and everything was a mess.

Except for the champagne bucket.

It remained untouched, sitting on that serving stand beside the railing right where the fake waiter had left it, shining like a bright silver beacon amid all the trampled food, dented platters, and upended furniture.

I rushed over to the bucket and clawed through the ice. I checked to make sure that there was just liquid in the champagne bottle, then threw it aside. The bottle shattered on the deck, the golden liquid inside hissing, fizzing, and bubbling like acid. It reminded me of Madeline's horrible magic. I flinched and kept searching through the ice.

Finally, just when I thought that I was wrong and there wasn't a bomb hidden inside, my hand closed around something small, square, and metal in the bottom of the bucket. Still holding on to my Stone magic to protect myself from any potential blast, I yanked the object out of the dark depths, wondering all the while why the sniper, the watcher, hadn't blown up the bomb already—and me along with it.

Or maybe he'd just been waiting for me to pick it up to ensure maximum damage to yours truly.

The thought made me flinch again, tense up, and reach for even more of my Stone magic. But the device still didn't explode, so I took a few precious seconds to examine it. I didn't know as much about bombs as Finn did, but it was a simple metal box with a cell phone duct-taped to the top to serve as the trigger. No doubt some sort of explosives had been packed into the container, but the box was still a lot heavier than it should have been. I gave it a gentle shake, and several items rattled around inside. They almost sounded like . . . nails, loose nails that would create deadly shrapnel the second the bomb exploded.

But even worse was the magic that coated the box.

Now that I was actually holding the bomb in my hands, I could identify the type of magic that had been used to make it: metal.

The cold, hard sensation pulsing off the box was eerily similar to my own Stone power. The only real difference was that this magic felt a bit more malleable than mine, just as metal could be shaped more easily than stone. A metal elemental had infused his magic into the box—a very strong one, judging from how much power rippled through the surface.

I looked over my shoulder, hoping that Phillip and Silvio had gotten everyone off the boat. But they were still struggling with Dimitri, Luiz, and their guards, with the *Delta Queen* waiters and other staff members also yelling, pushing, shoving, and trying to get to the gangplank.

I didn't know how powerful the bomb was or what the blast radius might be, but the watcher could blow it at any second, and I didn't want innocent people getting hurt in the explosion. I needed to get it away from the riverboat too, just to be sure that the blast didn't punch a hole in the side that would sink the vessel, taking anyone else who might still be inside or below deck down with it. My mind whirred and whirred, trying to think of the best way to contain the blast as much as possible, since I had no time to disarm the bomb—

Beep.

As if hearing my frantic thoughts, the cell phone lit up, confirming my fear that the watcher could detonate the bomb anytime he wanted. I wrapped my arms around the box, reached for even more of my Stone magic, and braced myself for detonation—

Nothing happened.

I glanced down and realized that a clock had appeared on the phone screen. Thirty seconds and counting down.

There was no more time, so I did the only thing I could think of.

Bomb still clutched in my arms, I hoisted myself up onto the railing, then leaped off the side of the riverboat into the cold depths of the Aneirin River below.

*   *   *

My legs churned and churned through the air for what felt like an eternity, although it couldn't have been more than a couple of seconds, and I hit the water with a loud *splash!*

The rough, jarring force of the impact almost tore the bomb out of my hands, but I managed to hang on to it. Instead of kicking toward the surface, I let the swift current drag me under, even as I counted off the seconds in my head.

Twenty-five . . . twenty-four . . . twenty-three . . .

The water was dark and murky, and I could barely make out the bomb. I didn't know if just being dunked in the river was enough to short out the phone and stop the explosion, but I was going to make sure that the bomb would do as little harm as possible.

There was no time to be subtle, so I reached for my Stone magic again. Normally, I used my power to harden my skin or make my hands as tough and heavy as cement blocks. This time, I coated the box with my power, hoping that my Stone magic would weigh it down and send it straight to the bottom of the river. The bright silvery glow of my magic cut through the darkness, clearly illuminating the countdown clock on the phone.

Fifteen . . . fourteen . . . thirteen . . .

My power easily covered the box, and once I had that first layer of Stone magic on top of it, I quickly coated it with several more, sending out surge after surge of magic. All the while, I kept ticking off the precious seconds in my mind.

Ten . . . nine . . . eight . . .

I'd done as much as I could to dampen the explosion.

I was out of air and almost out of time, so I dropped the bomb, letting it sink even deeper into the river. Then I kicked my legs and started clawing my way toward the surface as hard and fast as I could.

Five . . . four . . . three . . .

My head broke free of the water. I sucked down a desperate, ragged breath—

Boom!

The bomb must not have sunk as fast or as far down as I'd hoped, because it seemed to explode right below my feet. I didn't feel any nails or other shrapnel pounding against my skin, but the resulting shock wave ripped through the river, scooping up the surface of the water and me along with it, like a wave rising and breaking toward shore.

Only in this case, I wasn't going to land on a soft, sandy beach.

Instead, the gleaming white hull of the *Delta Queen* loomed up before me. There was no way that I could stop what was about to happen, so I threw my hands up and reached for more of my Stone magic, trying to harden my entire body as much as I possibly could, even though I knew exactly what little good it would do me against all those thick, heavy tons of wood—

My head slammed into the side of the riverboat, water cascaded down all around me, and the world blinked to black.

4

The pounding on my chest woke me.

Thump-thump-thump-thump.

Over and over again, a fist slammed into my heart, as though someone were beating me with a sledgehammer. I'd been through this same thing once before, so I knew exactly what was happening. Phillip really didn't know his own strength sometimes. If he hit me any harder, he was going to crack my ribs.

A final hard blow made me start choking and coughing up the good portion of the river that I'd swallowed. Hands rolled me over onto my side so I could spew all the disgusting, fish-flavored water out of my lungs. Once I was finished, those same hands gently rolled me the other way so that I was flat on my back again.

I wheezed, blinked, and stared up at a very wet Phillip. His blond hair was plastered to his head, while his white shirt was now see-through and clinging to his muscles.

More water dripped from the end of his ponytail and plopped onto the deck.

"You know," he said, his tense features slowly relaxing, "this is the second time now that I've fished you out of the water. You really need to learn how to swim, Gin."

"Oh, I can swim just fine. It's all the blows to the head that I need to avoid."

Phillip grinned, then helped me up into a seated position so that I was leaning against the brass railing. The sudden change in elevation made my head pound, and it took a few seconds for the world to stop spinning like a crazy carousel. Something warm trickled down the side of my face. I reached up, wincing and hissing with pain as my fingers probed the large, throbbing knot on my forehead, along with blood from what I assumed was a deep, nasty cut. Boat 1, Gin 0.

A white, fluffy towel appeared in front of me, and Silvio crouched down beside me, his gray suit neat and perfect, as though he hadn't just spent the last several minutes running around and trying to shove giants out of the way.

"For your head," he said.

I took the towel and gingerly wiped some of the blood and water off my face. Silvio's sharp gray gaze focused on my head wounds.

"I believe those will require some assistance from Ms. Deveraux," he said. "I'll call and ask her to come over."

I nodded, wincing at the pounding pain the small motion caused in my face and head.

Silvio got to his feet, pulled out his phone, and dialed Jolene "Jo-Jo" Deveraux, the dwarven Air elemental who healed me whenever I got into a serious scrape like this one. The vampire filled in Jo-Jo, then ended the call. But he didn't put his phone away. Instead, he started typing on it, his thumbs flying over the keys faster than I could talk.

"Who are you texting?" I asked, my voice slurring a bit.

"All the usual suspects. Owen, Finn, Bria."

I groaned. "Do you have to? It was just a bomb. And I only have a concussion . . . more or less."

Silvio gave me a sideways look. "Of course I have to. A good assistant always sees to his employer's needs."

"And I need my friends swarming all over me and making a fuss? This isn't the first time someone's tried to kill me, you know. It's not even the first time this week."

That honor had gone to the idiot who thought he could waylay me in the garage where I'd parked my car. He'd tried to crack open my skull with a tire iron, but I'd whacked him to death with it instead. He was still in the refrigerated cooler in an alley close to the Pork Pit, waiting to be disposed of by Sophia Deveraux.

"Of course you do," Silvio replied. "You just don't want to admit it."

I groaned again, but there was no stopping him. The vamp was infuriatingly efficient that way. While he texted everyone, I looked out over the deck, empty now except for the three of us and the mess around the conference table, which was still turned over onto its side, its wooden legs sticking out like a turtle that couldn't right itself.

"Where's everyone else?" I asked.

"Gone." Phillip snorted, crossing his arms over his chest. "Like the cowards they are."

"Dimitri, Luiz, and their guards finally managed to shove their way down the gangplank," Silvio said. "They got into their cars and peeled out of the parking lot as fast as they could. The last time I looked, the *Delta Queen* staff members were milling around down there. And I believe Lorelei Parker was still in the parking lot too."

I scoffed. "She probably stuck around hoping to see you two fish my body out of the river."

"Probably," Phillip said. "But let's focus on the most important thing right now."

"And what would that be?"

He stared at me. "Exactly who you've pissed off enough to warrant them coming after you like this. Bombs are nothing to mess around with, Gin."

"No, they are not."

I thought about his question for several seconds, then shrugged. "Beats me. I'm not without a significant number of enemies. It might be easier to eliminate the folks in Ashland who *don't* want me dead."

Phillip laughed, but his hearty chuckles quickly died down to somber silence. My words were all too true, and he knew it.

"What about Emery Slater?" Silvio chimed in, still tapping away on his phone. "I haven't been able to track her down, but she could have come back to town on the sly."

Emery Slater had been Madeline Monroe's right-hand woman, but the giant had fled Ashland after I'd taken down Madeline a few weeks ago. Emery hated me for killing her boss, and for taking credit for offing her uncle, Elliot Slater, last fall.

I shook my head and flinched, as the motion made my

knocked-around noggin start throbbing again. I really had to stop doing that. More blood oozed out of the wound, so I held the towel up to my head and put some pressure on the gash to try to stop the bleeding. It was several seconds before I could speak again.

"As much as I would like to lay the blame for this at Emery's feet, a bomb isn't really her style. She would much rather beat me to death with her fists than blow me up."

"True," Phillip agreed. "But she would be happy either way as long as you were dead."

"Absolutely." I lowered the towel from my forehead. "But I don't think it's her."

"What about Jonah McAllister?" Phillip suggested. "He's always been a fan of elaborate schemes. A bomb would be right up his alley."

Jonah had been Mab and Madeline's lawyer. He'd also tried to have me killed multiple times, including during a hostage situation at the Briartop art museum, but I'd exposed his schemes.

"I don't think it's him either," I replied. "Jonah mostly stays holed up in his mansion these days, working on his own defense. Besides, he's probably saving his money to bribe the judge and jury at his upcoming trial, not spending it on bombs and assassination attempts."

Silvio finished texting and slid his phone back into his pants pockets. "Well, what I don't understand is why you couldn't have just tossed the bomb overboard. That's what a normal person, a *sane* person, would have done. Why did you feel the need to throw it and yourself into the river at the same time?"

I started to shake my head again but stopped myself. "I didn't want you guys to get caught in the blast. Besides, it would have been just plain rude to mess up Philly's shiny boat any more than I already had."

I made my voice light and teasing, but Phillip picked up on what I wasn't saying.

"You think the bomb had enough explosives to sink the *Delta Queen*?" he asked.

"It had a lot of juice. At least it seemed to. The entire device was coated with elemental magic."

Silvio frowned. "What sort of magic? Fire?"

"Metal," I replied. "Whoever built that bomb is a metal elemental. A strong one."

They kept staring at me, their faces lined with increasing concern.

"I was worried that he was going to blow the bomb at any second and that it would take out everyone on deck—maybe even capsize the entire boat. I'd just let go of the box and was swimming away from it when . . . *boom*."

"But it seemed to be a relatively small, concentrated blast, as far as these things go," Phillip said. "Yeah, it blew up a whole lot of water, but there's no damage to the boat as far as I can tell. You're sure the bomb was covered in metal magic?"

"I'm sure. It felt exactly like Owen's power to me."

Phillip's frown deepened, the wheels churning in his mind to determine who in the Ashland underworld would have enough elemental juice to make a bomb that powerful. But his face remained blank, and he was coming up empty, just like I was. Metal was a fairly rare ability, just like my own Stone magic was, since metal was an offshoot of that major elemental power. Silvio also wore a thoughtful expression on his face, but he didn't come up with any ready suspects either.

"Besides," I continued, "I'm not so sure that this is about me."

"What do you mean?" Phillip asked.

"Someone was watching us from over there." I pointed to the woods on the far side of the river. "He had a sniper rifle, which he used to keep me from jumping into the river after the fake waiter who planted the bomb. The sniper, the watcher, could have put a bullet through my skull at any point during the meeting, when I was out here on deck. So why bother with the bomb? Why not just take me out with a head shot and be done with things? *Bing, bang, boom.* I'm dead."

Phillip stared out across the water. "You think that maybe you weren't the main target? That someone was trying to kill one of the other bosses or even me?"

"I don't know. Maybe the watcher wanted to kill me and didn't care about the collateral damage. Maybe he *likes* collateral damage. But something else is going on here, and I'm going to find out what it is."

I started to get to my feet, but Silvio leaned down, put a firm hand on my shoulder, and gave me a polite, if no-nonsense, scowl.

"You can find out what's going on *after* Ms. Deveraux gets here and heals you," he said. "And not a second before."

"You're not my mother, Silvio," I muttered. "I'm fine. I've been through worse than this."

He straightened back up and crossed his arms over his chest. "Well, I certainly feel like it sometimes. If my hair wasn't already gray, it would have turned that color working for you these past few weeks."

"Well, look on the bright side."

"What's that?"

I grinned. "There's never a dull moment in the employ of Gin Blanco."

Phillip snickered, but Silvio just sighed.

Twenty minutes later, a pair of heels *clack*ed in a familiar chorus, and a woman appeared at the top of the gangplank. Given the fall chill, she was wearing a white cashmere cardigan over a pale pink dress patterned with white roses. A string of pearls hung around her throat, while sensible, white patent-leather pumps encased her feet. A breeze whipped across the deck, but it didn't so much as ruffle the white-blond curls piled on top of her head in an artful chignon.

Jolene "Jo-Jo" Deveraux glanced around the deck, taking in the mess, then hurried over to me. Silvio had dragged out a chaise lounge from somewhere inside the riverboat and forced me to lie down on it. He'd also played the part of a good assistant and fetched some warm, dry clothes from a stash I kept in my car, along with my weapons.

My five silverstone knives were tucked into their usual slots—one up either sleeve, one in the small of my back, and one in either boot—so I was ready to rock 'n' roll as soon as Jo-Jo healed me.

The dwarf stopped, slapped her hands on her hips, and

gave me a critical once-over, her clear, almost colorless gaze lingering on the ugly gash on my forehead, along with the large knot that had puffed up all around it.

She shook her head. "And I thought you were just coming over here for a simple meeting. Trouble has a nasty habit of following you around, darling."

"What can I say? I'm popular that way."

Silvio pulled up a chair next to mine, and Jo-Jo took a seat and began assessing my injuries. She raised her hand, a milky-white glow coating her palm and swirling through her eyes as she reached for her Air magic.

I lay back on the chair while Jo-Jo worked on me, even though the uncomfortable, pins-and-needles sensation of her Air power stitching together the gash on my forehead made me wince and hiss almost as much as the original wound had. She also used her power to heal the knot on my face and fade out all the ugly bruising around it.

Even though I knew Jo-Jo was helping me, I was still sweating and swallowing down snarls by the time she finished. Air was the opposite element of Stone, so the dwarf's power would just never feel right to me, the way loud, chirping alarms drove some folks plumb crazy.

Jo-Jo dropped her hand, and the stabbing pins-and-needles of her Air magic vanished, along with the milky-white glow in her eyes and on her palm. "There you go, darling. Good as new."

I nodded, relieved that I could once again move my head without triggering a migraine. I had swung my feet over the side of the lounge chair, ready to get on with things, when another set of familiar footsteps hurried up the gangplank.

This time, a man stepped into view. With his blue-black hair, violet eyes, and rugged features, most women would have thought him handsome, especially when they noticed the way his navy suit jacket stretched across his broad, muscled shoulders and solid chest. I thought he was one of the most gorgeous men I'd ever seen, and the fact that he was mine warmed my heart in a way nothing else did.

Owen Grayson hurried over and dropped to a knee on the deck beside me. "Gin! Are you okay? I came as soon as Silvio texted me."

"I'm fine. Just a few bumps and bruises. Nothing too serious."

This time.

I didn't say the words because I didn't want to jinx myself. But who was I kidding? This was going to get a whole lot worse before it got better. It *always* did.

I'd killed the supposedly unkillable Mab Monroe. And Madeline. And a whole host of other dangerous giants, dwarves, vampires, and elementals in between. Even though I didn't want the job, I was now the big boss of the Ashland underworld. Given all that, I should have been . . . *safer*. At least for a few weeks, until the other criminals cooked up some new schemes to try to get rid of me. But I should have known that something like this would happen. It *always* did.

Story of my life.

Just when I thought I'd proven myself to everyone, just when I thought I was in the free and clear, just when I was finally ready to enjoy a little (relative) peace and quiet, another elemental had . . . what, exactly? Targeted me? Tried to assassinate me? Wanted to murder a bunch of mobsters at the same time? That remained to be seen. But whatever was going on, I was going to get to the bottom of it.

One body at a time.

Owen leaned in and pressed a gentle kiss to my forehead. I drew in a breath, letting his rich, metallic scent sink into my lungs.

He leaned back and gave me the same sort of critical once-over that Silvio and Jo-Jo had. Relief seeped into his face, replacing his tight, worried expression. Then he grinned and shook his head.

"I can't let you go anywhere, can I?" he murmured, a teasing note creeping into his deep, rumbling voice.

"Guess not," I drawled, determined to keep the mood light.

Owen got to his feet and looked at his best friend. "I thought I told you to take good care of my girl."

Phillip shrugged. "Kind of hard when she jumps overboard with a bomb in her hands. I can only do so much, you know."

Owen's grin faded a little, but he still lightly cuffed Phillip on the shoulder. "I know. Gin makes it hard sometimes, doesn't she?"

"Y'all do realize that I'm sitting right here?"

Phillip ignored me and cuffed him back. They grinned at each other, and then Owen looked at me, his smile slipping away and his face growing more serious.

"Who do you think did this?" he asked. "Emery Slater?"

"She does seem to be a popular choice among the peanut gallery, but I don't think so. It's just not her style. Not what I would expect from her. She's more brawn than bomb."

"Maybe that's exactly why it *is* her," Owen countered. "Doing something that you wouldn't expect. Catching you off guard."

"I don't know, but I'm going to find out." I looked at him. "You up for a little hike?"

"With you?" He winked at me. "Always."

"Good," I said. "Then let's go see if we can track us down a bomber."

❊ 5 ❊

Owen took my hand and helped me up out of the lounge chair. Silvio decided to stay on the riverboat to wait for Finn and Bria to arrive, while Jo-Jo left to go back home to work at her beauty salon.

Owen and I walked down the gangplank, with Phillip trailing along behind us. The *Delta Queen* staff members were standing in groups in the parking lot, talking, texting on their phones, and glancing up at the riverboat.

Phillip approached them, spreading his hands out wide. "Okay, folks, here's what I know so far . . ."

The waiters and guards clustered around him, hanging on to his every word. I looked over the crowd, scanning every single face and taking in everyone's body language. Wide eyes, tense shoulders, nervous tapping fingers and feet. All the workers seemed genuinely shocked and shaken up by what had happened. Even in Ashland, where violence was so common, no one expected to get blown up just going to work. It was enough to upset even me.

And the workers' worry told me something else: the watcher probably didn't have any of them on his payroll. Otherwise, he wouldn't have bothered sending that fake waiter onto the riverboat. And if one of the workers had known about the bomb beforehand, he or she wouldn't have stuck around to get an explanation and reassurances from Phillip that this was an isolated incident. I supposed that someone here could be faking their shock and distress, but it didn't seem likely. On one hand, I was relieved the staff wasn't involved, since I didn't want to trouble Phillip any more than I already had. On the other, it left me without someone to squeeze for easy answers.

But the workers weren't the only ones in the parking lot—so were Lorelei Parker and Jack Corbin.

The smuggler perched on the hood of a sleek royal-blue Dodge Charger, with her guard leaning against the driver's-side door, his arms crossed over his chest. Lorelei's eyes narrowed as she spotted me, and she looked me over from head to toe. Her lips puckered, and she pulled on the end of her black braid, lost in thought. I frowned. Strangely enough, the gesture reminded me of . . . something.

"Friends of yours?" Owen asked, staring at them.

I snorted. "Not bloody likely. Lorelei probably wishes that I'd drowned in the river."

Lorelei let go of her braid, hopped off the hood, and said something to Corbin. The two of them got into the car and peeled out of the parking lot, leaving the *Delta Queen* behind.

I stared at the empty street, wondering at the vague, uneasy feeling tickling my spine.

"Gin?" Owen asked.

I shook my head, putting all thoughts of Lorelei and her odd behavior out of my mind. "Come on. Let's go."

We got into Owen's car, and he drove out of the parking lot and over the nearest bridge to the opposite side of the river.

The highway curved past this part of the Aneirin River, and Owen steered his car off the road and into a gravel lot that fronted a series of wide stone steps leading up to a scenic overlook. A series of trails started at the lot and wound in either direction through the woods, rising and falling with the slope of the riverbank.

Given the number of trees that had already shed their leaves, I could see the gleaming white wood of the *Delta Queen* peeking through the brown tangles of branches, making the overlook and surrounding trails the perfect spots to spy on all the comings and goings on board the riverboat. Ambling along with a pair of binoculars slung around his neck, as though he were looking for birds, the watcher would have blended right in with the nature lovers on the trails, out for a fall stroll.

I'd have to talk to Phillip about rigging up security cameras or maybe even posting some guards over here— for his sake. I wasn't the only one with enemies who wanted me dead, and since Phillip had been so public in supporting me as the new big boss, no doubt his name had climbed to the top of several folks' hit lists too.

Owen and I got out of the car.

"Where do you want to start?" he asked. "The overlook?"

"Nah. Too many people come and go there all day long. The watcher wouldn't want to risk a jogger or biker seeing him and wondering what he was doing hanging around the same spot for so long. He'd go someplace more private where he wouldn't be disturbed. Let's try over there."

I pointed to the area where I thought I'd seen the flash of the watcher's binoculars, and we headed in that direction, meandering along the winding paths. It was after five now, and the trails were mostly deserted, except for a few dedicated outdoor types. I scanned the faces and body language of every person we passed, but they only seemed concerned with keeping their heart rates up or making sure that their dogs did their business before they headed home.

Owen and I moved farther down the path, and soon we were the only hikers on the trail. The sun was already weakening in the sky, its rays growing fainter and barely penetrating what was left of the fall foliage. The dappled shadows took advantage, clumping together and spreading out into murky pools that darkened and lengthened by the second. The air was cool, and the scent of the leaves and earth mixed pleasantly.

We followed the curving trail until it ended, then stepped off the asphalt and began making our way deeper into the woods.

Owen grabbed my arm. "Stop. Someone's been using magic here—metal magic. I can *feel* it. Much more of it than I should be able to. Almost like . . . he left something behind for us to find."

"Like another bomb?"

Given the fact that I'd survived the initial blast, the watcher had to realize that I would come here looking for clues. If I were him, I would have left behind a nasty surprise or two, if only on the off chance that he could blow me up that way.

Owen nodded. "Yeah. Like another bomb." He scanned the woods, his violet eyes glowing and his head tilting to one side as he reached out with his magic, trying to sense the other elemental's power trail. He pointed to the left. "Over there."

We headed in that direction, watching where we put our feet and scanning the surrounding trees. A hundred feet deeper into the woods, a fading patch of sunlight glinted off the corner of something metal, drawing my attention.

I pointed at the object, which was half-hidden underneath a pile of brown, curling leaves. "You were right. Someone left us a present."

"Some present," Owen muttered.

We crouched down and scanned the ground for trip-wires. A few seconds later, I spied a thin strand of fishing line strung ankle-high between two trees. A crude but effective trap. I palmed one of my knives and sliced through the fishing line, so we wouldn't accidentally trip the bomb.

I carefully brushed the leaves off the object, wincing at the faint *crackle-crackle*s they made at my touch. Just in case the bomb was booby-trapped some other way, I grabbed hold of my Stone magic and hardened my skin, ready to throw myself down on top of the bomb to protect Owen from any potential blast.

But there were no more traps, and I was able to study the bomb. It was identical to the one on the riverboat—a metal box with a cell phone taped to the top to serve as a timer and trigger. I hadn't had time to open the box that had been on the *Delta Queen*, and I reached for the simple latch on the side. It wasn't welded or magicked shut, and I slowly cracked open the top, still maintaining my grip on my Stone magic.

A small block of what looked like gray clay lay inside— the explosive—while several holes had been drilled into the lid. Red and black wires snaked through the openings, connecting the explosive to the cell phone. I unhooked the wires to disarm the bomb.

To my surprise, the explosive only took up about a third of the space inside the box. So if this device was the same as the one on the riverboat, Phillip had been right, and the blast from that bomb had been relatively small. I wondered what the damage would have been if it had detonated on deck. Enough to kill just me, since I'd been the person sitting closest to the bomb? Enough to take out half the folks at the conference table? Or maybe even everyone on deck? I didn't know, but I was glad I hadn't found out.

But I'd been right too, because the rest of the box was filled with nails, just like I'd thought the one on the *Delta Queen* had been. I slowly tilted the box to one side, and the nails rolled around, the sharp points glittering like diamonds in the fading sunlight.

Owen let out a low whistle. "That's a deadly bit of business. All those nails . . . they would have shredded everything and everyone they came into contact with."

"Maybe the watcher didn't want to kill me outright," I said. "Maybe he wanted to mess me up and watch me suffer first. Maybe that's why he had a sniper rifle. To put me down after the bomb went off."

Owen grimaced, but he didn't disagree with my assessment. I thought about my words to Phillip and Silvio, my musing that maybe the watcher liked collateral damage. The nails definitely proved that. Whoever the watcher was, he definitely had a sadistic streak, which only made me more determined to figure out who he was and what he wanted.

I rolled the nails around in the box again, listening to them *tink-tink-tink* together, the sound almost like a clock, ticking down the seconds to my death.

I left the bomb where I'd found it, and Owen and I searched the rest of the area. It was easy to tell where the fake waiter had slogged ashore, since he hadn't bothered to hide his muddy tracks. But they led back to the parking lot and vanished, which meant that he'd left in a car, so there was no way to trace him farther at the moment.

But it was the watcher's nest that interested me the most.

Owen and I followed the fake waiter's tracks straight to it. The watcher had chosen a good spot, on a slight rise just inside the trees that lined the shore. The area gave him a clear view of the riverboat from fore to aft but still had enough foliage to hide him from anyone on the *Delta Queen* looking in this direction. The flash of light on his binoculars had been his only giveaway. But even then, it was mostly luck that I'd spotted the reflection. If

I hadn't . . . well, I didn't want to think about what would have happened on the riverboat, especially to Phillip and Silvio.

But the watcher hadn't left any glaring clues behind. No restaurant receipts, no parking stubs, no hotel matchbooks. As far as I could tell, all he'd done was stand here, peer through his binoculars, and watch the riverboat before leaving. He'd even taken the time to pick up his shell casings and scuff over his footprints to hide what kind of shoes he was wearing. Smart.

And I didn't think anyone else had been here with him. No other tracks littered the ground, and the surrounding foliage wasn't trampled or disturbed enough for more than a couple of people to have passed this way. Besides, if the watcher had a group of men at his disposal, then why not send them to storm the riverboat and shoot me point-blank? No, this struck me as a two-man job: the waiter and the watcher.

I was betting that the watcher was also the metal elemental who had built the bombs. After all, why construct a bomb if you weren't going to stick around to watch it explode, and there hadn't been anyone else here to witness the blast. Besides, the metal elemental was smart enough to build a bomb, which meant that he was smart enough to get someone else—the fake waiter—to plant it on the riverboat so he could be sure to stay out of range of the destructive blast.

I crouched down and examined the same patch of ground for the fifth time, hoping that a clue would miraculously sprout up out of the earth like some magical fairy-tale rose. I'd even take a weed at this point. But of course that didn't happen, and I came up empty. Frustration surged through me. Another dead end—

"Hey, Gin," Owen called out. "Check this out."

I got to my feet and went over to where he was standing, about twenty feet to my right and another ten back in the woods. Owen pointed at a tree trunk, where a gnarled knot stuck out right at my heart level. At first, I didn't see what he was so interested in, but then I noticed the deep gouges in the wood. The bomber must have gotten bored while he'd been out here, because something had been carved into the knot. I leaned closer and squinted at the crude shape—a long line with a spiked ball on the end.

"Is that . . . a mace?" I asked.

I wasn't sure why that particular weapon popped into my head, but as soon as I said the word, my stomach clenched with a vague, uneasy feeling of . . . dread. But why would I be worried about some symbol carved into a tree? It wasn't the first one I'd seen, and I doubted it would be the last.

"Your guess is as good as mine." Owen flashed me a grin. "I was going with some sort of bomb or maybe even fireworks. Since there have been so many of those already today."

I laughed at his black humor, then stared at the carving again. It didn't look like it had been done with a knife, at least not a sharp one. Otherwise, the image would have been clearer, deeper, with more defined edges, and more curls of wood would have been littering the ground. This looked like scratches more than anything else, like it had been done with . . . a nail.

Like all the nails he'd packed into those two bombs.

As soon as the thought occurred to me, I knew that it was right. I wondered how many nails the watcher, the bomber, carried around with him—and why. Sure, they were practical tools for a metal elemental, but the nails had to mean *something* more, had to represent some sentiment or memory. Weapons always did to the people wielding them.

"You're sure it's not fireworks?" Owen joked again.

"No," I said. "Long line topped with a spiked ball. I really think it's a mace."

My stomach clenched again at the word, but I pushed my unease aside.

"A medieval weapon." Owen shook his head. "You don't see those every day. What does it mean?"

"I have no idea."

A mace wasn't something that was commonly used as a rune. Like Owen said, it wasn't a weapon that a lot of people wielded anymore. Guns, knives, swords, the occasional chainsaw, sure. But a mace? Even I didn't have a mace in my arsenal of weapons at Fletcher's house. Of course, it probably represented strength and power—most weapons did—or maybe some family or specific business. Or perhaps the watcher had drawn it simply because it represented his own affinity for metal—or, more likely, his twisted bombs.

"What made you look over here?" I asked. "I thought you were going over the trail that the fake waiter had made again."

Owen pointed through the trees. "This spot is directly across from the *Delta Queen*'s paddle wheel. If I had wanted to keep an eye on things, I would have started here at the back of the boat and worked my way forward toward the front."

I looked out across the river. He was right: we were lined up with the back edge of the paddle wheel. Owen's reasoning made perfect sense. No doubt the watcher had paced back and forth along this patch of woods, spying on all the happenings on the vessel.

"You find anything?" he asked.

I shook my head. "Whoever the elemental is, he didn't leave anything behind, except for his bomb in the leaves. I'll take it to Finn and see what he makes of it. He always likes to play with explosives. We've done all we can here. Let's go back to the riverboat. Finn and Bria should be there by now."

Owen nodded and headed toward the trail that would take us back to the parking lot. I had started to go retrieve the bomb from where I'd left it when a faint smoky scent tickled my nose.

I stopped and drew in a breath. An ashy sort of tang hung in the air, almost like someone had been smoking a cigarette. I drew in another breath. No, it was richer, deeper, stronger than that. Not a cigarette—a cigar.

I crouched down and scanned the ground, running my hands through the loose piles of leaves that were closest to the tree. A minute later, I found a cigar stub smushed into the dirt, as though the watcher had crushed it under the toe of his boot after he finished with his rune drawing. Jackpot.

I brought the stub up to my nose and sniffed it. I was by no means a cigar connoisseur, but it would have to be an expensive brand to have that sort of deep, dark, rich, coffee-like scent. Finn would know. Like alcohol, cigars were one of those things he thought made everything else better.

I wrapped the cigar in some dry leaves and slid the whole thing into my jacket pocket. Then I straightened up, pulled out my phone, and snapped several photos of the mace rune that had been carved into the tree.

I put my phone away and started to go catch up to Owen, but I found myself rooted in place, staring at the carving. The wind whistled through the trees, but that chill was nothing compared with the one slithering up my spine. The mace rune, the watcher's metal power, the boxes full of nails . . .

It all reminded me of . . . *something*.

I didn't think that the watcher was related to a job I'd done, since everyone I'd gone after as the Spider was dead. Of course, he could have been a friend or a relative of someone I'd assassinated, but the danger from those folks was almost always immediately after a hit, since that's when they would be most vehemently searching for whoever had killed their loved one. No, this was something else, some vague wisp of memory I couldn't quite bring into focus.

Still, the longer I stared at the crude mace, the more cold worry seeped through my body.

Because I had seen that weapon, that rune, somewhere before.

Now I just needed to remember where—before it was too late.

❊ 6 ❊

Phillip must have sent the majority of his staff home, because no one was in the parking lot next to the *Delta Queen* when we pulled back in there, and most of the cars were gone. But I did spot two familiar vehicles sitting side by side: a serviceable navy-blue sedan and a silver Aston Martin.

Owen and I walked up the gangplank to find two people talking with Phillip and Silvio on the main deck. One of them was a woman about my size, with shaggy blond hair, blue eyes, and rosy cheeks. She was dressed in black boots, dark jeans, and a white button-up shirt, with a gold detective's badge and a holstered gun clipped to her black leather belt. She was as no-nonsense as her sedan, a stark contrast to Mr. Aston Martin, who stood beside her in an expensive Fiona Fine suit, his walnut-brown hair slicked back into a carefully messy style, his sly green eyes taking in his surroundings.

Detective Bria Coolidge and Finnegan Lane both turned at the sound of our footsteps as Owen and I approached. They rushed over to us, and Bria, my baby sister, wrapped me up in a tight hug.

"Are you okay?" she asked. "I got Silvio's text and came straight over. He and Phillip just finished telling us what happened."

"I'm fine. I always make a habit of surviving nasty situations. You should know that by now."

She smiled at my joke, but the worried lines on her face didn't smooth out.

Finn reached over and clapped me on the shoulder. "See? I told you that Gin was all right. She always is."

"Ta-da." I swept my hand out to the side with an elaborate flourish, giving a not-so-modest bow.

"Hey," Finn protested. "That's *my* move."

"And now it's mine," I chirped.

He huffed in mock annoyance, then clapped me on the shoulder again, his firm grip telling me how worried he'd really been.

"Silvio said that you guys went across the river to check out where the bomber was set up," Bria said. "Did you find anything?"

Someone, probably Silvio, had set the conference table back up on its feet, and everyone gathered around while Owen and I laid out the second bomb and the cigar stub on top of the table.

Finn unwrapped the leaves from around the stub, then brought it up to his nose and drew in a deep breath. Even though the cigar had been smoked down to almost nothing, his green eyes glimmered in appreciation at the rich, lingering scent.

"I'll be more than happy to investigate where this beauty came from," he purred. "I've been meaning to re-stock my supply anyway."

He winked, but I rolled my eyes. "Only you would use my near-death experience as an excuse to go cigar shopping."

"You want me to be thorough, don't you?" Finn asked. "Leave no cigar store unturned?"

He kept a mostly straight face as he batted his eyes and pressed a hand to his heart, but his lips twitched, as he struggled to hold back his snickers.

"Yeah," I deadpanned. "That's *exactly* what I'm concerned about right now."

Finn pouted. "You're no fun."

I ignored him, pulled out my phone, and showed the mace rune photos to Bria. I didn't know why, but something about the symbol made me think of my sister. No, that wasn't right. It didn't make me think of Bria, not exactly, but it made me think about . . . *family*.

Once again, I tried to remember when and where I'd seen the rune before. I could almost feel the memory swimming around like a fish in the bottom of my brain. But the more I tried to hook it and reel it to the surface, the faster it slipped away.

Bria's eyebrows drew together in thought as she scrolled through the photos. "I don't recognize it. Email me the photos, and I'll run them through the department's system and see if they match any known gang runes in Ashland and beyond."

I nodded, took back my phone, and sent her the photos. Bria pulled out her own phone, hit some buttons, and held the device up to her ear.

"Hey, Xavier," she said, talking to her partner on the force. "I just sent you some photos. I need you to run them through the rune database for me . . ."

While she filled in Xavier, I went over to Owen, Finn, Phillip, and Silvio, who were huddled around the table, studying the second bomb.

"Anything?" I asked.

Finn shook his head. "The box, the nails, and the phone are all things you could buy anywhere. Nothing I can easily track down. I'll put out some feelers about the explosive, but I don't know how long it might take to get some concrete info about who bought it, when, and where. Maybe Bria will have more luck with the police records, looking for similar bombs, although the design is fairly simple."

I had expected as much, but frustration rippled through me. So I turned to Phillip, hoping that he would have better news. "What about the riverboat's security footage? I know you have cameras recording everything that happens on deck and in the parking lot."

"I've done a quick scan, but there's nothing useful on it," he said. "The guy was dressed like all the other waiters, and he walked into the parking lot from one of the side streets, so there's no car or license plate to trace. He had a backpack slung over his shoulder—which my guards have already found empty in a staff locker below deck—and he hung out and smoked until he saw some folks coming in for work. He approached one of the other waiters, claimed that he was a new hire, and walked right on board with the rest of them. The guards didn't even notice the new face or the extra body, much less search his backpack, something that I will be talking to them about at great length later on."

Phillip glowered at a pair of giant guards who were standing by the double doors that led into the riverboat. Both men shifted on their feet and ducked their heads in silent apology. I wouldn't want to be in their shoes. They'd be lucky if Phillip just fired them.

"Uh-oh. I know *that* look," Owen murmured. "If you're going to throw them overboard, you should at least give them life jackets first."

Phillip turned his glower to Owen, but his anger quickly melted into a sheepish grin. Tossing people into the river was one of Phillip's favorite ways of dealing with problems.

Silvio cleared this throat. "There might be another way to track down the bomber."

We all looked at him.

"How?" I asked.

"Well, you are the head of the underworld now . . ."

I winced at the reminder, but he kept on talking.

"So why don't you use all of the resources at your disposal?"

"What do you mean?"

Silvio shrugged. "Ask around. See if anyone's heard anything about the bombing or if there's a new elemental in town looking to make a name for himself by killing you. At the very least, ask folks to report back to you if they see or hear anything suspicious. Who knows? You might get lucky."

Silvio was right. Whether I liked it or not, I was the head of the underworld now, so I should at least get *some* small benefit out of dealing with the criminals and all their constant whining, crying, and turf wars. But I was still wary. It wouldn't have surprised me if one of the other bosses had hired the metal elemental to try to assassinate me. Inflicting horrific wounds on me with a bomb first, before moving in for the final kill, would have made a great many people in Ashland quite happy. I wasn't even particularly annoyed by the possibility. It was part of the job description. The other bosses had constantly plotted against Mab, despite how powerful she'd been, although their schemes had never really amounted to anything.

No, what really pissed me off was the fact that Phillip, Silvio, and all those innocent workers could have been seriously injured—or worse—by the bomb. After I killed Madeline, I had made it *exceptionally* clear to the entire underworld what would happen to anyone who went after my friends and my family—even by accident. Pain, blood, death. But apparently, the message hadn't sunk in. Well, this time, I was going to make sure that it did.

"And I know that look too," Owen murmured again, reaching out and squeezing my hand. "This is not your fault, Gin."

I shrugged and stared down at the deck instead of looking at my friends. They might not hold me responsible, but it *was* my fault. Death followed me wherever I went, whether I liked it or not. Still, I appreciated Owen's gesture, so I squeezed back, then dropped his hand and turned to Silvio.

"All right," I told the vampire. "Reach out to a few

folks, but do it discreetly. And only contact the ones who don't have any serious ambitions of their own. I'm sure that Lorelei, Dimitri, and Luiz have already spread rumors all over town about the bombing, but I don't want to confirm anything I don't have to."

I couldn't afford to look weak right now, or the sharks would start actively circling around me again. Not that they'd ever really left in the first place.

Silvio nodded and whipped out his phone, while Phillip and Owen started talking about the security footage again. Bria finished her call to Xavier, came back over to the table, and examined the second bomb with Finn.

I held up my phone, staring at the photo of the tree carving. I was grateful that my friends were going to help me run down all the available leads, but it seemed to me that the mace rune was the key to discovering the bomber's identity.

But more than that, staring at the symbol filled me with uneasy dread, as though I should have already known exactly who my enemy was and what he really wanted.

That night, Owen and I drove our cars over to Fletcher's house, my house now. We both parked in front of the ramshackle structure, but I signaled to Owen to stay in his vehicle as I got out and did a perimeter sweep. Normally, I would have just scanned the woods, the lawn, and the rocky ridge that dropped away from the front of the house before going inside.

Not tonight.

Instead, I made a slow, complete circuit of the house, crisscrossed the lawn several times, and even ventured into the woods to make absolutely sure that no one was lurking in the trees. All the while, I reached out with my Stone magic, listening to the emotional vibrations that had sunk into the gravel in the driveway, the small rocks hidden in the grass, and even the brick that made up parts of the house. But the stones only whispered of the whistling of the chilly autumn wind, the scurrying of animals in the underbrush, and the soft dropping of the leaves on top of the ground, slowly covering the stones up for the cold winter ahead.

When I was satisfied that no one had been near the house, I signaled to Owen, and we went inside. I took the extra precaution of making him wait by the front door while I swept the interior for intruders and any traps, including more bombs. But no one was hiding inside, and nothing had been disturbed since I'd left this morning.

I sighed, grateful that at least my house was safe and secure for the night.

"What are you thinking about?" Owen asked.

I was tired of speculating about the bomber, who he was, and why he'd tried to kill me, so I didn't tell Owen my real thoughts. Instead, I wrapped my arms around his neck.

"I was thinking that I'm glad we're finally alone together," I said in a low, husky voice, staring up into his eyes.

Owen's nose wrinkled, and he gave me a teasing grin. "As romantic as that sounds, don't you want to take a shower first? Don't take this the wrong way, but you sort of smell like . . . fish."

I sniffed. He was right. Even though I'd changed into

fresh clothes, the fishy scent of the river had soaked into my hair and skin.

I laughed, stood on my tiptoes, and kissed him on the nose. "All right, all right. Shower first. Lovin' later."

Owen headed into the den to watch some TV, while I went into the bathroom. I stripped off my clothes, turned the water on in the shower, and stepped into the hot spray, soaping up and washing off the lingering stench of the river. I also lathered and rinsed out my hair twice, just for good measure.

When I had finished, I slipped into a black microfleece robe patterned with silver skulls with red-sequined hearts for eyes—a birthday gift from Sophia—and padded into the den.

Owen had been busy while I was in the shower, and he'd put together several ham-and-turkey club sandwiches. He'd also heated up two bowls of broccoli-cheese soup, along with some cinnamon baked apples mixed with cranberries for dessert. Perfect comfort food after the day I'd had.

We took everything into the den, enjoying the warm, hearty meal and the easy silence that came with being in each other's company. Then we snuggled together on the couch, just holding each other, not saying anything at all. There was no need for words. Not now, not tonight.

But our innocent touches, lazy caresses, and soft kisses quickly turned longer, harder, deeper, until we were plastered together on the couch, making out like a couple of teenagers who couldn't get enough of each other. I loved everything about Owen—his firm touch, his rich metallic scent, the way his warm, hard muscles bunched and flexed under my fingers, even the hint of cinnamon that lingered on his tongue from the apples we'd eaten.

We broke apart after a particularly long, feverish kiss, and Owen wrapped his arm around my waist and pulled me onto his lap so that I was straddling him. My robe fell open, and he nipped at my exposed shoulder, even as his hand slid up my leg and under the hem of the black fabric.

I arched an eyebrow. "And what are you up to?"

Owen's hand crept higher up my thigh, then higher still. "Will it make you feel better if I promise you that it's something bad?"

I puckered my lips and pretended to think about it. "I don't know. Perhaps I need a demonstration. Just to be sure."

He flashed me a wicked grin, his violet eyes bright with the same desire that was simmering in my veins. "A demonstration?" he murmured. "Oh, I think that can be arranged."

He stroked the curls at the junction of my thighs, then slipped a finger inside me.

"Oh . . ."

I groaned, dug my hands into his shoulders, and rocked against him, even as he kept stroking me, his fingers moving in a slow, familiar pattern, one that he knew always drove me crazy. Waves of tension, pressure, and pleasure rippled through my body, but all I could do was hang on to him.

"More . . ." I whispered. "More . . ."

Owen leaned forward, his teeth nipping at my shoulder again. "Your wish is my command."

His hand began to move faster and faster, in more elaborate patterns, his fingers skimming the surface, then moving deeper inside me, only to retreat again. All the while, he kept kissing my neck and shoulder, his teeth playfully teasing my skin just like his hand was. Finally, it was all too much, and I shuddered, finding my release.

I slumped against him, my head buried against his neck, my entire body warm and boneless.

"I take it my demonstration was satisfactory?" he rumbled.

"'Satisfactory' is one way of putting it." I leaned back and winked. "Although I could always use another demonstration." I rocked forward on his lap again, feeling the hard length of him pressing up against me. "One with you wearing far less clothing."

This time, Owen was the one who groaned. "I could say the same thing about you."

I leaned forward and kissed him, my tongue slipping inside his mouth and thrusting against his. Owen growled low and deep in his throat, and that liquid heat burned through my veins again. I wanted to touch him—now—so I ripped his shirt open instead of bothering with the buttons and starting nipping at his neck and shoulders with my teeth.

"I think we've had enough teasing, don't you?" he rasped.

He picked me up and laid me back on the couch. I watched while he got to his feet, shrugged out of his clothes, and grabbed a condom from his wallet. I took my little white pills, but we always used extra protection.

I drank in the sight of his strong, muscled body,

my fingers itching to touch all his warm, supple skin. No matter how many times we were together, I always wanted more of him.

Owen covered himself with the condom, then leaned down and tugged open the belt on my robe, carefully peeling both sides away from my body, as though he were unwrapping a present. His hot violet gaze raked over me in appreciative fashion, and he leaned down to kiss me again, but I put a finger on his lips, stopping him.

"As you were," I ordered.

He quirked an eyebrow, but he sat back down on the couch. I gave him a slow, lazy smile, then got up and straddled him again. I looped my arms around his neck and swiveled my hips in a slow circle, pressing up against his hard length, then retreating.

"How do you like this demonstration?" I teased, making another slow circle. "Or do I need to take it up a notch?"

I leaned forward, as though I was finally going to join our bodies together, but stopped just short.

"Come here, you," Owen growled.

He grabbed my hips and pushed inside me with one long, smooth stroke that had us both moaning at how good it felt. Our mouths fused together, our tongues tangling as we devoured each other. Owen's hands cupped my breasts, kneading the already sensitive mounds, and he kissed his way down my chest, licking first one nipple, then the other.

I started to rock against him to find the release we were both so desperate for, but Owen's hands fell to my hips, keeping me in place.

"Hold still," he rasped against my skin. "I haven't finished my feast yet."

He leaned forward and kissed my breasts again. I groaned at not being able to move against him, with him, but waiting now would only make it that much better in the end.

The heat, the emotion, the connection between us built and built, until I was trembling with every soft whisper of his lips and every hot drag of his tongue across my skin. Finally, Owen picked me up and laid me back down on the couch again. We both couldn't wait any longer. I drew him down on top of me, and he entered me again with another long, hard thrust.

And this time, he didn't stop.

I locked my legs around his waist and pulled his head down to mine. Our lips and tongues and bodies crashed together, and every kiss and thrust fueled our frenzy. We couldn't get enough of each other, kissing harder, touching longer, pushing faster and faster together.

Then we both exploded, the world shattering around us as we reached our sweet, ultimate release.

We rode the afterglow for a long, long time before our bodies eased apart. I grabbed my black robe from where it had fallen on the floor and flipped it over both of us as a makeshift blanket. Then I wrapped my arms around Owen, holding him even tighter than before. He spooned his body against mine, and I slid my fingers through his silky black hair as his breathing evened out and deepened, telling me that he had gone to sleep.

But I didn't drift off along with him. Right now, I wanted to enjoy this precious time together. It would have been easy to take for granted how Owen made me feel, but today had proven I couldn't do that.

Not now, not ever.

I might be the new queen of the underworld, but I still had plenty of enemies who wanted me dead. So in a little while, I would wake up Owen and see if he wanted another demonstration. I would enjoy this night with him to the fullest and wring every drop of pleasure I could from it.

Then, tomorrow, I would track down my enemies and make them pay for what they'd tried to do to me and my friends.

* 7 *

I woke up the next morning feeling refreshed and cooked up a hearty breakfast of country-fried ham, scrambled eggs, and buttermilk pancakes. I was anticipating a long day, and I wanted some stick-to-my-ribs food to fuel whatever new problems might arise. I promised Owen I would call him if I learned anything important, then we kissed, said our good-byes, and went our separate ways to work.

I parked my car four blocks away from the Pork Pit, the barbecue restaurant that I ran in downtown Ashland. I chose an out-of-the-way spot on a little-used side street where I hoped no one would even think to look for my car, much less plant a bomb on it. Then I stuck my hands into the pockets of my black leather jacket and eased into the stream of commuters flowing down the sidewalk.

I scanned my surroundings, in case the bomber or the fake waiter might be lurking near the restaurant, but everyone was busy texting or gabbing on their phones, and no one paid me any mind. So I rounded the corner and stepped onto the street where the Pork Pit was located.

As far as I could tell, no one had noticed me, but I spotted a woman lingering on the sidewalk outside the restaurant, pretending to check her messages, although she kept glancing around. Blond hair, tight red suit jacket, short skirt, oversize sunglasses on her face.

I recognized her: Jade Jamison, a madam who ran hookers out in the suburbs. I'd helped her out a few weeks earlier when a minor mobster had been threatening her and her workers, despite the agreement they had that was supposed to prevent that sort of thing. I wouldn't have expected the guy to renege on the deal so quickly, especially since I'd put one of my knives up against his throat and told him to honor their arrangement—or else.

I sighed. I already had enough problems with the bomber. I didn't have time for underworld disputes right now too. Jade spotted me, but instead of hurrying over, she ducked her head and focused on her phone again, as though we were strangers.

I looked left and right, but I didn't see anyone out of the ordinary lingering on the sidewalks, and no cars idled at the curb in a suspicious manner. But if Jade wanted to pretend we didn't know each other, I'd play along.

So I pulled my keys out of my jacket pocket, approached the restaurant, and studied the front door, making sure that no runes had been carved into the wooden frame that would spew out elemental Fire, Ice, or some other magic that would kill me on the spot. But the door was clean, and so were the surrounding windows and what I could see of the storefront through the glass.

I was happy that I wouldn't have to try to disarm a rune trap this early in the morning. But it also made me suspicious. There should have been *some* sort of trap waiting for me here. Since the bomber had failed to assassinate me yesterday, he should have been trying again, as quickly as possible, before I found out who and especially where he was. But there were no runes, no traps, no bombs of any sort. More of that unease swirled through my stomach, that nagging little feeling that made me think that something else was going on besides someone simply wanting to kill me.

Or perhaps my own constant paranoia was the one trap that I could never truly escape.

Heels snapped on the sidewalk, and Jade strolled in my direction, still pretending to check her phone. She frowned and paused beside me, as though whatever she wasn't really looking at on her screen troubled her.

"Let me in through the back," she whispered, then sashayed down the sidewalk, rounded the corner, and disappeared from sight.

Not what I'd expected, but I was curious enough to see what she wanted.

So I stepped inside, locked the front door behind me, and flipped on the lights. Vinyl booths lined the windows, with tables and chairs sitting beyond them and a long counter with padded stools situated along the back wall. Blue and pink pig tracks curled every which way through the space, leading to the men's and women's restrooms, the cash register, and even into the back of the restaurant. I breathed in, letting the rich, spicy, smoky scent of all the meals I'd cooked seep deep into my lungs. Phillip might have the prettier view on the *Delta Queen*, but my gin joint certainly smelled far better than the Aneirin River.

Even though Jade was waiting, I took my sweet time checking the bathrooms, tables, chairs, and counter for runes, traps, and bombs. Satisfied that everything was clean, I pushed through the double doors and went into the back of the restaurant, scanning all the freezers and metal racks filled with foodstuffs, napkins, straws, and silverware. It would be rather embarrassing to be murdered in my own restaurant simply because I'd gotten sloppy and had assumed that no one would come after me here now that I was ostensibly the big boss.

When I was sure that everything was clean, I opened the back door to find Jade Jamison standing in the alley, her red clutch tucked under her right arm, impatiently *tap-tap-tapp*ing the toe of her red stiletto against the cracked, dirty asphalt.

"Took you long enough," she muttered. "What were you doing? Putting the pigs out to pasture?"

"Sorry," I drawled. "Just making sure that no one had left me a present inside overnight."

Jade pushed her sunglasses up onto her head, revealing her green eyes. "Oh, you mean like that bomb on the riverboat yesterday?"

I kept my face blank, although I was mentally wincing. I'd known that the rumors would fly hard and fast, but I'd underestimated the Ashland grapevine. "You heard about that?"

"Oh, I heard. The entire underworld has heard by now. Matter of fact, that's the reason I'm here."

"And why is that?"

She snorted. "Oh, please. Don't give me the stink-eye, and don't even *think* that I had something to do with it. I'm not stupid enough to believe I can kill you. And why would I want to anyway? You kept your word and got Leroy off my back. I haven't heard a peep from him since your little visit. As far as I'm concerned, you can be the big boss for as long as you live." She paused. "However brief a time that might actually turn out to be."

"Wow, thanks for the vote of confidence," I replied wryly. "But what's with all the cloak-and-dagger?"

She shrugged. "I didn't want anyone to see me talking to you. Just in case your reign is particularly short-lived."

"There you go again with all that confidence. It's enough to overinflate a girl's ego." Still, her words intrigued me. "Why do you want to talk to me?"

Jade looked me in the eye. "Because I know where you can find the guy who planted that bomb on the *Delta Queen*."

A hundred questions popped into my mind, most of them focused on where this guy was right this *second* and how quickly I could get him to give up the bomber's identity and location and kill them both.

But as urgently as I wanted that information, I decided to be polite about things. Besides, from what I knew of Jade Jamison, she was stubborn enough to dig in her heels if I rushed her. So I ushered her into the storefront, closed all the blinds on the windows so that no one would see her, and gestured for her to sit on one of the stools close to the old-fashioned cash register.

"Chocolate, strawberry, or vanilla?"

She frowned. "Um, strawberry? What kind of question is that?"

Instead of answering, I went into the back and returned with milk, ice cream, a carton of fresh strawberries, and more. I also grabbed a parfait glass from a rack of dishes in the corner.

"What are you doing?" she asked.

"Cooking," I said, dumping everything onto the counter in front of her. "It helps me think. So start talking."

Jade's sculpted blond eyebrows shot up in her forehead as I grabbed a bottle of homemade strawberry syrup. "Isn't it a little early for a milkshake?"

At her words, my fingers clenched around the ice-cream scoop in my hand, my grip so tight that I could feel the metal handle pressing into my spider rune scar.

I frowned and forced myself to relax my fingers. It was early for a milkshake. So why had I decided to make one for her? I couldn't come up with an answer. I'd just thought *milkshake* for some reason. Weird.

Jade cleared her throat. "Silvio texted me last night and told me what happened on the riverboat. He asked if I or any of my folks had heard about any new elementals in town, particularly one who can control metal."

"Have you?"

"No."

I looked at her. "Then why are you here? You said that you have information about the bombing."

"I do. At least I think I do." She drew in a breath. "One

of my girls went out on a job two nights ago. New client. Staying at the Blue Moon Hotel. You know it?"

I scooped out a generous portion of vanilla-bean ice cream and put it into a blender, along with some milk, fresh strawberries, and several squirts of strawberry syrup. "Yeah. Fancy place over on Carver Street. Has a nice view of the river which adds another hundred bucks to the bill every night."

She opened her mouth to continue, but I punched the button on the blender, cutting her off as I zapped the ingredients. When everything was combined, I poured the thick strawberry liquid into the parfait glass, then topped it off with whipped cream, several drizzles of strawberry syrup, and a couple of slices of fresh strawberries. I slid the milkshake across the counter to her.

Jade plucked a straw out of one of the dispensers, stuck it into the liquid, and took a cautious sip. The surprise on her face quickly melted into pleasure. "That's a really good milkshake."

"Of course it's good. I made it."

She rolled her eyes. "Your modesty is showing again."

I grinned and leaned my elbows down on the counter. Jade took another sip of her milkshake, then set it aside.

"So," she continued, "this guy at the Blue Moon Hotel. Bit of a slob but average-looking, a decent tipper, and so on."

"But?"

"But my girl noticed that he had a uniform hanging on the back of the bathroom door." Jade looked at me. "Black shirt, black pants, and a red tuxedo vest."

That got my attention. "A waiter uniform for the *Delta Queen*."

She nodded. "Of course, my girl didn't think anything of it at the time. But after Silvio called last night and I asked around, she told me about it."

"And you came down here to deliver the information to me in person." My eyes narrowed. "Why?"

Jade shrugged. "I wanted to make sure you realized that I didn't have anything to do with what happened on the *Delta Queen*, and neither did my girl."

"Duly noted. I appreciate the information."

Her red lips curved up into a sly grin. "I hope you'll remember that the next time I need your special brand of . . . assistance."

Suddenly, her reasons for tipping me off were crystal-clear. But that was just the way the world worked, especially in Ashland.

"Naturally," I replied in a wry tone.

Her grin widened. I couldn't help but like Jade Jamison. She was certainly ballsy, and she watched out for her people, both traits that I admired.

"So this guy, did he have a name?"

Jade snorted. "Mr. Smith."

I ground my teeth together at the likely alias. Just when I thought I was finally getting somewhere . . .

"Don't worry," she purred, sensing my frustration. "I haven't gotten to the best part yet."

"And what would that be?"

Jade reached into her red clutch, pulled out a slip of paper, and slid it across the counter. "He's still there. He called my girl again this morning and booked another session for this evening at her hotel, so it doesn't seem like he has any plans to leave town anytime soon."

I stared at the piece of paper. *Mr. Smith. Room 321. Blue Moon Hotel.*

Anticipation surged through me, but I calmly took the paper, tucked it under a slot in the cash register, and reached for the ice cream and the blender again.

"What are you doing?" Jade asked.

I grinned at her. "Making you another milkshake. You earned it."

* 8 *

Jade drank one of her strawberry milkshakes, complaining the whole time that it would go straight to her ass, but she left with a smile on her face, the other milkshake in a to-go cup, and a cardboard box full of barbecue sandwiches, sides, and all the fixings for her crew.

As much as I would have liked to have gone straight over to the Blue Moon Hotel, shown Mr. Smith the business end of one of my knives, and gotten some answers about what was going on, I still had a restaurant to run. Besides, if the bomber or someone else was watching the Pork Pit, he might see me leave, follow me over to the hotel, and warn Smith to skedaddle before I could get my hands on him. I didn't want anything to jeopardize the very pointed conversation I planned on having with Smith.

But even more than that, I wanted some time to think, to plot and plan, before I confronted Smith. I had a lot of puzzle pieces floating around in my mind, and I needed to put them in some sort of order—before the bomber tried again. So I stayed in the storefront and started my morning chores, including putting together a batch of Fletcher's secret barbecue sauce.

By the time Catalina Vasquez came in, along with the rest of the waitstaff, I knew what I wanted to do about Smith, even though I'd have to wait several hours to actually lay eyes on him. But I went ahead and texted Finn, asking him to drop by the restaurant so I could put the first part of my plan into action.

Finn strolled into the Pork Pit at about one-thirty and slid onto a stool next to the cash register. Silvio was sitting two seats down and typing on his tablet. The vampire was always perfectly punctual, and he had arrived earlier this morning, just as I was turning the sign on the front door over to *Open*.

Finn slapped him on the back. "Hey, Silvy. How's it going?"

Silvio grunted and went back to his tablet. Finn grinned at the annoyed pinch of the vampire's lips. The two of them had a bit of a rivalry going on, with each out to prove that he had more contacts, sources, and spies, and both of them racing to get all the scoop on the Ashland underworld before the other guy did. Today I was going to put their competition and connections to good use.

Silvio had already eaten a grilled chicken salad sandwich and sweet-potato fries, and I fixed Finn's order— a barbecue-chicken sandwich with a side of onion rings and a slice of peach crumb cake for dessert, along with a vanilla milkshake.

While Finn ate, I filled him in on everything Jade had told me. Silvio had heard it all before, but he still typed down a few more notes. I didn't really know why. Maybe it made him feel like more of an assistant. Or maybe Silvio wanted Finn to think that he had some insights that my foster brother didn't. Either way, Silvio had insisted on checking out Jade's information by calling the hotel and verifying that Smith was actually staying there, just to make sure that Jade wasn't trying to trap me in some way. But Jade was a smart woman. She knew how badly setting me up would end—for her.

"The Blue Moon Hotel?" Finn asked, popping the last of his onion rings into his mouth. "That makes sense."

"Why?"

He looked at me. "Because they have one of the best cigar bars in Ashland."

"So the bomber's cigar most likely came from there."

He nodded. "But wait. It gets better."

"And why is that?"

"Because I just happen to know the hotel manager," Finn crowed. He leaned over and elbowed Silvio in the side. "And I'm betting that you don't, right, Silvy?"

The vamp sniffed and straightened his tie. "No, I do not happen to know the manager of that particular hotel."

Finn's grin widened.

"It doesn't matter who knows who," I cut in. "Just that we get eyes and ears on Smith."

Finn frowned. "You mean you're not going to just bust into his hotel room and, you know . . ." He made a slashing motion across his throat, pantomiming me using one of my knives on someone, and threw in several choking gurgles for good measure.

I shook my head. "No. Not at first, anyway. I want to see exactly what Mr. Smith is up to before I have a face-to-face chat with him."

I didn't mention that the reason I was being so cautious was my nagging feeling that something wasn't right about this whole situation, that it was more than someone trying to kill me.

"Well, if you're not going to off the guy, then what are you going to do with him?" Finn asked.

I told him what I wanted. "Do you think you can arrange that?"

His chest puffed up with pride. "Of course I can. I'm Finnegan Lane, baby. The best in the business."

I rolled my eyes. So did Silvio, but Finn was too busy grinning, mentally patting himself on the back at his own cleverness, and slurping down the rest of his milkshake to care.

At eight o'clock that night, I found myself standing in an alley beside the Blue Moon Hotel. Despite the hotel's upscale reputation, this alley was like most in Ashland: dark, dingy, and filled with Dumpsters overflowing with all sorts of rotten garbage. Broken bottles littered the asphalt, the shards glimmering in the few beams of moonlight that managed to filter down into the corridor.

"Are you ready yet?" I groused. "You spend more time on your hair than I do."

Finn pulled his shaggy blond wig a little lower on his forehead. "You want me to look good, don't you?"

"Yes. That is my main concern at the moment. Your appearance."

"Just because we're standing in a dark, deserted alley doesn't mean that I shouldn't strive to look my very best." Finn sniffed and fluffed up the dyed strands of his wig.

Owen laughed at my bickering with Finn, but I sighed, crossed my arms over my chest, and *tap-tap-tap*ped my toe against the cracked pavement. Finn ignored the impatient sound.

Things were almost sure to get messy in the Blue Moon Hotel, and I wanted as little as possible to tie me, Finn, and Owen to Mr. Smith. But there were too many security cameras in the hotel's lobby, shops, restaurants, and elevators for us to avoid them all, so we all wore disguises—glasses and wigs that we'd borrowed from our friend Roslyn Phillips, who ran the Northern Aggression nightclub. Owen and Finn both sported shaggy blond dos and round silver glasses, while I was a redhead with square black frames.

The disguises wouldn't fool anyone for long, but it was an extra precaution and a bit of plausible deniability that I'd insisted on. Given what had happened on the riverboat, I needed to be as careful as possible from here on out.

"There," Finn announced, giving his wig one final pat. "All done."

"Finally," I muttered.

"The Blue Moon has certain standards, Gin," he replied. "Looking messy in a place like this is one of the quickest ways to attract unwanted attention."

Owen looked at him. "You've been to the hotel be-fore?"

"Certainly," Finn said, adjusting his cufflinks. "I am well acquainted with this and every other fine hotel in Ashland."

I snorted. "You mean you're acquainted with sneaking out of them, lest a jealous boyfriend or husband catch you in the act with their lady."

Finn clutched both hands to his heart. "Oh, Gin, you always wound me with your cynicism. Besides, I'm a changed man now, remember? A one-woman man. Right, Owen?"

Owen laughed again and shook his head. "Don't look at me for help. I *know* that the Snow women are not to be trifled with in any way, shape, or form. You're on your own here, my friend."

"One-woman man, huh?" I palmed a knife and flashed it at Finn before tucking it back up my sleeve. "Well, it better stay that way as long as you're dating my baby sister."

"It will, it will," Finn said in a hasty tone, holding up his hands in mock surrender. "Besides, you wouldn't get the chance to carve me up. Bria would blast my balls off with her Ice magic first if she ever even *thought* that I was cheating on her. Which I would never, ever do. And not just because I like all my love-machine man parts to be in working order and not frostbitten to the point of falling off." He shuddered.

Owen winced right along with him. "Like I said—not to be trifled with."

The two of them shared a commiserating look at the thought of facing down Bria's and my Ice magic, but I knew that Finn meant what he said. Despite his former womanizing ways, he really did love Bria, and she was just as crazy about him.

"Well, I think that is more than enough talk about your *man parts*," I sniped. "Let's get this show on the road."

Finn held his hand out. "Ladies first."

I stalked down the alley, strode out onto the sidewalk, and headed for the main entrance, with Finn and Owen a few steps behind me. One at a time, we pushed through the revolving doors and entered the hotel.

The Blue Moon was one of the finest hotels in Ashland, and every part of the expensive decor gleamed, from the old-fashioned chandeliers overhead to the gilded mirrors lining the walls to the marble floors, which featured thin veins of pale blue ribboning through the smooth white stone.

The lobby itself was an enormous circle, with the front desk across from the revolving doors and high-end shops and restaurants curving all the way around the area. They might be housed in the hotel, but the businesses in the lobby were their own destinations, and many folks came here to eat, browse, and spend way too much money on luxury goods.

People moved in and out of the stores, all dressed as professional businesspeople or professional shoppers, out to purchase more of the same designer brands and bling that they already wore. The staff members were gussied up in garments that were just as expensive, and the only way to tell a hotel worker from a guest was by the silver crescent-moon pin tacked to their suit jackets.

Finn was right. In a fancy place like this, blending in was the key to keeping a low profile and not attracting the attention of the roaming giant guards, who were always on the lookout for potential shoplifters. So Finn, Owen, and I had all dressed the part in dark suits, with Finn also carrying a silverstone briefcase to add to the illusion that we were corporate drones, in town for some sort of meeting, passing through the lobby on our way to get a drink, get dinner, and get back to the insanely expensive and exceptionally slow Wi-Fi in our rooms.

Finn glanced around the lobby, making sure that the guards were ignoring us, then pointed over at a shop to the right of the revolving doors. "There's the cigar bar. Let's go take a look."

We headed in that direction. The name of the place, Puff, was spelled out in bold, blocky letters that lit up one red neon light at a time. When the entire name was illuminated, the outline of a cigar flared to life at the end of the sign, complete with a gray spiral of smoke wafting up from its burning ember. The cigar sign and flashing letters cast a dull red glow onto the floor, making the blue veins in the marble look like blood running through the stone.

We reached the glass doors. Finn grinned and waggled his eyebrows at me, and I held out my hand, graciously telling him to go ahead. Owen looked back and forth between the two of us, not understanding our long-standing silent code.

"Owen, my man," Finn chirped, "I think it's high time

that I introduced you to the wide, wonderful world of cigars . . ."

Finn pushed through the doors, grabbed Owen's arm, and steered him inside. Owen looked at me, clearly wanting to stay outside, but I fluttered my fingers at him.

"You boys have fun," I drawled.

The glass doors swung shut behind them, and I moved over to the corner of the shop, leaning against the wall and pretending to check my phone. Finn made a beeline for a woman mixing drinks behind a wooden bar along the wall, with Owen following him. Finn favored the woman with a dazzling smile, then popped open his briefcase and pulled out a plastic bag that held the cigar stub I'd found in the woods. The woman stared at him a moment, and then a slow smile stretched across her face in return.

Finn was a natural schmoozer, and I was confident he'd be able to charm the woman into telling him what kind of cigar it was and who might have purchased one recently. Of course, if I were the bomber, I would have used a fake name and paid in cash, but maybe he wasn't that smart, and we'd get lucky. Hope sprang eternal, right?

I stood at the corner of the glass, still pretending to check my phone, although I was really scanning the storefront and everyone inside the place. In addition to the bar and the bottles of liquor on the mirrored glass shelves behind it, Puff featured clusters of oversize dark brown leather chairs and small tables, situated several feet away from one another. The chandeliers overhead were turned down low, and gray plumes of smoke snaked up into the air, adding to the hazy, elegant atmosphere.

The usual crowd had gathered inside—businesspeople conducting meetings, more casually dressed folks who looked like vacationers, and some very attractive men and women roaming around with drinks in their hands, hoping to pick up a paying date for the night.

No one stood out to me. I was about to turn my attention back to Finn and Owen, who were still at the bar, when I spotted a man in the shadows with his back to the wall.

He was the only person who was sitting by himself, and he was busy looking at his phone, so he didn't notice my staring. He wasn't smoking, but a crystal tumbler of Scotch sat on the table in front of him, along with a bottle. The man was tall, with a muscular build that was similar to Owen's. He wore a perfectly tailored dark blue suit with a pale blue shirt and matching tie, and a silverstone watch flashed on his left wrist, while a silverstone signet ring glimmered on his right hand. His black hair was slicked back from his forehead, revealing a square jaw, chiseled cheekbones, and overall movie-star good looks. Cary Grant had nothing on this guy. Everything about him whispered of understated elegance, money, and power.

I wasn't the only one who noticed him, and one of the working girls approached the man, flashing him an inviting smile. He looked up from his phone, revealing pale blue eyes, and shook his head. The woman pouted and leaned down, showing off the ample assets squeezed into her tight black minidress. The man didn't say anything, but he gave her a cold, flat look that had her standing up and moving away from him in search of more amenable prey for the evening.

The Puff door opened, and Finn and Owen walked over to me. Finn peered over my shoulder, trying to see who I was looking at.

"Uh-oh, Owen," Finn said, elbowing him in the side. "I think you might have some competition for Gin's affections."

"It's not like that," I protested.

"Sure." Finn drawled out the word, determined to tease me. "We just come out here and catch you ogling Mr. Tall, Slick, and Handsome like you want to take a long drag off him. I'm sure that's *nothing*."

I wasn't about to tell Finn that something about the guy nagged at me the way so many little things had been doing over the past two days. The bombs with their nail shrapnel, the mace rune carved into the tree, even the milkshakes I'd made for Jade Jamison. Finn would have said that I was being paranoid again. He might have been right about that.

"Should I be jealous?" Owen asked, joining in with Finn's teasing. "Because I am more than prepared to storm in there and challenge that guy to a duel. Pistols at dawn or something dramatic like that. Anything to defend my fair lady's honor and win her everlasting favor."

He pressed his fist to his heart and bowed low to me before straightening back up, grabbing my hand, and pressing a kiss to my knuckles.

I laughed. "As interesting as that would be, Sir Grayson, you have nothing to worry about."

"Good to hear, Lady Genevieve." Owen winked at me.

I turned away from the storefront. "What did you find out?"

Owen shook his head. "Dead end. They have the cigar—it's called Chicory Coffee, interestingly enough— but the clerk couldn't find a record of anyone ordering it in the past week."

"At least, no one with a credit card or charging it to their room," Finn added. "So the guy most likely paid cash for it."

I sighed. "So we still have nothing that might tell us who the bomber really is."

"You got it, sister." Finn shot his thumb and fore-finger at me, then perked up. "But on the bright side, I restocked my cigar supply with several of those exquisite Chicory Coffee smokes."

He held up a white plastic bag that featured the Puff name and cigar rune in red letters.

"Peachy," I muttered.

Finn grinned wider at my snarky tone.

"Now what?" Owen asked.

I glanced at my watch. "Now we go see what Mr. Smith is up to. His date should be wrapping up right about now, and he should be heading back to his room soon."

"Going to smoke the truth out of him, Gin?" Finn chuckled at his bad joke.

I sighed. "Please tell me that you are not going to make stupid cigar jokes the rest of the night."

Finn huffed, as though he were offended. "Of course not. There's nothing stupid about my jokes. Is there, Owen?"

Owen shook his head, but a grin spread across his face. "Don't ask me. I'm not getting in this middle of this . . . smelly situation."

I groaned, but Finn raised his hand, and Owen high-fived him.

"If you two are done being clever, maybe we can get on with things?" I groused.

"Sure, just give me a second to put away my smokes," Finn said. "I wouldn't want them to get damaged when we talk to Smith."

I frowned. "Damaged? Why would they get damaged? And with what?"

"Knives, magic, blood, big, fat, sloppy man tears as Smith begs for mercy," Finn said. "You know. All the Gin Blanco specialties."

He was right again. Those were my specialties.

Finn had Owen hold his briefcase so he could open it and slide the plastic bag full of cigars inside. The second he was done, I held out my hands, shooing the two of them toward the elevators. Finn put his arm around Owen's shoulder, already planning a time for them to get together to smoke some of the cigars.

Instead of following them, I looked through the windows of the cigar bar again. The man I'd noticed earlier was focused on his phone once more. He reached out, grabbed his glass of Scotch, and took a slow sip, making the signet ring flash on his hand. He wasn't doing anything out of the ordinary, but I still felt uneasy. There was just something about him that seemed so familiar—

A low whistle sounded. I looked over and realized that Finn was waving to me from the elevators.

I glanced at the man again, but he wasn't the one we

were here to see. That would be Mr. Smith, and he was waiting for me, even if he didn't know it yet.

So I moved away from the cigar bar, more than ready to put eyes on someone who could finally help me get to the bottom of things.

❈ 9 ❈

Owen, Finn, and I rode the elevator up to the seventh floor, acting casual but keeping our heads down so as not to give the security cameras a good look at our faces. The doors opened, but the hallway was empty, so we were able to go over to the fire stairs and walk down to the third floor without anyone seeing us. The Blue Moon was one of those places that prided itself on its guests—and all their activities, legal and otherwise—staying anonymous, so no cameras monitored the stairwells or the room floors.

Finn drew an electronic key card out of his jacket pocket, slid it through the reader, and opened the door. He stepped inside, and Owen shut the door behind us. The room was empty, but that was to be expected.

Because we weren't in Mr. Smith's room—we were in the one next door.

I'd told Finn and Silvio that I didn't want to question

Smith. Not just yet. Instead, I wanted to watch him first and get a sense of what he was like. And, more important, who he was working for. Dead men tell few tales, and I wanted as much information as I could get before I went into the next room and put the squeeze on Smith in person.

So, wearing his disguise, Finn had come over to the hotel earlier today and lifted a master key card off one of the housekeepers. Making sure that Smith was out, he'd let himself into the other man's room and made a few, well, adjustments to certain items inside.

Finn and Owen took off their jackets and threw them onto the bed, but I kept mine on, to hide the knives up my sleeves just in case I had to leave the room in a hurry. Three chairs had been arranged in front of the TV, and we all sat down, with me in the seat closest to the door. If Smith realized that someone had been in his room, he might bolt, and I wanted to be able to run him down.

Finn picked up the remote and clicked on the flat-screen TV. A mirror image of our room popped up onto the screen, thanks to the bug that he had planted in the TV next door.

"And now, allow me to proudly present our newest viewing channel," Finn pronounced, giving an elegant flourish of his hand. "And it won't even cost you extra."

"Cost me extra? It already costs five hundred bucks a night, which you put on one of my credit cards," I grumbled. "For that much money, they should have real, live people come to your room and act out the movies."

"You mean on the credit card of one of your many

aliases," Finn chirped back. "It's not like you actually have to *pay* for it."

"I do if I want to keep using this alias."

He waved away my concerns, hopped to his feet, and strolled over to the minibar. "Who's thirsty? I certainly am."

He pulled out several small bottles and tossed one over to Owen, keeping the rest for himself. Twenty dollars a bottle times three, four, five . . . I sighed and stopped counting. I was not looking forward to getting the bill for tonight.

Finn and Owen cracked open their overpriced, under-sized bottles of booze, but I stared at the TV screen.

The room on the other side of the wall was a mess. Tangled sheets trailed off the king-size bed, pillows had been strewn everywhere, silver room-service platters crowded together on the desk, and several pairs of silk leopard-print boxers had been draped over the tops of the lampshades, as if to dry.

"What a slob," Owen said.

"You don't have to be neat to plant a bomb. Just sneaky. When is he supposed to be back in his room?"

Finn glanced at his watch. "According to the info that the lovely Ms. Jamison texted me earlier tonight, Smith's date with her employee was supposed to wrap up fifteen minutes ago. They were meeting at a hotel a block over, so he should be back here anytime now."

Sure enough, out in the hallway, I heard the loud bang of a door slamming shut. On the screen, a shadow moved across the floor in the other room, indicating that some-one had opened the door. A second later, a man stepped within view of the TV. Sandy hair, dark eyes, plain features, modest suit, with a garish leopard-print tie. Hello, Mr. Smith.

"That's him," I said. "That's the fake waiter from the riverboat."

Finn hit another button on the remote. "Did I mention that we have picture and sound? So let's sit back and watch the show."

Smith must have enjoyed his paid date, because he was grinning from ear to ear and whistling a jaunty, happy tune. He even went over to the mirror and winked at himself, as if he was proud of his stud-muffin ways. Smith was far too busy basking in his own prowess to suspect that he was in trouble—or that someone was watching him.

Finn, Owen, and I settled in for our evening's viewing, but Smith didn't do anything remotely interesting. All he did was plop down on the unmade bed, pull out his cell phone, and start scrolling through his messages, texting several folks and chuckling at some silly cat video, judging from the *meows* streaming out of his phone.

Finally, he got tired of that and threw his phone down on top of the nightstand, not noticing that it slipped off the side and fell into the crack between the nightstand and the wall. Smith scooted down into the center of the bed and picked up the remote.

Click.

Click-click.

Click.

He jabbed and jabbed at the buttons, but nothing happened, thanks to the rewiring job Finn had done on his TV.

"Aw, nuts," Smith muttered. "Stupid TV's broken."

I tensed, wondering if he might call the front desk to have someone from maintenance come up and look at the TV. If that happened, our spy mission was over, and I'd have to grab Smith and get him out of his room before one of the hotel staff showed up.

But instead of calling for help, Smith got up and stripped off his suit in view of the TV, revealing zebra-striped boxers. At least he was consistent with his jungle theme.

"Woot, woot. Take it off, baby!" Finn called out. "Bow-chicka-wow-wow!"

"I didn't think he was your type." Owen chuckled. "Especially considering that conversation we had earlier about you being a one-woman man now."

"Oh, he's not." Finn grinned. "But somebody had to say it."

I glared at him, but he cracked open another miniature bottle of booze and saluted me with it.

Smith finished stripping, leaving his suit and silk boxers on the floor, then headed into the bathroom. Through the TV, I could hear the squeaking of the faucets turning on, then the steady hissing of water running in the shower.

Owen looked at me. "Now would be the perfect time to slip into his room."

I shook my head. "Not yet."

"What are you waiting for? An invitation?" Finn asked. "We've been here thirty minutes already, and he hasn't done anything entertaining, much less incriminating. I don't think that Smith is going to get out of the shower, call up his comrades in crime, and ask them to come over for poker night so you can kill them all in one fell swoop."

"I know that," I snapped. "But Fletcher always said that there was no harm in waiting if you weren't sure about things. So that's what we're going to do."

"*Wait*? Until you feel *sure* about things? With your paranoia, Christmas will come sooner," Finn groused.

"And you never could sit still for more than five minutes without fidgeting," I shot back.

My foster brother huffed, got up from his chair, and propped some pillows up against the headboard before launching himself ass-first onto the bed. He punched the pillows several times to flatten them into submission and made a big show of positioning them just so, before he finally settled back against them, stretched out his legs, and crossed his ankles.

"Well, if we have to wait, then I'm going to be comfortable while I do it," Finn said, leaning over and plucking a room-service menu off the nightstand. "I wonder if they have popcorn in this joint. Since we're here to watch a show, we *totally* need some popcorn to go along with it. Don't you think?"

"I think the only thing corny in here is *you*," I muttered.

Owen snickered. "Maybe Finn would like some cheese to go along with his whine."

"Nice," I said.

I held out my hand, and Owen high-fived me.

Finn shot us both a dirty look, but he contented himself with the minibar liquor. We all settled back down and sat there in silence while Smith took his shower.

I hadn't lied. I didn't really know what I was waiting for. Maybe for the bomber to make a personal appearance. Because if my minion had been going around town trashing hotel rooms, having a good time, and attracting attention, then I would have made it a point to come and tell him to knock it off. That discretion was the better part of valor—and the only thing that would keep me from killing him. Besides, guys like Smith always squealed the second anyone put any kind of pressure on them. And I was betting that the bomber didn't want anyone knowing who he was—before he killed me, anyway.

So I would wait and watch and hope that I got a lucky break.

But of course, the bomber could already be long gone, and Smith could be on his own now, blowing through whatever money he'd made by planting the bomb on the riverboat—

Another shadow moved across the floor of Smith's room.

I leaned forward, peering at the screen. I hadn't heard a door click shut in the hallway, indicating that someone had entered the room. I wondered if my eyes were playing tricks on me.

But they weren't.

A second later, a man stepped within view of the TV. Smith was still in the shower, so he was oblivious to the guy's arrival.

Black hair, blue eyes, handsome face, snazzy suit. Lo and behold, it was the same guy I'd noticed in the cigar bar. I might be paranoid, but more often than not, my hunches paid off.

Still, the longer I looked at him, the more my stomach tightened with tension. Something about this guy seriously worried me, something beyond the suspicion that he was the bomber. Once again, I felt some sort of vague memory swimming around and around in the bottom of my brain, but the more I tried to pull it up, the deeper it sank. In an instant, it had vanished completely. But the tension, the worry, the dread remained.

The mystery man glanced around the room, his mouth twisting with disgust at the mess Smith had made. But he shoved several pairs of socks off the desk chair and sat down in it. Waiting, just like we were.

Owen frowned. "Hey, isn't that—"

"The guy from downstairs." Finn finished his thought. "Who is he?"

"I don't know," I replied. "But your TV channel just got a lot more interesting."

✣ 10 ✣

The mystery man watched the bathroom door, waiting for Smith to finish his shower, so I took the opportunity to study him.

I had a better view now than I'd had in the cigar bar, and the man was even more handsome than I'd originally thought. Add in his suit, expensive watch, and silverstone signet ring, and you had an exceptionally attractive package. But his perfect features couldn't quite hide the coldness lurking in his eyes, and I thought of the flat glare he'd given the woman who tried to pick him up downstairs. Pretty polish aside, I knew a predator when I saw one.

The guy leaned back in the chair, put his arm on the desk, and started drumming his fingers on the wooden surface. His eyes narrowed as he stared at the bathroom door, and his mouth puckered with annoyance at having to wait for Smith, who was taking what felt like the world's longest shower. At first, his finger tapping seemed harmless enough.

Then I noticed the spoon.

A few inches from his hand, a spoon laid across an empty saucer trembled, then started to shake violently, as though it were being rattled around by an earthquake. I could hear the silverware clanging around, even through the TV screen. There was no way that the guy simply drumming his fingers would cause the spoon to move around like that. He'd have to repeatedly bang his fist against the desk to get that kind of result . . . unless he had some sort of magic.

Some elementals constantly leaked magic, their power rippling off their bodies in invisible waves and affecting their surroundings in small ways even when they weren't doing anything other than blinking and breathing. Or, say, tapping their fingers on a desktop. It was worrisome enough that the guy was an elemental, but what really troubled me was the fact that there was only one kind of power that would affect a simple spoon that way.

Metal magic.

Which meant I'd just found the bomber.

I pointed at the screen. "Do you guys see that? What he's doing to that spoon?"

Finn sat up on the bed. "He's a metal elemental."

"Yeah," Owen said, his face creasing with worry. "And I can *feel* his magic, even in here. Can't you, Gin? The guy's strong. Certainly stronger than I am. Stronger than any other metal elemental I've ever met."

Owen was right. Not only could I sense the guy's

cold, hard power, but I could feel it pulsing through the wall that separated us, which meant that he had some serious juice, especially since he wasn't actively using his magic. Oh, I didn't think he had as much raw power as Madeline Monroe, but he had enough to do some serious damage—and enough to make even me think twice about taking him on face-to-face.

The squeaking of the faucets sounded again, and the water stopped running. A minute later, Smith stepped back out into the main part of his room, wearing a fluffy white robe and toweling off his face and hair. He was still whistling, and it took him several seconds to spot the mystery man sitting at the desk. But when he did, he dropped his towel and let out a surprised, high-pitched shriek that made Finn, Owen, and me all wince.

"Pike!" Smith said, clutching a hand to his heart. "You scared the shit out of me!"

"I really hope not," the mystery man, Pike, drawled in a cool voice. "That would be very unpleasant for both of us."

Smith paused, as if he wasn't sure whether or not Pike was making a joke. He decided to play if off as a joke, because he grinned. "Anyway, Pike, dude, I'm glad you got my message," Smith said. "And I really appreciate you putting me up in these swanky digs these past few days. It's been primo all the way around. I just wish that I had been able to help you kill that chick like you wanted."

Kill that chick? Maybe this was just about murdering me after all.

I took another look at Pike, examining his face, clothes, and posture. I even tried to see what, if anything, might be engraved on his silverstone signet ring, but his hand was turned the wrong way. Still, no matter how hard I tried, I just couldn't place him. As far as I knew, I'd never even met the man. Granted, lots of people whom I'd never met before had tried to kill me over the past few months, but I at least knew about their or their bosses' reputations and that they all wanted to take over the Ashland underworld.

But Pike? I didn't get that greedy, jealous, *kill Gin Blanco to get to the top* vibe from him at all. Instead, he struck me as the sort who would hold a grudge at the smallest perceived slight, take it very, very personally, and spend a great deal of time plotting how to exact maximum retribution for it.

But try as I might, I couldn't imagine what I could have possibly done to piss him off enough to plant a bomb on the *Delta Queen*. Pike was a total mystery to me—a fact that I didn't like and definitely one that I couldn't afford. Not if I wanted to keep on breathing and, more important, keep my friends safe from whatever plots he might have hatched.

"No, you didn't manage to *kill that chick*," Pike murmured. "Things took an unexpected turn. I didn't think that my plan would be uncovered—or that you would abandon your post at the first sign of trouble."

His face was calm, but clear menace rippled through his voice, and he never stopped drumming his fingers on the desk. Smith eyed the spoon, which was still rattling around on that saucer, but he swallowed his nervousness. Fool. He was already dead. He just didn't know it yet.

Smith held up his hands and gave an apologetic shrug. "What was I supposed to do? That chick has a serious reputation, and she came at me like she wanted to tear my head off with her bare hands. I wasn't going to stick around to let her make it a reality. Know what I mean?"

"Hmm," Pike replied. "Yes, I suppose you're right. It was better to run away and live to fight another day. I actually think that this will work out better. Now I can regroup. Refocus my efforts and really make the statement that I want."

Smith perked up. "See? I knew that you'd see things my way. That's why I texted and asked you to come over. So we could clear the air."

Pike gave the other man a flat look, but Smith didn't notice it. Then again, it was obvious that he wasn't the brains of this operation.

"So are you here to give me the rest of my payment, like we agreed?" Smith asked, a wheedling tone creeping into his voice. "Because I want double what you promised me."

Pike's fingers stilled. "And why should I pay you double?"

"Because you didn't tell me that I was planting an actual *bomb* on that tub. You said that it was just a smoke grenade that would add to the confusion after you shot that chick in the head." Smith threw up his hands in indignation. "I could have been killed!"

So Pike hadn't told Smith the truth about the bomb, which meant that he'd probably planned for his hired hand to stay right by that champagne bucket and die in the explosion. Well, that would have been a neat, effective way of tying up any loose ends that might lead back to him.

"That was the idea," Pike said. "But since you let *that chick*, as you call her, spook you into running, I guess I'll just have to take care of things myself."

Smith swallowed again, his face suddenly pale, despite his hot shower. He stepped back and dropped his hand down into the pocket of his white robe. "Now, Pike, there's no need to be hasty. Just because I didn't finish the job is no reason for this to turn ugly."

"Oh," Pike said. "I think that it is every reason for it to turn *ugly*. I pay for results . . . not disappointments like you."

Smith huffed, then yanked his hand up out of the pocket of his robe, revealing a small black pistol.

On the bed, Finn perked up. "Now it's getting interesting."

Owen and I both shushed him.

Smith pointed the gun at Pike. "Now what are you going to do, tough guy?" Smith crowed. "Because I have a gun, and you don't."

Pike gave him a bored look, then reached over and picked up the spoon from the saucer. "A gun? I don't need a gun. All I need is this one simple spoon."

Smith's finger curled back on the trigger, and his sneer widened. "I always thought that you were an arrogant, hoity-toity son of a bitch—"

A pale blue light flashed around Pike's fingers, and another, stronger surge of his metal magic pulsed through the wall. Given the intense glow, I couldn't see exactly what he was doing, but he almost seemed to be . . . twisting the spoon in his hands, as though it were a dishrag he was wringing out, instead of solid metal. For some reason, he also pressed his signet ring up against the spoon.

A second later, the light winked out, and he raised his hand, still holding the dirty piece of silverware.

But it wasn't a simple spoon anymore.

Instead, Pike was now holding a long, thin piece of metal with a sharp point that looked remarkably similar to one of my silverstone knives.

"Did he just . . ." My voice trailed off.

"Use his metal magic to reshape that spoon into a dagger?" Owen finished my thought. "Yeah. That's exactly what he did."

"Cool," Finn chimed in.

Owen and I both turned around in our chairs and gave him a look.

"What?" Finn protested. "It is cool in a completely sneaky, underhanded, deadly sort of way. I admire such things."

Owen and I both turned back around and stared at the TV screen again.

Smith looked at the thin bit of metal and barked out a laugh. "And what do you think you're going to do with that? I still have a gun, in case you haven't noticed."

Pike flicked his hand in a short, quick throwing motion. The spoon-turned-dagger zipped through the air—and sank right into the middle of Smith's throat.

Smith dropped his gun and clutched his hands to his neck. He stupidly yanked the dagger out, causing even more damage and hastening his own death. Dark arterial blood spattered down the front of his white robe, but

Smith still tried to fight the inevitable—or at least take Pike with him.

Wheezing all the while, Smith staggered forward and raised the dagger, as though he was going to stab the other man with it. But his feet got tangled in the clothes he'd stripped off earlier, and he tripped and toppled to the floor, landing at Pike's feet.

Still sitting in the desk chair, Pike swiveled around so that he wouldn't get any blood on his glossy black wing tips. Then he pulled out his phone and started checking his messages while he waited for Smith to bleed out.

It didn't take long.

After sending a few texts, Pike tucked his phone away and stared at Smith for several seconds, making sure that he was dead.

Then he got to his feet, buttoned his blue suit jacket, stepped over Smith's body, and left the hotel room.

Smith's blood continued to ooze across the floor, the growing puddle soaking into the white sheets lying at the foot of the bed.

Owen and Finn sat there staring at the monitor, but I surged to my feet and hurried over to the door of our room, not wanting to lose this opportunity to take care of Pike. The door to Smith's room slammed shut, and I cracked open the one to our room.

Pike was striding down the hall, and there was already about thirty feet of space between us. He would hear me coming up behind him, but it was a risk I was going to have to take—

A small *beep-beep* sounded, and Pike stopped and pulled his phone out of his jacket. I wasn't about to ignore this lucky break, so I stepped through the door, making sure that it didn't bang shut behind me, palmed one of my knives, and headed in his direction.

Pike started walking again, but he was still looking at his phone, so I managed to close the gap between us to twenty-five feet . . . twenty feet . . . fifteen . . . ten . . .

I tightened my grip on my knife, ready to jam the blade into his back and keep right on stabbing until he was down and bleeding out.

Pike stopped.

I hesitated, and he turned his head, as though he was going to look over his shoulder. Too late, I realized that he could probably sense my knife, since it was made out of metal, but I started forward again, hoping that I could get to him before he realized what was happening—

Click.

A handle turned, a door opened, and an elderly couple stepped out of a room and into the hallway, right in front of me.

I had to pull up short to keep from mowing them down. I tried to skirt around them, but of course, they moved right in front of me again, completely oblivious to the fact that I was standing behind them and, worst of all, cutting me off from Pike. A frustrated snarl rose in my throat, but I clamped my lips together. Maybe there was still a chance I could get to him.

"Are you sure you have the key card, Peggy?" the old man asked.

Maybe not.

"I've got it right here, Fred," the woman replied, holding the plastic up where he could see it.

Once again, I tried to maneuver past the couple, but they blocked me without even realizing it. All I could do was glare over their shoulders and watch while Pike pocketed his phone and continued down the hallway. He didn't look back, but he was moving fast, almost as if he'd sensed the danger he was in.

A second later, he pushed through the door to the same fire stairs that Finn, Owen, and I had used earlier and vanished. From there, he could go down to the lobby or disappear into a room on an upper floor, and I had no way of guessing which one it might be.

Gone—the bastard was gone.

"Oh, excuse us, young lady," the woman said, finally noticing me. She grabbed the man's jacket and yanked him back out of my way. "Let her through, Fred. She looks like she has places to be."

"Not anymore," I muttered.

My target had escaped, so all I could do now was slide my knife back up my sleeve, give the old couple a bland smile, turn around, and head back to our room.

❄ 11 ❄

"Well, that was anticlimactic," Finn drawled as he and Owen walked down the hallway to meet me.

"Tell me about it," I muttered.

"Don't worry," Owen said. "We'll track him down. He won't be so lucky next time."

I nodded, then glanced over my shoulder. The elderly couple had finally made it to the elevators, and they stepped inside one of the cars, the doors sliding shut behind them.

"C'mon," I said, jerking my head at Smith's room. "We need to get in there, nose around, and get out before anyone else realizes what's happened to him."

Finn ducked back into our room to grab some latex gloves from his briefcase, while Owen and I looked up and down the hallway, making sure the coast was clear. Finn came back out, gloves already on, and waited while Owen and I pulled on our own gloves. Then Finn whipped out his master key card, and the three of us slipped into the dead man's room.

Smith lay where he had fallen, his dark, sightless eyes fixed on the chair where Pike had sat and watched him bleed to death. I didn't waste time examining his body, since I'd already witnessed his murder. But Pike hadn't bothered to search the room before he left, and I was going to cash in on his sloppiness. Because there was one thing in here that might actually tell me more about the metal elemental.

So I went over, stuck my hand into the space between the nightstand and the wall, and fished out Smith's phone, which he'd dropped before Pike paid him a visit. It was a burner cell, but I still passed it over to Finn.

"See what info you can get off that. Like Pike's number and any texts he might have sent to Smith."

Finn nodded and tucked the phone away in his jacket pocket. "Anything else?"

"Well, there's this." Owen pointed to the spoon-turned-dagger that Smith was still clutching in his dead hand.

He crouched down and plucked the makeshift weapon out of Smith's fingers, careful not to disturb the rest of the body. Owen got to his feet and held the dagger out where we could all examine it.

I'd assumed that the weapon was crude when I saw it on the TV monitor, but it was anything but. Long, light, thin, with razor-sharp edges that tapered to a deadly point. Oh, the craftsmanship wasn't nearly as good as the five knives that Owen had forged for me, but it wasn't some plastic toy you'd get out of a cereal box either. Pike was even more dangerous than I'd thought.

"He did that with just one little burst of his metal magic?" Finn let out a low whistle. "Impressive."

"Look closer at it," Owen said, pointing at the bottom of the knife. "Right there. See it?"

Finn and I leaned down, and I noticed a symbol stamped into the metal—a long line topped by a spiked ball. I thought of how Pike had pressed his signet ring into the spoon when he was shaping it. He'd been marking his impromptu weapon. Well, now I knew exactly what was engraved on his jewelry.

"A fucking mace," I snarled.

The rune was more confirmation that Pike was the bomber and another reminder of my failure to kill him. Frustration surged through me, and my fingers itched to grab every single thing in the room that wasn't nailed down and throw it as hard as I could. The dirty dishes, the room-service platters, all those ridiculous leopard-print boxers.

But I drew in a couple of deep breaths and let them out, pushing down my anger. Trashing Smith's room even more than it already was would make far too much noise. It wouldn't solve anything, and it certainly wouldn't help me track down Pike before he struck again.

So I searched through all the cabinets and drawers, then patted down the pockets of Smith's clothes in case we'd missed something, but there were no other clues to be found.

"All right," I said. "Time to go."

Finn nodded, went over to the TV, and started messing with the wires, unhooking his spy gear and putting everything back the way it was supposed to be. Owen nestled the spoon-turned-dagger back in Smith's hand in the same position as before.

A couple of minutes later, Finn finished with the TV. He made sure the hallway was clear, then slipped next door to our room. Owen followed him, but I lingered next to Smith's body, staring at the pool of blood that had spread out around the dead man. It almost looked like he was sleeping on red satin sheets.

I just wondered whose blood would be spilled next—Pike's or mine.

An hour later, Finn, Owen, and I were among the gawkers standing outside the Blue Moon Hotel, watching as a stretcher bearing a black body bag was carted out of the main entrance.

A man wearing dark blue coveralls steered the stretcher across the sidewalk and over to a van waiting at the curb. The flashing blue and white lights of the hotel marquee and its crescent-moon rune made his black hair and skin gleam like polished jet. Silver glasses perched on his nose, and a small black goatee clung to his chin, giving him a serious, distinguished air.

Dr. Ryan Colson handed the stretcher off to one of his workers, then turned and looked out over the crowd. His hazel gaze locked with mine. I'd ditched my wig-and-glasses disguise, so he could see exactly who I was. He blinked a few times, as if to make sure that his eyes weren't playing tricks on him. When he realized that it was indeed me, Colson crossed his arms over his chest and quirked his eyebrows, silently asking if I was the one who'd left behind such a bloody mess. A valid question, given the jagged wound in Smith's neck, which was similar to many that I'd dished out over the years.

I shook my head. I hadn't killed anyone tonight—for a change.

The corners of Colson's lips curled up into a small, wry smile. He nodded at me, then went over to help his worker load the stretcher into the coroner's van.

Bria pushed through the revolving doors, having finished her questioning of the hotel staff. She headed in my direction, trailed by a giant who was around seven feet tall with a shaved head and ebony skin. Despite the late hour, a pair of aviator sunglasses was hooked into the neck of his white polo shirt. Xavier, Bria's partner on the force.

"Anything?" I asked Bria.

After Finn, Owen, and I left the hotel, I'd called Bria and given her a heads-up about Smith's murder. We'd hung around until she, Xavier, and the rest of the cops arrived.

Bria checked the notes on the small pad in her hand. "Nothing out of the ordinary. Guy's name was Harold Smith, according to his credit card and driver's license. It looks to be his real name. Been staying here for the past few days. Didn't hassle the staff, although one of the housekeepers told me what a slob he was. No bomb-making materials and no trace of any explosives ever being in his room."

I rubbed my head, which was suddenly aching. "That's because Pike was the one who actually built the bombs, probably somewhere else. Smith was just his delivery boy. When I messed up his plan and Smith didn't die in the explosion, Pike came here and finished the job."

Not for the first time, I wish that I'd moved quicker and managed to catch Pike in the hallway outside Smith's room. A couple of swipes with my knife, and I could have ended this whole thing before anyone else got hurt. But I'd wanted to watch Pike, to see if I could figure out why he seemed so familiar, and I'd blown my chance. Well, that and I didn't want to plow through that elderly couple and traumatize them by stabbing Pike right in front of them. Or worse, put them in the crossfire. Unlike Pike, I tried to keep collateral damage—and witnesses—to a minimum. Either way, he was in the wind, and I was back to square one.

"Anything on a guest named Pike staying at the hotel?" I asked, even though I knew that he wouldn't be dumb enough to stay at the same hotel as his minion.

Xavier shook his head. "No one by that name is registered here, but I'll start checking the other hotels. You think that's his real name or an alias?"

"Real name," I said automatically.

Xavier frowned. "Are you sure? How do you know that?"

How *did* I know that? I couldn't come up with a reasonable answer. But the more I thought about it, the more certain I felt that Pike was his real name.

But I couldn't explain to Xavier what I didn't know myself, so I shrugged. "I just do. Call it a hunch."

But it was more than a hunch, which didn't make any sense either. And the name *Pike* nagged at me, the same way the mace rune had been nagging at me since yesterday. Most of the time, I was good at remembering names and faces, especially of dangerous elementals. It was practically a job requirement, both as an assassin and as the head of the underworld. I knew this guy—I *knew* I did—but I'd be damned if I could recall when or where we'd met or why he wanted to blast me into oblivion.

"I'll let you know if we find out anything else or if Pike shows up at any of the local hotels," Bria said.

"Just be careful. Okay, guys?"

She and Xavier both nodded at me, then headed back to the hotel, pushed through the revolving doors, and disappeared inside to see what other leads they might come up with.

There was nothing else to see or do here, so Finn, Owen, and I got into Finn's car, and he drove us over to Fletcher's house before heading back to his apartment.

Owen had promised Eva, his baby sister, that they would hang out after her last evening class, so he kissed me good night and went home. After he left, I checked in with Silvio, who promised to reach out to his sources and meet me at the Pork Pit bright and early the next morning with a complete update. Sometimes I wondered if the vampire ever actually slept. If he did, he probably had his tablet and phone nestled on the pillow next to him.

But Silvio wasn't the only one with resources, so I tossed my phone onto the coffee table in the den, got up off the couch, and went to Fletcher's office.

I flipped on the lights and looked out over the old man's personal space. A battered desk, bookcases, filing cabinets. Given our life of crime, Fletcher had spent a fair amount of time keeping tabs on our enemies, in addition to spying on and collecting information about all the folks in the Ashland underworld. So his office was a veritable treasure trove of dirty little secrets, despite the benign furnishings.

For the longest time, I didn't have the heart to tidy up Fletcher's cluttered office, but I'd finally had to start going through all the papers and folders that he'd accumulated over the years. 'Assassin Smothered by Piles of Papers' was not a headline I wanted to read.

Plus, Fletcher had had his own unique filing system, organizing most—but not all—of the files by the runes people used to represent their magic, family, business, or crew. I'd never understood why he did things that way, rather than just using people's names, but I supposed it was the system that worked for him.

Over the past several weeks, I'd slowly started sorting through all the files and reorganizing them in a way that would let me understand and access the information more easily when needed. But I'd left the majority of the furniture, pens, pads, paperweights, and other knickknacks in their usual spots, as an homage to him, and every once in a while, I would brew a cup of chicory coffee, bring it back here, set it on his desk, and let the fumes permeate the office, just as they had when Fletcher was alive.

As a final touch, I'd framed a photo of the old man that I'd taken on Bone Mountain and placed it on the corner of his desk, so I could see it and be reminded of him. In the picture, Fletcher stood on a snowy mountain ridge, his hands in the pockets of his blue work pants, his green eyes bright, and a soft smile creasing his face, as he looked out over the scenic landscape. It was my favorite picture of him.

I ran my fingers over the glass and his smiling face before digging into the files. I went through all the ones I had organized first, looking for the name *Pike* and the mace rune, but I didn't find either one. I sighed. I should have known it wouldn't be that easy. My life never, ever was.

So I started in on the files that I hadn't organized yet, the ones that were still in Fletcher's old system. An angry growl rumbled out of my throat with every folder I opened, closed, and set aside because it wasn't the right one. Soon I had flipped through them all and had nothing to show for it. I growled again, longer and louder. Once—*just once*—I would like to come in here, grab the file I needed, and start reading it without all the rigmarole of searching high and low for it.

But Fletcher had stuffed files in odd locations before, hiding the really important ones for me to find in case I ever needed them. In fact, it seemed like a game that he'd arranged to play with me, even from beyond the grave. So I ransacked the rest of the office, opening all the desk drawers, peering in, under, and around all the furniture, looking for secret compartments everywhere I searched.

And I found some.

Several, as a matter of fact. False bottoms in the filing cabinet drawers, hollow panels in the bookcases, even an empty space under a loose floorboard. And all the hidey-holes had at least one folder tucked away inside them—if not more.

I sat with my back to Fletcher's desk and eagerly flipped

through them, eyeing the runes the old man had drawn on the tabs, which included everything from knives dripping blood to lightning bolts shooting through skulls to a heart made out of jagged icicles that had been arranged together like the pieces of a jigsaw puzzle. That last file was hidden by itself in a secret compartment in the very bottom of the lowest drawer in Fletcher's desk, as if it was particularly special.

But there was no mace rune and no Pike.

Nothing. Once again, I had nothing.

I punched the side of Fletcher's desk in frustration. Of course, my hand had a lot more give to it than the thick, solid wood did, and I hissed in pain and glared down at my bruised knuckles.

After a moment, I shook the pain away and forced myself to think things through.

Fletcher had kept files on everyone who was anyone in the Ashland underworld, along with all the folks we'd gone after as the Tin Man and the Spider, just in case someone came looking for payback. But there was nothing in any of the folders about anyone named Pike. As far as I could tell, no Pikes had ever been part of the Ashland underworld.

It could be that Fletcher simply hadn't known about Pike. Maybe the metal elemental wasn't from Ashland and thus had never pinged the old man's radar. But I *still* felt like I knew Pike, or had at least heard of him, even if I couldn't remember when or where. And I was firmly convinced that the memory, as vague and hazy as it was, was the key to figuring out exactly who Pike was and what he wanted.

Or maybe Finn was right, and my crazy paranoia was showing again.

Either way, my failure in Fletcher's office was just another in a string of missed opportunities. If only I'd taken Pike out in the hotel, I wouldn't be sitting on the floor with busted knuckles and a bad attitude. Yep, Gin Blanco was batting exactly .000 tonight.

Out in the hallway, one of the grandfather clocks chimed out the late hour. I sighed and got to my feet, throwing the stack of hidden files on top of Fletcher's desk. Then I slapped off the lights, left the office, and headed upstairs to try to get some sleep.

All I wanted to do was forget about all the mistakes I'd already made regarding the mysterious Mr. Pike—and what they might cost me.

❊ 12 ❊

Feeling more frustrated than ever before, I trudged upstairs, took a long, hot shower, and went to bed. For
the longest time, I lay in the dark, glaring at the ceiling, thinking about all of Fletcher's files that I'd looked
through and how useless they had all been.

But the thing that made me the angriest was that I
knew there was something in his files that would tell me
all about Pike. Just like I *knew* I'd seen Pike somewhere
before, along with his mace rune. I just couldn't quite arrange all the puzzle pieces and vague wisps of memories
together into one clear, solid picture. So I lay in bed and
tried again, but the answers were as elusive as ever.

Eventually I drifted off to sleep, although I wasn't quite
sure when the dreams began, the memories that so often
plagued me about all the things I'd seen, done, and survived over the years . . .

"What are we doing here?" I asked.

Fletcher looked at me, his green eyes dark and serious. "I've got a job to do, Gin. A very dangerous one. So you're going to stay here until I finish it."

Here *was a cabin out in the woods in the middle of nowhere. Fletcher had woken me up early this Friday morning, told me to pack whatever I needed for a couple of days, and driven us out here in his old white van. Finn was at some outdoor adventure camp in Cypress Mountain, so he wouldn't be back until late Sunday.*

The cabin was nothing special, just thick logs that had been stacked together, the sort of quaint, rustic structure that leaf-lookers, bird-watchers, and other folks would pay an obscene amount of money to vacation in. I was surprised that someone wasn't staying in it already, since it was late October and the height of the autumn tourist season in Ashland.

As I looked over the cabin, I realized that someone was here already. The back fins of Sophia's classic convertible peeked around the far side of the structure.

"What's Sophia doing here? Is Jo-Jo here too?"

Fletcher shook his head, not really answering me. "Let's get you squared away inside."

We got out of the van and headed toward the cabin. Fletcher climbed the stairs, then scuffed his feet on the porch, making plenty of noise. I wondered what he was doing, but he kept right on scuffing his feet, even though his boots weren't dirty.

The front door cracked open, revealing a black eye.

A welcoming grunt sounded, and Sophia Deveraux opened the door the rest of the way. Sophia might be Jo-Jo's younger sister, but she had a completely different style—Goth. She sported black boots, black jeans, and a black T-shirt with a cute Dalmatian puppy that was grinning and showing off its bloody vampire fangs. Her lips were painted a dark crimson, the color matching the glittery streaks in her black hair. A white collar studded with red hearts ringed her throat, completing the look. Black and white and red all over.

But the thing that interested me the most was the shotgun in Sophia's hand.

She leaned the weapon up against the wall before stepping aside so that Fletcher and I could enter the cabin. I'd been staying with the old man for several months now, and in all that time, I'd never seen Sophia handle a gun. Not even once. If there was a problem, she used her fists and massive strength to take care of it. But today, for this job, Sophia had a gun.

That told me everything I needed to know about how dangerous Fletcher's assignment really was.

I clutched my backpack a little more tightly to my chest, wishing that I'd thought to bring a weapon, even if it was just a kitchen knife. After all, the old man was teaching me how to be an assassin like him. It was time I started acting like one, which meant having a weapon handy at all times. I vowed to find a knife as soon as possible.

"Where are they?" Fletcher asked.

Sophia stuck her thumb over her shoulder. Fletcher headed toward the back of the cabin, stopping when he came to a bathroom. That's where Jo-Jo was.

Along with the girl.

She was sitting on the closed toilet lid, with Jo-Jo kneeling on the floor beside her. The girl was dressed like me, in sneakers, jeans, and a long-sleeved T-shirt, although her black hair was pulled back into a pretty French braid and studded with sparkly red-rose-and-thorn pins, instead of being in a boring *old ponytail like mine was. I even thought that she was the same age as me—fourteen or so—although it was hard to tell since her face was such a mess.*

Someone had brutally beaten the girl.

Both of her eyes were blackened, her nose was broken, and deep scratches crisscrossed her forehead, cheeks, and chin, as though a wild animal had clawed her over and over again, digging deeper and deeper into her skin every single time. Blood oozed out of the scratches and dripped out of her pulpy nose, spattering onto her pale blue T-shirt and turning it an ugly brown. Tears also streamed down her bruised, swollen face, and every once in a while, the girl would let out a choked sob, her fingers digging into the bloody towel she was clutching in her lap.

"It's okay, darling," Jo-Jo crooned. "I'm going to fix you right up. I'll be done in a few minutes, and then you'll feel a whole lot better. Okay?"

The girl sniffled, but she finally nodded.

"All right, then. Here we go."

Jo-Jo held up her hand. A milky-white glow coated her palm, and the familiar sensation of her Air magic gusted through the bathroom.

"Gin," Fletcher said. "Can you help Jo-Jo, please?"

I slipped into the bathroom, knowing what he really wanted me to do. I skirted around Jo-Jo and went over to the girl. She tensed at my approach, but I sat down on the edge of the bathtub and gently took one of her hands in both of mine. Her skin was hot and clammy, and the rapid throbbing of her pulse in her wrist beat like a drum against my fingers.

"It's okay," I said. "Jo-Jo heals me all the time. It hurts a little in the beginning, but she'll make you all better."

The girl stared at me, and I realized that her eyes were a very pale, very pretty blue. She sniffled again, curled her fingers into mine, and tightened her grip. With her other hand, she reached up and took hold of her braid, tugging on the end of it in a nervous habit.

Jo-Jo reached for even more of her Air magic and leaned forward. The girl whimpered, and a fresh wave of tears slid down her cheeks, but she sat still while Jo-Jo used her power to stitch her skin together, straighten her nose, and fade out all the bruises and swelling.

About halfway through, I noticed that the girl's hand had gone cold against mine and that a faint trace of magic rippled through her fingers where they pressed against my own. The girl kept her head down, gritting her teeth. She didn't like the pins-and-needles feel of Jo-Jo's Air magic any more than I did, so she must have Ice or Stone power, like me, or perhaps water or metal. It made me even more curious about who she was and who had hurt her.

It didn't take Jo-Jo long to heal the girl. The dwarf released her hold on her Air magic and patted the girl on the shoulder.

"There you go, darling," Jo-Jo crooned in a soft voice, as though she were soothing a wounded animal. "You're all better now. Why don't you take a shower? I put some fresh clothes on the sink. If you need anything else, just holler. Come on, Gin."

The girl dropped the end of her braid and slipped her other hand out of both of mine. I smiled, trying to reassure her, but she gave me a dull, flat stare in return. Jo-Jo and I *left the bathroom, and the dwarf shut the door behind us. A few seconds later, I heard the water in the shower hiss on— and the girl's choked sobs as she started crying in earnest.*

"What happened to her?" I whispered.

Jo-Jo shook her head, and a bit of annoyance spurted through me. I was getting tired of people not answering me.

I followed her back out into the front of the cabin, where Fletcher and Sophia were talking in low voices.

"Now what?" Jo-Jo asked.

"I'm going after him," Fletcher said. "Right now. Before he finds her and kills her too."

Too? Who had this mystery man already killed?

Jo-Jo nodded, knowing exactly what he was talking about. Well, that made one of us.

"Sophia's going with me," Fletcher said. "To deal with his guards while I go after Renaldo."

Well, at least the mystery man had a name now.

Jo-Jo lifted her chin. "I'm coming too."

"No," Fletcher said. "It's too dangerous."

Her clear eyes glowed with determination, and her mouth flattened out into a harsh line. "Which is all the more reason for me to come. In case you and Sophia need healing."

Fletcher stared at her, then sighed. "All right. I know there's no changing your mind once it's made up about something."

Jo-Jo tipped her head. "Smart man."

"Girls?" Sophia rasped, pointing at me.

"He can't find them here, can he?" Jo-Jo asked, her face creasing with worry.

"He shouldn't," Fletcher said. "Especially if we leave now and hit him first. We get in, I kill Renaldo, then we get out. Are we all agreed?"

"Agreed," the Deveraux sisters replied in unison.

The three of them moved around the cabin, Sophia grabbing her shotgun while Jo-Jo went into one of the back rooms and returned carrying a large pink satchel. From the way the contents clanked together, the satchel appeared to be full of tins of her healing ointment. Fletcher checked and rechecked the weapons he'd brought along in his black duffel bag. Some of the items surprised me. Oh, there were the usual guns, knives, and boxes of ammo, but he also had several wooden stakes and a long sword that was made out of hard gray stone instead of metal.

"What's that for?" I asked, pointing to the stone sword.

"In case I can't take him by surprise," Fletcher said, sliding the weapon back into the bag and zipping up the whole thing.

"Renaldo, right? That's the guy you're going after?"

He tried to skirt around me, but I crossed my arms over my chest and stepped in front of him. Fletcher stopped, knowing that I could be as stubborn as all get-out when I really wanted to. I was a teenager, after all. He grabbed my arm and drew me off to one side of the cabin, away from the couch where Jo-Jo and Sophia were sorting through their own supplies.

"The girl in the bathroom? She's in some serious trouble," he said. "Her mom contacted me a few days ago. Her husband, the girl's father, is a man named Renaldo Pike. He was hitting them—both of them—and has been for a long time. The mom wanted to leave him, but she couldn't get away by herself, so she got in touch with me through Jo-Jo."

"So where's the mom? Why isn't she here?"

Fletcher's lips pinched together, and his shoulders slumped.

My stomach twisted. "Oh. She didn't make it."

"Renaldo found out what she was planning, and he decided to teach them both a lesson. I didn't get there in time. The woman . . . what he did to her . . ." Fletcher's voice trailed off, and tears gleamed in his eyes before he was able to blink them away. "I'll be hearing her screams in my nightmares for a long time to come."

I stared at him, my own eyes wide, my mouth hanging open, my heart aching for the woman—and for the girl who'd lost her mom in such a horrific way.

Fletcher cleared his throat. "Now I'm going to go make sure that Renaldo never hurts his daughter again."

"What do you need me to do?"

He reached over, hugged me tight, and pressed a kiss to the top of my head. "That's my Gin. Stay with the girl, okay? The two of you should be safe here, and we won't be gone long, if everything goes according to plan."

"Be careful."

He flashed me a grin. "Always."

Fletcher grabbed his bag. Sophia and Jo-Jo met him at the front door, and the three of them headed outside. I watched through the windows as Fletcher went over to a small shed, opened it, and rummaged through the items inside, gathering up a few more supplies.

Deeper in the cabin, a door clicked open, and I heard the squeaking of sneakers on the floor. The girl came up to stand beside me. Sophia had clearly lent her some clothes, since her black jeans and long-sleeved T-shirt were a couple of sizes too big and covered with white skulls. The sides of her wet hair were pinned back with those red rose pins I'd noticed earlier, while the rest of her black locks hung loose around her shoulders.

Panic sparked in the girl's gaze as she realized that Fletcher, Jo-Jo, and Sophia were getting ready to leave. "Where are they going?"

"Don't worry. They'll be back soon. You're safe here. I won't let anything happen to you. I promise."

She looked me up and down, disbelief clouding her pretty face.

We stood there, staring at each other, the silence between us growing and growing. I didn't know what to say to her. What could you say to someone whose dad had killed her mom and almost beaten her to death? It wasn't like I could suggest that we watch TV or something.

A low rumble sounded, and I realized that the girl's stomach was growling.

"Why don't we get something to eat? You must be hungry after everything . . . that's happened." I winced at my own stupid words.

The girl gave me a flat stare, her features dull, drawn, and tired. She swayed on her feet, and she glanced at the floor like she wanted to lie down there, curl into a ball, and die. I knew that look, that feeling. It was the same one I'd had after my family was murdered. The deep, bone-weary, heart-crushing ache that never truly left me. The one that made me even more determined to ease her pain in whatever small way I could.

"Come on," I coaxed. "You might feel better if you eat something."

She kept staring at me, that dull, distant look still on her face, so I grabbed her hand and tugged her through the cabin until I found the kitchen in the back. I led the girl over to the table, and she dropped down into a chair, slumping one shoulder against the wall, as if it and the chair were the only things holding her up. Maybe they were.

"My name is Gin. What's yours?"

She didn't answer.

"Okay . . . well, maybe you'll feel like telling me later."

I opened the refrigerator and cabinets. Fletcher always kept his hidey-holes well stocked with food, so there was plenty to choose from. Peanut butter, boxes of mac and cheese, frozen pizzas. I didn't know what the girl would like, but I spotted a bottle of Jo-Jo's homemade chocolate syrup on one of the shelves, and I figured that I couldn't go wrong with a chocolate milkshake. So I pulled out the ice cream and milk from the fridge, plugged in a blender on the counter, and whipped everything together.

I poured the shake into a glass, stuck a straw in it, and took it over to the table.

"There you go," I said, talking to the girl in the same soft, soothing tone that Jo-Jo had used.

"It's too early for a milkshake," she said, her voice barely above a whisper.

I scooted it a little closer to her. "Just try it, okay?"

She dutifully took a sip. She stopped and frowned, as if she was surprised by how good it was or how hungry she was after all. But she must have liked it, because she kept sipping and sipping it. She didn't act like she wanted to talk, so I made a second chocolate shake for myself.

When the girl wasn't looking, I reached over, grabbed one of the kitchen knives out of the butcher's block on the counter, *and slipped it into one of the back pockets on my jeans. It wasn't as good as one of Fletcher's silverstone knives, but it was better than no knife at all.*

I finished making my own milkshake and poured it into a glass. Outside, I heard car doors slamming shut, then an engine rumbling to life and tires crunching on gravel. Fletcher, Jo-Jo, and Sophia must finally be leaving—

Beep-beep-beep-beep.

The horn on Sophia's convertible blared and blared, as though someone were hitting it over and over again in warning. I froze, but the horn was quickly drowned out by the squealing of tires and the screeching of metal slamming into something.

"Fletcher," I whispered.

I dropped my milkshake, not caring that the glass shattered on the floor, and ran out of the kitchen. I skidded to a stop at the front cabin windows, with the girl right next to me.

Sophia's convertible was wrapped around a tree— literally.

Somehow the car had slammed into and then curled around the tree trunk like a plastic tie twisted on the end of a loaf of bread. Broken glass and bent pieces of metal littered the ground, while black smoke boiled up from the hood. I couldn't see through the smoke, so I couldn't tell how badly Fletcher and the Deveraux sisters might be hurt.

"Oh, no," the girl whispered, her trembling finger pointing. "*He's* here."

A man was walking up the gravel driveway toward the cabin. He was dressed in a dark blue suit, with a silverstone ring flashing on his finger. Both were at odds with the old-fashioned weapon he was carrying, a long, thick wooden stick topped with a spiked metal ball. His black hair was swept back from his face, revealing the bright blue burn of magic in his eyes.

The man didn't give the crumpled car a second look as he passed it, and he kept striding toward the house with steady, certain steps. No emotion showed on his face. No hate, no rage, nothing but the cold, certain promise of pain and death.

"That's your dad?"

The girl nodded, tears streaming down her pale face.

Another plume of smoke caught my eye, and hot, hungry flames started shooting out of the hood of Sophia's convertible. My heart twisted, and I sucked in a breath, waiting for the doors to wrench open and for Fletcher, Jo-Jo, and Sophia to spill out of the wrecked car and sprint away from the growing fire.

But they didn't.

"Your friends are probably dead," the girl said in a dull voice. "He can control metal. That's what he did to their car. Crushed it around them like a tin can. He's done it before. My mom . . . he used that mace on her. He beat her to death with it right in front of me, and he laughed the whole time. Now he's going to kill us too. There's no stopping him. There never is."

More and more tears streaked down her face, her gaze locked onto her father as he drew closer to the cabin.

Cold rage pulsed through me, overpowering my grief and fear. This man, this Renaldo Pike, had murdered his wife, beaten his daughter, and hurt Fletcher, Jo-Jo, and Sophia. Maybe even killed them.

I'd be damned *if he was going to do the same thing to us.*

This was *exactly the sort of situation Fletcher had been training me for. So I could take care of myself. And if the girl wouldn't do the same, then I'd just have to do it for her. I glanced around the room for a weapon, but Fletcher, Jo-Jo, and Sophia had taken everything with them.*

"He's reaching for his magic," the girl whispered. "He's going to play with us first. He likes to do that."

At her words, a nail worked its way loose from the wall and tinked to the floor at my feet, rolling around and around, almost like a grenade waiting to explode.

And it wasn't the only one.

The closer Renaldo Pike got to the cabin, the more nails ripped out of the walls, shooting out of the wood like bullets. They hit the couch, the chairs, even the TV, shattering the monitor. Everything shuddered, splintered, and cracked apart, and glass, fabric, and other shrapnel flew through the air. It was like being in the center of a bomb that kept exploding over and over again.

I ducked down, but the girl stood at the windows, as if she'd already accepted the fact that there was nothing she could do to keep him from killing her.

I yanked her down beside me, out of the path of the flying nails. "Do you have a death wish?" I hissed. "Move!"

I grabbed the girl's hand. Still crouching low, I headed toward the kitchen, dragging her along behind me, determined to get out of the cabin before her father killed us both—

My eyes snapped open, the squealing of all those nails tearing out of the cabin walls still echoing in my mind, the scent of sawdust still filling my nose, and the cold, sweaty feel of the girl's hand still imprinted on my skin as though I'd touched her just a moment ago.

I remembered now—I remembered *everything*.

The girl, her father, all the terrible things that had happened that day.

But with the dream, the memories, came some startling revelations.

I wasn't the one Pike wanted to kill. I hadn't been the target of the bomb on the *Delta Queen*.

In fact, this wasn't about me at all.

It was all about *her*.

I lay in bed for several minutes, thinking about the day I'd met the girl, reviewing all the facts from back then and trying to piece them together with what I knew—or at least suspected—now.

Then I threw back the sheets, got up, pulled on my black skull robe, and hurried downstairs to Fletcher's office. I slapped on the lights, went over to one of the cabinets, and yanked open a drawer of files still organized by Fletcher's old method.

This time, I didn't look for the name *Pike* or the mace rune. No, this time, I looked for a completely different rune—a rose wrapped in thorns dripping blood—a warning about how deadly beauty could be.

And I found it, right where I thought it would be. Looked like I'd finally gotten my wish about finding the correct file on the first try. Lucky me.

I stared at the rune Fletcher had drawn on the folder's tab. I'd never noticed it before, but the very top corner of the tab had been creased down. Something that couldn't have been done by accident. Unease pooled in the pit of my stomach, and I slowly flipped it up with my thumb.

My spider rune was inked on the hidden part of the tab.

I had been so sure that a ghost from my past had come back to haunt me. But this time, the ghost wasn't mine—it was *hers*.

My hands were shaking, and I took several deep breaths to steady myself. Then I plopped down in the old man's chair, snapped on the light on his desk, opened the file, and started reading.

It wasn't an excessively thick file, not compared with the one he'd compiled on Mab Monroe, but there was still plenty of heft to it. The first several pages outlined all her criminal enterprises. Gambling, money laundering, the occasional art or jewelry theft.

It wasn't until I got close to the back of the file that the information changed. Because it wasn't about *her* anymore; it was all about her dead mother. Several pages had been torn from a notebook, and all of them featured Fletcher's distinctive handwriting. Just seeing the old man's script made my heart squeeze, and it took me a few seconds to focus on the words enough to actually read them.

Lily Rose Pike. Contact made through Jo-Jo's beauty salon. Married to an abusive man. Afraid for her life and her daughter's life. Desperate to leave her husband but worried what he might do if he catches her. Only in town for a few more days before heading back to their home in West Virginia. Need to extract the mother and daughter at the same time . . .

Fletcher went on from there, mulling over various plans to get Lily Rose and her daughter safely away from her husband. I flipped through a few more pages, which detailed Lily Rose's murder and everything that happened that day at the cabin. Another one of the old man's scribbled notes jumped out at me.

Girl sent to live with her grandmother here in Ashland. New name/identity given to the girl for added protection.

A photo of the grandmother was included, one that made me blink in surprise. I knew her—she was one of Finn's clients. In fact, I'd seen her at more than one society event over the years, even though I'd never actually spoken to her.

But it was the very last thing in the file that held my attention: a photo of the girl.

It was an old Polaroid, one that Jo-Jo or maybe Sophia had taken when the girl first arrived at the cabin, since her face was still a bruised, bloody mess in the shot. A little arrow marked the white strip at the bottom of the photo, pointing to the back.

I drew in a breath and flipped the photo over. Sure enough, Fletcher had taped a note to the back of the picture, along with one of the red-rose-and-thorn pins the girl had worn in her hair that day. I ran my fingers over the sharp edges of the pin before focusing on the note.

Gin—Remember the cabin in the woods. And that even an enemy can sometimes need our help. Fletcher.

This wasn't the first message the old man had left me from beyond the grave, but it was one of the most surprising. So many questions crowded into my mind, but he wasn't around to answer them. So I flipped the photo back over, studying the girl's features. Even though it had been taken more than fifteen years ago, I still recognized her.

The sad, haunted, battered face of Lorelei Parker stared back at me.

☼ 13 ☼

I sat in the dark and waited, just as I had so many times before.

After reviewing Lorelei Parker's file several times, I'd gone back to bed. But my sleep had been fitful, so I'd gotten up, dressed, and come to the one place where I might get some answers: Jo-Jo's beauty salon. Now I was politely waiting for the Deveraux sisters to wake up.

Jo-Jo and Sophia must have been dead asleep, because they hadn't heard me open the front door an hour ago, slip inside, and rustle around in the kitchen before taking my seat in one of the salon chairs. Even Rosco, Jo-Jo's basset hound, hadn't roused at my intrusion, and he was still grunting and snoring softly in his basket in the corner. Then again, I was very good at being quiet and invisible. Fletcher hadn't dubbed me the Spider for nothing.

Oh, I could have gone upstairs and woken up the sisters the second I arrived, but that would have been rude.

Besides, sitting alone in the dark gave me more time to think and try to wrap my mind around what was happening.

Because of all the things I'd done, suffered, and lived through, what had happened at the cabin had seemed to be finished long ago. But now it had reared its ugly head again, proving once again that the past was never truly past, at least not where my life was concerned.

Upstairs, a bedframe creaked, as someone turned over on her mattress, telling me that she was finally waking up. Sure enough, a few minutes later, soft footsteps padded down the stairs, and a loud, sleepy yawn sounded. The footsteps crept closer, and a familiar figure appeared in the hallway, heading in my direction.

"Sophia?" Jo-Jo's soft voice floated over to me as she entered the room. "Did you put on the coffee already? I swear that I smell chicory."

She snapped on the lights. The bright glare revealed me sitting in a cherry-red salon chair, my legs crossed at the ankles, a manila file folder in my lap.

Jo-Jo sucked down a breath, staggered back, and clutched a hand to her heart. "Gin! You scared me!"

It was just after seven on this chilly November morning, and the dwarf was bundled up in a pale pink microfleece robe, although her feet were bare, as usual. Her middle-aged face was free of makeup, but her white-blond hair was done up in pink sponge rollers. She never went to bed without rolling up her hair for the next day.

At the sound of Jo-Jo's voice, Rosco raised his head, wondering who his mistress was talking to. But the basset hound realized that it was just me, *woof*ed at us for interrupting his sleep, laid his head back down, and started snoring again.

"Gin?" Jo-Jo asked. "What are you doing here?"

I held up the photo that had been in Fletcher's file. "Lorelei Parker."

She frowned, making the laugh lines around her mouth deepen. "Lorelei Parker? Why would you want to know about her?" Her face cleared, and understanding flashed in her eyes. "The metal elemental. The one who planted that bomb on the riverboat."

"His last name is Pike, and I watched him kill a man last night using nothing but a spoon and a little bit of his metal magic. And all the while, I kept thinking that I knew him from somewhere. That he was connected to me somehow. I finally found the answer in one of Fletcher's files, but it wasn't the one that I expected. Turns out that Pike doesn't care about me at all. He's here for *her*." I raised the photo of Lorelei again.

Jo-Jo rubbed her forehead. "I was always afraid this might happen. That he might find her and finally make good on his promise."

"What promise? Who is he, exactly?" I asked, wanting her to confirm my suspicions. "And what does he want with Lorelei?"

She sighed. "His name is Raymond Pike. He's Lorelei's half brother, and he vowed to kill her for murdering their father."

The sound of our voices woke Sophia, who came downstairs wearing a black skull robe just like mine. Jo-Jo told her why I was here, and the three of us ended up in the kitchen. The Deveraux sisters sipped the chicory coffee I'd put on earlier, while I whipped up some buttermilk biscuits and peppery gravy. The sizzling sounds and the smoky scent of sausage frying were enough to get Rosco to abandon his warm, comfy basket, trot into the kitchen, and plop down at my feet, hoping that I'd slip him some scraps.

Sophia dug into my breakfast feast, with Rosco now perched at her feet, his stubby tail thumping against her legs as if the steady motion would make a spoonful of gravy magically jump off her plate and into his waiting mouth.

I fixed myself a plate too. Normally, I would have enjoyed the food, but I kept thinking about that day at the cabin and the absolute terror in Lorelei's eyes when her father had come for her. That was enough to ruin my appetite, but I made myself choke down the food anyway. It was most likely going to be a long day, and I needed to keep up my strength for whatever bad thing might happen next.

Similar memories must have haunted Jo-Jo, because she only picked at her food before pushing her plate away. Rosco whined, and she absently plucked a small piece of sausage off her plate and tossed it down to him. The basset hound downed it in one gulp.

Jo-Jo cradled her coffee cup in her hands, the tiny clouds painted on her pale pink nails matching the larger ones on the blue mug, all of them symbols of her Air magic. She studied the wisps of steam curling up out of the dark chicory brew for the better part of a minute. Then she drew in a breath, let it out, and finally raised her eyes to mine.

"Her name was Lily Rose," Jo-Jo began. "She was a sweet little girl who used to spend summers in Ashland with Mallory, her grandmother, who was and still is a client of mine. Mallory is a dwarf like me, so there were actually several generations in between her and Lily Rose, and Mallory was the girl's great-grandmother several times over. But she adored Lily Rose and would bring the girl here whenever she got her hair and nails done."

Dwarves had long life spans, and most of them just went with *grandmother* and *grandfather*, instead of trying to keep track of all the generations in between them and their kinfolk.

"Mallory would be the grandmother you and Fletcher sent Lorelei to live with after her mother was murdered," I said.

"Mallory Parker. You might know her. She's one of—"

"Finn's clients at his bank," I finished. "I've seen him talking to her at various events."

Jo-Jo nodded. "Anyway, the years passed, and Lily Rose grew up. Mallory mentioned that she had moved away, married a man named Renaldo Pike, and had a daughter, but I didn't see Lily Rose again for a long time."

"Until?"

"Until one day, someone started pounding on my door, about an hour before the salon was supposed to open," Jo-Jo said. "It's not unusual. Sometimes my clients come early if they have a special event they need to get dolled up for. So I opened the door, not thinking anything of it."

"And Lily Rose was there," I guessed.

She nodded again. "At first, I didn't think that anything was wrong, and I took her back to the salon. Then I noticed how much makeup she was wearing. She was trying to cover up a black eye. And she was all bundled up, in these thick, long clothes, even though it wasn't all that cold. She was hiding other marks too. Deep scratches and puncture wounds, all over her arms, legs, and chest."

"Nails," Sophia rasped in her eerie, broken voice. "From where he'd tortured her."

Like all other forms of magic, metal could be used in various ways, to build or destroy, to help or injure, to heal or hurt. I thought of how easily Renaldo Pike had ripped all those nails out of the cabin walls. Even I shuddered a little at that.

"But the worst part was that Lily Rose wasn't alone," Jo-Jo said, her voice so soft that I had to lean forward to hear her. "She had her daughter with her—and she'd been tortured too."

"Lorelei."

Jo-Jo and Sophia both nodded, their faces dark with memories of the awful sight.

"Lily Rose started crying, telling me that her husband had been abusing her. That he'd slowly changed from the man she'd loved and married into someone else, someone cruel, someone she didn't even recognize anymore. That she'd tried to leave him several times, but he always found her and dragged her back. She'd told him that she was coming to the salon to get her hair fixed for a business dinner they were supposed to go to that night. That was the only reason he'd let her and Lorelei out of the mansion they were staying in while they were in Ashland.

But even then, he'd sent a giant driver with her, to stay outside the salon and make sure she didn't try to run away again."

I frowned. "But why come to the salon? Why did she think that you would be able to help her?"

Jo-Jo and Sophia glanced at each other.

"Lily Rose remembered Fletcher from the salon, from when she was a little girl," Jo-Jo said. "She'd heard the rumors that there was an assassin in Ashland who could help her, and she begged me to put her in touch with him."

"But why didn't she ask her great-grandmother for help? From what I know of Mallory Parker, she has lots of money and connections."

Jo-Jo shook her head, making her pink sponge curlers sway back and forth. "As the years passed and the abuse got worse, Renaldo slowly made Lily Rose cut off all contact with her friends and family. It was only her and her mama, Laura, anyway, and Laura had died the year before."

"How did her mother die?"

Jo-Jo's lips pinched together. "Hit-and-run. Someone plowed into Laura while she was crossing the street. The cops never found the driver, but . . ."

"But Lily Rose thought that Renaldo did it, that he killed her mother."

The dwarf nodded. "She told me that he was insanely jealous of anyone she cared about, even if they were just casual friends. Even on the rare occasions when she would talk to someone, Renaldo watched her constantly, monitoring her phone calls, mail, everything.

She was basically his prisoner, and she was always afraid of being too friendly with other people, lest Renaldo get jealous and go after them. So Lily Rose couldn't get in touch with Mallory too often without fear of Renaldo tracking down Mallory and killing her the way he had killed Laura."

Rosco whined, and Sophia reached out and started petting him with her foot.

"So I called Fletcher and asked him to come over." A ghost of a smile flitted across Jo-Jo's face. "You can imagine what happened next."

"Fletcher would have taken one look at Lily Rose and Lorelei and wanted to help them."

Jo-Jo and Sophia both nodded.

"I also called Mallory and told her what was going on," Jo-Jo said. "Turns out, she already knew. She'd gotten worried when she hadn't seen or heard from Lily Rose in months, so she'd hired a private investigator. He told her that he suspected Renaldo was abusing his wife and daughter, and Mallory had been making her own plans to help them."

"So what went wrong?" I asked. "How did Lorelei end up at the cabin without her mother?"

Jo-Jo and Sophia exchanged another look, sadness filling both their faces.

"Renaldo somehow found out that Lily Rose was planning to leave him, and he started beating her," Jo-Jo said. "Fletcher was watching the house, and he went in as soon as he realized what was happening. But there were too many guards, and by the time he got through them, Lily Rose was already dead."

Silence fell over the kitchen. I hadn't known Lily Rose, but I could imagine the pain, fear, and terror that she'd experienced, being hurt, beaten, and tortured by someone who was supposed to love her. She hadn't deserved that, and neither had Lorelei. No one did.

Jo-Jo wiped away the tears that had trickled down her cheeks. "Fletcher managed to stop Renaldo before he killed Lorelei too. He would have finished off the bastard then and there, if it hadn't been for Raymond, Renaldo's son from his first marriage. He stopped Fletcher from killing his father, so Fletcher decided to get Lorelei out while he still could."

"Raymond Pike," I murmured. "I've never heard of him."

"You wouldn't have," Jo-Jo said. "The Pikes lived up in West Virginia, well away from Ashland."

"Is that why Fletcher didn't give Lorelei a new first name? I thought it was curious that he only changed her last name."

"Fletcher thought it would be better for Lorelei to keep her first name. That it would be easier for her to remember and one fewer thing that she had to lose, since everything else had been ripped away from her," Jo-Jo said. "But Fletcher didn't just give Lorelei a new last name and forget about her. He kept tabs on Raymond. From what he told me, Raymond is just as ruthless as his father ever was. And worse, just as strong in his metal magic."

"And now he's here in Ashland," I said. "To finally get revenge for his father's death."

"Revenge on Lorelei," Jo-Jo corrected. "Since she holds her responsible."

I couldn't help but bark out a humorless laugh at the irony of *that*.

Just when I thought that I'd finally taken care of all the bad things in my past, just when I thought that I was finally fucking *free* of them, something totally unexpected like this popped up. Something I'd all but forgotten about. But my past was never truly *over*. It was nothing but a giant pool of quicksand, one that perpetually tried to pull me under and drown me. Right now, I was up to my neck in it and sinking fast.

And the truth was that I wasn't all that different from Raymond Pike. I'd killed Mab because she'd murdered my mom and my older sister, and I'd killed Madeline because she had threatened me and my friends. So I could understand Pike's desire for revenge. Appreciate it, even. But I'd never tried to blow up a riverboat full of innocent people just to get back at one person. I didn't have many limits, but Pike had stepped way over the line.

Jo-Jo and Sophia watched the play of emotions on my face. Shock. Disbelief. Anger. Weariness. Guilt.

So much *guilt*.

They could guess what I was thinking. Part of it, anyway.

"What are you going to do, Gin?" Jo-Jo asked.

I rubbed my head, which was suddenly aching. "I have no idea. There's never been any love lost between Lorelei and me. She's sent plenty of her men to kill me the past few months."

I'd never done anything to Lorelei, but she'd tried to murder me the same as all the other bosses had. Just for that, part of me wanted to let her and her half brother have at each other. Either Pike would kill her and eliminate one of my enemies, or Lorelei would be too busy taking him out to plot against me for a while. Win-win for me either way.

Then there was the fact that Lorelei had never shown me anything but sneering disdain whenever our paths had crossed. I'd always wondered why she hated me so much, and I was beginning to think that it had everything to do with her father's death.

But even more important, Lorelei had surely realized that her brother was behind the attack on the riverboat. That he was in Ashland and gunning for her. I was ostensibly the big boss now. If someone in the underworld had a problem, she was supposed to come to me about it. Lorelei should have immediately told me about Pike, but she hadn't.

And I wanted to know why.

"Talk to her?" Sophia suggested.

I let out a tense breath. "Yeah. I need to talk to Lorelei. About a lot of things."

Jo-Jo perked up. "Excellent. I know exactly where she's going to be today. I was invited myself."

I frowned. "You and Lorelei Parker were invited to the same shindig? What could that possibly be?"

Instead of answering me, the dwarf gave me a once-over, taking in my boots, jeans, long-sleeved T-shirt, and black leather jacket. "It's a good thing you're already here, darling."

"Why?"

She grinned. "Because you can't go looking like that."

❋ 14 ❋

At two o'clock that afternoon, I found myself someplace I had never been before in all my thirty-one years.

An old-fashioned Southern garden party.

Lilies, pansies, hydrangeas, forsythias, mums, and other flowers in all shapes, sizes, and colors spread out as far as the eye could see, interspersed with all sorts of curling vines, green leaves, and perfectly pruned bushes. Maple, oak, and poplar trees towered over the area, providing a bit of shade from the autumn sun. The warm rays lent the remaining red, orange, and yellow leaves a rich, vibrant shimmer, making them seem as though they had been sculpted out of polished metal. A faint breeze gusted through the lush garden, teasing the green tendrils of the weeping willows and mixing the blossoms' scents into one strong, heady perfume. Black wrought-iron benches crouched here and there in shady spots under the trees, while white flagstones had been set into the manicured lawn, in paths winding through the garden and out into the landscapes beyond.

But roses were by far the most prominent flowers here. A series of arched whitewashed trellises circled the area like soldiers standing at attention, each featuring a different color of rose, starting with white and slowly deepening to pale pink, sunny yellow, and blood-red before giving way to midnight-black blooms on the final trellis. Naturally, this spot was known as the Rose Garden, one of more than three dozen different themed areas that made up the Ashland Botanical Gardens.

And what was a gorgeous garden without a fancy party?

Round tables clustered together in the center of the trellises, each one covered with a white silk cloth embroidered with shimmering silver roses—the rune for this particular garden. Dainty white china tea sets hand-painted with different colors of roses perched on each table, along with silver platters of pimiento-cheese sandwiches and buttery scones and crystal bowls filled with fresh strawberries and cream. White rose-shaped candles flickered in glass hurricane lamps in the middle of each table, the melting wax adding more rosy perfume to the air.

I shifted on my feet, my black stilettos sinking like spikes into the grass. "I've never seen so many rose-covered whatnots in one place before. Including me. I feel ridiculous," I grumbled.

Jo-Jo threaded her arm through mine. "Well, I think you look fabulous, darling."

Fabulous was not the word I would use to describe myself right now. For one thing, I was wearing a dress.

And not just any dress. The pinkest, laciest, frilliest thing you could possibly imagine, patterned with, you guessed it, roses. Not only that, but there was a fair amount of crinoline under the full, flowing skirt, making it poof out that much more, as though I were a human bell. I half-expected the fabric to go *ding-ding-ding* every time it swished against my legs. A large black hat with a floppy brim topped my head, and Jo-Jo had insisted that I also don black satin elbow-length gloves and one of her pearl chokers. All put together, I felt like an extra from *Gone with the Wind*. Fiddle-dee-dee.

"I do not look *fabulous*," I grumbled again. "I look like a doll on top of someone's wedding cake but without the creepy fake smile."

Jo-Jo patted my gloved hand. "We'll have to work on that, then. Fake smiles are practically a requirement at these parties."

I shot her a dirty look, but she chuckled.

"Well, I think you look great too," another voice chimed in.

I glanced to my right at the woman standing next to me: Roslyn Phillips, the owner of the Northern Aggression nightclub and significant other to Xavier. She'd been invited to the party too, and she looked every inch the sweet Southern belle in a mint-green dress with a long, flowing skirt that featured a rose pattern. A matching hat perched on top of her head, while a diamond solitaire nestled in the hollow of her throat. All the green brought out the lovely color of her toffee eyes and skin and her black hair, which was curled into loose waves. I'd always thought that Roslyn was beautiful, but she looked truly stunning today, the perfect picture of feminine elegance, grace, and beauty.

"You're just saying that because you came through with the dress and heels for me at the last minute." I paused. "People really pay your workers to dress up like this at Northern Aggression?"

Roslyn's nightclub was a place where you could pay for anything your heart desired, which apparently included pink frou-frou garden dresses.

Roslyn grinned, showing off the small pearl-white fangs in her mouth. "Everyone has their fantasies, Gin. Prim and proper Southern lady is a lot more popular than you'd expect, especially in Ashland."

I blanched at the thought.

"Just think of it as another disguise, darling," Jo-Jo said. "All the better to blend in with the crowd. Fletcher taught you that, remember?"

"Oh, great," I muttered. "Bring the old man into it. I'm sure wherever he is, he's laughing his ass off at me right now."

Still, the thought of Fletcher brought a smile to my face, and I let Jo-Jo and Roslyn lead me deeper into the garden.

The Ashland Botanical Gardens were located on some lush acreage up in Northtown, close to Jo-Jo's salon. Ostensibly, today's event was a fund-raiser to benefit the gardens and help with other local charity and conservation efforts, but really, it was just an excuse for the rich society types to mix, mingle, and talk trash about each other behind their white gloved hands.

The event was also ladies-only, much to Finn's disappointment. He'd called to let me know that Harold Smith's burner phone was another dead end, with only a few cryptic texts from Pike on it, and I'd told him what I was up to.

"What is it with all these girls-only parties?" Finn had grumbled. "First, y'all have your spa day at Jo-Jo's salon a few months ago, and now this. I can look fabulous, eat cucumber sandwiches, and drink mint juleps with the best of them."

"If you want to dress in drag and do the job for me, you are more than welcome to," I'd replied in a sweet, syrupy tone.

"You're just jealous that I would rock a garden dress way better than you ever could," he'd countered.

"I'm frightened that you even know what a garden dress is."

"Oh, baby," Finn had crooned. "I know *all* about the finer things in life—and the ladies who enjoy them. I happen to be one of those finer things, you know."

"I think I just threw up a little in my mouth."

Finn had laughed, but he'd agreed to be on call in case I needed him. So had Owen. But I didn't anticipate any problems. All I wanted to do was talk to Lorelei. After that, I didn't know what might happen, but I figured that I deserved to hear her side of things. Yep, that was me these days. Mediation queen.

Jo-Jo, Roslyn, and I had arrived late, so all the boring speeches were already over with, and folks were now mixing and mingling, sipping drinks, and munching on their cute little sandwiches. The crustless pimiento-cheese creations had even been cut and pressed into the shape of roses. Somebody here had *way* too much time on her hands.

I scanned the crowd. Every woman in the garden was wearing the same sort of stupid floppy hat that I was. We all looked like Stepford Wives. And Jo-Jo was right too. There were plenty of fake smiles to go around, and I heard more than a few folks murmur, *Why, bless your heart.* Which is the classic Southern way of pretending to sympathize with someone when you're really just putting the other woman down and driving your stiletto straight through her heart at the same time.

Finally, I spotted Lorelei sitting with an elderly dwarf at a table that was front and center in the garden.

"Ladies, go enjoy yourselves," I told Jo-Jo and Roslyn. "I have some business to attend to."

They both grinned, then moved off to talk to their own friends and business associates.

I threaded my way through the crowd, a bland smile plastered on my face. The society ladies all smiled back at me, but their eyes sharpened, and their minds churned as they tried to figure out who I was, what I was doing there, and how they might benefit from it. The sharks smelled fresh blood in the water.

But I made it over to the table without getting waylaid by anyone, and I dropped into a seat across from Lorelei, who kept right on talking to the dwarf.

Mallory Parker, her great-grandmother.

A sign posted next to the podium a few feet away bore a picture of Mallory's smiling face, proclaiming her as the proud sponsor of today's event, the annual Lily Rose

Memorial Fund-Raiser. Several charities were listed on the sign, the most prominent being the botanical gardens and a battered women's shelter. I wondered how many folks here knew that Lily Rose had been an actual person and not just a name. Or maybe everyone thought Lily Rose was some sort of fancy hybrid flower that Mallory had picked to match the garden setting.

I focused on Mallory, who had removed her white hat and set it aside. I couldn't tell how old she was, but I was betting well more than three hundred, given the deep wrinkles that grooved into her face. She was small, even for a dwarf, and her skin had the brown, weathered look of someone who'd done her fair share of work outdoors over the years. And she must have been richly rewarded for that work, since she had enough diamonds flashing on her neck, wrists, and fingers to fund a small army. Her satin dress was pale blue, with scads of matching lace, and her hair was a white, fluffy, teased cloud around her head, although I could see the pink of her skull here and there.

Mallory Parker was the perfect picture of an old-school Southern grandmother. Someone who was always polite, punctual, and oh-so-proper in everything from her speech to her dress to the way her pinkie crooked out just so as she sipped her tea.

Still, the longer I looked at her, the more I got the sense that there was more to Mallory than satin, lace, and diamonds. She might seem as old and fragile as the tea set on the table, but her blue eyes were sharp and bright as she took in everything around her.

". . . go ahead with your Hawaiian vacation," Lorelei said in a low, sultry tone that was similar to my own. "I can change your ticket so that you leave tonight."

"But what about you, sweetheart?" Mallory said in a twangy voice that was far more hillbilly than high society. "We were supposed to take our annual trip together after the fund-raiser today, just like we always do."

Lorelei flashed her grandmother a smile, even though it didn't reach her eyes. "I have some business to wrap up, but I can fly out and meet you in a few days. So what do you say?"

"I say that it sounds like a grand old time," I drawled. "I've always wanted to visit Hawaii. Aloha."

Lorelei shot me an annoyed look. She didn't like me eavesdropping. Too bad. I was going to do a lot worse than that today. My frilly getup must have thrown her off, because confusion filled her face as she tried to figure out who I was. I tipped up the brim of my hat to reveal my face.

Her jaw clenched. "What are you doing here?"

Instead of answering, I flagged down a passing waitress and plucked a tall, frosty mint julep off her tray. I took my sweet time leaning back in my chair and arranging my ridiculous skirt around my legs before sipping the drink. The cold, tart liquid slid down my throat, leaving behind a refreshing zing of mint in my mouth. Mmm. Perfect.

"Why, just enjoying the party," I drawled again. "I always like to come out and support a good cause, don't you? And there are *so* many listed on that sign. Although I find myself most intrigued by the name of the event itself. Lily Rose. Such a pretty name for such a pretty party."

I took another sip of my mint julep. Lorelei kept glaring at me, admittedly with good reason. My words had been far more cruel than kind. Maybe I fit in with the society sharks better than I thought, even if I wasn't bothering with fake smiles and syrupy-sweet *bless your hearts.*

Mallory Parker stared at me, wondering who was upsetting her granddaughter so very much. Her eyes narrowed with recognition. "Gin Blanco."

I stared back, surprised that she knew me. We didn't exactly move in the same social circles. But there was a knowing tone in Mallory's voice, telling me that she knew exactly who I was and what I did. Interesting. Then again, I supposed that I shouldn't have been surprised, given what Fletcher had tried to do for Lily Rose and Lorelei all those years ago.

"Ms. Blanco," the dwarf said, leaning forward and holding her small, weathered hand out over the table to me. "I've seen you at various events with Mr. Lane, but I don't think that we've ever been formally introduced. Mallory Parker."

"Ma'am," I murmured, shaking her hand.

Her grip was much firmer than I expected. Then again, she was a dwarf. Even at more than three hundred years old, she still had enough inherent strength to break every bone in my hand if she wanted to. And she was also smart enough to realize that I wasn't here for the mint juleps.

"Lorelei?" Mallory asked, a hint of steel hardening her hillbilly voice. "What's going on? Why is Ms. Blanco here?"

Lorelei opened her mouth, but I beat her to the punch.

"I'm here because Raymond Pike is trying to kill your granddaughter."

All around us, the society ladies flitted to and fro like colorful butterflies, each one twitching the wings of her billowing skirt to attract maximum attention as they talked, laughed, and cut one another to pieces with soft words and sly smiles. A breeze gusted through the garden, causing a set of silver wind chimes dangling from one of the trellises to *tinkle-tinkle* together, but the notes sounded more mournful than cheery. Farther out in the garden, the tree branches tangled together, then scraped apart, while the limbs on a nearby rhododendron bush quivered, as if chilled by the cool fall wind.

But our table was completely quiet, except for Mallory's sharp, sudden intake of breath.

Her gaze swung back to Lorelei. "Is this true? Has Raymond finally tracked you down?"

Lorelei shook her head, making the brim of her white hat bob up and down like a ship riding the ocean waves. "It's nothing I can't handle."

"That's not the question I asked, young lady," Mallory snapped in true grandmotherly fashion.

Lorelei sighed. "Yes, Raymond is in Ashland."

"How do you know for sure?" Mallory asked.

"There was an . . . incident on the *Delta Queen* riverboat a couple of days ago."

The dwarf's eyes narrowed. "What sort of *incident?*"

The way Lorelei was skirting around things, she'd never tell her grandmother what had really happened, so I decided to cut to the chase.

"Raymond Pike planted a bomb on the riverboat," I said. "One that was full of potential shrapnel. Nails, to be exact."

Mallory blinked. "Nails. Are you sure?"

"I got an up-close-and-personal view of the device, along with a second one that he left behind in the woods. Trust me, I'm sure."

Lorelei kept her posture easy and relaxed, but her fingers fisted around the linen napkin in her hand, making the diamonds in her rose-and-thorn rune ring flash in warning.

And the faintest bit of magic surged off her.

It was just a brief pulse of power, like the chill you would feel if you opened a refrigerator door and then quickly shut it again, but it was there. Curious. Lorelei wasn't known to be an elemental. Perhaps hiding her power had been Fletcher's idea, another way to protect her from her brother. I wondered if she had the same metal magic that Pike did—and if she was as strong in her power as he was.

Lorelei got a grip on her magic, smothering it, but she didn't bother to hide the death stare she was giving me. She was plenty pissed at me for dropping the dime on Raymond being in town. Too damn bad. Yeah, ratting out Lorelei to the old lady wasn't exactly the nicest thing I'd ever done, but I doubted that Lorelei would have agreed to see me otherwise, much less answer any of my questions about her half brother. She still probably wouldn't do that, now that I'd riled her up.

Mallory drummed her gnarled fingers on the table, deep in thought. "So that's why you want me on a plane to Hawaii. You're trying to get me out of the way. So you can do what, exactly? Stay behind and kill Raymond yourself?"

"That is *exactly* what I'm going to do," Lorelei snapped. "Just like I've been dreaming about for *years* now. My only regret is that my father isn't still alive so I could do the same to him."

The cold venom in Lorelei's voice shouldn't have surprised me, but somehow it did. It was hard for me to reconcile what I knew about Lorelei Parker, suave smuggler to the stars, with that beaten, battered girl I'd met all those years ago. But as I looked at Lorelei, her features slowly darkened, bruises ringing out from around her eyes to blacken her entire face, just as it had been back then. I blinked, and the illusion vanished, although not the memories it left behind.

Mallory stabbed her finger at her granddaughter. "Well, you can forget about it, sweetheart. I'm not going anywhere. Not until that bastard is dead. And you are absolutely *not* taking him on by yourself."

Lorelei sighed. "Now, Grandma . . ."

"Don't you *Grandma* me," Mallory snapped. "I already lost one granddaughter to a Pike. I'm not going to lose another one."

She sucked in a deep breath, then let loose with a string of salty curses that let us know *exactly* what she thought of the not-so-dearly-departed Renaldo Pike and his son, Raymond. Mallory's voice wasn't all that loud, but her hillbilly tone was sharp and vicious enough to attract the attention of the society sharks, who were always hungry for more drama and gossip. The other ladies stared and whispered behind their white-gloved hands, but Mallory ignored them and kept right on cursing.

I grinned, making mental note of her words. I'd have to remember them for later.

Finally, Mallory wound down, although she kept muttering to herself and tapping her fingers on the table. Suddenly, she stopped and focused on me again.

"Why are you here, Ms. Blanco? What's your interest in all this? I would think that such matters would be beneath your notice, given your new position as the head of the underworld."

I arched an eyebrow. "And I would think that someone like you wouldn't know anything at all about the Ashland underworld."

"Bah." She waved her hand, making her many rings sparkle. "Where do you think I got all these diamonds from? I *earned* them, with every shipment of booze and guns and money that I smuggled into Ashland. I didn't marry or sleep my way into them, like so many of these simpering fools here did."

She glared at the ladies who'd been staring at us, and they quickly returned to their previous conversations, although they kept sneaking glances at us.

I looked at her with new appreciation. So Mallory Parker had been a smuggler, and she'd no doubt taught her great-granddaughter all the tricks of the trade. Maybe she'd even passed her business on to Lorelei, just as Fletcher had done to me. Another way Lorelei and I were more alike than I'd ever thought possible.

When it seemed everyone was minding her own business again, Mallory turned her steely blue gaze back to me. "I will repeat my question. Why do you care about Raymond Pike and what he's up to in Ashland?"

"Normally, I wouldn't care who was trying to kill your granddaughter. In fact, I would cheer them on, given all the men she's sent to try to murder me over the past several months."

Mallory looked at Lorelei, who shrugged.

"It's just business, Grandma. Eliminating threats. You're the one who taught me how to do that, remember?"

Lorelei's calm, nonchalant tone caught my attention, as did her specific words. *Eliminating threats.* What did she mean by *that*? Because she hadn't eliminated *me*. That's what *I* had done to every person she'd sicced on me. Or was there more to her attempts to take me out than I'd realized? And if so, what, exactly?

The dwarf's lips puckered at Lorelei's words, but warm pride flashed in her eyes, making them sparkle even brighter than her diamonds. The same sort of pride that had always lit up Fletcher's face whenever I'd mastered or used one of his lessons. I wondered what Mallory had taught her granddaughter about eliminating threats.

The old woman waved her hand, telling me to continue.

"As I said, I wouldn't normally care about Lorelei and her enemies."

"But?" Mallory asked.

"But Raymond Pike planted his bomb on the *Delta Queen*, which happens to belong to Phillip Kincaid, a friend of mine. I take attacks on my friends *very* personally."

"I've heard that about you," Mallory scoffed. "Idiot. I

hope you know that such sentimental foolishness isn't a luxury someone like you can afford to indulge in. Especially in your current position. Not if you want to survive. You're hanging on to control of the underworld by a thread, and it is a thin, tenuous thread at best."

I shifted in my chair, uncomfortable at just how right she was. "And you're an expert on survival?" I sniped back.

Mallory's thin chest puffed up. "I am in Ashland, sweetheart. I was here in the beginning, back when this town was founded, and I'll be here for many more years to come."

I couldn't argue with that, since she was at least two hundred fifty years older than I was—and smarter and far more sly than her garden dress and her soft Southern demeanor implied.

Mallory gave me a syrupy smile, the kind that was almost always accompanied by a knife in the back. Lorelei winced, apparently having seen that smile before. And I suspected that, old lady or not, Mallory Parker was as hard-core as they came and could outthink and outplot almost anyone, including me.

"Tell me one thing," she purred. "Since we're all just businesswomen sitting here shooting the breeze."

"What?" I didn't bother to keep the wariness out of my voice.

Her smile widened, and I realized that I'd stepped right into her sticky web, whatever it was. "How much is your going rate, Ms. Blanco? Or do you prefer to be called the Spider when actually negotiating?"

My danger radar immediately *ping*ed up into the red-alert level. "Why do you want to know?"

"Because I want to hire you."

"For what?" I asked, even though I already knew the answer.

Mallory's smile widened, her expression sweeter, softer, and more innocent than ever before, even as her eyes gleamed with the cold satisfaction of a hunter having snared something in her trap. "Why, to kill Raymond Pike, of course."

❋ 15 ❋

An angry blush bloomed in Lorelei's cheeks, which turned as blood-red as the roses on the white trellis closest to our table. She shot me another hate-filled glare, as though this ridiculous proposal had come from me and not her grandmother.

"Absolutely not," Lorelei ground out the words. "I don't need Blanco's help, Grandma. I can take care of myself—and you too. I've been doing it for years now."

Mallory crossed her arms over her chest. "You are my granddaughter, and I will do whatever is necessary to protect you from that man. I've kept track of him. From what I've heard, he's even more dangerous and depraved than his father ever was."

Lorelei's jaw clenched tightly. "And you think that I haven't been watching out for Raymond too? That I haven't been waiting for him to find me? I know *exactly* how twisted he is. I'm the one who lived in that house with him, remember? He always hated Mom and me. Was always jealous of how much attention our father paid her. Raymond tore Mom down with his cruel words and stupid pranks every chance he got. For *years*. Making Mom look bad and getting us both in trouble with my father was the thing he loved best."

Mallory's face softened at the mention of Lily Rose and the torture she and Lorelei had endured. "I know you can take care of yourself, sweetheart. But you should let me do my job and take care of you too. I love you too much to lose you to him."

She reached over, put her brown, wrinkled hand on top of Lorelei's pale, smooth one, and gave it a gentle squeeze. Another bit of power rolled off Lorelei, this blast even colder and stronger than the first one had been.

My eyes narrowed. I knew Ice magic when I felt it, but her previous pulse of power had been different, more like Pike's metal magic. Ice and metal . . . Could Lorelei actually be gifted in two elements? Like me? If so, how had she managed to keep that hidden all these years? Especially given her position in the Ashland underworld? I'd underestimated her. It seemed she was even better at keeping secrets than I was.

For a moment, Lorelei's face filled with raw, naked emotion, along with a bone-deep weariness. In that instant, I saw the wounded girl she had once been—and how part of her ached to just let Mallory handle everything. To stop being tough and strong, just for a little while, and let someone else take care of things for a change.

Take care of *her*.

Her hurt and heartache punched me in the gut and

stole my breath away. Because they were feelings that I knew all too well, ones that had been building inside me ever since I'd taken out Mab and the Ashland underworld had discovered that I was the Spider and decided that they wanted me dead no matter what.

But Lorelei couldn't step aside any more than I could, especially not now. The moment passed, the feel of her Ice magic vanished, and her face hardened again. She squeezed Mallory's hand back, then released it and took hold of her black satin clutch sitting on the table.

"I'll take care of Raymond," Lorelei said. "Don't worry about him—or me. When the time's right, I'll kill him. Like I should have done all those years ago."

Once again, Lorelei shot me a harsh, accusing look, as if this was all my fault.

Mallory waved her hand, causing her diamond rings to flash again. "That's all well and good, but there's no reason not to get some added insurance by hiring Ms. Blanco. It's not like we can't afford her. That's why we've done so many nasty things over the years—to have money to pay for little incidentals like these."

"*Incidentals?* Let me make one thing clear: I'm not your hired help," I snapped. "So don't talk about me like I'm not sitting right here."

Mallory sniffed, then picked up her teacup and took a dainty sip, her pinkie perfectly positioned, as though she really were the sweet, innocent old lady she appeared to be and not a former smuggler who could curse better than a sailor and was trying to hire me to do a hit.

Across the garden, a woman said Mallory's name and waved to her.

"Why, Delilah!" Mallory called out. "Bless your heart! Don't you look lovely!"

Delilah beamed and gestured for Mallory to join the group of women she was chatting with. Mallory smiled and waved back. But as soon as Delilah turned her head, a dark scowl crinkled the dwarf's face.

"I can't *stand* that woman," Mallory muttered. "All she does is talk about her stupid horses. But she gives the gardens a hefty annual donation, so I have to go make nice. You two should do the same. After all, we're all on the same side now."

I snorted. "I doubt that."

Mallory ignored me and got to her feet. "Ten million should do it," she said. "Ten million dollars for you to kill Raymond. It's really quite generous, considering that it's several times more than your going rate."

"And how do you know my going rate?"

"I did several friendly deals with Fletcher Lane over the years, and I inquired about your services from time to time. Besides, I like to stay on top of these things for professional reasons. Helps keep me young."

Fletcher hadn't told me about any deals he'd ever done with Mallory Parker, and had never mentioned anything regarding her asking about hiring me. Then again, the old man had never told me anything about Lorelei either.

Mallory noticed the surprise and suspicion on my face and let out a small, trilling laugh. "I might be old, but I'm not dead yet, sweetheart. At least not until someone like you comes to visit me in the black of the night."

I didn't respond.

"I'll arrange for you to receive the money any way you

like. Cash, gold, bearer bonds." She paused, then waggled her fingers again, showing off her rings. "Although I prefer diamonds myself. They are a girl's best friend for a reason. Several, actually. Easy to transport, easy to fence. After all, you just never know when you might need the money to leave town in a hurry. I've found that it's best to be prepared for anything, haven't you?"

I still didn't respond.

Mallory picked up her white hat and arranged it on top of her head before turning her steely blue eyes back to me. "Think about my offer, Ms. Blanco. It's one of the most lucrative you will ever receive. I will expect an answer by the end of the day. Finnegan knows how to reach me. Until then. Ta-ta, y'all."

She nodded at Lorelei and me, plastered another syrupy smile on her face, and moved off into the crowd to swim with all the other sharks.

Across the garden, Jo-Jo waved her hand to catch my attention. She tilted her head at Mallory, who was now holding court in the middle of a pack of society dames. I shook my head, telling Jo-Jo that nothing had been resolved. She nodded back, then turned and started talking to Roslyn.

"Well, well, well. Your pet dwarf and your nightclub madam," Lorelei said in a snarky tone. "I see that the Gin Blanco gang is out in full force today."

"Jo-Jo healed you at the cabin that day," I snarked right back. "And you do business with Roslyn just like all the other bosses do. So shut your mouth about my friends before I shut it for you. Permanently."

Lorelei leaned back in her chair, unconcerned by the cold threat of violence in my voice, although she kept one hand on the table, next to her clutch. "I guess you remember me now, huh? I was wondering how long it would take you to figure it out. Why, given all the hype surrounding the great Spider, I would have thought that you would have been knocking on my door long before now. But it's been, what, two days? And you're just now confronting me?" She clucked her tongue, mocking me. "Very disappointing, Gin. Mab Monroe would have already resolved this whole situation."

"I'm not Mab," I said, in an even icier tone than before. "Something you should be extremely grateful for, sugar."

"And why is that?"

"Because you'd be dead, along with Mallory—and Raymond too. Mab never was very merciful to trouble-makers *or* their targets."

Lorelei scoffed. "Well, at least she would have killed him. And that is definitely something I could drink to."

She dragged over the mint julep she'd been sipping before I sat down, raised it to her lips, and threw back the rest of it. Lorelei put the empty glass down and pushed it away so hard that it snagged on a wrinkle in the table-cloth and almost tipped over before slowly righting itself. The teetering motion made the ice inside the glass rattle around like dominoes.

"All these months, you've known that I was the Spider, all the times our paths have crossed, Mab's funeral, that night at the Briartop art museum, the Monroe mansion a few weeks ago . . . Why didn't you tell me who you really were?"

Lorelei gave me a flat look. "Tell you what, exactly? That my father abused me and my mom? That he basically kept us prisoners? That every time she tried to leave him, he only got more jealous, violent, and vicious? That he finally murdered her right in front of me? Forgive me for not bringing up my unhappy childhood."

The longer I stared at her, the more anger tightened her face.

"Besides, I always thought you knew who I was," she said in a harsh voice. "How could you have forgotten?"

Her words came out as a bitter accusation, one that made my stomach tense up with guilt and shame. Because I had forgotten—completely.

Oh, back when I was younger, I'd wondered what had happened to the girl and had constantly pestered Fletcher for updates about her. But all the old man ever told me was that she was safe, so I'd slowly quit thinking and asking about her and had moved on to other things the way that kids, people, so often do. And I'd had plenty of other things to focus on. My assassin training, all the jobs I'd done, getting my revenge on Mab, all the other folks I'd gone up against over the past year. I doubted that I would have ever realized that Lorelei was that same girl, if not for Pike trying to bomb the *Delta Queen*.

But I wasn't about to admit any of that to her, and I certainly wasn't going to let her see my guilt over it. So I shrugged. "What can I say? I've killed a lot of people since then."

"So have I," she snapped. "Funny, though, how that one day is still branded in my mind, like it just happened yesterday."

For the third time, magic rolled off her body, a mix of cold and hard power that confirmed my suspicions about her having both Ice and metal magic. The power cut off as quickly as it had before, but Lorelei couldn't hide the slight sag of her shoulders, the twist of her mouth, or all the horrible memories that darkened her eyes, just like the blood and bruises that had blackened her face all those years ago. So her magic was tied to her emotions, and she only lost her grip on it and let it show when she was particularly upset.

Like now.

"Is that why you hate me so much?" I asked. "Because I didn't remember you?"

Lorelei let out a bitter laugh. "Of course not. I'm not *that* petty."

"Then why?"

"You really don't know?"

I shook my head.

She leaned forward, anger glittering in her blue eyes. "I hate you because you're Gin Blanco, the great assassin, the Spider. I hate you because you're the head of the underworld now, a job that you are extremely ill suited for and obviously don't want but lucked into anyway, just like you seemingly luck into everything else in life. Killing Mab Monroe, snagging Owen Grayson, becoming some sort of fucking folk hero to the downtrodden. Some of us have to work our asses off for every single thing we have in this life, but not you, not Gin Blanco. You are the luckiest damn person I've ever *met*. But most of all, I hate you because it should have been me that day."

She stabbed her finger into her chest, right where her heart was. The diamonds in her rose-and-thorn rune ring winked accusingly at me. "It should have been *me*, not you. But you took that away from me without even trying."

I frowned. "What do you mean? What did I take away from you?"

She huffed and gave me a sneering look like I was the dumbest person alive. "Forget it. The great Gin Blanco wouldn't understand anyway."

As much as I wanted to snap right back and tell her to cut out the cryptic shit, already, I tried to get my temper under control, struggling to find some common ground with her. Because Lorelei was hurting and had been for years, and I'd forgotten all about her.

"But why didn't you at least tell me that the bomb on the *Delta Queen* was meant for you and not me? I am allegedly the head of the underworld. Those sorts of things are rather pertinent to me now."

She snorted. "Please. You're the big boss in name only. None of the heavyweights are going to come to you with anything *important*. Besides, I have my own plans for Raymond—and they don't involve you."

I stared her down. "My friends could have been killed on the riverboat. So I'm *involved* now, whether you like it or not."

"Forget it," she said, sneering. "And forget what my grandmother offered you. I don't need your so-called *protection*, and I certainly don't want your damn *help*. I'm quite capable of taking care of myself."

"Is that why you keep touching that gun in your purse?"

Startled, Lorelei wrapped her hand around the black satin clutch on the table in front of her. It was just the right size to hold a phone, a compact, a lipstick, and a small pistol. The top of the bag was open, and I could see something glinting inside, although it seemed pale, even opaque, instead of the gunmetal-gray I would expect. But what was even stranger was the chill that radiated off the bag, as though it were full of ice cubes. Curious.

Lorelei had been touching the bag off and on ever since Mallory left, as though she was thinking about pulling out whatever weapon was inside and going to town on me with it. But she must have realized how badly that would end for her, because she moved her hand away from the bag.

"Just stay away from Mallory and me." Lorelei shoved her chair back, surged to her feet, and whirled around to storm away.

"I'm sorry for what happened to you—and your mother," I said in a soft voice. "I know . . . how hard it is to lose someone you love. I know what it's like to have them ripped away so brutally, so viciously. I know how helpless that can make you feel, how vulnerable, how victimized."

Her back stiffened. She paused, as if debating whether or not to respond, then stared at me over her shoulder, her pretty features hard and determined. "I'm nobody's *victim*." She spat out the words. "Not anymore. Never again."

Lorelei whipped back around and hurried off without another word, making her way over to Mallory, Delilah, and the other society gals. She plastered a fake smile on her face, as though she didn't have a care in the world, then grabbed another mint julep from a waitress and downed it in one gulp. I kept staring at her, comparing her with the girl I'd met so long ago.

She was right. The Lorelei Parker I knew was no victim. She was a criminal who made people shake in their shoes, and she ran her smuggling operations with brutal, ruthless efficiency, often taking care of her problems herself and making an example out of anyone who didn't meet her expectations. According to Fletcher's file, she'd dropped almost as many bodies in and around Ashland as I had. We were two sides of the same coin.

Lorelei didn't need my protection. She was perfectly capable of taking care of herself, and she had Jack Corbin and a whole host of giant guards to help her do it. And it wasn't like I needed or even wanted the fat payday Mallory had offered me.

Still, the longer I looked at Lorelei, the more acidic guilt bubbled up inside my chest, eating into the blackened shards of my heart.

Because, like it or not, everything that was happening to her now was partially my fault.

❋ 16 ❋

I needed some time to think, so I got to my feet and headed toward the large trellis that arched over the garden's entrance and exit. Jo-Jo and Roslyn watched me go, their faces filled with concern, but I waved to them, letting them know that I was okay.

I left the Rose Garden and meandered along one of the white flagstone paths, admiring the contrast of the red, orange, and yellow leaves against the tropical vibrancy of the flowers below. The botanical gardens featured everything from an elaborate hedge maze to a rock garden, and I could have headed into the other themed areas, but I made a slow circuit around the perimeter of the Rose Garden instead.

This might have been the first formal garden soiree I'd ever attended, but I was well acquainted with all the winding paths, since I'd killed more than a couple of folks here. The botanical gardens were a popular party spot, especially in the spring and summer, and I'd skulked through the trees and hunkered down in the bushes more than once, waiting for someone to get within knife's reach, so I could clamp my hand over his mouth, drag him back into the greenery, and cut his throat. Simpler times.

As I walked, I peered into the dancing, dappled shadows, remembering how easy it had been to slip from one section of the gardens to the next without anyone ever suspecting that I was watching them. It would be the perfect place for Pike to take out Lorelei.

My steps slowed, my eyes cutting left and right as I considered all the ways Pike could get close to his sister. Oh, he couldn't enter the Rose Garden itself, not without attracting attention during the ladies-only fund-raiser, but there were plenty of spots where he could spy on the event and then raise his gun and put a bullet through Lorelei's heart when the moment was right. Or, worse, watch while the bomb he'd planted earlier finally exploded . . .

My nose twitched, and I realized that another strong scent had intruded on all the heavy floral perfumes: smoke.

I stopped and drew in another breath, wondering if I'd just imagined the scent. One breath, two breaths, three breaths, four . . . I drew air deep down into my lungs again and again, turning in a slow circle, but all I could smell were the roses, lilies, and other blooms fighting for olfactory dominance. No smoke. I shook my head and started walking again. Sometimes my overly developed sense of paranoia surprised even me—

A gray spiral of smoke wafted up into the air off to my right.

I squinted in that direction, wondering if both my eyes and my nose were playing tricks on me. Another spiral of smoke curled up, and the scent swirled through my nose again, stronger than before. I picked up my skirt and hurried over, searching for the source of the smoke.

A cigar butt smoldered in the grass.

My stomach clenched, but I forced myself to scan the area and think things through. He must have taken one final drag off the cigar before tossing the butt aside and stepping off the path. I spotted a narrow trail of broken branches and fallen leaves a few feet away, where someone must have carelessly plowed through the row of bushes. A bit of silver also shimmered in the grass there, so I went over, crouched down, and brushed the leaves off the object.

A single nail gleamed in the black earth, confirming what I'd suspected and bringing another, more chilling thought with it.

Raymond Pike was here—and Jo-Jo and Roslyn were still at the garden party.

I surged to my feet, whipped around, and ran back the way I'd come. I could have followed Pike's trail through the bushes, but there was no telling where he might have ended up, and I wanted to get back to the garden—and my friends—as fast as possible.

My stilettos *click-click-click*ed on the flagstones, making far too much noise, so I hopped on first one foot, then the other, until I could yank them off and toss them into the bushes. I lifted up the ridiculous, billowing skirt of my dress and grabbed one of the silverstone knives strapped to my thighs. Unlike Jo-Jo and Roslyn, I hadn't brought a purse, and I was cursing that decision now. If I'd brought my phone, I could have called my friends to warn them.

The main entrance to the Rose Garden loomed up ahead, another white trellis with blood-red roses twining through the arch. As much as I wanted to barge into the middle of the party and tell everyone to run, I forced myself to slow down and scan my surroundings.

Waitresses moved in and out through the arch, leaving with empty trays and returning with fresh ones, and the murmur of conversation and faint trills of laughter floated over to me. Everyone else was still enjoying themselves at the party, which meant that Pike hadn't struck.

Yet.

I had started to leave the path so I could hunt him down when a low tree branch snagged on the brim of my floppy black hat, yanking me backward. I cursed, reached up, ripped off the stupid hat, and tossed it aside. The wind picked it up, whipping the hat up into the air before neatly dropping it onto an arrow-shaped bronze trail marker that pointed in the direction of the rock garden. I couldn't have done that on purpose if I'd tried a million times. I huffed, stepped off the flagstone path, and wiggled my way through the thick clusters of rhododendron bushes that ringed the garden.

Normally, it wouldn't have been a problem for me to move quickly and quietly through the dense foliage. But every single branch seemed determined to snag my oversize skirt, while broken twigs scraped and stabbed into the bottoms of my bare feet. I was going nowhere fast and sounding like a rampaging bull doing it. So I lifted my skirt again and used my knife to hack away the crinoline underneath. Once the stiffer, poofier fabric was gone, the skirt fell flat against my legs, allowing me to slip between the branches without getting caught. I also peeled off my black satin gloves and tossed them into the bushes so I could have a better grip on my knife. Twigs still stabbed my bare feet every third step or so, but I pushed the discomfort to the back of my mind. I'd be hurting a lot worse—we all would—if Pike went through with his latest devious plan.

Knife in hand, I skulked through the shadows, searching for him. Every few feet, I stopped and sniffed the air, but between the Southern belles and the flowers, there were too many floral perfumes for me to detect any cigar smoke that might be clinging to him.

Finally, I reached a break in the rhododendron bushes that let me peer into the Rose Garden. The party was still going strong, and everyone was drinking, gossiping, and moving from one clique to the next. Jo-Jo and Roslyn were talking to some women I didn't recognize, while Lorelei was schmoozing with another group.

I crouched down, scanning everyone and everything in the garden, and considered what I knew about Raymond Pike. Not much, just that he was a cruel, ruthless metal elemental who wanted to kill his half sister. Then again, what else did I really need to know?

A waitress carrying a silver champagne bucket walked in front of my hiding spot. My gaze locked on the bucket, and I wondered if it contained another bomb. But the waitress promptly carried it over to the bar area, pulled out the bottle, and popped it open.

My worry lingered. Given the bomb Pike had planted on the *Delta Queen*, it was entirely possible that he'd done the same thing here. I frowned. Why a bomb, though? When he murdered Smith at the hotel, Pike had proven that he had more than enough magic to take someone out face-to-face, given the spoon-turned-dagger that he'd thrown into Smith's throat. So why go to all the trouble of building a bomb and trying to kill Lorelei with it on the riverboat? Especially when he had a sniper rifle that he could have used to blow out her skull?

Unless . . . he didn't really *want* to kill her?

After all, the bomb had been planted at the opposite end of the conference table from Lorelei's seat. And Phillip and Silvio had said that the resulting explosion had seemed small. So the bomb would have probably killed me, since I'd been sitting the closest to it, and maybe some other folks. But Lorelei probably would have escaped largely unscathed. Jack Corbin too.

Maybe . . . Pike hadn't been trying to kill his sister. Maybe . . . he just wanted to scare her. Maybe . . . he just wanted her to realize that he was in Ashland and coming for her. Maybe . . . he wanted to torture her before he finally moved in for the kill.

There were no *maybes* about it.

From all accounts, Raymond Pike had grown up to be just like his father. But Renaldo had been taken away from him, and he'd spent years searching for Lorelei so he could take his revenge. Now he'd finally found her. It wouldn't be enough for Pike simply to kill his sister. Oh, no. He would want her to *suffer* first, the way he had suffered all these years.

And the best way to make Lorelei suffer would be by taking away the person she loved most: Mallory.

I scanned the garden, searching for Mallory. She was sitting at her table, sipping tea, about twenty feet away from my position. I studied the bushes and trees around her, but I didn't see anything suspicious. No branches moving back and forth, no bright swatches of clothing peeking through the limbs, no telltale flash from a set of binoculars.

Maybe I was wrong. Maybe Pike was here to kill Lorelei after all—

A waitress separated herself from the crowd and headed in Mallory's direction. Instead of a bottle of champagne or a tray of food, she clutched a small box in her hand. My breath caught in my throat.

"Here you go, ma'am," the waitress said, putting the box down on the table in front of the elderly dwarf. "A special party favor just for you."

She bobbed her head at Mallory, then went back over to the bar.

So Pike was getting someone else to do his dirty work, just like he had on the *Delta Queen*. I wondered if he intended for the waitress to live through what he had planned. Probably not.

Mallory glanced at the box, but she didn't make a move to actually open it. The so-called party favor was made out of rose quartz and looked like a fancy jewelry box. Even from here, I could hear the delicate murmurs of the stone, singing proudly of its own beauty.

But those weren't the only murmurs I could hear.

Dark, devious notes of mischief and malice also emanated from the stone, telling me exactly what was inside: another bomb.

I held my breath, waiting for the bomb to explode, but Mallory kept sipping her tea, the box sitting innocently on the table. I exhaled. Pike wasn't going to detonate it just yet. Why not?

I looked around and spotted Lorelei on the other side of the garden, her back to Mallory. That's why. Pike would want Lorelei to actually *see* her grandmother being blown to bits. I wouldn't be surprised if he called Lorelei on her phone, told her to turn around, and then *boom!*

Of course, I thought about running forward, snatching up the box, and throwing it as deep and far as I could into the trees. But Pike might recognize me if I approached Mallory and tried to take the box away. Either way, if he blew the bomb, a lot of people here were going to get hurt—or worse.

No, I had to find Pike and take him out before he could trigger the blast. So I circled the garden, moving from one bush to the next as quickly and quietly as I could, looking for his hiding spot.

Thirty seconds later, I found him.

He was leaning against a tree about fifty feet away from Mallory, staring out through the screen of leaves. His head swiveled from side to side as he looked back and forth between Lorelei and her grandmother.

My knife still in my hand, I crept toward Pike. The one good thing about my filmy dress and bare feet was that I didn't make any noise as I sidled closer and closer to him.

Pike kept his relaxed stance, a phone in his hand. He was dressed in a dark blue suit, and the sun streaming in through the trees made his black hair as glossy as a crow's wing. A photographer couldn't have positioned Pike any better to show off his chiseled features and muscled body. A faint chill of metal magic wafted off him, but the sensation didn't bother me, since it felt so similar to my own Stone power.

Pike straightened up. I stopped and tensed, ready to throw my knife at his throat, just like he'd done to Smith at the hotel. But the risk was that he might still be able to trigger the bomb before he died or I managed to get that phone away from him—

"That knife in your hand is quite impressive," he murmured in a cool, smooth voice. "Silverstone is a favorite metal of mine."

Raymond Pike turned to look at me. I twirled my knife around in my hand and stepped forward so that he could see me, easing closer to him. I didn't look at the phone in his hand—didn't so much as glance at it—but I was aware of it all the while.

"Mine too," I replied. "Especially when I'm killing people with it."

He chuckled, his face creasing into a wide smile. Most people would have thought the expression charming, but his eyes stayed cold, and the curve of his lips was more sinister than sincere. This was not a man to be trifled with. Well, I wasn't to be trifled with either.

"I don't think we've been formally introduced," he said in that same suave voice. "I'm Raymond Pike."

"Gin," I replied. "Like the liquor."

He arched his eyebrows. "How quaint."

He crossed his arms over his chest. I kept staring at his face, even though I was thinking about distances and angles and how I could best get that phone away from him.

Pike's blue gaze swept over me, taking in my tangled hair, torn dress, and bare, dirt-crusted feet. "Why, aren't you the very epitome of Southern womanhood," he drawled, his cultured tone making even the sarcastic insult sound classy. "A veritable flower of perfection in this fine, fine garden."

I grinned, but my smile was as sharp as the knife in my hand. "Bless your heart. What a lovely compliment. I'm actually not looking my best right now, but I expect that to change in another minute or two."

"Really? How so?"

My grin widened. "Because that's when I'll be figuring out how to wash your blood out of my dress. Red really is my best color."

He chuckled, unconcerned by my threat. "You're confident. I like that. It always makes the game so much more interesting."

"The game?"

He nodded. "Life and death. The one that people like you and me play with all the puppets and pawns out there."

"Well, if that's your game, then why didn't you blow me to bits on the riverboat?" I asked, creeping forward another step. "You had plenty of opportunity. Not to mention that sniper rifle you used to take those shots at me."

Pike shrugged. "You weren't my target. Besides, I was rather curious to see what you would do. Most people would have run screaming once they realized there was a bomb on board. But not you. I found it most interesting. And amusing, watching your pitiful efforts to save everyone, even if it cost you your own life. And it almost did. Lucky for you that friend of yours jumped into the river to save you. Or you'd be as dead as Lorelei will be very, very soon."

"Oh, yes. Lorelei. I've heard of family feuds before and have been involved in a few myself, but I've never wanted to kill my own sister. What did she ever do to you?"

The coldness lurking beneath his handsome mask of a face rose to the surface and spread out like ice coating his skin. His eyes narrowed, his nostrils flared, and his jaw clenched. In that moment, there was a complete and utter stillness to him, like a snake waiting to strike. I might have thought him a statue planted in the gardens, if not for the hate burning in his blue eyes.

"*Half* sister," he corrected in that ever-smooth voice. "She killed my father, and instead of having the guts to face up to what she'd done, she went into hiding. She should die for that alone."

"But there's more."

"You're damn right there's *more*," he snarled. "After my father's death, I was put into foster care. Some fool psychiatrist said that I was a danger to myself and others. They locked me up in juvie until I was eighteen. You can imagine the sorts of things that happened to me in there."

Nothing good. Being locked up, at other people's mercy, or lack thereof . . . It would have warped Pike even more than his father already had.

"Lorelei is to blame for it all. Every second I was locked up, every time I was beaten, every bad thing that happened to me inside," he continued. "It's taken years for me to track her down. Years of dead ends and false leads and being led on a merry fucking goose chase. But now I've found her, and I intend to finish what my father started all those years ago. For him and especially for me."

Memories from that day filled my mind. The horn on Sophia's convertible beeping in warning. Her car crumpled around that tree, smoke boiling up from the hood. Renaldo Pike striding toward the cabin, using his metal magic to rip all the nails out of the walls and send them shooting out like bullets. And then, everything that had happened after I'd dragged Lorelei out of the cabin and into the woods . . .

I blinked, forcing away the memories. Raymond Pike was wrong about so many things. As far as I was concerned, his father had gotten *exactly* what he deserved. But of course, Pike wouldn't see it that way.

I shook my head. "I'm afraid it's too late for that. You should have killed Lorelei on the riverboat. You would have gotten away with it then. But not now."

"Why? Because you're here, and you're going to stop me?" Pike laughed. "Don't flatter yourself. All you've done so far is run around, stick your nose where it doesn't belong, and try to *save* people."

He raised his phone. I tensed, expecting him to detonate the bomb, but all he did was clutch that hand to his heart, phone and all, mocking me.

"It's been very *noble* of you, though," he said. "Even if it all was a waste of time."

I tightened my grip on my knife and eased forward another foot. Three more steps, and I'd be close enough to gut him. "That's the difference between you and me. I don't think that saving people is a waste of time. More like time well spent."

Pike scoffed, then dropped his hand from his heart and glanced down at his phone. I was out of time, so I raised my knife, ready to lunge toward him and drive the blade through his heart—

A cold, hard force took hold of my knife, as though an invisible hand were peeling my fingers off the hilt. Before I could tighten my grip again, the force jerked the knife completely out of my hand and sent it zipping over to Pike, who plucked it effortlessly out of midair.

"An impressive weapon," he murmured, hefting it in his hand. "Light, lethal, perfectly balanced. How about I take it for a spin?"

Pike grinned, snapped his arm up, and threw the knife right back at me, aiming for my throat, the same way he'd done when he killed Smith. There was no time to duck, so I threw up my forearm as I reached for my Stone magic, hardening my skin.

I didn't know if Pike used his metal magic to direct the weapon or if he was just that good a marksman, but the knife slammed into my forearm, tip first, in a perfect throw.

Bull's-eye.

I hadn't brought enough of my magic to bear to completely block the blow, and the knife sliced through my skin, the blade lodging deep in the tendons close to my elbow with a hard, sickening impact. I felt like someone had jabbed an icy poker right into the middle of my funny bone. Ha-ha-ha-ha.

I staggered back, my breath escaping in a hissing yelp of pain, as blood spurted out of my arm and spattered all over my dress. As an added bonus, a sharp bit of rock buried under a pile of leaves sliced into my left foot. Injury and insult.

But I swallowed my screams, reached down, and yanked my own knife out of my arm. The coppery stink of my blood filled my nose, overpowering all the sweet floral perfumes. I tightened my grip on the blade, using my Stone magic to harden my fist around the hilt and make sure the weapon stayed put.

Every movement, every breath, every blink of my eyes sent more and more pain spiraling through my body. Still, it could have been worse. If I hadn't used my magic, the weapon would have broken my arm outright. If I hadn't raised my arm, the knife would have lodged in my throat—and I'd be on the ground, bleeding out.

Instead of using his metal magic to rip the weapon away from me again, Pike did something far, far worse: he held up his phone. The screen was large enough for me to see a timer there. Two minutes and *tick-tick-tick*ing down.

"Since you seem to enjoy saving people so much, I'm giving you a chance to do just that," he purred. "You have two choices. You can try to kill me right now, or you can try to stop my bomb. I'll give you a hint. This one packs a lot more punch than the one on the riverboat. Up to you, hero."

A wave of magic rolled off him, and the phone disintegrated in his hand, with bits of plastic, glass, and metal *ping*ing off the surrounding trees and bushes. Pike backed up, his hands held up in front of him, ready to blast me with magic if I came at him.

For a mad, mad moment, I thought about going after him and ending this here and now. But he was right—I would rather save everyone than try to kill him. Besides, there would be plenty of time for that later.

"Tell Lorelei that her big brother says hello," Pike purred again, realizing he'd won this round. "And that I'll be seeing her again real soon."

He waggled his fingers, then raised his hand to his lips and blew me a kiss before disappearing into the trees. Smug bastard.

I plunged through the bushes, shoving my way through the tight branches and staggering out into the middle of the garden.

For a second, nothing happened. Then someone noticed me, my knife, and the blood dripping all over me.

"Look out!" someone screamed. "She has a knife!"

Everyone turned to stare at me. The society ladies. The waitresses. Jo-Jo, Roslyn, Lorelei, and Mallory. They all froze, and the only sounds were my hoarse, raspy breaths and the faint tinkling of the wind chimes in the distance.

Then chaos erupted.

Everyone screamed and stampeded away from me as fast as they could. But they didn't get far; in their haste, the partygoers slammed into one another, rattling around like bowling pins, upending chairs, tipping over tables, and sending all those pretty tea sets crashing to the ground. One woman—Delilah—tripped and did a header into the podium, knocking herself unconscious. In an instant, the elegant soiree was reduced to a giant rose-and-tea-themed mess, with broken dishes, trampled food, and overturned furniture strewn in the midst of all the colorful flowers.

There was no time to explain, so I shoved through the women standing between me and that box that was still sitting in front of Mallory, who was getting to her feet. By some stroke of luck, hers was the only table that had remained upright and untouched during the stampede. I just hoped it stayed that way. If the box fell to the ground, if someone accidentally kicked it . . . I didn't know what might trigger the bomb other than the cell-phone timer, and I didn't want to find out.

Out of the corner of my eye, I spotted Jo-Jo and Roslyn moving against the crowd, trying to get to me. So was Lorelei, although she was heading toward Mallory. But I was closer to the dwarf than any of them, so I shut them out of my mind and focused on the bomb.

"Move!" I yelled, although my voice was lost among the shrieks and screams. "Move! Move! Move!"

I pushed a couple of middle-aged matrons out of my way and staggered over to the table. Mallory sidestepped away from me, clearly wondering what I was doing, but I only had eyes for the bomb. More women streamed past the table, carrying Mallory along in their wake. Good. The farther away she was, the more likely she was to survive.

Just as I'd thought, the bomb was housed inside a jewelry box made out of pale rose quartz. Flowers and vines swirled through the sides, while a small silver clasp held the lid closed. It would have been quite beautiful, if not for the ugly rune carved into the top.

A mace—Pike's rune.

As my gaze locked onto the symbol, a pale blue light flared, growing brighter and brighter and slowly filling in the lines of the mace rune. Cold, hard power leaked out of the box, building and building like a wave rising up. Pike must have coated the box with his metal magic to make the blast even more powerful, to send the nails inside shooting out in all directions for maximum effect.

No collateral damage this time—just utter *destruction*.

I'd been trying to keep a mental clock running in my head, but I didn't know how accurate my timing was. I thought that I had about thirty seconds left to do something with the bomb—other than watch it explode and rip people to shreds, including me.

Desperation filled me. My eyes flicked left and right, but there was no place to throw the bomb. Even if I managed to find an empty area, I couldn't throw it far enough to keep everyone out of the blast radius. The blowback would still kill people, along with the resulting shrapnel.

Twenty-five . . . twenty-four . . . twenty-three . . .

Lorelei reached my side. She'd lost her floppy hat and one of her heels, but her mouth was set into a determined slash as she stared down at the bomb.

"Encase it with your Ice magic!" she yelled above the screams. "As much as you can! I'll use my metal magic to keep it from blowing outright! That's the only way to contain the blast!"

Twenty . . . nineteen . . . eighteen . . .

I reached for the box and wrapped my hands around one side of it. Lorelei slapped her hands down on the other side, and we both blasted the box with our magic.

There was no time for subtlety and skill. If the bomb blew, it would kill both of us, regardless of the fact that I was using my Stone magic to harden my skin. But better me than all these innocent people. So I slammed a layer of Ice around the jewelry box, hoping that the force of my magic wouldn't make it detonate in my hands.

And it didn't, thanks to Lorelei.

Pike's metal magic started to react to my Ice power, and the entire box trembled, as though it were about to explode, even though the lines on the mace rune weren't completely filled in yet. But Lorelei sent a wave of her metal magic into the heart of the symbol, pushing back against Pike's power. She didn't seem to be as strong as her brother, but her magic was enough to slow his down.

Fifteen . . . fourteen . . . thirteen . . .

The rose quartz wailed at the sudden, brutal assault, but I shut the stone's cries out of my mind and hit it with another round of magic. Then another, then another, as though I were wrapping a Christmas present, only with elemental Ice instead of pretty paper. Lorelei worked beside me the whole time, holding off her brother's magic as long as she could.

Best-case scenario, my Ice would throttle the blast, and

it wouldn't be any worse than a pipe bomb some juvenile delinquents stuck in a toilet. Worst-case, Raymond Pike had a whole lot more magic than I did, and I'd be seeing Fletcher in a few more seconds.

Ten . . . nine . . . eight . . .

Through all my layers of Ice, Pike's mace rune burned an even brighter blue, the entire symbol now fully lit up with his metal power, indicating that the bomb was about to explode.

Five . . . four . . . three . . .

"Throw it!" Lorelei screamed, ripping her hands off the box. "Throw it now!"

I snatched up the Ice-coated jewelry box, reared back my hand, and pitched it as hard, high, and far away as I could. It didn't travel all that far, getting stuck in a tree branch behind one of the trellises—

BOOM!

✳ 17 ✳

The force of the blast knocked me back into Lorelei and sent us both tumbling to the ground.

The tree disintegrated into the sum of its splinters. So did the trellis in front of it and all the surrounding bushes. Ash and cinders fluttered through the air like confetti, along with burned leaves, blackened petals, and smoldering bits of bark. Lorelei and I were the closest to the blast, and the smoke boiled over us, making me cough and cough. Strangely enough, the smoke smelled like roses.

The explosion seemed to go on forever, although it couldn't have lasted more than a few seconds. I didn't know how long it was before I was able to pick myself up and stagger to my feet.

I wobbled back and forth, my ears ringing from the blast and my head swimming in a way that told me that I had another concussion. But I was still in one piece, and so were Lorelei and everyone else. So I forced myself to ignore my injuries and focus on the damage.

The smoldering remains of the tree were studded with nails, the charred trunk bristling with them like a pin-cushion. I half expected blood to come pouring out of the wounds, but of course, it didn't. Still, a shiver raced up my spine. That could have been me studded with nails—or, worse, Jo-Jo and Roslyn.

My friends rushed over to me, Jo-Jo reaching for her Air magic to heal my injuries. Her power surged over me much the same way my Ice magic had blasted over the jewelry box. I grimaced at the pins-and-needles sensation of her magic sweeping over my body and stitching back what was cut, bloody, and bruised.

I looked at Lorelei, who was slowly getting to her feet. She'd been behind me, so she'd been spared the brunt of the blast. All it seemed to have done was to knock her down and dirty her dress.

Lorelei gave me a guarded look, her gaze lingering on the bloody gash on my arm as it slowly healed. Once she realized that I was still in one piece, she hurried over to Mallory, who was calling her name. Lorelei hugged her grandmother tightly, then bent down and started whis-pering in her ear. Mallory's face was pale, but her blue eyes glittered with determination. So did Lorelei's.

"Now what happens?" Roslyn asked, staring at them the same way I was.

Despite Jo-Jo's healing magic, my head was still ach-ing, and it wasn't from the bomb blast or the resulting concussion. "I have no clue."

*   *   *

Naturally, all the panicked society ladies called the cops, and the po-po showed up about ten minutes later. Bria and Xavier were the lead investigators on the scene, with uniformed officers moving through the crowd and taking witness statements. Still more folks dressed in bomb gear swept through the Rose Garden, then spread out to the other sections, searching for more explosive devices. I doubted they would find any, though. Pike had only wanted to kill Mallory. He wouldn't have cared enough about anyone else to make more than one bomb.

Bria came over to me, while Xavier split off to check on Roslyn. My sister hugged me tightly, then looked me over, her blue gaze taking in the blood, soot, and ash that streaked my face, arms, and pink dress.

"It's nothing," I said. "Just some dirt and grime. Jo-Jo already healed me."

Bria's worry seemed to lessen but only a little bit.

She focused on the still-smoldering tree and all the nails glinting in the ruined tree stump. "Another bomb."

"Yep. Compliments of one Raymond Pike."

I filled Bria in on my encounter with Pike. The only thing I didn't mention was how he'd used his metal magic to turn my own knife against me. I was the only one who needed to know that troubling fact. It had been a long time since I'd been up against a metal elemental, and I'd been in such a hurry to kill Pike that I hadn't thought about him being able to neutralize my knives, much less control them.

I should have, though. Pike had taught me a painful lesson, one that rattled me far more than I liked. My knives were such a big part of who and what I was that

I didn't know quite what to do without them. How to protect, how to attack, how to *win*. But I'd figure it out. I always did.

And then Raymond Pike would die.

"Well," Bria said, cutting into my dark thoughts, "I should talk to Lorelei."

"Good luck with that."

My sister shrugged, but it was her job, so she headed in Lorelei's direction. I followed her, curious about what the smuggler would—or wouldn't—say.

Lorelei and Mallory were seated at the same table they'd occupied when I first arrived. Lorelei was whispering to her grandmother, but she stopped talking once she noticed Bria approaching. Her face was blank and shuttered. So was Mallory's.

"Ms. Parker," Bria said. "Mrs. Parker. I'd like to talk to you about the bombing. My sister tells me that you were the intended targets."

"I have no idea what you're talking about," Lorelei said, somehow managing to look down her nose at Bria, even though she was seated. "I don't know what your sister thinks she saw or overheard, but my grandmother and I don't know anything about the bombing. We were just in the wrong place at the wrong time. Right, Grandma?"

Mallory nodded.

Anger surged through me. "Don't be an idiot, Lorelei. Tell the cops about Raymond. Maybe you'll get lucky, and they can arrest him for the bombing before he takes another crack at you and Mallory."

Lorelei shrugged. "I don't know what you're talking about."

Mallory looked back and forth between me and her granddaughter, but she didn't say anything. And I realized that she wouldn't. Neither would Lorelei.

"You should let me help you, Ms. Parker," Bria said. "It's what I do, and I'm pretty good at it."

Lorelei snorted. "The police? Help *me*? The police have *never* helped me—and especially not my mother. She called the police for help. More than once. But do you know what they did?"

Bria shook her head.

"Nothing," Lorelei spat out. "Not a damn thing except take the bribes that my father doled out to get them to ignore the bruises on my mom's face—and on mine too. So forgive me if I don't put much stock in the police, especially the Ashland police. Let me save you some time and energy. We didn't see anything, we didn't hear anything, and we don't know anything. Now, if you'll excuse us, my grandmother needs her rest."

Lorelei helped Mallory to her feet, then waved at Jack Corbin, who was standing at the garden entrance. He came over and took Mallory's arm. The dwarf smiled up at him and patted his hand. Corbin tried to smile back, but his expression was more of a miserable wince, and he glanced over at the ruined tree. His eyes widened, and then he wet his lips and quickly looked away from the damage. Curious.

They walked past me, and Mallory turned her head to stare at me. Corbin was looking straight ahead, clearly wanting to get out of here as fast as possible, so he didn't see her mouth the words to me.

Help her. Please.

Mallory stared at me another second, then she and Corbin swept past me and out of the garden.

"You're sure you don't know anything about the bombing?" Bria asked again, still trying to get Lorelei to open up.

"I'm sure." Lorelei gave her the same kind of syrupy smile that Mallory had used on me and the society ladies. "Bless your heart for asking, though."

Bria recognized the insult for what it was, and she gave Lorelei an even sweeter, more syrupy smile in return. "And bless *your* heart for being *so* cooperative and *so* very helpful."

Lorelei's eyes narrowed, but Bria just cranked up the wattage on her smile. Score one for my baby sister.

Bria stared down Lorelei for a few more seconds, then moved off to speak to the next witness. She couldn't make Lorelei talk if she didn't want to.

But I could.

Lorelei started to walk away, but I latched onto her arm. She shook me off, but I grabbed hold of her again. She shook me off a second time but finally faced me, crossing her arms over her chest.

"Why can't you just leave me alone?" she snapped.

"Because your revenge-seeking half brother keeps planting bombs in close proximity to me and my friends," I snapped back. "That happens to concern me. I might be an assassin, but I don't deal in collateral damage, and I especially don't like to see innocent people almost get blown up just because they're in the wrong place with the wrong people at the wrong time."

"Well, you don't have to worry about that anymore," Lorelei retorted. "I said that I would take care of Raymond, and I will."

"It seems to me like Raymond is going to take care of you first. Are you even doing anything to track him down?"

Lorelei laughed, but it was a soft, ugly sound. "That's the beauty of this whole thing. I don't have to track him down. I don't have to do anything. He'll find me soon enough, and I'll be ready when he does. Count on it."

Her voice held a poison promise that I knew all too well. Her hands were clenched into fists, and anger blazed in her eyes. I didn't know if the emotion was directed at her brother or me. Probably both of us.

"I can't believe that you're standing here, wanting to help me *now*," she snarled. "If it weren't for you and your friends, none of this would even be happening. I could have gotten on with my life *years* ago, instead of waiting for this day to come."

This time, I knew exactly what she was talking about. Her words weren't completely correct, but they had enough truth in them to make me flinch.

"That wasn't my fault. You know it wasn't. And neither is any of this."

Lorelei let out another, even uglier laugh. "Well, I suppose that quibbling over who's to blame doesn't make much sense now that Raymond has finally found me."

More of that acidic guilt flooded my heart, chewing through what was left of it, but I couldn't argue with her logic.

She gave me a disgusted look. "Just . . . stay out of my way. Okay? For once in your miserable life. I can take care of Raymond."

"Sure," I sniped. "Before or after he kills you and Mallory? Because he's not going to stop until the two of you are dead."

Lorelei didn't say anything, but anger, pain, and guilt flashed in her eyes, smoldering like the ruined tree. Her mouth tightened into a hard, determined line.

I drew in a breath and tried to rein in my anger. "Listen, I just want to help—"

"Forget it." She cut me off. "I don't want or need your help. I can take care of myself. Stay out of my way, or you'll regret it."

Lorelei gave me one more disgusted glare, then stormed out of the garden.

❄ 18 ❄

A hot shower and several worried voice mails awaited me when I got home to Fletcher's. Everyone and his brother had heard about the explosion, and Finn, Owen, and Silvio had all called to check on me—Finn wanting all the juicy details, Owen making sure that I was okay, and Silvio chiding me because I hadn't brought him along to the party.

I dealt with all their questions and concerns, told them that I wanted to be alone tonight, and went to bed, even though it was just after six. I fell asleep almost immediately, but when the dreams started, dredged up by everything that had happened over the past few days, they felt as vivid as if I were wide awake . . .

I dragged Lorelei down the hallway, through the kitchen, and out the back door of the cabin. We stumbled down the steps, both of us sprawling in the dirt, but I kept crabbing forward the whole time, yanking her along with me as best and as fast as I could.

Behind us, more and more nails shot out of the cabin walls, the floorboards, and even the roof, the sharp projectiles punching through the windows and raining shards of glass down on us. The entire wooden structure moaned and groaned, threatening to collapse in on itself.

And then, with a single ominous creak, it did.

Without all those nails to hold them in place, the walls toppled together, pulling the supports down with them, and the whole cabin caved in like a house of cards. Thick, choking clouds of dust puffed up, while split pieces of wood zoomed through the air like warped arrows.

I threw one arm up to protect my head, still crawling forward and pulling Lorelei along with me, trying to get us clear of the debris. What was left of the cabin quickly settled down, although the resulting dust churned like a storm cloud above our heads. I let go of Lorelei's hand. She curled into a ball, crying, but I staggered up onto my feet, coughing and trying to clear the dust out of my lungs.

At first, I didn't see anything but the collapsed cabin, then a figure emerged out of the dust. Renaldo Pike stopped and stared at the splintered structure, smiling at the destruction he'd caused. He caught sight of Lorelei and me. His cruel smile widened, and he headed in our direction, twirling that mace around in his hand.

"It's no use," Lorelei mumbled, staring at her father with dull, blank eyes. "He'll find us wherever we go. And then he'll kill us. Just like he killed my mom."

"He's not going to kill us!" I hissed. "All we have to do is outrun him. Now, come on!"

I grabbed her arm, yanked her to her feet, and pulled her with me into the woods. She stumbled along behind me, barely keeping up, but I tightened my grip on her hand and increased my pace, ruthlessly tuning out her sobs. Yeah, I was hurting her, and I felt bad about that, but it was better than the alternative. No way was I letting some mace-wielding elemental murder me. Renaldo had already hurt Fletcher, Jo-Jo, and Sophia—maybe even killed them—but he wasn't getting us too.

I scanned the woods, trying to come up with a better plan than just running blindly, but all I saw were trees and rocks—and more trees and rocks. Nothing that would help me slow down the monster behind us, much less stop him for good.

With every step, the knife I'd grabbed from the kitchen rode up and down in the back pocket of my jeans. I could kill Renaldo with the weapon. I'd done it before. All I had to do was get close enough to stab him before he realized what was happening—

I leaped over a tree root sticking up out of the earth, but Lorelei didn't see it and hooked her foot through it. She stumbled, her cold, shaking hand tearing free of my grasp, and hit the ground hard. I ran back to help her up.

Magic surged through the air.

I threw myself down on the ground just in time to avoid the nails that zipped over my head like a swarm of angry bees and then thunked *into a nearby tree.*

I scrambled back up onto my feet. Renaldo was thirty feet behind us, calmly walking along as if he had all the time in the world. His eyes burned an even brighter blue as he reached for more of his metal magic. He waved his hand,

and the nails embedded in the tree trunk started working themselves free for another strike.

"Get up! Get up! Get up!" I screamed at Lorelei, hauling her upright.

She tried to stand on her own but fell back down, sobbing and clutching her foot. She must have twisted her ankle. Behind her, Renaldo kept striding toward us at that slow, steady pace, his grin sharpening with evil intent. He wanted to kill us both, and she couldn't run away anymore. Only one thing to do.

Leave her behind.

I kept staring at Renaldo as I backed out of the clearing we were in and headed toward the trees on the far side.

Lorelei realized what I was doing, and her eyes widened with fear and panic. "No! Don't go! Don't leave me here with him!"

I tuned out her tearful pleas, turned, and vanished into the trees.

"Wait! Please! Come back!" she said, her voice dissolving into a choked sob. "Please don't leave me!"

My heart twisted at her words, but I knew that I was doing the right thing.

I darted about thirty feet into the woods, then cut to my right, circling back around. Of course, I wasn't going to leave her. That wasn't what Fletcher had taught me to do. Not at all.

What he had taught me was that it was better to get the drop on a powerful enemy, rather than take him on face-to-face. All I needed was a few seconds of stealth and surprise, and I could plunge my knife into Renaldo's back. Then Lorelei and I would both be safe. I didn't like using her as bait, but it was the only way I could think of to save us both.

So I crept through the woods, forcing myself to look and listen, in case Renaldo had figured out what I was up to and was waiting for me. I crept back to the spot where I'd vanished into the trees, but the metal elemental had his back to me. He stood over his daughter, who was huddled on her knees. He kicked a wad of dirt right into her face, causing her to cringe and choke at the small pebbles that pelted her cheeks and the dust that filled her nose and mouth. Then he started circling around her.

"Cringing and groveling, just like your mother," Renaldo said in a disgusted voice. "She always was weak. Just like you are."

Lorelei lifted her head, rage making her blue eyes burn even brighter than her father's. She managed to get back up onto her feet, although she could hardly stand on her twisted ankle. But she raised her chin and glared right back at her father. In that moment, she wasn't weak. Not anymore. Never again.

"Mom never did anything wrong," she spat. "You're the one who's a complete monster. Always claiming that you loved her even though all you did was hit and yell and make fun of her. She hated you, and so do I."

Renaldo stopped his circling and laughed, the mocking sound low and evil. "Well, you'll be joining her soon enough."

I pulled the kitchen knife from the back pocket of my jeans and slipped out into the clearing. Lorelei saw me, and her eyes widened, realizing that I hadn't abandoned her after all.

She focused on her father again. "Yeah, well, I'd rather be dead than have to spend one more miserable minute with you and Raymond. You both think that your metal magic *makes you sooo strong, sooo special. But all you do is hurt people with it. You're disgusting, and so is he."*

Renaldo scoffed. *"You don't have enough metal magic to speak of. And that weak bit of Ice power you inherited from your mother isn't any better. You always were jealous of Raymond's power."*

She snorted. *"Jealous? Of Raymond? Please."*

"He's here with me," Renaldo continued, as though she hadn't spoken. *"Dealing with the people in the car. Making sure they're dead. The ones who foolishly thought that they could take away what was mine. I punished your mother for her insolence, for thinking that she could dare to leave me. And now I'm going to do the same to you."*

Renaldo twirled the mace in his hand, building up momentum for a powerful, deadly strike.

I drew in a breath and crept closer to him. I was twenty feet away and closing fast. Fifteen feet . . . ten . . . five . . .

I raised my knife, ready to plunge it deep into his back. I'd only have one shot, and I needed to make it count.

Lorelei's eyes flicked to me again, and her father realized that she was looking at something behind him.

Renaldo whipped around and caught my arm in his hand. I struggled with all my might, trying to slam the knife forward into his body, but he was stronger than I was. He stared at me, completely unconcerned about the blade hovering inches from his heart. Then he snapped my right wrist back, breaking it. I screamed, the knife slipping from my fingers and hitting the dirt.

Renaldo gave me another bored look, then rammed his mace into my body. The impact was bad enough, but the real pain came from the wicked spikes on the metal ball *that stabbed deep into my right shoulder. I screamed, then screamed again, as he yanked the weapon back out, tearing the spikes through my muscles.*

I dropped to the ground, still screaming. Every single part of my right arm, from my broken wrist to my mangled shoulder, burned, pulsed, and throbbed with pain.

Renaldo reared his foot back to kick me in the ribs, but I managed to roll out of the way, my one good hand scrabbling over the ground, trying to pull myself out of his range. Every movement sent more agony slicing through my shoulder. Cries of pain bubbled out of my lips, and sweat streamed down my face, the salty drops stinging my eyes and adding to my misery. Nausea boiled in my stomach, and gray spots flashed in front of my eyes in warning. I was this close *to blacking out, and if that happened, I was dead.*

"Stop it! Leave her alone!"

Lorelei snatched up my knife. Despite how badly she was wobbling on her twisted ankle, she still lashed out with the weapon, trying to stab her father to death. But Renaldo blocked her blow, then slapped her across the face, sending her tumbling to the ground. Her moans of pain matched mine.

Renaldo leaned down and picked up my knife, flipping it end-over-end in his hand, before turning and throwing it across the clearing. Thwack. The knife sank deep into a tree trunk.

Despair filled me. There went my only weapon and my best chance of killing him—

Something sharp stabbed into my right palm, in the center of my spider rune scar. I hissed and raised my hand, to find a nail sticking out of my skin. I ground my teeth together and yanked it free, causing myself even more pain, but I didn't let go of it. Renaldo had used nails against us, and I was going to do the same thing to him. Yeah, a single nail wasn't much of a weapon, but it was all I had.

I let out a weak little whimper that wasn't really all that fake and kept dragging myself through the dirt, rocks, and leaves.

Renaldo laughed. "Running away? I don't think so. No one runs away from me."

His footsteps scuffed on the ground, as his shadow slid closer and closer to me on the forest floor. I forced down the pain of my injuries and tightened my grip on the nail, waiting for him to get within reach.

Renaldo's hand clamped onto my injured arm, and he hauled me upright. He turned me around and held his mace up against my face, one of the points digging into my cheek, close to my eye.

"You should be grateful that I'm going to kill you first. You won't suffer nearly as much as my daughter will."

He grinned, then reared back his arm to slam the mace into my face.

But I was quicker.

I snapped my hand up and rammed the nail into the side of his neck.

It was a crude weapon, but the tip was sharp enough to cut through his skin just as it had cut through mine. Renaldo yelped, blood spewing out of the wound. He was so surprised that his mace slipped from his hand, hit the ground, and rolled away.

My fingers were too slick with blood to yank the nail back out of his neck, so I shoved him away. His feet caught on *another tree root sticking up out of the ground, and he fell backward.*

Right on top of his own mace.

Renaldo screamed and arched his back, as if he could push the deadly spikes out of his body, but all he did was sink even deeper down on top of them. Blood bubbled up out of his lips, and I knew that at least one of those spikes had hit something vital.

Good.

Renaldo rolled to his side, the spiked ball of the mace sticking out of his back. His gaze locked on his daughter, and he started crawling toward her, stretching his hand out. Lorelei scrambled backward out of the way, shrieking all the while.

But there was no need to be afraid of him anymore.

Renaldo's hand dropped to the dirt, his body stilled, and his head lolled to the side, the glossy glaze of death dimming his eyes . . .

Lorelei's shrieks startled me out of my own sleep. I lay in bed, gasping for air, my wrist and shoulder throbbing, as though those spikes had torn through my muscles just moments ago.

I let out a long, weary breath and scrubbed my hands over my face, as if that would somehow get rid of the awful memories—or my growing guilt.

Raymond Pike wanted to kill Lorelei for murdering their father. That was the sole reason he'd come to Ashland.

But he was targeting the wrong person.

Lorelei hadn't done anything to their father. *I* was the one who'd killed Renaldo, and Lorelei knew it as well as I did. So why wasn't she shouting the truth to the rooftops?

Why hadn't she found some way to let Raymond know that it was really me who'd killed their father? Why was she sitting back and waiting for him to try to murder her again for something that she didn't even do?

If she really wanted to *eliminate threats*, as she'd put it, then Lorelei should have whispered in Raymond's ear that I was the one he really wanted. That way, she could have killed two birds with one truth. She could have let Raymond have his revenge and gotten rid of me at the same time.

But she hadn't done any of that, and I wondered why.

Oh, the *why*s. They had caused me many a sleepless night.

And this one was going to be no exception.

✤ 19 ✤

Despite all the questions bouncing around in my mind, I managed to get a little sleep. I still had a barbecue restaurant to run, so I got up, took a shower, and went to the Pork Pit on schedule the next morning.

I did my usual check for booby traps, being extra cautious in case Pike had decided to leave me a little present like the ones he'd been dropping for Lorelei all over town. But the restaurant was clean, so I opened the front door, went inside, and started cooking.

The familiar rhythms of mixing, stirring, baking, and frying soothed me the way they always did. The thing I loved about cooking was that it was predictable, reliable, dependable. Measure the ingredients, follow the directions, set the oven to the right temperature, and everything always came out just fine. Too bad there wasn't a recipe for life and all its messy complications.

So I threw myself into my routine to try to quiet my

troubled thoughts. And it worked. By the time Sophia, Catalina, and the rest of the waitstaff came in, I'd already made two vats of Fletcher's secret barbecue sauce, put the day's sourdough rolls in the ovens to bake, and sliced up the vegetables for the burgers and other sandwiches. But most important, I felt much calmer, and I'd made an important decision.

To leave Lorelei Parker to her own fate.

I'd already saved her twice from her brother and his bombs, and she'd been an ungrateful snot every step of the way. She didn't want my help? Well, that was just fine and dandy with me. She was an underworld boss. She had Ice and metal magic. She could take care of herself. Besides, it wasn't my problem. Her feud with her brother didn't have anything to do with me.

Even if a stubborn little voice in the very back of my mind kept insisting that it did.

Stupid voice. Stupid head. Stupid everything.

Silvio cleared his throat, interrupting my thoughts. He'd come in with Catalina a few minutes ago and was sitting on his usual stool, arranging his phone and tablet on the counter. "It's nice to see that you are actually where you're supposed to be. For a change."

"Don't tell me that you're still bent out of shape because I didn't take you to the garden party yesterday. It was ladies-only, if you'll recall."

Silvio sniffed, letting me know that he was indeed still miffed. "I'm not upset that I couldn't attend the actual event. I find those sorts of social activities rather abhorrent." His nose twitched in disgust. "It's just that you didn't check in with me before you went."

"So?"

The vampire gave me a chiding look. "So how can I be your assistant and actually *assist* you if I don't know where you are or what you're doing?"

I sighed. "I appreciate your wanting to help, Silvio. Really, I do. But you should know by now that I'm more of a do-it-myselfer. I'm still not used to having an assistant, especially not one as . . . dedicated as you."

That was my diplomatic way of not saying that Silvio's obsessive love of lists, schedules, plans, and details sometimes drove me crazy. I didn't know if I would ever get used to having an assistant, but I didn't want to hurt his feelings.

My apology seemed to satisfy Silvio, who fired up his tablet for the morning briefing. For once, I listened carefully to everything he said, since almost all of it had to do with Pike.

"If he's staying in a hotel in Ashland, he's using an alias," Silvio said. "More likely, he's rented an apartment or a house under a fake name. Either way, there's no trace of him anywhere in the city. No hotel sightings, no credit-card charges, nothing."

I tapped my fingers against the counter. Not surprising. Pike had struck me as a careful sort who didn't leave anything to chance, especially not the revenge he'd been planning for so many years. The fact that I'd mucked up his plans to hurt Lorelei and hadn't been seriously injured myself was somewhat amazing. I just wondered how long it would be before my luck ran out.

No, I thought. My luck wasn't going to run out, because *this wasn't my problem*. Lorelei wanted me to stay out of her affairs; well, I was going to cede to her wishes. Besides, I still had enough problems of my own to worry about with the other bosses.

Still, that didn't mean that I wasn't going to keep an eye on the situation. After all, I'd messed up Pike's schemes twice now. It wasn't out of the realm of possibility that he might turn his attention to me after he was done with Lorelei.

"Keep looking for Pike," I told Silvio. "If you find him, don't approach him. He's too dangerous for that. Just let me know where he is."

He made a note on his tablet. "I'll ask Ms. Jamison again too, since her organization was the one that located Harold Smith."

I nodded. It made sense. Not only did Jade Jamison run guys and girls, but she also owned several cleaning and service businesses that supplied workers to restaurants, hotels, apartment buildings, and more throughout Ashland.

While Silvio texted Jade, I crossed the storefront, flipped over the sign on the door to *Open*, and greeted the day's first customers.

The lunch rush came and went with no problems, unless you counted Dimitri Barkov and Luiz Ramos strolling into the restaurant together, sitting down, and ordering heaping plates of barbecue. In between bites, the gangsters stared at me, obviously wanting me to come over and talk to them, but my cold glower had them staying in their seats and concentrating on their vittles—for the time being.

Silvio's lips quirked up into a small, amused smile.

"You never did tell them who was getting the coin laundries."

"Well, they'll just have to wait until I'm good and ready to decide," I snapped. "I'm sure they've heard that I have other problems right now."

I kept cooking, cleaning, and cashing out customers. By the time two o'clock rolled around and Owen and Finn showed up at the restaurant, I had settled into a mellow mood.

"How are you feeling?" Owen asked, giving me a slow once-over to make sure that I was really okay.

"Fine, just like I told you last night. I'm not even sore from the bombing, thanks to Jo-Jo and her healing magic."

Owen nodded, but he knew me too well to let me get away with such a simple, easy answer. "And how are you feeling on the inside?" he asked in a softer voice.

I gave him a tight smile. "Those wounds always tend to linger with me."

"I thought so."

Owen stepped around the counter and drew me into his arms, just holding me for a second and offering me the comfort he knew that I needed. He dipped his head to mine, and we shared a long, lingering kiss that had Finn making gagging sounds. So I kissed Owen again, even deeper, just for good measure.

"Please, Gin," Finn whined, clutching his flat stomach. "Stop sucking face with your boy toy before I lose my appetite."

"Why, to hear you tell it, wading through raw sewage wouldn't make the great Finnegan Lane lose his appetite."

He considered my words, then brightened. "You know, you're right. I could always eat."

Finn grabbed a menu and started scanning through the choices, even though he'd memorized them all long ago.

He and Owen slid onto the two stools closest to the cash register, with Silvio sitting beside them, and ordered their food. A bacon cheeseburger for Owen, with onion rings and potato salad, barbecue chicken with a side of mac and cheese for Finn, and a grilled chicken salad sandwich for Silvio, with some chocolate chip cookies that I'd baked fresh this morning.

My friends chatted back and forth with each other and across the counter to me while I fixed their food. Eventually, Finn jerked his thumb over his shoulder at the booth where Dimitri and Luiz were still sitting.

"What's with the Wonder Twins?" he snarked. "I thought they hated each other."

"Oh, they're probably just disappointed that Pike didn't blow me to smithereens yesterday. They'll get over it."

Another dark, pointed glare from me had Dimitri and Luiz pulling out fat wads of bills to pay for their food and skedaddling out the front door. Good riddance. I was tired of them and their whining. Especially when there was a far more dangerous threat in Ashland.

I rubbed my aching head. As much as I tried to stop thinking about Lorelei, Pike, and all the rest of it, my mind kept going back to everything that had happened, both over the past few days and all those years ago.

But I pushed those thoughts away and concentrated on finishing my friends' food. I had just slid the hot plates over to them when the bell over the front door chimed, indicating that I had a new customer.

I wasn't all that surprised when Mallory Parker strolled through the door. My friends glanced over their shoulders at the new arrival, and Finn let out a low whistle.

"I wonder what she wants," he murmured.

"Nothing good," I muttered.

Mallory was decked out in diamonds, just as she had been at the garden party, although she wore a blue pantsuit today instead of a frilly frock. Still, she was way overdressed for my gin joint, and everyone stared at her, including a few low-level thugs who eyed her jewelry with obvious interest.

At least, until they realized that Sophia was staring at them from behind the counter with her arms crossed over her chest, a butcher's knife clutched in her hand. The Goth dwarf stabbed the knife toward the thugs, then toward the door. They couldn't climb out of their booth and run outside fast enough. Sophia snickered and went back to work.

Catalina seated Mallory and took her order, before handing the ticket over to me. The dwarf had skipped all the lunch items and gone straight to dessert, ordering a piece of apple pie with a cinnamon-sugar crumb topping, vanilla-bean ice cream, and a hearty drizzle of rich homemade caramel sauce.

I fixed her pie, along with the glass of milk she'd ordered, and took it over to her. Mallory waved her hand, and I slid into the booth across from her. She nodded at me, then reached out, dragged her plate closer, and dug into the apple pie. I watched her eat in silence.

Mallory finished about half of her pie before she put down her fork and pushed her plate away. She sighed in contentment and delicately dabbed at her lips with a white paper napkin. "The pie is just as good as I remember. I see that you've kept Mr. Lane's recipe."

"I've kept all his recipes. You don't mess with the classics."

"No, you don't." She fixed me with a steely look. "You know why I'm here."

"Lorelei."

She nodded. "I want you to reconsider my offer. Given everything that happened yesterday, we never did get a chance to finish our discussion."

"You mean Pike setting off his bomb?" I snarked. "That did put a damper on the festivities."

Mallory arched her thin white eyebrows. "I see you have the same bad sarcasm as Lorelei."

I sighed. "Look, I appreciate your wanting to protect your granddaughter. I even admire you for it. But I'm not the person for the job. You do realize that Lorelei is one of the most feared underworld bosses in Ashland, right? She is more than capable of taking care of herself."

"Of course, I realize that. I taught her everything she knows." Mallory waved her hand, flashing her rings. "And I certainly didn't get all these diamonds by playing nice."

"So if Lorelei is so capable, then why ask me for help?"

She shrugged. "It never hurts to have a little extra insurance."

I barked out a laugh. "*Insurance*? Is that what I am to you? Lady, you need to work on your sales pitch."

Mallory gave me another stern look. "I think you're the person who has the best chance of killing Raymond—after Lorelei, of course—and I always like to back a winner. Besides, you're not thinking about the big picture and what I can do for you."

"I don't need or want your ten million smackeroos."

She steepled her hands together. "Oh, sweetheart, I'm not talking about mere *money*."

"So what *are* you talking about?"

She whipped out that sweet, sly, dangerous smile of hers. "Respectability."

"What do you mean?"

Mallory leaned forward. "Do you really want to spend the rest of your life tiptoeing around the cops and everyone else in town? Clinging to the shadows, even though you know they can't hide you anymore? Mab Monroe never did that. Instead, she let everyone—and I do mean *everyone*—know exactly how powerful she was. And they all welcomed her with open arms, whether it was the cops or the criminals or the crème de la crème of Ashland society. Admittedly, that last group was too stupid to realize that Mab would kill them just as soon as look at them. But they and everyone else were all too afraid of her not to do exactly what she wanted when she wanted something done."

"So?"

"So you're the big boss now. Act like it." Mallory clenched her tiny hand into a tight fist. "Take control, seize power, and hold on to it with an iron grip, instead of letting others dictate how much of it you have."

She wasn't wrong. In fact, she was far too right—about

everything. Not that I would ever admit that to her, though. I might be the big boss now, but it was in name only, and my grasp on the crown was tenuous at best, just as Lorelei had said in the gardens.

"Well, Gin?" Mallory asked. "What do you say?"

"You really think you can do all that?" I asked, crossing my arms over my chest and leaning back against the booth. "Just wave your hand and have people welcome me with open arms, no matter how hoity-toity they are."

She gave me a thin smile. "Of course I can. It's one of the privileges of being part of the rich old guard—deciding who gets invited to the party. Trust me. I can make it happen."

I stifled a groan. So not only would I have the other bosses to contend with, but I'd be the belle of Ashland society too. Talk about something I had never, *ever* wanted for myself.

"Forgive me if I find that hard to believe, given your own criminal background. Not to mention your granddaughter's current, less-than-legal endeavors."

"Bah. I've been around so long that no one remembers how I got my start or where my money came from. Or, if they do remember, they're smart enough to keep their mouths shut about my running guns, moonshine, and everything else I could make a cold red cent on," she said, her hillbilly twang becoming more pronounced the longer she talked. "Besides, it's not like any of their hands are cleaner than mine. Just think about it, Gin. You could be powerful, feared, *and* legitimate. In this town, I'd say that's better than winning the lottery."

She kept that sweet, serene smile on her face, thinking that I would see the wisdom of her offer . . . sooner or later. Yeah. That was going to be later—a whole lot later. Like the tenth of never.

"Your generous proposal aside, Lorelei has made it abundantly clear that she doesn't want my help." I shrugged. "That settles the matter, as far as I'm concerned. If she wants to go toe-to-toe with her brother, then more power to her."

Mallory shook her head. "You don't understand how dangerous Raymond is—"

"I understand *perfectly*," I snapped. "A couple of nights ago, I watched him murder a man using nothing more than a spoon and a little bit of his metal magic, and he's almost killed me twice now with his bombs. Believe me, I am well acquainted with how dangerous he is. And your dropping the danger card and asking me to risk myself for Lorelei still isn't selling it to me."

Mallory's jaw clenched, and she leaned forward again. "And you're also well acquainted with the fact that he's targeting the wrong woman. Does *that* sell it to you, Ms. Blanco?"

She'd just slapped down her trump card, and we both knew it. She waited, expecting some sort of emotion to flicker across my face. Guilt, most likely. Yeah, more than a little of that churned in my stomach, but I kept my features cold and hard and stared her down.

Mallory realized that I wasn't going to back down or give in, and she just . . . deflated. Her head dropped, her shoulders slumped, and her entire body seemed to draw in on itself. Even the white, fluffy cloud of her hair seemed to droop. Suddenly, she looked every one of her three-hundred-and-some years. Still, she tried once more to convince me.

"There's nothing I can do or say to change your mind?" she asked in a soft, almost trembling voice.

"I'm sorry, but no."

For a moment, tears gleamed in her eyes, but she blinked them back. "Then I'm sorry too."

Mallory reached into her purse, plucked out some bills, and threw them onto the table. She slid out of the booth, got to her feet, and left the restaurant. I thought she might slam the door behind her, but she opened and closed it so quietly that the bell barely made a whisper at her passing.

I watched her plod down the sidewalk, her face pale and haggard, her body seeming more stooped and frail than ever before. Maybe it was cynical, but I wondered if the whole wounded-old-lady routine was just an act to sucker me in. But Mallory's pace and posture didn't change as she rounded the corner and disappeared.

I sighed. I'd done the right thing by telling her no. I knew I had.

So why did I feel so guilty about it?

* 20 *

I waited until Mallory had vanished, then got out of the booth, grabbed her dirty dishes, and went back over to where Owen, Finn, and Silvio were sitting at the counter.

"That didn't look like it went well," Owen said.

I dumped the half-eaten apple pie into a trash can behind the counter, along with the milk. "She still wants me to help Lorelei. I told her no."

Owen nodded, but his violet gaze never left my face. I held on to my blank mask, not wanting him or anyone else to see my inner turmoil. Because no matter how hard I tried, I couldn't help but feel like I was abandoning Lorelei to her own death at Pike's hands. Running away, just like I had that day in the woods, only this time with no plans to double back to try to save her.

Fletcher would have been so disappointed in me.

"Uh-oh," Finn said. "I know that look."

"What look?"

"The look that says you're feeling guilty about turning down Mallory, even though you had every right to." Finn's green eyes narrowed. "Why do you feel so responsible for Lorelei Parker all of a sudden?"

"I don't. Not anymore."

He frowned. "Not anymore? What does that mean?"

I shook my head. Fletcher and I had never told Finn what happened that weekend he'd been gone, and I wasn't about to clue him in now. Not when I was still trying to figure out how I felt about things.

"Forget it," I muttered. "It doesn't matter. Lorelei doesn't want my help, and I have too many other things to worry about. Besides, let someone else face down the dangerous elemental for a change. I'm out, and that's that."

Owen, Finn, and Silvio looked back and forth at one other.

"If that's how you feel, then of course we will support you," Silvio said. "It's a wise decision. There's no need to put yourself at further risk. Especially not now."

"What do you mean?"

Silvio held up his phone. "Dimitri and Luiz apparently didn't enjoy their lunch all that much. They are spreading some rather nasty rumors about how you tried to kill them on the riverboat. Add that to what happened at the botanical gardens yesterday, and, well, some of the bosses are questioning your intentions again."

I massaged my temples. There wasn't enough aspirin in the world for all the headaches the Ashland underworld caused me. I'd never thought of myself as a masochist before, but I must be, deep down inside. That was the only reason I could think of for why things just kept getting worse and worse, no matter how hard I tried to make them better.

"What do you suggest?" I asked.

Silvio shrugged. "You'll have to set up another meeting with Dimitri and Luiz and decide who gets the coin laundries. Schmooze them, allay their fears, the whole shebang. That's the only way to quiet the rumblings. For now."

I sighed, knowing that I was beaten. "All right. Call their people, and set it up."

"Are you sure, Gin?" Owen asked. "You want to focus on that instead of Lorelei?"

I shook my head again, more emphatically this time, despite the fact that it increased the shooting pains in my temples. "Lorelei's a big girl. She can take care of herself. I have enough headaches right now."

Owen and Finn left to go back to their respective offices, while Silvio moved over to a booth to start making calls. The rest of the day passed quietly. No one tried to kill me, and no more mobsters came into the Pork Pit to eat and glower at me. I was grateful that it was a relatively slow day.

Bria and Xavier stopped by at around five to eat dinner, but they didn't have anything new to report on the garden party bombing. The waitress who'd given Mallory the jewelry box had had no idea there was a bomb inside. Pike had approached her outside the Rose Garden and said that he had a special delivery for Mallory, which was all the waitress knew.

The po-po were looking for Pike, but Bria said that there hadn't been any sign of him. The tension in her voice told me that she didn't expect the cops to find him either. Pike was smart enough to build bombs with his metal magic. Using a fake ID and avoiding the police would be child's play. Besides, it wasn't like any of the cops besides Bria and Xavier would look all that hard for him. Not without some serious financial incentive.

After Bria and Xavier left, I closed down the restaurant early and sent the staff home for the night, along with Sophia and Catalina. I shooed Silvio home too, despite his protests that he should stay by my side on the off chance that somebody spotted Pike.

I turned off the appliances, put all the extra food away, and spent an hour washing dishes, wiping down tables, and straightening up to get the restaurant ready to open again in the morning. Normally, the familiar motions would have marked the end of another busy day and a quiet time to rest, relax, and recharge.

Not tonight.

Because I *still* couldn't stop thinking about Lorelei.

I finished my chores, left the restaurant, and walked over to my car a couple of blocks away, checking it for rune traps and bombs. But there were no explosives on the vehicle, so I got in and drove home.

I checked the woods, the yard, and all the doors and windows, but no one had been near the house all day. Good. I didn't feel like dealing with any would-be assassins tonight. Or, worse, some mobster who wanted to whine to me in person about something.

I stepped inside, toed off my boots, and headed back

to the kitchen. I didn't feel like making anything complicated, so I put together a Southwestern salad of shredded
barbecue chicken, black beans, diced tomatoes, and other
veggies, along with several slices of Sophia's sourdough
bread, toasted and topped with tangy melted parmesan
and mozzarella cheese. A glass of blackberry lemonade
and some chocolate chip cookies completed my meal.
Chocolate chip cookies always made everything better.

I put my food on a tray and took it into the den, determined to enjoy my dinner. I set my tray down on the
coffee table and arranged everything just the way I liked
it. Lemonade and silverware on the right, salad in the
middle, toast and cookies off to the left, napkin draped
across my lap. Then I leaned over, reaching for the remote.

Lorelei Parker's face stared up at me.

I'd forgotten that I'd dropped her photo and Fletcher's
file onto the table when I'd come home from the garden
party yesterday. My hand hovered in the air above Lorelei's bruised, battered face.

"You again," I muttered.

I nudged the photo aside with my index finger, picked
up the remote, and turned on the TV. I found one of my
favorite superhero movies and settled in to watch all the
caped crusaders and their daring escapades while I ate.

All the while, though, I kept looking at that photo of
Lorelei.

She looked so young in the picture, so wounded, vulnerable, frightened. But she wasn't the same person, the
same innocent girl she'd been back then, any more than
I was. Lorelei had clawed her way up through the under-

world ranks, and she had stayed there by being cold, hard, and ruthless. Just as I'd become an assassin and survived the same way. Lorelei and I had both killed our fair share of people for money, revenge, survival, and more. When it came right down to it, we were almost mirror images of each other.

Murdered mothers. Check. Criminal mentors. Check. Criminals ourselves. Double check.

Lorelei didn't need my help any more than I needed hers to solve my problems. I should stick with what I'd told Mallory and the guys at the Pork Pit. I should stay out of things and let Lorelei and Raymond settle their family feud by themselves.

But I'd be damned if I could do that.

I'd never denied all the bad things I'd done, and I'd especially never let someone else take the blame for them. Fletcher had taught me better than that. But that's exactly what I'd be doing if I didn't at least try to help Lorelei, if I left her at the mercy of her brother when I was the one he should have been targeting all along.

I looked at that photo of Lorelei a final time. Then I grabbed my dirty dishes, took them into the kitchen, and set them in the sink. I'd have to wash them later.

Right now, I had a metal man to find and kill.

❋ 21 ❋

I went upstairs, stripped off my clothes, and put on my gear for the night. Black boots, black jeans, and a long-sleeved black T-shirt topped with a black vest lined with silverstone.

Wearing the vest was a calculated risk, but I was hoping that it would absorb whatever magic Pike might throw at me, instead of giving him a tool for his metal magic. I left my silverstone spider rune ring on my right index finger and the matching necklace around my throat. More risks, but I didn't know how much raw power Pike might have, and it would be better to have the reserves of Ice and Stone magic stored in my jewelry than not.

Then came the most important question: whether or not to wear my knives.

I held up one of the blades. The silverstone glinted under the lights, with my rune stamped in the hilt almost looking like a real spider perched on the metal. Pike had already demonstrated that he could disarm me, but I decided to take my usual set of knives anyway. I'd just have to kill him before he got a chance to use his magic on my weapons. Simple as that.

I packed up a few more things I might need, then headed out.

Bria, Xavier, and the cops hadn't been able to find Pike, and neither had Finn or Silvio, but I knew exactly where he would be: wherever Lorelei was.

So I drove over to Lorelei's mansion in Northtown. I parked about half a mile away from the edge of her property, which butted up against the Aneirin River, not too far away from Salina Dubois's former estate, which I'd had the misfortune to visit earlier this year. I just hoped things went better tonight than they had back then.

Fletcher had included several photos of Lorelei and Mallory's estate in his file, and I'd studied the images before I left the house. As with most Northtown mansions, thick stands of trees separated their home from their closest neighbor's, giving the illusion of privacy—and plenty of places for an assassin to hide.

A full moon glimmered in the sky, along with a bright blanket of stars, giving me enough light to navigate through the woods. Good thing, since I didn't dare use a flashlight. If Pike was out here, I wanted to take him by surprise, which meant no lights and no noise of any kind.

I reached the edge of the tree line and hunkered down behind a large maple. I pulled a pair of night-vision goggles out of my black duffel bag, held them up to my eyes, and scanned the estate.

The mansion was modest by Northtown standards,

three sprawling stories with about thirty rooms total. A pool was at the right side of the house, along with an impressive garden filled with bird baths and feeders. Thick, padded chairs shaded by umbrellas were arranged on a stone patio. I could easily picture Mallory sitting outside and watching the flowers and birds for hours on end.

To my surprise, Lorelei didn't have all that many giant guards patrolling the perimeter. I only spotted three doing a slow circuit around the house, stepping into and out of the golden glows cast out by the numerous lights mounted on the mansion's exterior. Given that Pike was gunning for her, I'd assumed that she'd have at least a dozen men on the premises, if not more. Or maybe she really did think she could take care of Pike by herself. If that was the case, I admired her confidence, even if it was most likely going to get her killed.

Once I'd scanned the grounds, I put away the night-vision goggles and pulled out a pair of binoculars, training them on the mansion itself. Some of the windows were covered with lace curtains, but it looked like every single light in the entire house was on. I wondered if that was because Lorelei wanted to see her brother coming.

I moved my binoculars back and forth, peering at all the doors and windows, until I spotted Lorelei sitting at a desk in a library on the first floor. She held her hand out in front of her, and a pale blue light flickered on her fingertips. A second later, the light vanished, leaving behind a rectangular piece of elemental Ice in her hand. She studied it a moment, then reached for her power again, creating another piece of Ice, this one shaped like a short cylinder.

Then another one, then another one.

I watched while she created and assembled all the odd bits of Ice, as though she were working a jigsaw puzzle. But the end result was far more interesting than a pretty picture.

It was a gun.

It looked like a small revolver, but it was made entirely out of elemental Ice, including the single bullet that she created and then loaded it with. An Ice gun . . . that must have been what I'd seen glinting in her clutch at the garden party. It would also explain the chill that had been radiating off her bag.

Impressive. I'd heard of such weapons, but I'd never seen one being made before, and I certainly didn't have the skill to do something like that. An Ice dagger was about as complicated a shape as I ever made. Lorelei might not have as much raw magic as I did, but she more than made up for it with her finesse. Maybe she was better prepared than I'd thought. Maybe she was even better prepared than me. At least she wasn't carrying around metal weapons that could potentially be used against her.

I scanned the other rooms, but I didn't see Mallory. She must be somewhere deeper in the mansion. She wouldn't leave Lorelei as long as Pike was alive.

So far, her brother had been playing games with her. Since he'd failed in his previous attempts, it would make sense for Pike to come here and finish what he'd started by trying to kill Lorelei. I was counting on it, and it looked like she was too.

Since the mansion was secure, I switched back to my night-vision goggles and scanned the woods around me again, but I didn't see or hear anything unusual. Just the rustling of the wind dancing through the branches, the *bzz-bzz-bzz* of a few bugs droning defiantly against the growing cold, and the mournful hoots of an owl hidden in a tree.

So I left my hiding spot and did a perimeter sweep, keeping one eye on the guards patrolling the mansion and the other on my surroundings, just in case Pike had slipped into the woods without me spotting him. I reached out with my Stone magic, listening to the whispers of the rocks hidden under the brown, brittle leaves, but they only reflected back my own tension at what might happen here tonight.

I completed my circuit and was about to return to my initial hiding spot when a branch snapped off to my left. But what was even more interesting was the faint cursing that followed.

I frowned. Surely Pike wouldn't be that sloppy, but perhaps the terrain had undermined him. Either way, I was going to take advantage of his blunder, so I palmed a knife and headed in that direction. Maybe this would be an earlier, easier night than I'd thought.

I sidled through the trees like a ghost, taking care where I stepped so that I wouldn't give myself away like Pike had. When I was close to where the telltale *crack* had come from, I stopped and dropped into a crouch, looking, listening, and waiting for Pike to move and make another mistake.

One minute passed, then two, then three.

I didn't hear any more *crack*s or cursing. Pike must have finally realized that it would be best to be quiet.

Scanning the woods, I spotted a shadow moving off

to my left, creeping closer and closer to my location. My frown deepened. How could he possibly know where I was? I was wearing black from head to toe and staying perfectly still. I should have been just another bit of darkness to him.

But the shadow kept approaching, slowly sharpening into a distinct, familiar figure—a tall, muscular man.

I sighed, stood up, leaned against the closest tree, and tucked my knife back up my sleeve. I waited until the shadow had moved past me, then scuffed my feet through the leaves, making enough noise to attract his attention.

"You want to tell me what you're doing here?" I drawled.

Owen whipped around.

We stared at each other for several seconds. Me calm and unruffled, Owen tense and wound up. Like me, he was dressed in black from head to toe and geared up for a night of skulking. He had his phone clutched in one hand and his blacksmith hammer raised high in the other.

He let out a breath and lowered the weapon to his side. "You could have just called out to me."

"I would have, if I'd known you were going to be creeping through the woods." I crossed my arms over my chest. "What are you doing here?"

"You mean how did I find you when you thought that you had snuck off without telling anyone what you were up to? Silvio helped me with that." Owen held up his phone, the light illuminating his face. "While you were taking out the trash today at the restaurant, Silvio installed a new app on your phone, one that lets him track where it and you currently are to within fifty feet."

"You guys *bugged* me?"

Owen nodded, not the least bit apologetic, and brought the phone up to his ear. "Hey, Silvio. I found her, right where you said she would be. I'll take it from here. Thanks, man."

Silvio murmured something back, and Owen ended the call and slid the phone into his pants pocket.

My eyes narrowed. "And why did you and Silvio decide to track my phone tonight? I told everyone that I was going home and staying put."

"It was Finn's idea. All three of us knew as soon as Mallory came into the restaurant that you were going to help Lorelei. Finn had to wine and dine some big new client, and Silvio said he was looking into some stuff for you. So I decided to come and back you up."

"But how did you know for sure that I would be out here? I didn't even know myself until a couple of hours ago."

"Finn kept talking about what a soft touch you are. That somebody spins you a sob story, and you go rushing off all by your lonesome to help them." A faint grin curved Owen's lips. "Finn said that it's your own little spider's trap that you fall into every single time."

"I am *not* a soft touch," I growled.

"What Finn was trying to say was that it was obvious at the Pork Pit that you somehow feel responsible for what's happening to Lorelei. And we all know that when you feel responsible for something, you'll do anything to make it right," Owen finished in a soft voice. "That's one of the things I admire most about you."

Frustration surged through me, and I ground my teeth together. I hadn't called anyone because I didn't want any of my friends involved in this—none of them. Because Raymond Pike was a dangerous enemy, and it was my responsibility to take care of him. Not theirs.

"You need to leave," I growled again. "Right now. Pike could be here any second."

"You know that's not going to happen. I'm here, and I'm staying." Owen reached out and took my hand in his. "What's going on, Gin? Something's up. I can tell. What happened with you and Lorelei? Why are you so interested in Pike?"

He gave my fingers a gentle, knowing squeeze. Care, concern, and understanding shimmered in his violet eyes, melting the last of my defenses.

I sighed. "Because Pike has the wrong person. He thinks that Lorelei killed their father, but she didn't— I did."

He nodded. "I figured it might be something like that. But how did you even meet Lorelei's father? Was he one of your jobs as the Spider?"

"Not one of my jobs, one of Fletcher's."

His features sharpened with understanding. "Finn said that his dad knew Mallory. That Fletcher was the one who introduced Finn to her, back when Finn was first starting out at his bank. What else did Fletcher do for Mallory?"

I shook my head. "Not here. Let's get into position, and I'll tell you all about it."

*   *   *

I led Owen over to my hiding spot, which gave us the best view of the mansion and grounds. We hunkered down inside the tree line, and I used my night-vision goggles and binoculars to make sure that the coast was still clear.

A car drove up to the mansion, but a quick look revealed that Jack Corbin was behind the wheel. Lorelei must have called him over for added protection, since he was her second-in-command. Corbin steered his car into the garage attached to the far side of the house. A few seconds later, the door slid shut, hiding him and the vehicle from view.

While I finished my scan, I told Owen everything that had happened that day in the woods. How Renaldo Pike had torn the cabin apart, how Lorelei and I had tried to run away from him, how I'd eventually killed him.

Owen let out a low whistle. "He really did all those horrible things to his own wife and daughter?"

I nodded. "And a lot of other people too. Fletcher showed me some crime-scene photos of Renaldo's victims. Business rivals, mostly. They weren't pretty. He scratched them up with nails, then used his mace to smash in their skulls."

"And Lorelei?"

I shrugged. "I never saw her again after that day. Fletcher told me that he'd given her a new identity and she'd gone to live with her grandmother. I was happy that she was safe, but I eventually put her out of my mind. I didn't recognize or really remember her until a few days ago. And now here we are."

"And now here you are, helping her again."

"Yeah," I replied in a tired voice. "Caught in my own little spider's trap again."

Owen smiled, the moonlight highlighting the rough, rugged planes of his face. "It's not really a trap, you know. More like doing the right thing."

I sighed. "Sometimes it feels like it."

He reached out and squeezed my hand again in a silent show of support.

I squeezed back, then picked up my binoculars and focused on the mansion. After a minute, I lowered them, then checked the time on my phone.

"It's after midnight," I said, putting my phone away. "You'd think that Pike would have shown himself by now, if he was going to try to kill Lorelei tonight."

"Maybe he wants to terrorize her some more first," Owen said. "So far, that seems to be making him pretty happy."

"And it would have made a lot of people pretty dead, if I hadn't been able to stop him," I muttered, looking at the mansion. "But I can only get lucky so many times before Pike puts one over on me—"

The shadow of a man detached itself from the corner of the garage, raising his arm back and throwing something across the lawn. The object landed on the grass and tumbled end over end before finally stopping about ten feet away from where one of the giant guards was patrolling. The guard turned in that direction, his gaze drawn by the motion just like mine had been—

Boom!

* 22 *

A ball of fire erupted on the lawn.

The burst of red-orange light illuminated Pike standing at the corner of the garage, a gun in his hand and a satisfied smirk on his face as he watched the flames shoot into the air.

How had Pike gotten that close to the mansion without me seeing him? Had he been here the whole time I'd been watching? Maybe he'd arrived before I had. But if so, where had he been hiding that I hadn't spotted him?

Compared with Pike's garden party bomb, this was a relatively small blast, probably from a grenade rather than a full-fledged explosive device. But it was loud and bright enough to get the first guard and the other two to grab their weapons and race in that direction.

Crack!
Crack! Crack!
Crack! Crack! Crack!

But the explosion was a lure, just a trap to get all three guards to come investigate at once. With all of them in one place, it was easy for Pike to raise his gun and mow them down like weeds. The giants never even knew what hit them.

The second the guards were down, Pike sauntered over to the nearest door, smashed the glass with his gun so he could unlock it, and stepped inside.

Through the fire and boiling smoke, I could see Lorelei jump to her feet in the library, the elemental Ice gun glinting in her hand. Perhaps it was just my imagination, but she looked grim, determined, and almost . . . *happy*. As if she was finally getting to do something that she'd waited a long, long time for.

And I realized that Pike wasn't the only one hungry for revenge.

I pulled out my phone and texted Bria, Finn, and Silvio, letting them know that Pike was here. Then I surged forward, but I'd only taken three steps when I thought better of things and stopped. If Pike had indeed gotten here before me, he might have planted some explosives in the lawn to keep people from rushing to the mansion, just like he'd left that booby-trapped bomb in the woods across the river from the *Delta Queen*. So I turned to Owen.

"Can you scan the ground?" I asked. "In case Pike hid any bombs in the grass?"

He nodded. "Yeah, I can use my own metal magic to sense his power. Follow me, and step exactly where I step."

I didn't like Owen being out front, where he would be an easy target if Pike came back outside and decided to shoot him, but this was the safest and quickest way for us to get to the mansion.

Owen's eyes started glowing a vivid violet, and his gaze dropped to the ground and swept from side to side. He was reaching out with his power, trying to sense any bits of metal that might be buried in the grass and what they might whisper back to him about potential dangers. Still holding his blacksmith hammer, Owen stepped out onto the lawn. I followed him closely, palming a knife.

Pike's hail of bullets had killed the three guards instantly, so no screams, shrieks, or shouts of pain tore through the air, although a small cluster of flames still crackled at the explosion site. It looked like a cheery campfire, instead of the funeral pyre it really was, marking where the giants had fallen.

I frowned. Pike had picked the perfect spot at the garage to ambush the giants, almost as if he'd known how many guards would be here, along with their exact routes. The garage . . . A suspicion bubbled up in my mind about where Pike might have gotten that information, but I had no way of confirming it right now, so I pushed the thought aside.

Owen didn't find any bombs hidden in the grass, and we reached the stone patio at the side of the mansion.

I flashed my knife at him. "Now it's my turn to be in the lead."

He nodded, his hammer propped up on his shoulder, ready to back me up, just like always, despite the trouble I'd gone looking for tonight.

The grenade had blown the glass out of the patio doors, and I carefully stepped through the jagged opening to the other side, minimizing the crunching of my boots in the shards. I didn't spot Pike, Lorelei, Corbin, or even Mallory in the hallway in front of me. The popping and hissing of the fire still burning on the lawn faded away, and the mansion was as silent as a tomb.

I sidled along one wall, stopping and peering into every room we passed, with Owen behind me. The interior was quite lovely, each room boasting a different color and theme, from a rose living room with pink sofas to a beach sunroom with white wicker chairs stuffed with blue starfish-shaped pillows.

But the deeper we went into the mansion, the more I noticed that there was one thing missing from all the fine furnishings.

Metal.

Oh, bits of metal flashed here and there, but most everything was made out of glass, ceramic, or plastic. No silver picture frames adorned the walls, no iron sculptures perched in the corners, no brass lamps sat on the tables. I didn't see so much as an aluminum soda can squatting on a coaster—

Footsteps slapped on the floor, heading toward us. I dropped down into a crouch and peered around the table situated at the corner of the hallway, Owen next to me.

Jack Corbin raced in our direction, his legs and arms pumping hard. Behind him, a man appeared at the far end of the hallway.

Raymond Pike.

Pike had ditched his usual suit and was dressed just like I was—black boots, black pants, long-sleeved black shirt. A gun was holstered at his waist, while a mace dangled from his hand. An open black sack was slung across his chest, the sort that a farmer would fill with seeds, so he could reach in and scatter them as he walked through a field. Weird. What did he have in there?

Pike's blue eyes glowed with magic. He waved his hand, and a cold, hard surge of power blasted off his body and rolled down the hallway. In a normal house, that one wave of his magic would have been enough to make anything metal shake, rattle, and vibrate. Picture frames would have ripped off the walls, sculptures would have toppled over, chandeliers would have crashed down from the ceiling.

But nothing happened here—no crashes, no bangs, no destruction of any sort. Well, that explained why Lorelei had so little metal in her mansion. She'd wanted to neutralize her half brother's power as much as possible. Smart.

But Pike wasn't worried by the lack of metal—because he'd brought his own.

He dropped his hand down into the black sack on his chest, then drew it back out. The bag *tink*ed at his movements, and my stomach clenched as I realized exactly what was inside it.

"Nails," I whispered.

Sure enough, Pike tossed a handful of nails out in front of him, even as he let loose with another wave of metal magic. The nails blasted down the hallway like bullets—straight into Corbin's back.

Punch-punch-punch-punch.

Nail after nail slammed into Corbin's back, and he screamed out in pain. Owen and I ducked, but the table hid us from Pike's line of sight. None of the nails even came close to hitting us, since Pike placed each and every one of the projectiles *exactly* where he wanted them to go, given how much precise control he had over his magic.

Pike waved his hand again, using the nails in Corbin's back to propel the other man forward and slam his head into the wall. Corbin dropped to the floor, unconscious.

I expected Pike to move in for the kill, but he eyed Corbin a moment, then turned and vanished into another hallway.

Owen and I darted forward. He knelt next to Corbin, while I kept an eye out for Pike. When I was sure that the metal elemental wasn't coming back, I glanced at Corbin. A dozen nails stuck up out of his back. Blood had already soaked through his blue shirt, but it didn't look like the nails had hit anything vital. Lucky man.

"Leave him be," I whispered. "He's unconscious, which is for the best right now. And forget a frontal assault on Pike. We have to take him by surprise. He's too strong in his magic, and we brought too much metal with us."

I held up my knife. Owen stared at it before looking at his own blacksmith hammer. He nodded.

We moved forward and peered around the corner where Pike had disappeared, but he was already gone. We crept down the hallway. Once again, I took care where I put my feet, not wanting a floorboard to creak and give away our position. As far as Pike knew, he, Lorelei, and Mallory were the only people left in the mansion, and I wanted to keep it that way.

"Oh, Lorelei . . ." Pike's voice rang out with an eerie,

singsong quality. "Come out, come out, wherever you are . . ."

I tried to follow the sound, but the mansion had an open floor plan, with lots of wide archways, and his voice rattled around and bounced off the walls, making it hard to pinpoint exactly where he was. So I reached out with my magic, listening to the marble, brick, and granite, searching for any disturbances in the stone that would tell me which way Pike had gone.

Owen and I reached another hallway, this one running front to back through the house. Dark mutters echoed through the stone at the back, so I pointed in that direction. Owen nodded, and we headed that way.

"Lorelei . . ." Pike's voice rang out again. "You can't hide from me. Not for long. You never could. Not even when we were kids."

"And you always were a sick son of a bitch." Lorelei finally spoke up. "Even back then, I knew that there was something seriously wrong with you. And all the years since haven't changed my opinion one bit."

Her voice was tinny, with more than a little static. Owen pointed to an intercom box on the wall. The whole mansion was probably wired, which meant that Lorelei could be anywhere inside.

"You shouldn't have run away after you murdered our father," Pike called out. "If you had just accepted your punishment back then, I might have killed you quickly. But not now. Not after I got locked up. Not after having to chase you all these years."

"How did you find me?" Lorelei asked.

"It was a bit of blind luck," he replied. "I recently entered into a new business venture with an interesting group of people. One of my conditions in adding my resources to theirs was their help in finding you. It was surprisingly easy, since one of the members knew all about your new identity. She'd even done some business with you."

I wondered who Pike was talking about and how that person could know who Lorelei really was. Fletcher had never been a slouch when it came to helping people disappear. So who had been able to see through the new identity he'd given Lorelei all those years ago?

Owen and I reached the end of the hallway, and I glanced around the corner. Pike stood in the middle of the next hallway over, about twenty feet ahead of us. Too far for me to try to stab him in the back. He'd hear me coming and pelt me with nails, just like he had done to Corbin. I thought back to the mansion blueprints in Fletcher's file, but there wasn't another room or hallway that would let me get any closer to Pike or come at him from a different angle. So I was stuck, waiting for him to either go forward or head back in this direction.

"Oh, Lorelei . . ." Pike called out in that creepy voice again. "Where are you . . ."

A door opened at the far end of the hallway, and something *tink-tink-tink*ed across the floor. A grenade spun to a stop right at Pike's feet, twirling around and around like a toy top. Looked like Lorelei had stocked up on some of those weapons she smuggled.

But it didn't work.

Pike cursed and flung his hand out. His metal magic

sent the grenade skittering back down the hallway in the direction it had come from. The door at the far end slammed shut. I counted off the seconds in my head. Five . . . four . . . three . . . two . . . one . . .

Boom!

The grenade exploded, blowing large chunks out of the walls and incinerating the closed door. But Pike didn't flinch at the shooting flames and resulting debris. Then again, he built bombs. He probably enjoyed those sorts of things.

"Oh, Lorelei," Pike purred, once the noise of the explosion died down. "Your weapons won't do you any good. Not against my magic. Metal is in practically *everything*. Just the smallest trace of it, and I can control it with ease. Even here, in your carefully arranged house, there's still more than enough of it for my purposes. And you know how creative Dad taught us to be with our magic, all the tricks he made us learn, even you, with your weak powers."

A floorboard creaked, and Lorelei darted from one room to the next in front of Pike. He growled and went after her—

But Lorelei must have dropped another grenade behind her, because Pike lurched back out into the hallway and flattened himself against the wall.

Boom!

Another explosion ripped through the mansion.

"Enough of your stupid games!" Pike roared. "Come out and fight me!"

Lorelei's mocking laughter floated out of the intercom system. "You always were a sore loser, even when we were kids and Dad would pit us against each other. If you couldn't win the game right off the bat, then you just didn't want to play at all, did you, Raymond? You might have more raw magic, but I was always more creative with my power. All you were ever interested in making were those stupid spikes, maces, and bombs. Dad was always *so* disappointed in you about that."

Tink-tink-tink.

Lorelei tossed another grenade into the hallway, but Pike used his magic to send the device skittering back into the room it had come from.

Boom!

The grenade exploded, and a loud scream sounded, as though Lorelei had been caught in the blast. Pike laughed and rushed forward, with Owen and me hurrying to follow.

We reached a wide archway that led into a kitchen, with a series of glass patio doors that overlooked the backyard. What looked like blood was spattered on the white tile floor, with a smear of it going behind the island in the middle of the room, as though Lorelei had dragged herself back there to hide. Pike headed in that direction.

I motioned to Owen to circle around and approach Pike from a door on the far side of the kitchen so we could flank him. Owen nodded and hurried down the hallway.

Pike crept closer to the bloody trail. His back was still to me, so I eased into the kitchen. Approaching him was a calculated risk, but I had to get to him before he noticed the knives I was carrying and tried to use the metal against me. But he was moving slowly, and I was coming on fast. Another ten seconds, and he'd be mine.

Ten . . . seven . . . five . . .

I tightened my grip and raised my knife.

Three . . . two . . . one . . .

Pike whipped around and snapped up his hand, magic surging off his body. My knife got stuck in mid-air, as though I were trying to slice through a brick wall instead of empty space. I grunted and struggled, pushing back against his power with my own Stone magic. It took me a second to break free of his invisible hold and stagger back.

Pike arched an eyebrow, more amused than concerned. "You again with the knives. When are you going to learn? You can't sneak up on me with those."

I bared my teeth. "Oh, I don't know. Maybe when you're dead."

I faked that I was coming at him with my knife again, then raised my free hand and blasted him with Ice magic. But Pike was as quick as I was, and he reached into his satchel and flung out a handful of nails. The metal met my Ice, crushing the deadly shards and sending them all crashing to the floor between us.

Even as I started forward again, trying to get close enough to just stab him already, Pike darted around the island, reached down, and yanked Lorelei to her feet. I stopped short.

"Hello, sis," he crooned, holding the spiked ball of his mace up against her throat. "So good to finally see you again after all these long years apart."

"I wish I could say the same," Lorelei muttered.

If Pike and I resembled commandos in our black clothes, then Lorelei was loaded for bear. She too was dressed in black and wearing enough weapons to start a small war. A bandolier studded with grenades was cinched across her chest, a brace of knives circled her waist, and her elemental Ice gun was holstered to her thigh.

Despite her previous scream and the blood on the floor, Lorelei didn't have a scratch on her. No blood, no cuts, no bruises of any kind. I knew a feint when I saw one, and there was still one other person in the mansion who hadn't made an appearance yet: Mallory.

Lorelei stared at me, then deliberately flicked her eyes to the right, toward the glass patio doors. Out of the corner of my eye, I spotted a small shadow creeping up to the doors, and I realized what their plan was. Lorelei would lure Raymond into the kitchen with her fake scream and blood trail. Then Mallory would step up to the doors and shoot him.

It might have worked too—if me and my do-gooder intentions hadn't come along and messed up the whole thing.

Even as I cursed myself for ruining their plan, Raymond dug the mace's spikes into Lorelei's throat, making her tilt her head to the side to keep from getting skewered.

"I was already going to kill you slowly," he hissed. "Draw it out for a few hours. Now I'm going to make it last for *days*."

Even if Mallory had been in the kitchen instead of outside, she couldn't have taken out Pike now, not with Lorelei in the line of fire. It would have been a difficult shot even for Finn.

Good thing I had some backup.

Owen slipped through the kitchen's back entrance, raised his hammer, and crept toward Pike. I stared at the metal elemental, not giving any indication that he was about to get his skull smashed in.

"You wanted to help me, Gin," Lorelei drawled. "I'd be all right with that happening any old time now."

"Don't rush me," I drawled back. "These things take time—"

Pike's eyes lit up with his magic again, and another wave of power rolled off his body, ripping Owen's hammer out of his hand. Pike had sensed the metal weapon the same way he had sensed my knife.

I surged forward, hoping to take him by surprise, but Pike saw me move and let loose with another burst of power.

Even though Lorelei had eliminated as much of the metal as she could from her home, there was still one room where there was plenty of it: the kitchen.

At Pike's command, a butcher's block of knives zoomed off the counter and slammed into my right arm, opening up deep cuts. One of the knives stuck in the tendons in my wrist, and I barely managed to hold on to my own weapon.

"Gin!" Owen yelled, and stepped forward, his hands clenched into fists.

Pike turned and threw his mace, causing Owen to drop to the floor. The heavy weapon zipped over his head and *thunk*ed into one of the cabinets behind him.

While Pike was distracted, Lorelei grabbed her elemental Ice gun, pressed the muzzle against his leg, and pulled the trigger. The gun shattered in her hand as the icy bullet punched into his thigh just like a metal one would have. Nice.

He screamed and let go of her. Lorelei ducked.

"Now!" she yelled.

Crack! Crack! Crack!

The glass doors shattered as bullets punched through them, and I spotted Mallory standing outside, revolvers in her hands. But Pike held up his own hands, sending out blast after blast of magic, the invisible waves of his power catching the metal bullets and sending them *ping-ping-ping*ing all over the kitchen. Owen and I both ducked to keep from getting shot by accident.

Click-click-click.

Mallory ran out of ammo. She cursed, tossed her guns away, and reached for two more that were holstered to her waist, but Pike was quicker. He shoved his hand into his satchel, came up with a handful of nails, and tossed them at her. He used a much stronger blast of magic than he had used with Corbin, and the nails zipped through the air and punched straight into Mallory's chest.

The dwarf grunted at the hard, brutal impacts and staggered back, out of my line of sight.

"Grandma!" Lorelei yelled, scrambling to her feet and running around the island.

Pike sent an iron rack full of pots and pans mounted to the ceiling crashing down on top of her. Lorelei hit the floor, groaning.

"You're not getting away this time," he growled.

I got to my feet and darted forward. Pike let out another soft, deadly laugh and raised his hand.

The kitchen knife still stuck in my wrist jerked loose, and I screamed as it sliced through my tendons. The pain was so intense that my own silverstone knife slipped from my bloody, nerveless fingers. It clattered onto the top of the island, and Pike used his magic to send it skittering off the countertop and right into his hand.

Owen yelled, surged back up to his feet, and charged at Pike, who whipped around and sliced out with my knife. Owen jumped back, but his foot caught in the bottom of one of the pans on the floor, and he lurched to one side, his knee letting out an ugly *pop*. Owen yelped, clinging to one of the counters just to stay upright.

Pike put his back to a row of cabinets, his eyes flicking back and forth between Owen and me as he flipped my knife end over end in his hand.

I grabbed hold of my Stone magic and used it to harden my skin, just in case he decided to throw my own knife at me.

"Whom to kill first?" Pike murmured.

He was so busy looking at us that he didn't notice Lorelei reach out from under the rack of pots and pans and start fumbling with a drawer in the bottom of the island.

But I wasn't going to wait for her to act. My hands curled into tight fists, blood squeezing out between the fingers of my injured right arm. I didn't bother palming the knife hidden up my left sleeve. The way this fight was going, Pike would just use his metal magic to disarm me again. So this time, I reached for my Ice power. A silver light flared, and a long, sharp dagger appeared in my left hand.

I flashed the cold, glittering Ice at Pike. "Try to take this one away from me, you son of a bitch," I hissed.

Pike looked at the Ice dagger, then at my face, his eyes narrowing in thought. Too late, I realized what I'd done—and all the memories I'd triggered.

"You . . . you were in the woods!" he accused.

"Guilty as charged," I hissed again. "I should have killed you back then when I had the chance. But I'm going to rectify that mistake right now."

"Oh, I don't think so."

Pike waved his hand again. This time, the refrigerator wrenched free of the wall and zipped across the floor, coming straight at me. I staggered out of the way as it toppled over, the doors opening and spilling vegetables, mayonnaise, milk, and more all over the floor.

Lorelei finally yanked open a freezer drawer in the bottom of the island and pulled out another elemental Ice gun. A row of identical weapons were lined up inside the frosty space. Cool arsenal.

Even though she was still tangled up in all those pots and pans, Lorelei flipped over onto her back and raised the weapon to fire at Pike.

He grabbed a toaster off the counter and tossed it at her. The appliance hit her hand, shattering her Ice gun and making her yelp with pain.

At this point, I was starting to wonder if any of us were going to be able to kill Pike—

Woo-woo. Woo-woo.

Maybe we wouldn't have to. The distinctive wail of a police siren blared in the distance. For once, I welcomed the sound.

"Looks like the party's over for you, Ray," I said. "All we have to do is keep you pinned in here until the cops arrive. I'm sure that they have a nice cell waiting for you downtown. You should enjoy it, what with all those metal bars. It'll be just like juvie all over again."

Rage flashed in Pike's eyes, but he gave me a cold smile and flipped my knife end over end in his hand again. "One more lesson, then, before I go. You helped take my father away from me. Now I'm going to return the favor and take someone away from you."

I sucked in a breath, knowing exactly what he was going to do. But I couldn't stop him.

I couldn't stop him.

Pike flipped my knife over in his hand a final time, then whipped around and threw it at Owen.

But Owen realized that it was coming. Still wobbling on his injured knee, he snapped up his hand, his eyes glowing an intense violet with his own metal power.

My knife stopped in midair a foot in front of him.

"Owen!" I screamed.

I started forward, but this time, my foot got caught in the bottom of a pan. My feet flew out from under me, and I hit the floor.

Lorelei cursed, reaching into the freezer drawer for another elemental Ice gun, but her movements were slow and awkward, and she wasn't going to be able to stop her brother.

Pike tilted his head to the side and studied Owen with new interest. "Another metal elemental. How quaint."

His eyes burned an even brighter blue as he sent out another surge of magic, but Owen pushed back with his own power, and my knife hovered in midair between them.

Sweat beaded on Owen's forehead, lines of tension and pain grooving deeply into his face. I could feel how much magic he was using just to keep my knife from coming any closer.

But it wasn't working.

Inch by inch, my knife slid forward through the air, swimming toward Owen like a hungry shark.

I scrambled to my feet, hoping that I could put my body in front of Owen's and take the blow meant for him.

Too late.

With a cold, hard rush, Pike's power overcame Owen's and blasted right through his defenses.

Pike sent out a final burst of magic, and my knife zipped through the air and plunged into Owen's chest.

❄ 23 ❄

"No!" I screamed. "No! No! No!"

Owen staggered back against the counter. His feet slipped out from under him, and he slid to the floor, my knife buried in his chest.

I started toward Owen, but Pike raised both his hands and sent out another blast of magic, one that ripped through the entire kitchen. Pots, pans, appliances. Anything that had the slightest bit of metal in it rattled, rolled, and tumbled to the floor.

But it was nothing compared with my magic.

My power erupted as I screamed, surging through every piece of stone that made up the mansion. The floor bucked and heaved, the walls shook, and deep cracks zipped through the ceiling.

The vibrations threw Pike off balance and made him lose his grip on his magic, giving Lorelei enough time to grab another Ice gun and fire it at him. But the rippling floor spoiled her aim, and the bullet *thunk*ed into one of the cabinets instead of his skull.

In the distance, the police siren kept wailing, getting closer and closer, louder and louder. Pike growled, yanked his mace out of the cabinet, and plunged through the shattered glass patio doors. But I didn't care about chasing after him.

I didn't care about anything but Owen.

I swallowed down my screams, tossed my Ice dagger aside, waded through the debris, and sank down beside him. The mansion kept shaking, though, the stones still vibrating from my violent burst of power.

Owen looked up at me, his violet eyes bright with pain. "Gin . . ." he rasped. "Gin . . . it's not . . . your fault . . ."

He coughed, more and more blood gushing out from the wound on his chest. Pike hadn't hit his heart with the knife, but he'd come close enough. I knew exactly what would happen next. Owen's lungs would fill with fluid, and he'd choke to death on his own blood—if he didn't bleed out before then.

He was going to bleed out in another minute, two tops.

And I had no idea how to save him.

Fear and grief crushed my heart and made my stomach roil, but I grabbed Owen's hand and stared into his eyes, trying to come up with some sort of plan that would miraculously help him escape death the way I had so many times before. Tears slid down my face and plopped onto our entwined hands, smearing all the blood there. Owen opened his mouth, but I put my fingers against his lips.

"Save your strength," I whispered.

He coughed up another mouthful of blood in response.

Lorelei shimmied out from under the metal rack Pike had dropped on her. She started to run outside to check on Mallory, but her eyes widened as she realized just how much blood was pouring out of Owen's wound. She changed course, hurried over, and fell to her knees beside me.

She gave Owen the same critical once-over I had. "Forget the knife. You have to stop the bleeding—right now—or he's dead."

"Don't you think I know that?" I snapped, my voice rising to a near scream that shook the entire mansion again. "Get me some towels! Now!"

Lorelei gave me a cold look. "Unless you want to kill us all with your Stone power, *stop screaming*."

Another cry of fear and rage bubbled up in my throat, but I choked it down. She was right. If I didn't get control of my emotions, I could collapse the entire mansion on top of us. Then Owen would be dead for sure.

"All right," Lorelei said, once I was calmer. "Forget about towels. You need to freeze the wound."

"Freeze it?"

She nodded. "With your Ice magic. Freeze the wound, and lower his body temperature until you can get him to a healer. You know how kids and animals always fall into frozen rivers and ponds up north, then the rescue crews drag them out of the water and heat them back up? It's like that, only a little different. My mom taught me how to do it, for when I would scrape my knees playing out in the woods." Her voice dropped. "Or for when my dad would hit us."

In theory, it should work, but I'd never attempted anything like that before with my magic. Most of the time, I just blasted people with my power or used it to protect myself. Even though I'd been practicing using my magic in all sorts of different ways, I didn't know if I had enough finesse and control to freeze Owen without killing him outright.

"Do it," Owen rasped. "Getting weaker . . . by the second. It's the only way . . ."

His voice trailed off, and his eyes grew glassy and unfocused. My heart dropped.

"Do it!" Lorelei snapped. "Now, before it's too late."

Still, I hesitated, wondering if I could really do such a thing, especially to Owen.

"Don't be an idiot!" Lorelei snapped again. "I'll show you what to do. Just follow my lead, and use your magic. I don't have enough raw power to freeze him, but you do."

She reached out and ripped Owen's shirt away, exposing the deep, ugly wound. Then she grabbed my hands, squeezed them once, and gently laid them on Owen's chest on either side of my knife. I stared at her with wide eyes.

"You saved me once," Lorelei growled, putting her hands next to mine on Owen's body. "You're going to do the same for him. Right now, Gin."

I nodded and let out a tense breath, pushing my fear away. I focused on Owen, staring into his eyes, then let loose with a small trickle of my Ice magic. In an instant, the cold crystals of my power coated his chest, like frost on a window. Beside me, Lorelei reached for her own Ice power, sending a small wave of it shooting down into Owen's wound.

If my magic was a frigid hammer, then hers was a cool, delicate chisel. I was already sweating from the effort of trying not to use too much magic on him at once, but Lorelei trickled her Ice into one side of his injury, then the other, as easily and expertly as she had made all those small pieces of her Ice gun and then assembled them together.

Owen whimpered as our combined cold invaded his body, the sound tearing at my heart, and he started thrashing around, trying to escape the power that was freezing him bit by bit. Lorelei slid her hands up to his shoulders, leaning down and anchoring him in place.

"Keep going," she ordered. "It's working."

Sure enough, her Ice had frozen the blood oozing out of Owen's wound, making the drops look like rubies clinging to his chest. Lorelei pulled back on her power, leaving the rest up to me. I drew in a breath and let loose with another wave of my magic, this time sending the cold crystals shooting out across his skin and then down through his entire body, cooling his core temperature.

Owen's eyes fluttered closed, his breath puffed out in frosty gasps, and his skin took on an eerie silvery tint as my Ice magic slowly invaded his body. His head lolled to one side, and his shoulders sagged in a way that told me he'd lost consciousness, but I kept funneling my power into him. The trick was to use just enough magic to stabilize him without putting so much of my power into him that he would never thaw out again.

"That's it," Lorelei murmured. "Slow and steady, Gin. Slow and steady."

I didn't know how much time passed. All I was aware of was Lorelei's soft words of encouragement and the waves of my Ice magic sinking through Owen's body, one muscle and tendon at a time, trying to preserve him on the brink of death.

Finally, Lorelei let go of Owen's shoulders, grabbed my hands, and pried my numb fingers off his frozen chest.

"That's enough, Gin," she whispered. "That's enough."

I nodded, just hoping it would save him.

Footsteps crunched on glass, and Mallory entered the kitchen. Nails studded the dwarf's chest, but she didn't seem to be injured at all.

"I told you these silverstone vests would come in handy, sweetheart," Mallory called out to Lorelei, thumping her fist on her chest. "Even if we did have to pay an arm and a leg for them . . ."

Her voice trailed off as she caught sight of Owen. Lorelei squeezed my shoulder, then went over to check on her grandmother.

Bria and Xavier rushed into the kitchen, guns drawn, with Finn and Silvio right behind them. They'd all gotten my text message and had come to help.

Bria, Finn, and Silvio hurried over to me, while Xavier moved through the kitchen and then the rest of the house, making sure that Pike hadn't doubled back. Shocked gasps rang out as my friends caught sight of Owen's frosted form.

"Gin," Bria whispered. "What did you do to him?"

"I saved him." My voice came out as a strangled gasp. "I hope. We have to get him over to Jo-Jo's. And call

Cooper Stills. He'll have to come and help her with Owen."

"I'm on it," Silvio said, already dialing the number on his phone.

"Owen's strong," Finn said, putting a comforting hand on my shoulder. "He'll pull through this."

But the worry in his face matched the fear squeezing my heart.

Xavier came back into the kitchen, bent down, and carefully scooped up Owen in his arms. I stared at all the blood on the floor—Owen's blood.

"Come on, Gin," Bria said in a gentle voice. "We need to go."

She put her arm around my shoulder. I shuddered and let her lead me out of the kitchen.

Everything that happened after that seemed disjointed and far away, as though I had stepped out of my own body and was seeing things from someone's else point of view. Xavier putting Owen in the back of a police sedan, then getting in the front. Me crawling into the backseat with Owen, cradling his head in my lap, stroking his stiff, frozen black hair back off his face. Lorelei on the other side of him, sending a small, steady trickle of her Ice magic into the wound to keep the knife frozen in place so that it wouldn't move and kill him outright. Bria turning on the siren and hauling ass over to Jo-Jo's. Finn, Silvio, and Mallory following us in another car.

All the while, I kept whispering to Owen that I loved him. That he couldn't let someone like Raymond Pike be the end of us. I didn't know if he heard me or not, but it seemed like some of the tense lines of pain on his face smoothed out. Or maybe that was just wishful thinking on my part.

Thanks to Silvio's calls, all the lights were on at Jo-Jo's house, and she was pacing back and forth on the front porch, waiting for us, along with Sophia and another dwarf with salt-and-pepper hair and rust-colored eyes: Cooper Stills, Jo-Jo's gentleman friend and Owen's blacksmith mentor.

Xavier and Silvio carefully pulled Owen out of the backseat and carried him over to the porch. Jo-Jo, Sophia, and Cooper all sucked in their breath at the sight of my knife sticking out of his chest, but Jo-Jo took control of the situation. She opened the door and waved us on through.

"Take him to the salon," she said. "I've already set up a spot for him."

Xavier and Silvio nodded, hurried into the back of the house, and gently placed Owen on a cherry-red chair. I tried not to notice how the fabric matched the bloodstains covering his chest.

Jo-Jo sank down into a seat next to Owen. Cooper, who was also an Air elemental, sat next to her, ready to help. She looked at him and nodded, and he reached out and put a hand on her shoulder, his eyes glowing an intense copper as he started feeding her his power. Jo-Jo reached for her own Air magic, and a milky-white glow coated her palm.

Bria, Finn, Sophia, Lorelei, and Mallory also crowded into the salon. We all stood there, quiet and still, and watched. Even Rosco, in his basket in the corner, didn't make a sound.

I felt the pins-and-needles of Jo-Jo's Air power prodding at the mass of Ice in Owen's chest and seeping through the rest of his battered body. I curled my hands into tight fists, digging my fingers into the spider rune scars embedded in my palms, resisting the urge to scream out all my grief, fear, and rage.

Jo-Jo assessed the wound for the better part of three minutes, trying to figure out the best way to get my knife out of Owen's chest without killing him in the process.

"All right," she said. "I've cleaned up as much of the damage as I can while the knife is still in there."

"Now what?" I whispered.

"You let me worry about that, darling," she replied. "All you have to do is pull the knife out when I tell you to."

She stared at Cooper. "When Gin pulls the knife free, we both need to flood the wound with our Air magic. I'll do the hard part, stitching everything back together. You just keep feeding me your power, okay? Don't stop. Not even for an instant."

Cooper nodded. "Anything you need, doll. Anything for Owen. You know that."

Jo-Jo flashed him a grateful smile, then looked at me. "Anytime you're ready, darling."

It took me several seconds to unclench my fists, but I finally stepped forward, leaned down, and gripped my knife with my left, uninjured hand. The spider rune stamped into the hilt dug into the larger, matching scar on my palm, but for once, the sensation didn't comfort me. Owen hadn't stirred the whole time Jo-Jo had been working on him, but I kept staring at him, willing him to open his eyes—

"Gin," Jo-Jo prodded in a soft voice.

I nodded, then tightened my grip and slid the knife out of Owen's chest as quickly and gently as I could.

Blood gushed up out of the wound but not nearly as much as there would have been if Lorelei and I hadn't used our Ice magic to stop the bleeding. The knife slipped out of my fingers and clattered to the floor. Finn grabbed the weapon, while Bria took hold of my shoulders and moved me back out of the way so Jo-Jo and Cooper could resume their work.

The feel of Jo-Jo's Air magic flooded the room, and everyone stood absolutely quiet and still again, not daring to move or do anything to interrupt her concentration. Seconds passed and turned into minutes, and I stayed rooted in place, as cold and frozen as Owen's heart.

The gushing blood slowed to a trickle, then stopped. The milky-white glow of Jo-Jo's Air power burned as bright as a star in the center of Owen's chest, and streaks of coppery red flickered in the mass of magic as Cooper poured his own power into healing Owen. With their combined strength, the jagged edges of the knife wound closed together, and the mark faded away completely.

But there was still more work to be done thawing out the rest of him.

Ten minutes later, Jo-Jo slumped forward in her chair, the milky-white glow snuffing out of her eyes and fading from the palm of her hand. The wound on Owen's chest was healed, and his skin, while still pale, was a more normal color, free of the frozen crystals of my Ice magic.

Jo-Jo got up and gestured for me to take her seat next to him. I sank down onto the chair and clutched his hand, a sigh escaping my lips when I felt the warmth of his skin. I leaned closer, expecting his eyes to flutter open and for him to make some teasing remark about how I'd almost killed him.

Nothing happened.

Owen's eyes remained closed, although his chest rose and fell with a steady rhythm. Worry shot through me, and I wondered if I'd used too much Ice magic on him after all.

"I've repaired the damage from the knife wound and raised his body temperature back up to where it should be," Jo-Jo said.

"But?"

"But he was right on the edge of death when you froze him, and he lost a lot of blood." She bit her lip. "Maybe too much blood."

"What about giving him a transfusion?" I asked, throwing my hand out wide and gesturing at my friends. "Surely one of us here has the same blood type as his."

The dwarf shook her head. "It's not that simple. One of us might have the same blood type, but nobody else has metal magic. I'm worried that Owen will have a bad reaction if I try to give him someone else's blood, especially blood that contains a different kind of elemental magic. He's so weak right now that it might kill him outright."

I knew she was right, that we couldn't take the risk, but frustration pulsed through my body all the same. I felt so damn *useless* right now. The knowledge that there was nothing I could do to help Owen burned through my heart like acid.

"Will he wake up?" I whispered. "Did I kill him after all?"

Jo-Jo gave me a helpless look. "I don't know, darling. Let's give it a few hours and see. Okay? He's been through a hard trauma. Maybe his brain just needs a little time to catch up with his body."

I nodded and dropped my head, tears scalding my eyes and streaking down my face.

Jo-Jo reached down, took hold of my injured arm, and used her magic to heal my own wounds. It only took a minute. She laid her hand on my shoulder a moment, then left, Rosco trotting after her. The others followed, and Bria shut the doors behind them, so that I was the only one left with Owen in the salon.

I gripped his hand in mine, waiting for him to open his eyes. But he didn't, and I didn't know when he would—if ever.

More tears streaked down my cheeks, but I scooted my chair up as close as possible to Owen, tightened my grip on his hand, and willed him to wake up with all the love I had.

❋24❋

For a long time, I sat by Owen's side, my gaze locked on his face, my body rigid and tense, ready to run and get Jo-Jo at the slightest sign that something was wrong and that he was getting worse.

He still looked far too pale, but his breathing remained clear and even, his chest rising and falling in a reassuring rhythm. Every once in a while, his closed eyes would twitch, as though he were squinting at something only he could see. I wondered what he was dreaming about. I hoped that it was something good—and anything other than what had happened to him tonight.

His steady, continued breathing slowly lulled me into relaxing and putting my head down on his shoulder. The tension leaked out of my body, and I found myself sinking into my own dreams, my own memories . . .

I stared down at Renaldo Pike's body, his own mace still sticking out of his back.

"You killed him," Lorelei whispered. "You actually killed him."

I grunted and cradled my broken wrist to my chest. I hadn't killed him so much as I'd gotten lucky and survived him, but I'd let her think what she wanted.

Lorelei got to her feet and hobbled over to her father. She stared at him with wide, frightened eyes, as if she were afraid that he was going to leap up like a zombie and attack her again. Maybe he was a zombie to her—a nightmare that just kept coming back no matter how many times you tried to forget about it.

Footsteps crashed through the woods. My heart lifted, and I hoped it was Fletcher or one of the Deveraux sisters, but instead, a boy ran into the clearing. Black hair, blue eyes, handsome face. I knew at once that it was Raymond, who'd wrecked Sophia's convertible with her, Jo-Jo, and Fletcher inside.

He stopped short at the sight of Lorelei standing over their father's body. "You little bitch!" he hissed. "You're dead! I'll kill you for this!"

He opened his fist, revealing a hand full of nails. Instead of running or trying to get out of the way, Lorelei stared at him like he was the same sort of zombie their father was.

Raymond reared his hand back, metal magic swirling around him the same way it had his father. I shuddered at the resemblance.

He let the nails fly. I reached for my Stone magic, using it to harden my skin. Then I stepped in front of Lorelei, shoving her out of the way. I tried to dive to the ground, but I wasn't fast enough.

I screamed and fell to the ground as the nails punched

into my back, ripping through what little Stone magic I'd brought to bear. I felt like a porcupine, only I couldn't get rid of my quills.

A pair of boots planted themselves in front of my face. I peered up and realized that Raymond was glaring down at me—and that he had more nails in his hand. Desperate, I reached for my Ice magic, trying to make a dagger to fend him off, but that power was much weaker than my Stone magic, and all I ended up with was a cold twig. Raymond stomped down on my hand, crushing the Ice and my fingers along with it. I yelped in pain.

"You stupid fool," he hissed again. "You should have stayed out of the way. Now I'm going to kill you too for protecting her—"

Crack!

Lorelei smashed a thick, heavy tree limb across the back of his skull, and her brother's eyes rolled up in his head. He let out an audible oof, *as though she'd driven all the air out of his lungs, and toppled to the ground.*

But she kept right on hitting him.

Lorelei slammed the branch into his arms, legs, and back, over and over again, before finally concentrating on his head.

"You killed her!" she screamed. "You both killed my mother! I hate you! I hate you both!"

Blood poured out of Raymond's wounds, but he remained unconscious. All I could do was lie there and watch her beat him. I couldn't move, not with all the nails in my back, and I was lucky that I hadn't passed out. Or maybe not so lucky, given all the pain that pulsed through my back, shoulder, arm, and wrist.

Footsteps crashed through the woods, and I tensed, wondering if Renaldo and Raymond had brought more men with them. But Fletcher, Jo-Jo, and Sophia ran into the clearing. They had blackened faces, singed hair, and ugly red burns from the convertible crash, but they were all standing, and some of the terror and hurt in my heart eased at the sight of them.

Fletcher pried the stick out of Lorelei's hands and tossed it aside. It landed on the ground next to me, Raymond's blood dripping off the wood.

"That's enough," the old man said. "That's enough. You're safe now. You're safe."

"No!" she screamed. "Let me kill him! Please! Please, let me kill him . . ."

Her voice choked off, and she started sobbing. Sophia grabbed Lorelei, cradling the girl to her chest, shushing her, and telling her that everything was going to be all right, even if we all knew that it wasn't.

Fletcher stared at Lorelei, an unreadable expression on his face, then hurried over and dropped to his knees beside me. He placed a gentle hand on my shoulder, staring at all the nails sticking out of my back.

"Gin, are you all right?"

"Just peachy," I drawled, although my voice came out as a hoarse wheeze. "I always wanted to try acupuncture."

Fletcher laughed, the harsh sound full of worry. "You just lie still. Jo-Jo will help you."

The dwarf dropped to her knees beside me. "We'll fix you right up, darling."

Jo-Jo used her Air magic to fish the nails out of my back,

one by one. It hurt—horribly—like getting dozens of shots in reverse, but Fletcher held my hand the whole time.

Finally, Jo-Jo finished, and Fletcher helped me sit up. Lorelei was still crying against Sophia's chest, and the Goth dwarf jerked her head at Raymond, who was still unconscious.

"What about him?" Sophia rasped. "Kill him now?"

Fletcher stood over the boy, staring down at him, a silverstone knife glinting in his brown, weathered hand. Finally, he shook his head. "No kids—ever," he murmured. "The boy is only sixteen."

"No!" Lorelei shouted, her hands clenching into fists. "You have to kill him now! Or else he'll just come back later and try to kill us all again. I know he will. I know it!"

Fletcher looked at her tear-streaked face, then back at the boy. I could see the struggle in his eyes. He wanted to do as Lorelei asked—he wanted to kill Raymond and end things right here, right now. We all knew that Raymond was going to grow up to be just another sadistic version of his father.

But Fletcher shook his head again and dropped his knife to his side. "No kids—ever," he repeated in a firmer voice. "Don't worry about your brother. We're going to give you a new last name and make sure that he can never find you. You'll never see him again after today. I promise you that. Okay?"

Lorelei's shoulders slumped. Because it wasn't okay with her. Because she didn't believe that Fletcher could keep her safe.

On the ground, Raymond groaned, starting to come around. "Kill you for this," he mumbled. "Kill you . . ."

Lorelei shuddered and turned away, as though she couldn't stand to look at him—and the danger he still represented.

For the first time since I'd known him, I thought that Fletcher had made the wrong decision. But he always taught me that an assassin without limits was just a monster, and he was keeping to his code . . .

"Gin?" a low, raspy voice said.

At first, I thought that I was still dreaming, that Fletcher was saying something else to me. But then I realized that I was in Jo-Jo's salon, still clutching Owen's hand, having fallen asleep next to him. I slowly lifted my head from his shoulder, wondering if I had just imagined the sound of his voice.

But his violet eyes were open and steady on mine.

"Hey," Owen rasped again, giving me that familiar, crooked grin I loved so much.

"Hey," I whispered back, tears streaming down my face. "How do you feel?"

"Like a human shish kebab."

I laughed at his bad joke, but the ache in my heart eased. He was going to be okay.

Owen was still lying in the salon chair, so I got up and carefully lay down next to him, fitting my body against his. He wrapped one arm around me, but even that small motion exhausted him, so I scooted closer and pressed a soft kiss to his lips. Then I laid my head down on his shoulder, splayed my fingers across his chest, and listened to the steady *thump-thump-thump* of his heart.

Beating strongly, just like always.

*   *   *

Owen drifted back to sleep, and I lay there, spooned next to him, for the better part of an hour before the front door banged open. Quick footsteps hurried in our direction.

"Owen! Owen!" a familiar voice called out.

His eyes snapped open as a college-age girl with blue-black hair, porcelain skin, and blue eyes burst into the salon. Eva Grayson, his baby sister.

"Owen!" she yelled again.

I got up out of the chair. Eva hurried over and threw herself down on top of Owen, even though he was still lying in the chair.

"I'm so glad you're okay!" Eva said. "You had me worried sick!"

Owen laughed. "I'm fine, Eva. Really, I am. Jo-Jo fixed me right up."

Eva drew back and gave him some breathing room. "What happened? I got a call from Silvio saying that you and Gin had been in some sort of fight and that you were hurt real bad. I was up at Country Daze, spending the night with Violet, but I got here as soon as I could."

I cleared my throat. "I'll give you two some time alone."

Eva nodded at me, then took my chair next to Owen.

He reached out and grabbed my hand. "Hey," he said in a soft voice. "It's not your fault. Don't you think for one second that it was. I knew exactly what I was getting into."

I leaned down and brushed my lips across his forehead. "And I love you for that—for backing me up no matter what. Just get some rest. I'll fix us all something to eat while you two talk."

Owen nodded and focused his attention on Eva, re-assuring her that he was fine and that everything was okay.

I stood in the salon doorway and watched them a moment, then closed the doors so I could get started on what needed to be done now.

Finding and killing Raymond Pike—once and for all.

* 25 *

I headed into the kitchen. Jo-Jo had brewed a pot of coffee, and the rich chicory scent filled the air. I drew in a deep breath, thinking of Fletcher, who had drunk the same dark brew. The scent and all the memories it called up of the old man steadied me. I knew what he would do now in my shoes, and I was finally ready to embrace it myself.

Jo-Jo, Sophia, Cooper, and Finn were talking to Mallory in soft voices, while Silvio texted on his phone, with Rosco sitting at his feet. Lorelei stood off by herself a few feet away.

The only people missing were Bria and Xavier. They must have headed back to Lorelei's mansion to deal with the aftermath of Pike's attack. I wondered if they had found Corbin unconscious inside the house yet. But I wasn't worried about him. Corbin hadn't been injured nearly as badly as Owen had.

The others stopped talking at the sight of my cold, hard face. I nodded at everyone, then washed my hands and opened the fridge, wondering what sort of nibbles I could make. Something light but healthy, I decided. Owen would need his fruits and veggies to get his strength back up. So I grabbed some pineapple out of the fridge, along with strawberries, mangoes, a couple of kiwis, and a lime. I plucked a knife from one of the drawers and started cutting up the fruit, sticking it all in a large bowl.

My friends stared at me, wondering what I was doing making fruit salad at a time like this. But it was either this or go out into the backyard and stab one of Jo-Jo's trees to death to work out some of my anger. Even now that I knew that Owen was going to be okay, I still wanted to pulverize everything and everyone within spitting distance just so they could feel a small portion of the anguish that I had felt tonight.

But instead of doing that, I grabbed a mango and started cutting into it.

"Um, Gin?" Finn asked. "Are you okay?"

"Yep."

I whacked my way through another mango, slicing off the thick skin, then filleting the fruit off the troublesome seed inside. Everyone would be over to see about Owen in the morning, so we were going to need a lot of fruit salad. And bacon. And pancakes. Stacks of them. I frowned, wondering if I had time to run out to the grocery store to make sure I had enough for everyone. Later, I decided. After Owen was asleep.

Finn cleared his throat. "Far be it from me to distract

you from butchering poor, defenseless fruit, but what are you going to do now, Gin?"

I kept right on slicing. "What I should have done all along—kill Raymond Pike."

He shook his head. "That might be harder than you think. I just finished talking to Bria and Xavier. The cops are looking for him, but there's been no sign of him around Lorelei's estate. It's like he grew wings and just vanished."

I'd expected as much, since Pike hadn't ever turned up at any of the local hotels. Whatever his cover alias was, it was a good one, and he wouldn't be found through regular methods.

But I didn't have to play by the rules. Not anymore.

"Don't worry about finding Pike. I'll take care of that."

"How?" Mallory asked.

I stared at her. "You told me earlier that I should step up and start acting like the big boss. Well, consider this my first official command. Everyone's always whining and crying to me about their problems. Now they're going to help me solve one of mine."

"What do you have in mind?" Silvio asked.

"Put the word out," I said in an icy voice. "To everyone in the underworld, from the top dogs all the way down to the corner con artists. I want Raymond Pike found. Whatever it takes."

Jo-Jo sucked in a breath, while Finn, Silvio, Sophia, Cooper, and Lorelei all looked worried. Mallory stared at me, then slowly nodded her approval. She understood what I was doing better than anyone else.

Finally laying claim to the underworld.

Finally becoming the big boss.

Finally seizing control, the way Mab Monroe had done so long ago.

I glanced at Silvio again. "Tell everyone that whoever finds Pike first will earn my gratitude—and a hundred thousand dollars."

Finn winced. "Gin, are you sure you want to do that? You'll have every crazy person from here to Bigtime calling in with a supposed sighting of Pike."

I considered his words. "You know, you're right. Make it a million."

Finn's eyes widened. His face paled, his hand clutched at his chest as though he were about to have a heart attack, and he actually whimpered. He didn't like the thought of me giving away all that money, but it would be worth every penny I had to pinpoint Pike.

I stared at my foster brother, and he finally nodded.

"I'll call the bank in the morning and have the money ready and waiting," Finn said.

"Good."

"Although . . ."

"What?"

Finn shook his head again, playing devil's advocate. "Say you find Pike. Then what? You saw what he did at the riverboat, at the garden party, and tonight at Lorelei's mansion. He's sure to have a contingency plan in case someone comes looking for him, probably one that involves more bombs. And if he's holed up in a hotel or an apartment building, then there will be too many innocent people around to try to take him out. Not without causing a whole lot of collateral damage."

"I know that. But I don't have to go after Pike. He's going to come to me."

Finn frowned. "And why would he be stupid enough to do that?"

I stabbed my knife toward Lorelei. "Because I still have something he wants."

Silence descended over the kitchen.

Surprise flashed across Finn's, Jo-Jo's, and Sophia's faces before they could hide it. They'd seen me do a lot of bad things over the years—cheat, steal, lie, kill—and they'd done their share of bad things themselves. But my cold determination to serve up Lorelei to her abusive brother shocked even them.

Lorelei crossed her arms over her chest. "Going to make me the bait in your little spider's trap? Well, it wouldn't be the first time, would it?"

"You'd better fucking believe it, sugar."

I looked over at Mallory, expecting her to protest, but something like respect flickered in her eyes.

She cleared her throat. "I think we should let the girls talk. Why don't we go check on Mr. Grayson?"

Mallory waved her hand. My friends shot me uneasy looks, but they followed her out of the kitchen and into the salon. Rosco trotted after them, leaving me alone with Lorelei. I stared at her, expecting her to make some snarky comment, but instead, her features softened a bit.

"I'm glad that Grayson is okay," she said. "That you were able to save him."

I nodded stiffly. "With your help. He would have died

if you hadn't told me what to do. Thank you. I owe you for that. More than you know."

"It's not your fault, what happened to him."

"Of course it is," I said, slicing up a kiwi and adding the green, jeweled pieces to my fruit salad. "Because you've been right all along. Fletcher should have let you kill Raymond that day. It would have saved us all a lot of grief and misery now, wouldn't it?"

"I'm glad that Fletcher didn't let me kill Raymond back then," Lorelei said in a quiet voice.

Startled, I looked up. That was about the last thing I'd expected her to say.

"I was afraid for a long time," she continued. "Knowing that Raymond was still out there and that he was doing his best to find me . . . knowing that he wanted revenge for our father's death . . . I was afraid to do *anything*. I couldn't even go into the backyard without worrying that Raymond might be watching me from the trees. I had nightmares like you wouldn't believe."

Oh, I knew all about nightmares, but I couldn't help but ask the inevitable question. "So what changed?"

She straightened her shoulders and lifted her chin. "I did. It took a while—it took a long while—but I got sick and tired of being afraid, and I got angry instead, at how stupid I was being for letting Raymond control my life, even though he wasn't even around anymore. It was like I was still stuck in that house growing up with him, worrying what I would do or say that would set him or our father off. So I decided that if he was coming for me, then I was damn sure going to be ready for him."

"But you didn't have to worry so much. Fletcher was

always good at hiding people." Another thought occurred to me. "You were safe as Lorelei Parker for years. How do you think Raymond finally found you?"

She shrugged. "I have no idea. You heard what he said about doing business with someone who knows me."

"Any idea who that could be?"

She shrugged again. "I've smuggled a lot of stuff for a lot of people, from here to Cypress Mountain to Cloudburst Falls, all the way up to Bigtime. It could be anyone."

So no leads there. I wanted to know who knew so much about the Ashland underworld—and especially Fletcher's methods—that they could put two and two together regarding Lorelei's real identity, but that was a question for another day.

"You were ready for Raymond tonight," I said. "You wanted him to come to your mansion. You set a trap for him, one that I completely messed up. Something that you have every right to be angry about."

"Absolutely. I told you that I could handle him. You should have trusted me." She smirked again. "After all, I have a reputation too, you know."

"Point taken."

To my surprise, a small smile flickered across her face. "You were wrong at the garden party too. I don't actually *hate* you."

I snorted. "Well, you could have fooled me. I suppose that you sent all those men to the Pork Pit to kill me over the summer because you secretly want to be my new best friend?"

She laughed, the sound lighter than I would have expected, given everything that had happened tonight.

"Of course not. The people I sent after you were causing certain . . . problems in my organization. Taking bribes, informing on me to my competitors, skimming from my shipments."

My eyebrows shot up in my face. "So you sicced them on me, knowing that I would kill them instead? That's cold, sugar."

"It was the quickest, easiest way to eliminate threats. Don't get all pissy about it. I didn't send anyone your way I knew you couldn't handle." Lorelei leaned back against the counter. "If it makes you feel any better, I did the same thing with my guards tonight. Those three giants Raymond killed? They were after Mallory's diamonds. They thought tonight was finally the night that they were going to rob us." She let out a small, satisfied chuckle. "They were dead wrong."

"Three birds, one brother," I murmured. "Impressive. But what about Corbin? He was there too."

"Jack called, said that he was worried about me and Mallory, and insisted on coming over," she replied. "I didn't mean for Raymond to hurt him too. But your sister has called and said he's going to be fine."

Suspicion swirled through my mind at her words, but I decided to focus on one thing at a time. "Well, I'm so very glad that I could help out and be your own private pest exterminator all these months."

I gave her a disgusted look, then chopped up another kiwi.

"You should consider it a compliment, a testament to your skills," she countered.

"I'm sensing an *and* in there."

"And . . . it also had the added effect of making it look as though I wanted you dead as badly as the other bosses do."

"Don't you?"

Her brow furrowed, and she stared at me like I'd suddenly started speaking pig Latin. "Of course not. Why would you think that?"

"Oh, I don't know," I snarked. "All the snotty glares and cold looks you grace me with whenever our paths cross."

Lorelei waved her hand, making her diamond rose-and-thorn ring glimmer and looking for a moment just like Mallory. "Just keeping up appearances. I have zero interest in running the Ashland underworld. All the bosses covet the job, but nobody in their right mind would *actually* want it. They don't realize that all they'd be doing is managing other people's problems instead of their own."

"You have no idea," I muttered.

I finished with the last of my kiwis, then moved on to the strawberries. Lorelei watched me slice and dice in silence, but she kept tugging on the end of her black braid, crossing and uncrossing her arms, stepping toward me, then easing back up against the counter. Something else was on her mind, but I ignored her pensive movements and kept right on slicing strawberries.

I had no desire to make things easy for her. Not after what she'd just told me. Not after realizing just how effectively she'd used me to get rid of her problems—and for how long she'd been doing it. Anger and a little shame burned through me at being such an *idiot* and not realizing what she was really up to. Lorelei had always been a little over-the-top in her dislike of me. I should have picked up on that. I should have realized that there was more going on than her just hating my guts.

Then again, I should have done a lot of things differently over the past few days.

But whacking through things while I was cooking almost always soothed me, and tonight was no different. By the time I had all the fruit in a bowl, I felt much calmer and could almost appreciate Lorelei's slick moves. Almost.

Ignoring Lorelei, I mixed together some sourwood honey and lime juice, then zested the lime and whisked it into my dressing. I tossed the whole thing together, enjoying the bright mix of colors and the citrusy tang of the lime coating all the fruit. If this didn't make Owen feel better, nothing would.

When I finished, I washed the sticky fruit juice off my hands. Lorelei crept forward, stepping up to the opposite side of the butcher's block table, her fingers tapping on the smooth surface. I dried off my hands, crossed my arms over my chest, and stared her down.

"You got something else to say, now is the time."

She wet her lips. "Appearances aside, I shouldn't have been quite so nasty to you. I admit that. But I just couldn't help myself."

"And why is that?"

She wouldn't meet my cold gaze. "Because I've always been jealous of you, Gin."

I blinked. Once again, that was just about the last thing I'd expected her to say. "Why in the world would you be jealous of *me*? I'm the most hunted woman in Ashland. People try to kill me on a monthly, if not weekly, basis. There's blood on my clothes more often than not, and I'm always waiting for the next attack. Mine is not a healthy, stress-free lifestyle."

"And all of that just adds to my jealousy." A bitter laugh escaped her lips. When she spoke again, her voice was whisper-soft. "Because you've always been stronger than me."

I didn't say anything. After a moment, Lorelei exhaled and raised her eyes to mine.

"That day at the cabin, when my father came after us, I wanted to stand and fight," she said. "I'd dreamed of doing it so many times. Of standing up for me and my mom. Of finally stopping him. But in the end, I just . . . *froze*. All I could think about was how he'd already killed my mom and was going to do the same thing to me. But you . . . you didn't even *think* about giving up. Not for a *second*. Not even when it looked like he and Raymond had killed your friends."

I thought of her cryptic words at the garden party. Now I finally understood what they meant. "You wanted it to be you—*you* wanted to be the one to kill your father."

She gave me a sharp nod. "And I was ashamed that you did it instead. That you *had* to do it, since I was so useless that day."

"You weren't useless," I countered. "You saved me from Raymond. He would have killed me if you hadn't stopped him."

"It wasn't enough. Not for me." She let out another long, tense breath. "So I, of course, have been doing the mature thing and shooting you dirty looks every time I've seen you these past few months. Instead of just stepping up and admitting to myself how weak I was that day."

"I don't think you're weak. Not now and not back then either."

Her mouth twisted with disgust. "Then what am I?"

I stepped forward and placed my hand on top of hers. "A survivor. Just like me."

Surprise flashed in her eyes, along with gratitude. But her expression slowly darkened with grief and regret for all the things she'd lost. Her mom, her childhood, her innocence. But most of all, there was strength, the strength that had helped her survive her father, the same strength that would help her survive her brother.

Her hand tightened around mine for a moment, and then we both let go. Because we knew what we had to do now: figure out how to kill Pike.

"You should just let me handle this by myself," Lorelei said. "Raymond's not your problem. He never was."

"He almost killed Owen. I would hunt him to the ends of the earth for that alone."

Lorelei nodded, hearing the venom in my voice. "Raymond is no fool. He's sure to realize that you'll be gunning for him now, and he'll have done his homework on you. He'll see you coming a mile away."

"I don't care whether he knows that I'm coming," I growled. "All I want is a level playing field. Someplace where his metal magic can be neutralized or at least minimized. And I know just the spot."

"Where?"

Instead of answering, I opened the refrigerator, then the freezer and a couple of the cabinets, grabbing everything I needed.

"Now what are you making?" she asked in an exasperated tone.

"You'll see."

Lorelei watched me put milk, cinnamon sticks, and cocoa powder into a saucepan on the stove. I also filled a blender with some vanilla-bean ice cream and a few ice cubes, and her nose scrunched up in confusion.

A couple of minutes later, I handed her a parfait glass filled with a decadent drink topped with marshmallows, mini chocolate chips, and graham-cracker crumbs.

She let out the first genuine laugh I'd heard all night. "You and your milkshakes. I should have known."

"Hot chocolate milkshakes," I corrected her. "The best of both worlds. They're good for what ails you. Who knows? Maybe they'll become my official good luck drink. It worked before that day in the woods."

"Yeah," Lorelei said in a thoughtful voice. "I suppose it did. Well, cheers."

"Cheers.

We clinked our glasses together, then sipped the shakes, which were just as good as they looked. Cold and sweet but with a lingering hint of cinnamon warmth from the hot chocolate.

Lorelei slurped down half of hers, then let out a happy sigh. "You know, this doesn't make us friends."

"Of course not," I replied. "I would never presume *that*. But we don't have to be friends to kill your brother. Just willing to do whatever it takes to end him."

"Believe me, I am more than willing, and I will certainly drink to that."

Lorelei grinned and held her glass up again. I clinked mine against hers and returned her grin with a wider one of my own.

"Good. Now, here's what we're going to do."

☀ 26 ☀

Once Lorelei and I had hammered out the details of our plan, we went into the salon to fill in the others. By that point, it was after three in the morning. Sophia helped Owen upstairs to one of the spare bedrooms, and the rest of us crashed in other beds and sofas throughout the house for what was left of the night.

I got up around nine o'clock and made a hearty Southern brunch of fried chicken, fried green tomatoes, bacon, and waffles, along with the fruit salad I'd already put together. One by one, the others plodded into the kitchen, still bleary-eyed from the long night but irresistibly drawn to the scents of sizzling meat and baking batter. Jo-Jo, Sophia, Mallory, and Lorelei ate in the kitchen, while Finn and Silvio fixed their food to go, since they had several things to check on for me this morning. So did Cooper, who had to get back to his blacksmith forge, and Eva, who headed to the community college for her morning classes.

Owen was still resting, so I took a tray up to the spare bedroom where he'd spent the night. Jo-Jo had checked him again and declared that he was fully healed, but I still wanted him to take it easy for as long as possible.

He sat up in bed, and I placed the tray on his lap.

He looked at all the food, then grinned. "It was just a little knife wound, Gin. Hardly worth all this effort. Although if I knew that it would mean breakfast in bed, I would have gotten myself stabbed a long time ago."

I smoothed his black hair off his face, then kissed him, so he wouldn't notice how forced my laughter was. "You're always worth the effort, stab wound or no stab wound."

I kept my words light and teasing, just like his, but I could still picture him bleeding out from that knife—*my knife*—sticking out of his chest. It was one of the most horrible things I'd ever seen, and I wouldn't be able to get the image out of my head anytime soon—if ever. Lorelei had her nightmares about Raymond and her father. Well, now I had another one for my collection too.

Owen scarfed down his food. I wasn't all that hungry, but I forced myself to swallow bite after bite, knowing that I would need to keep my strength up for the long day ahead.

He finished the last of his orange juice, then eased his head back against the pillows, his violet eyes sliding shut. He was still tired, and his body needed time to recover from all the trauma it had received, both from the stab wound and from the elemental Ice that Lorelei and I had used on him.

I removed the tray and pulled the sheets and blankets back up to his chin.

"Gin?" Owen mumbled in a sleepy voice.

"Yeah?"

"Be careful when you kill that bastard."

I kissed him again. "Don't you worry your pretty little head about a thing now. Because I promise you this— Raymond Pike will be dead by midnight."

As much as I wanted to stay with Owen and reassure myself that he was okay, I wasn't going to find Pike by sitting around the salon. So I went home to Fletcher's, showered, and threw on some fresh clothes before going downtown and opening up the Pork Pit for the day.

After all, nobody could snitch to the big boss if she wasn't in her office.

It was almost eleven when I got to the restaurant, and a dozen people were already waiting outside. Some of them just wanted to get their barbecue on, but more than a few had shifty eyes and nervous grins that told me they were here with information they hoped would score them a fat payday.

Silvio handled them in true assistant fashion. While I cooked, cleaned, and went about my chores, the vamp sat in a booth at the back of the restaurant near the restrooms, listening to all the stories the underworld boys and girls urgently whispered to him. Silvio faithfully listened and took copious notes on his tablet. Sometimes he would make a call or two to check on something. But after every person had said his or her piece, he would look over at me and shake his head no, indicating that they didn't have any valid info on Pike.

Frustration surged through me, but I forced myself to

rein in my temper and keep on running my restaurant as though nothing were wrong and I wasn't itching to kill a man by sundown. This was my home turf, and I was going to use that to my advantage. Raymond Pike couldn't hide forever. Not in *my* city.

Finally, at about two o'clock, the front door opened, and Jade Jamison sashayed into the Pork Pit. She looked at the man sitting with Silvio, then over at me. Silvio raised his eyebrows in a silent question, but I waved Jade over, and she plopped down on the stool closest to the cash register.

"Come by for another milkshake? Those have been a real crowd pleaser these past few days."

"Sure," she chirped. "With a side of information."

I groaned. "Wow. That was really bad."

She grinned. "I know, but I always wanted to say a cheesy line like that, and it seemed like the perfect time."

She requested a strawberry shake, and I started fixing it. Whatever info Jade had, it was enough to make her grin from ear to ear. That alone told me that she had the goods about where Pike was hiding. Some of the tension in my chest eased. I'd waited hours for someone to bring me Pike's head on a platter, and it looked like she was finally going to deliver.

"So," Jade said, after she'd taken a long, appreciative sip of her milkshake, "I hear that you're looking for someone else now. A guy named Raymond Pike."

"Yep."

"What do you want with him?"

"Nothing good."

She flinched at the venom in my voice. Her smile faded, and she pushed her milkshake aside.

"Well, I don't know anything about anyone named Raymond Pike," she said, picking up her phone from the counter. "But this guy is staying at the Peach Blossom. He's in a penthouse suite that's rented out to some private investment group."

The Peach Blossom was one of Ashland's many luxury apartment buildings, down the street from the *Delta Queen*.

Jade pulled up an image on her phone, then turned the screen around so I could see it. Black hair, blue eyes, smug smirk. The photo was grainy, as if it had been taken with another, cheaper phone, but it was still sharp enough to let me make out Pike sitting at a table, eating breakfast and reading a newspaper, as if he hadn't murdered three people last night and almost succeeded in doing the same to Owen.

"That's my guy. How did you find him?"

"One of my guys works as a doorman at the Peach Blossom," she said. "Cleaning, delivering food, and the like. After I got Silvio's message last night, I passed it along to all my folks and told them to keep their eyes peeled. My guy served this man a late breakfast about ninety minutes ago."

"Does your guy have access to the apartment building's security footage? Who comes and goes?" I wasn't satisfied with just getting Pike. Not after what he'd done to Owen. Now I was going to take down everyone who'd helped him.

"Of course," Jade said. "What are you looking for?"

"A right-hand man."

She frowned, not understanding my cryptic words. "Okay . . . but I'm telling you the truth. Your guy is there."

"Oh, I believe you, but there are a few other things I need to confirm. Looking at the security footage for the past few days will help me with that. So can you get it for me or not?" I asked.

"Sure. I can have my guy send it to your phone."

"Do it."

I waved Silvio over, and Jade stopped texting long enough to show him the photo of Pike. The vampire nodded, then told the cluster of folks still waiting that the person in question had been found and the reward had been claimed. Disappointed groans rose from the crowd, making some of the customers stare curiously in that direction, but everyone gave me curt nods and left the restaurant in a somewhat orderly and almost respectful fashion.

"Congratulations," I said. "You've just earned yourself one million smackeroos."

Jade beamed at me for several seconds, but her expression quickly melted into a wary look. "Just like that? You're actually going to honor the deal just based on my word and a cell-phone photo?"

"Sure." I shrugged. "Of course, if I were to find out that you or your guy were lying to me, well, that wouldn't work out so well for the two of you."

She flinched again.

"But you're much too smart for that," I continued in a soft, silky voice. "Aren't you, Jade?"

She nodded, her expression tense. "You'd better fucking believe it."

"Good. Then Silvio will see about getting you your money."

I slid off my stool and untied the strings of my blue work apron, pulling it up and over my head. I hung it on a hook sticking out from the back wall, then pulled out my phone and texted Lorelei, telling her that I knew where Pike was and asking if it was time to put our plan into motion.

She hit me back a second later. *All set on my end. Come on over.*

I slid the phone back into my pocket, more than ready to rock 'n' roll.

"What are you going to do?" Jade asked, eyeing the long sleeves of my black T-shirt like she expected me to flash one of my knives at her.

I grinned. "Nothing much. Just making sure that Raymond Pike has everything he needs for his last night in Ashland."

"Are you sure this is a good idea?" Jack Corbin asked. "Leaving town like this? So . . . suddenly?"

It was an hour later, and I was in the library in Lorelei's mansion, watching her pack up a laptop, a tablet, and some other gear. Mallory was off in another room, gathering up her own things, which consisted of boxes filled with all sorts of jewelry, most of it crusted with impressive diamonds. At least she was consistent that way.

"I mean, what happened last night was horrible," Corbin continued. "The guards dying, Pike storming into the mansion, him attacking me and you and Mallory. But I can hire more guards, increase your security. He won't get past me again, Lorelei. I promise you that."

After we'd rushed Owen to Jo-Jo's last night, Bria and Xavier had returned to the mansion. They'd taken Corbin to an Air elemental the police had on call, and the healer had fished all of Pike's nails out of Corbin's back and stitched up his wounds. Corbin had been lucky—very lucky—that the nails hadn't hit anything vital.

Then again, I didn't believe in such good luck.

Lorelei slipped her laptop into a bag, careful not to look at him. "I appreciate your concern, Jack. Really, I do. But there's no stopping Raymond or his metal magic. I always knew that it would come to this. That Raymond would find me one day and that I would have to run. Besides, Gin thinks this is for the best. Right, Gin?"

"Right," I drawled.

Corbin ran a hand through his dark brown hair, then started pacing back and forth in front of Lorelei's desk. "But why do you have to leave today? You haven't given me any time to prepare. If I'd known this was what you wanted, I would have made the arrangements for you and Mallory."

"That's why I've taken care of everything," I cut in, annoyed by the whining tone creeping into his voice. "I've already hired the moving vans, and my friends are coming over later to help Lorelei and Mallory pack up some more of their things. Lorelei will ride in the front van with me, and we'll make Mallory comfortable in the back of another van."

Lorelei zipped up her laptop bag, then moved over and

started pulling books off one of the shelves along the wall. "Mallory wants to stop by the botanical gardens before we leave for good. She and my mom spent a lot of time there when Mom was younger. And so have Mallory and I over the years."

"I suppose we have time for one last nostalgia stop before we get you out of town," I said. "We'll take Huckleberry Road. It runs right by the gardens, and there's never a lot of traffic on it. We'll stop, let Mallory say her goodbyes, and be on our way. By the time Pike realizes that you're gone, you and Mallory will be in another state, with new identities, and he'll never be able to find you again."

Lorelei nodded and kept pulling books off the shelves. I eyed the titles. Lots of fantasy and spy books, along with a sprinkling of Southern literature. I approved of her reading choices, especially since I spotted a copy of *Where the Red Fern Grows*. My heart squeezed as I thought of Fletcher. The old man would have been happy that I was here, helping Lorelei. And so was I.

Corbin looked back and forth between us. "It sounds like you've thought of everything."

I turned away so he wouldn't see my sly smile. "Yeah, I think we have."

"Well, if you're sure that there's nothing I can do . . ." Corbin's voice trailed off.

"I'm sure," Lorelei said.

She stopped her packing, walked over, and laid her hand on Corbin's shoulder. "You've been a big help already, Jack. Don't think that I haven't noticed—or that I don't appreciate all your hard work for me."

She reached out and hugged him. I was facing Lorelei, and I arched my eyebrows at her sweet, syrupy words. Lorelei rolled her eyes before her face smoothed out into a neutral expression. She drew back and stared at Corbin.

"I've arranged for you to receive a nice bonus. One that should tide you over until you can join someone else's crew. I'll also put in a good word for you with the folks I know."

"Thanks, boss," Corbin said. "Well, if you don't need me for anything, I guess I'll leave you to it, then."

Corbin smiled at Lorelei, nodded at me, then left the library and shut the door behind him. Lorelei opened her mouth, but I held up a finger in warning. I hadn't heard Corbin walk away.

"Let me help you with those books," I said. "They look heavy."

"Sure."

Lorelei and I moved around the office, lugging books from one side to the other. After about a minute, a floorboard creaked, and I heard soft footsteps retreating down the hall.

I dropped the books I'd been holding onto a nearby sofa and cracked open the library door. Corbin was gone, and the hallway was deserted. Good.

Closing the door, I turned to face Lorelei, who'd dumped her own armful of books onto her desk.

"Do you think he bought it?" I asked. "That we weren't too obvious?"

Lorelei snorted. "I didn't hire him for his brains. He bought it, all right. Hook, line, and sinker."

I grinned. "Well, then, let's see what our bait catches us."

☼ 27 ☼

At six o'clock that evening, I was sitting shotgun next to
Bria in a white moving van, watching the world pass by.
We were in Northtown, on Huckleberry Road, driving by
the lush landscape of the botanical gardens, although the
setting sun was already turning the thick clusters of plants
more gray than green. Iron streetlights had already sputtered to life along this narrow, curvy stretch of road, their
golden glow doing little to banish the growing shadows.

"Are you sure this is going to work, Gin?" Bria asked.
"It seems like a big risk to take."

"This is our best option. Trust me."

"But what if Pike does something unexpected?" Bria
pressed, worry creasing her face. "What if things go
wrong?"

"Pike has been fairly predictable up to this point. I
don't expect him to deviate too much from his standard
plan of attack. Even if he does exactly what I think he

will, things will still undoubtedly go wrong. That's just how my bad luck rolls. But that's why we're doing it this way. To minimize the risk to everyone."

I glanced in the side mirror. Two vans identical to ours cruised down the road behind us. Finn was driving the second vehicle, Xavier riding shotgun, while Sophia was steering the last one, with Owen and Silvio as her wingmen. Despite the fact that he'd almost died last night, Owen had insisted on coming. I loved him for it, but it also made my stomach churn with worry, just like it did for the rest of my friends. Because as long as Pike was alive, they were all in danger, especially being here with me.

Bria didn't say anything else, but she alternated between looking at me, at the road ahead, and in the rearview mirror. One of her hands wrapped around the steering wheel, while the other crept up to fiddle with her wig—a dark brown ponytail. I thought it went rather well with the head-to-toe black clothes she was wearing.

"You're going to mess up your hair if you keep pulling on it like that."

Bria dropped her hand from the wig. "Sorry."

"Don't worry about it. These things itch like crazy."

I reached up and patted my own wig—a black one that had been styled into a French braid—before tugging down my leather jacket, the royal-blue color bright enough to be seen clearly through the windshield.

I hadn't exactly told Corbin the truth about what I was up to tonight.

Bria drove on, and the road straightened out, with a four-way stop up ahead. Directly across from us, a black sedan was already sitting at the intersection, another identical sedan idling behind it. Bria slowed the van and stopped at the appropriate spot. We looked at each other, then focused on the other cars.

The first black sedan cruised forward, passing us.

Thunk.

The sound of metal sticking to metal cut through the air. At the same time, the driver of the sedan gunned his engine, tires squealing as he zoomed away from us.

"What was that?" Bria glanced in her side mirror. "Hey, there's some sort of box stuck to the side of our van—"

Boom!

An explosion rocked the van. The two back tires lifted off the ground, and I thought the vehicle was going to flip. But instead, gravity took over, and the tires crashed back onto the road. That jolting motion sent the van skittering sideways, taking Bria and me for a very wild and bumpy ride. For a second, all I could see was a swirling mix of greens, grays, blacks, and browns as the vehicle careened off the road and spun around and around through the grass, churning up thick wads of dirt.

But just as quickly as it had started, the ride ended, and the van abruptly jerked to a halt.

The violent, sudden stop would have thrown Bria and me through the now-cracked windshield if we hadn't been wearing our seat belts. Even as it was, I felt as if my head was trying to wrench itself away from the rest of my body.

Thick, black smoke boiled into the van, and the stench of burned rubber filled the air, sinking deep into my lungs.

I coughed and looked at Bria. "Are you okay?"

She blinked, her eyes a bit unfocused, and she reached up and patted her brown ponytail again. "I'm okay. How about you?"

I didn't see any blood on my clothes, although my chest ached from where the seat belt had caught me. Like Bria, I also reached up and patted my hair, making sure the black braid was still where it was supposed to be.

"Yeah," I croaked out. "Just a few bruises—"

Screech!

My door was wrenched open, and a knife flashed in front of my face. I tensed and lashed out at the weapon, but I must have been more dazed than I'd realized, because I completely missed and ended up slapping the dashboard instead.

Zip-zip.

While I flailed around, the knife made two quick, neat cuts through my seat belt. Then a hand reached inside, grabbed me, and yanked me out of the van. I tumbled out and landed facedown in the grass.

"Hey!" Bria yelled. "Leave her alone!"

She cursed, trying to get free of her own seat belt, but it was too late.

A hand fisted in the back of my jacket and hauled me to my feet, making my brain spin around in my skull again.

"Come along quietly, and you'll get to live a few minutes longer," Raymond Pike hissed in my ear.

A hand clamped down on my left shoulder, and something pricked my side, drawing blood and making me hiss with pain. I glanced down. Pike had the spikes on the ball of his mace pressed up against my left kidney. If he stabbed me there, I was done for.

"You've caused me enough problems already. I won't hesitate to end you at the slightest sign of trouble. Do you understand?" he hissed again, his fingers digging into my shoulder with a tight, bruising grip.

I nodded, not trusting myself to speak right now.

"Good. Now, let's get out of here and go somewhere a little more private."

Somewhere he could get on with the business of killing me, but I wasn't exactly in a position to quibble right now.

But my friends weren't about to let him just march me off to my death.

Engines roared and tires squealed as Finn and Sophia raced their vans up the road to our position, then screeched to a stop. Doors snapped open, and their loud, worried shouts drifted over to me.

"Hey!"

"There he is!"

"He's got her!"

Inside the first van, Bria was still trying to get free of her seat belt, although she kept cursing and shouting at Pike to leave me alone.

Screech.

The second black sedan fishtailed to a stop in the middle of the street, forming a roadblock with the first car and cutting Bria and me off from the rest of our friends. Five giants with guns spilled out of the vehicle. Three of the men hunkered down behind the car, using it as a shield, but the other two raced in our direction.

Pike took his hand off my shoulder long enough to stab his finger at the giants, then over at the other two vans still on the road. "What am I paying you fools for?" he snapped. "Kill them! Now!"

The two giants raised their guns and started firing at my friends. So did the men still stationed behind the second sedan on the road.

Crack!

Crack! Crack!

Crack!

"Take cover!" Finn yelled.

He ducked behind his open van door, then raised his gun and fired back at the giants. Xavier was out of their vehicle too, returning fire, and I saw Sophia, Owen, and Silvio open the doors of the third van and raise their own guns.

"Get him!" Owen roared over the *crack-crack-crack* of bullets. "Get Pike before he gets away with her!"

Pike cursed, realizing that he couldn't get back to his sedan and that the giants wouldn't be able to hold off my friends forever. He spun me toward the trees.

"Move!" he yelled. "Now! Before I kill you where you stand!"

I nodded, telling him that I would do exactly what he wanted.

Then he grabbed my shoulder, shoved the mace spikes into my side again, and forced me into the woods.

Pike's fingers dug into my shoulder socket like he wanted to rip off my arm, but I kept my head down and concentrated on moving forward and not doing anything to further enrage him. There was no use trying to escape. Not when he had those spikes pressed up against my side, ready to ram them through me if I put up any kind of struggle.

Behind us, steady sounds of gunfire still ripped through the air, along with an occasional shout, but the trees muted the sounds, so I shut them out of my mind. Besides, my friends couldn't help me now.

We'd gone about two hundred feet when the trees gave way to a smooth lawn crisscrossed with white flagstones. Old-fashioned streetlights lined the paths, the golden glows hovering over the stones like fireflies suspended in a spider's web.

"The botanical gardens?" Pike muttered. "How did we wind up back here—"

Crack-crack-crack.

More gunfire sounded, along with several shouts, the voices getting closer and closer.

"Where are they?"

"Do you see them?"

"We're coming for you!"

Pike cursed and shoved me forward again, forcing me down one of the paths that led into a hedge maze. Rows of thick, impenetrable bushes rose up eight feet on both sides, cutting us off from everyone and everything else. Only a few lights were spaced here and there along the path, adding to the gloom. Pike's hot breath rasped against my cheek. The stink of cigar smoke clung to his body, overpowering the far more pleasing aromas of the garden.

A few smaller paths split off left and right, but Pike pushed me along the center trail. We'd gone about fifty feet when the maze opened up into a large circular area. White picket fences ran along the path, cordoning off flowerbeds full of pansies, mums, and fat pumpkins with leafy green vines curling all around them. Embedded in the center of the garden was a round mosaic made out of jagged, colorful bits of red, orange, and yellow glass that had been fitted together to form a cornucopia.

Pike marched me over to the mosaic and threw me down face-first in the center of the glass. I used my hands to break my fall, but I still felt the hard, jarring impact. My palms scraped against the words *Harvest Time* that curved over the top of the cornucopia.

Pike circled around me, his boots tapping on the glass. He was wearing another black satchel of nails across his chest, and the metal pieces *tink*ed in time to his footsteps. All the while, he kept swinging his mace back and forth like a scythe of death hanging over my head. Finally, he stopped in front of me.

"Now, bitch," he growled, "I think it's time for our long-awaited family reunion—and for you to finally pay for killing our father."

Instead of begging for mercy like he wanted, I started laughing. Deep, hearty chuckles spewed out of my lips.

"What's so funny?" he growled again.

It took me another few seconds to stop laughing. "Well," I said, lifting my head to look at him. "You finally got one thing right. I did kill your father, but he wasn't my daddy too. Something that I am extremely grateful for."

His black eyebrows drew together, confusion filling his face.

I reached up and yanked off the black wig I was wearing, which Jo-Jo had braided to look just like Lorelei's hair.

Pike sucked in a breath, finally realizing how thoroughly he'd been fooled—and that he had kidnapped the wrong woman.

"Surprise," I drawled. "I'm not the bitch you're looking for."

* 28 *

I surged to my feet, palmed the knife hidden up my sleeve, and lashed out with it.

I wanted to gut Pike and end the fight before it even got started, but he ducked out of the way. I raised my knife again, but he was quicker and swung his mace out in a wicked arc. This time, I was the one who stepped back, and we started circling around and around, each of us searching for an opening to take the other down.

Pike's eyes narrowed. "You're not Lorelei."

"Way to state the obvious. Aren't you the observant one."

"But there was a woman in the van with you," he accused. "One dressed in black clothes with a brown ponytail just like yours. I saw her when I planted the bomb on the back of the van."

"My sister, Bria, dressed up to look like me." I gestured with my knife at the black boots, dark jeans, and blue leather jacket I was wearing. "With me dressed up to look like Lorelei. A simple trick, but you totally fell for it."

Pike's face hardened. "Lorelei was supposed to be in the lead van."

I smirked. "That's what we told your boy Corbin, and he spoon-fed it right to you."

He blinked, surprise flickering in his face. "How do you know about Corbin?"

"That he's been keeping tabs on Lorelei for you? Feeding you all her movements and plans? Please." I scoffed. "Paranoia is my middle name. You had to have *some* way of tracking her, since you kept showing up every single place she went, and how better to do that than by turning Lorelei's right-hand man? Plus, I thought it was odd that you appeared right after Corbin drove up to the mansion last night. The only way you could have snuck past me was if you were hidden in his car. You also spared Corbin, when you could have easily killed him with your nails. You really should have offed him, instead of giving him all those superficial wounds."

His mouth twisted. Looked like we agreed on one thing.

"So I had my guys do a little digging into his finances. And guess what? Corbin has received several large cash deposits over the past week. Not to mention the fact that the security cameras at the Peach Blossom caught him going in and out of your penthouse several times. You only get that much money and take those kinds of meetings on the sly when you sell someone out. Besides, I saw him on the road. He was driving that black sedan you were in."

A muscle ticked in Pike's jaw. This wasn't going at all how he'd imagined it.

"Now, one of the things I admire about Lorelei is her creative problem solving," I said. "She really is very clever about getting other people to do her dirty work, myself included. It was her idea to get Corbin to tell you all about her supposed plan to leave Ashland. We gave him all the juicy details, including our route and which van she was supposedly going to be in, which Corbin oh-so-obligingly passed on to you. And what do you know? You totally bought it, and here we are."

"Where is she?" Pike growled, looking around the garden. "Where is that bitch?"

"If I were you, sugar, I'd be more concerned about me right now."

"You? You think I'm scared of *you*?" This time, he was the one who laughed. "Oh, I know all about you. Gin Blanco, the Spider. *Ooh*. Just saying your name gives me chills." He gave a fake shudder with his shoulders.

"It should, since you walked right into my trap."

He laughed again. "Trap? What trap? All I see is you, with one knife and no one to help you."

"I don't need anyone to help me with you. All I needed was this lovely little garden spot."

Pike frowned, his brows knitting in confusion again. His gaze flicked back and forth between me and the white picket fences, flowerbeds, and glass mosaic. His eyes glowed bright blue for a second. Realization dawned on his face.

"No metal," he growled.

I stabbed my knife at him. "*Ding-ding-ding*. We have

a winner. Did you really think that I would just let you kidnap me and take me any old place you wanted? Your ambush on the road, bombing the van, thinking that I was Lorelei and grabbing me, marching me all the way back here. I planned it all, with every single thing designed to drive you into the gardens. So far, everything's gone off without a hitch."

"Not everything." He sneered. "What about your friends? My giants should be done shooting them to death by now."

I tilted my head to the side. "Funny. I don't hear anything. Do you?"

Pike listened, but the *crack-crack-crack* of gunfire had stopped, and the only sound was the soft slapping of our footsteps as we kept circling each other.

"Do you know what the one good thing about being the head of the Ashland underworld is?" I asked.

He glared at me.

"Everyone more or less reports to me now. I figured that you might try to hire some local muscle to help you this time around, especially since you'd already offed Smith, your previous stooge. So I put the word out and offered a very generous payday to anyone who came forward with information about you. Those giants you thought were on your payroll? They're really on *mine*."

Pike's mouth dropped open. "But—but they were firing at your friends! I saw them!"

"Your smuggler sister has access to all kinds of interesting things. Fake ammunition is one of them. Those giants you thought you hired? They were shooting blanks. Just like you're doing, sugar."

Shock flashed across Pike's face, along with more than a little embarrassment. His cheeks flushed a mottled red, although it was nothing compared with the rage sparking in his eyes.

"You bitch," he growled. "You think you can put one over on me? No fucking way."

"Not just me," I purred, stabbing my knife off to the side. "Look. The rest of our garden party has finally arrived."

Pike glanced over at the entrance, his mouth dropping open again.

My friends were here.

Finn, Bria, Xavier, Sophia, Jo-Jo, Silvio, and Owen stood in a loose semicircle, all of them armed with elemental Ice guns. Mallory was with them too, wearing the same sort of black clothes as the rest of us, along with her usual array of diamonds. She looked like a cat burglar who'd just lifted the biggest score of her life.

Mallory had her Ice gun trained on Corbin, who looked utterly miserable. Cuts and bruises marred his face, and his eyes were dull and dim. He'd bet on the wrong side, and he knew how badly he'd lost.

And then there was Lorelei.

She left my friends behind, heading for the center of the garden where Pike and I stood. She too was carrying an Ice gun, with a couple more holstered to her thighs and a brace of knives circling her waist. After this was all over with, I'd have to tell her how much I approved of her wardrobe choices.

Pike cursed and backpedaled so that he could keep both of us in sight at the same time.

Lorelei stopped beside me and smirked at him. "Hello, Raymond. You wanted to see me?"

Pike looked back and forth between us before focusing on his sister. "You think you're so smart, with your schemes and your new friends and your pet assassin. But you know what? You're still the same weak, whiny little bitch you always were, too afraid to face me by yourself."

Ice magic rolled off Lorelei's body, and her fingers tightened around her gun. "Weak? I was never weak. *I* was the one who got hit over and over again. *I* was the one who got beaten by our father for every little thing he thought I did wrong. *I* was the one he tortured, right along with my mother. You? All you ever did was pucker up and kiss his ass. You were too afraid of him not to. I'd say that makes *you* the weak, whiny little bitch. Not me."

More of that hot, embarrassed rage stained Pike's cheeks a dark, ugly red.

Lorelei shook her head, her braid swishing against her shoulder. "I don't know why I was ever afraid of you, Raymond. You don't have any real strength, any real power. Not the kind that truly matters. All you have is your ego, and it's not going to be enough to save you. Not this time."

But Pike laughed, the sound soft yet confident. He gestured out at the gardens. "You think you've beaten me by bringing me here? I don't need any metal here to kill you. I brought plenty of my own. I always do."

His eyes flashed a wicked blue, and he chucked his mace at us.

For a second, I thought that he was a complete idiot,

throwing away his one weapon, especially with such a halfhearted attempt. But then I felt a wave of magic surge off him, and I realized what he was really targeting with it: the mace.

"Bomb!" I screamed.

I reached for my Stone magic and used it to harden my skin, even as I tackled Lorelei, driving her to the ground and covering her body with mine—

Boom!

Fire, heat, smoke, noise.

Shrapnel.

The mace's metal spikes shot out from the force of the explosion, while the rest of the weapon splintered into jagged pieces that cut through the air like knives.

I grunted as the dangerous mix of shrapnel pelted my back, along with wads of dirt and rocks. The hailstorm punched into my body, leaving bruises behind, but my Stone magic kept the pieces from actually slicing into my skin. As soon as the last of the shrapnel fell, I rolled off Lorelei and scrambled to my feet. She did the same, both of us searching for her brother.

But Pike wasn't there.

Lorelei whirled around, searching for him. I looked over at my friends.

Mallory was down on the ground, with Jo-Jo, Silvio, and Owen trying to help her up. Corbin must have used the explosion to make a break for it, and he was running for the entrance, with Finn, Bria, Xavier, and Sophia chasing after him.

My gaze locked with Owen's.

He pointed to the hedge maze tunnel on the far side of the garden. "Pike went that way! Go! Go!"

Lorelei and I looked at each other, then sprinted in that direction.

❖ 29 ❖

Lorelei and I plunged into the hedge maze.

As we ran deeper into the maze, the hedges became taller and thicker, the tight tangle of limbs impenetrable, and the path twisted and turned, with new branches splitting off from it every few feet in no discernible order or pattern. A sign planted at one of the junctions said that the maze was designed to look like a rose when viewed from above.

Wasn't that ironic.

The silvery light of the full moon frosted the tops of the hedges, outshining the iron streetlights that were planted throughout the maze. The air smelled crisp and green, with a metallic hint of the night's coming frost. Leaves had fallen off the trees farther out in the gardens and blown down into the maze corridors, the brown curls creating spiderweb patterns on the white flagstones.

Lorelei and I came to a junction. I looked left and right down the murky, shadow-strewn corridors, but I didn't see Pike or hear anything but our harsh, raspy breaths. If we went the wrong way, he was gone—until the next time he decided to plant a bomb somewhere.

I reached out with my Stone magic, listening to the rocks in the ground and hidden in the bushes. But they only murmured of the night's growing chill. Pike's passage hadn't been long or distinctive enough to resonate with them. I cursed and bent down, hoping there would be some sort of scuff mark or bootprint on the flagstones that would indicate which way he'd gone.

Nothing.

I got to my feet and stalked back and forth in both directions, but I didn't see so much as a broken branch. I let out another curse. Given my luck, I'd pick the wrong direction, and Pike would get away.

Lorelei pointed to the right. "He went that way."

"Are you sure?"

She nodded, her eyes glinting like pale sapphires, and I realized that she was using her own metal magic, weak though it was. "I'm sure. I spent years tracking him and his magic all through our house so I could avoid him as much as possible. He's still holding on to his power, trying to find some metal to use with it. It's faint, but I can sense his trail. Trust me."

"Lead the way."

Lorelei headed down the right passageway.

We moved quickly and quietly. We didn't speak. We didn't need to. The only thing that mattered now was finding Pike—and finishing him.

But the maze made it difficult.

Time and time again, we came to junctions where the hedges split into two or three or sometimes even four new directions. I would have been floundering around for hours, trying to track him, but Lorelei never wavered, and she never hesitated.

The whole trek reminded me of that day in the woods, except this time, Lorelei was the hunter, the unstoppable force. No matter how many different directions Pike took, no matter how he maneuvered through the maze, she followed the faint trail of his magic like a bloodhound glued to a scent that only she could detect.

Finally, we rounded a corner and spotted Pike darting through a patch of light. He quickly disappeared into another corridor.

"There he is!" Lorelei yelled, raising her Ice gun. "There he is!"

She ran after him. I reached for her, but I wasn't quick enough to grab and yank her back. In an instant, she was several feet past me and sprinting even deeper into the maze.

"Wait!" I hissed. "Wait!"

There might not be any metal around, but Pike still had that bag of nails draped across his chest, and, worse, he could always have another bomb on him. Besides, he was as fond of traps as I was, and I was willing to bet that the only reason we'd seen him now was so he could try to lure us into some sort of kill spot.

"Lorelei!" I hissed again. "Stop!"

But she didn't.

So I went after her. She was going to get herself killed,

being so reckless and blindly chasing after Pike, but I could understand why she did it. She was tired—tired of hiding and waiting and wondering when and where he might strike next.

She wanted to end this.

But I crept forward at a more cautious pace. We might have trapped Pike in the maze, but a rabid animal was always the most dangerous when it was cornered—

Lorelei's scream shattered the silence.

I forgot about being cautious and sprinted forward. She kept screaming, and a cold, hard burst of magic filled the section of the maze up ahead, like an invisible mushroom cloud arcing up into the sky.

Please! . . . Please don't leave me!

Lorelei's voice echoed in my mind, even as her screams assaulted my ears.

The corridor opened up into another garden, one with a Japanese theme, given the clusters of cherry and bonsai trees that lined the paths and the wooden pagoda sitting in the middle. I spotted a rock garden behind the pagoda, the stones glowing like opals in the moonlight.

Lorelei was on her knees near the pagoda, her hands raised and her eyes glowing a pale blue as she tried to fight off her brother. But she was losing badly, her face and hands already crisscrossed with deep, bloody scratches. Pike drew a handful of nails out of his bag and sent them slicing through the air toward her. Lorelei screamed as they stuck into her shoulder, like pins in a cushion.

I raced toward them. The second I was in range, I shot a spray of Ice daggers out of my left hand.

Pike's head snapped up at the sudden surge of magic,

and he tossed a handful of nails at me, driving them into my Ice daggers and shattering my cold weapons. Bits of Ice and metal *tink-tink-tink*ed to the ground between us.

While Pike was distracted, Lorelei reached for one of the Ice guns holstered to her thighs, but he kicked her in the ribs. The blow threw her back, and her head clipped the side of an iron bench close to the pagoda. Lorelei dropped to the ground and didn't move.

Pike stepped over her still form, stopping in front of me. He shook his head. "You must have a serious death wish."

"I am rather fatalistic that way," I admitted. "Mostly, though, I just don't like bullies. People like you who think that their magic makes them better than everyone else. Folks who enjoy hurting other people with their power."

"A bully? I'm so much more than *that*." He laughed, the sound chilling me far more than the night air did. "Although I've been extremely disappointed in *you* so far. I thought that the mighty Gin Blanco would be tougher. Stronger. Smarter. From what I've been told, you were supposed to be quite the powerhouse. But I haven't seen any evidence of that at all."

"And who's been spreading tales about me all the way up in West Virginia?" I asked. "Is it the same person who told you about Lorelei's new last name and location?"

He grinned. "My new friend? Let's just say that . . . she's as coldhearted as they come."

Well, that told me absolutely nothing. I thought about pressing him for more information, but he wouldn't tell me. In fact, he would delight in *not* telling me, and I didn't want to give him any more of a thrill than what he'd already gotten from torturing Lorelei, who was still out cold.

I bared my teeth at him. "Funny, but I would say the same thing about me. It's too bad your friend's not here, though. She could die right alongside you tonight."

Pike regarded me with an amused look. "You really believe that, don't you? That you can kill me, despite all the times I've bested you over the past few days."

"Why shouldn't I? Everyone's luck runs out sooner or later, and I'd be happy to help you extinguish what little is left of yours. Besides, you won't be the first Pike I've killed."

He frowned. "What do you mean?"

"Haven't you figured it out yet?" I shook my head and clucked my tongue, mocking him. "Little slow on the uptake, aren't you, Ray? I already told you once, but let me say it again: *I* killed your father. Not Lorelei. Dear Daddy Renaldo was about to beat her to death. He almost got me too, before I shoved him down on top of that mace he was so fond of carrying around. He didn't much like all those spikes digging into him for a change, instead of Lily Rose and Lorelei."

It was a calculated jab to try to enrage him enough to rush blindly at me, but he didn't fall for it. Pike stared at me, memories darkening his eyes and the wheels of his mind churning as he thought back to that day.

"And you think that *I'm* not smart?" I let out a light, pealing laugh. "Look at you. You're the one who's been trying to get your revenge on the wrong woman. For *years*. Not the sharpest nail in the shed, are you, Ray?"

Pike kept staring at me, but the certainty in my voice and the cold, cruel curve of my lips finally convinced him.

"You bitch!" His voice teetered on a scream. "You killed my father!"

"Damn right I did," I snarled back. "Just like I'm going to kill you."

Pike took a step forward, as though he was finally going to charge me. But he must have thought better of it, because he stopped, threw back his head, and laughed instead.

"Oh, give it up." He sneered. "Because you're still trying to kill me with a knife—and I have more than enough magic to rip that pretty metal away and drive it right through your heart."

Pike waved his hand, expecting the force of his magic to pop the knife out of my hand just as it had done before during the garden party.

Nothing happened.

Pike frowned and waved his hand again.

And still, nothing happened.

His eyes narrowed. "You switched knives. That one you're holding, it's not metal. I should have realized that something was wrong with it the second I saw it."

"This old thing?" I held up the weapon. "You're right. It's not my usual silverstone knife."

I tapped my nail against the blade. Instead of the usual *tink-tink-tink*, the sound was flat and hollow, as though the knife weren't solid at all.

"It's ceramic," I said, tilting the weapon back and forth, letting the moonlight bounce off the metallic-looking paint I'd sprayed all over the surface. "Your sister gave it to me, along with a couple of others. She thought they might come in handy when we suckered you out here tonight."

"Still thinking you've won just because we're in a garden." Pike gave me an evil grin. "Don't you know that metal is in practically *everything*? You might have switched to ceramic knives, but there's still metal on your clothes, in your shoes, and wrapped around your throat, given that pretty rune necklace you're wearing."

Pike raised his hand again, and a blast of power rolled off him, streaked through the air, and surrounded me like a force field. The invisible fingers of his metal magic rifled through my clothes, snaked through my hair, and even tugged on the laces of my black boots.

But once again, they came up empty.

Confusion flickered in Pike's eyes.

"You know what? It's difficult, but it's not impossible to find clothes that don't have any metal in them."

"But your ring, your necklace!" he sputtered.

"Plastic knockoffs," I said, tapping the tip of my ceramic knife against my spider rune pendant. "But you're right. They are pretty, nonetheless, don't you think?"

He growled, grabbed a handful of nails out of his satchel, and sent them shooting straight at my face.

❖ 30 ❖

Pike wanted to take me by surprise, but I had been waiting for the move. After all, sneak attacks were what he did best. Me too.

The nails bounced off my body, thanks to my Stone-hardened skin, and I whipped my knife out in a quick counterstrike.

Pike lunged back, so that my knife only sliced through the strap of his satchel instead of him. The bag of nails dropped to the ground, and I kicked it off into the bushes. Pike lashed out with his own kick, which would have blown out my knee if it had connected. While I was recovering my balance, he reached around to the small of his back and came out with his own knife—silverstone, judging by the way it glinted in the moonlight.

He grinned. "I was going to use this to cut Lorelei's throat when I finally decided to finish her off. But I guess I'll just have to practice on you first."

"Bring it on, you sick son of a bitch," I hissed.

Pike and I circled each other again, our booted feet scraping through all the dried leaves. I might have largely neutralized his metal magic, but he was still a dangerous enemy, and the way he held that knife told me that he knew how to use it. Even with my Stone magic protecting me, one mistake, one second of hesitation, one lapse in concentration, and I'd be on the ground and bleeding out from the vicious wounds he would inflict on me.

Pike lunged in, but I recognized it as an opening feint, meant to test my resolve and skill, and I held my ground, easily slapping the blade of his knife away with mine.

He flashed me a cool look. "Well, at least my source got one thing right. You actually seem to know what you're doing with that knife."

There he went again, talking as if he actually knew me. I wondered who his chatty source was and where she had gotten so much information about me. Maybe I could carve the answer out of him before I put him down for good.

He lunged in with his knife again. I ducked, but I wasn't quick enough to avoid the blow. The tip of his knife dragged along my forearm, the silverstone soaking up just enough of my Stone magic to let the blade break through the surface of my skin.

I yelped and staggered back. Pike swung his knife in a powerful arc, trying to lay my guts open with one long, smooth slice, but I twisted my body to the side, avoiding the blow. He leaned in too far, and I jabbed the hilt of my knife into his left temple.

This time, Pike staggered back, and I pressed my advantage, swinging, swinging, swinging my knife in an elaborate pattern, all three strikes meant to kill, kill, kill. But he was just as good with a knife as I was, and he side-stepped my blows the same way I had eluded his.

I risked a glance at Lorelei, but she was still slumped unconscious on the ground.

Pike darted forward, and I stepped up to meet him. Our blades flashed in the air, his bright and pure, mine dull and fake. He nicked my shoulder, and I got in a long slice in his forearm. He twisted his knife into my thigh, while I rammed mine deep into his shoulder. He slapped me across the face, and I punched him in the kidneys. And so the fight went on and on, and neither one of us could get enough of an advantage to end the other.

Until my knife broke.

Pike and I were locked together, trying to overpower each other. Cold, hard, invisible waves of our magic pulsed through the air, even as our knives slid back and forth, the blades screeching together. But my ceramic wasn't as strong as his silverstone, and the metal finally sawed through my weapon, leaving nothing behind but a jagged, useless hilt.

The snap of the knife threw me off balance. I grunted and tried to spin away, but Pike grabbed my hair and yanked me back toward him.

Then the bastard punched his blade into my side.

I screamed and flung my hand back, trying to shoot Ice daggers into his face to blind him. I missed the mark, but I blasted him with enough magic to make him growl and let go of me.

The knife tore free, hurting just as much coming out as it had going in. I fell to the ground, clutching my side and trying to ignore the pain flooding my body from the brutal wound. Pike hadn't hit anything terribly vital, but he'd come far too close for my liking. I needed to end the fight—and him—now.

Pike loomed over me, my blood dripping off the end of his knife. "Now what are you going to do, bitch?"

"This."

I put my hands on the ground and lashed out with my foot, driving my boot into his ankle. The blow wasn't all that hard, but Pike yelped in surprise, his feet skidded through a patch of dead leaves, and he landed hard on his hands and knees.

I lurched back up onto my feet. A troubling amount of blood had already soaked into my blue T-shirt, with even more oozing out of the wound.

Pike scrambled upright, flipped his knife over, grabbed it by the blade, and hurled it at me. I snapped up my hands, reached for my magic, and sent out dozens of Ice daggers. My Ice knocked the knife off course, and it clattered harmlessly to the ground.

Too late, I realized the attack had just been a distraction so that Pike could get to what he really wanted: the iron bench near the pagoda.

I didn't think he had the strength, but Pike wrenched the bench free of its foundation and lifted the whole thing off the ground. Then he ripped the metal apart with his bare hands and put it back together.

All over *himself.*

The wrought-iron bands uncurled from their original shapes, crawling up Pike's arms like snakes. And that was only the beginning. His blue eyes glowed, and his magic blasted off him in cold, hard waves. The iron bands began to move, writhing faster than any snake ever could and taking shape over his body.

And I finally realized what he was doing: creating a suit of armor for himself.

In seconds, Pike was encased in metal from head to toe, the pieces of the bench covering most of his body as though he had rolled himself up in the slats.

But he wasn't content with just his new metal shell.

Two snakes of iron curled across his knuckles, forming two solid bands there before sprouting spikes—the same sort of spikes that had been on his mace before he'd blown it to bits. Spikes also appeared along his arms, legs, and chest, but the ones on his hands were the most worrisome. They swayed like two undulating cobras, as though they were waiting for me to get within striking distance.

I grabbed a ceramic knife from against the small of my back, even though I couldn't get close enough to Pike to stab him now. Not without getting a spike through some part of me in return.

Pike laughed at my obvious frustration. "Not exactly what you were expecting, huh, Gin? My source told me that you were clever. Well, thanks to my father, so am I. And now it's time for me to finally avenge him."

He threw his hands forward. A blast of magic rolled off him, and the metal spikes hissed out from his body, straight at my heart.

I did what anyone would do in this situation.

I hit the ground.

The deadly spikes shot out over my head, but I still

landed hard on my injured side. I groaned but forced the throbbing, aching sting of the wound away and got back up onto my hands and knees. Since I was already on the ground, the best thing to do would be to drag Pike down to my level. Driving my knife through his heart, his throat, his eye would do the trick. I wasn't picky. All I had to do was get close enough to hit one of those sweet spots, and he'd be as dead as his father was.

So I drew back my foot, determined to ram it into Pike's knee. But the spikes on his legs zipped out, and I had to roll out of the way to keep from impaling my foot on the moving pieces of metal.

Pike stepped up and slammed his foot into my ribs. More pain erupted from my wound, along with an agonizing spurt of blood. I groaned again but forced myself to keep moving, to keep fighting. I hadn't given up that day in the woods, and I wasn't going to give up now.

Raymond Pike was *not* going to be the death of me.

Since I couldn't kick his legs out from under him, I staggered back up onto my own feet. I tightened my grip on my ceramic knife and darted forward, but once again, his lashing metal spikes drove me back.

And again, and again.

Every time I found a vulnerable spot, an opening, Pike used his magic—and his snakelike spikes—to take away my advantage. The bastard also plunged the sharp tips into my skin, cutting me again and again and bleeding me dry one small slice at a time.

He knocked my knife out of my hand, and I screamed, frustration mixing in with the increasing pain. Pike laughed the whole time—just laughed and laughed. The mocking sound only added to my anger, but there was nothing I could do to shut him up.

Finally, Pike grew tired of letting me try to kill him, and he went on the offensive. He flexed his hands, then curled them into tight fists. The metal ringing his knuckles shifted into two long blades, more like swords than spikes.

He shoved his arms forward, trying to skewer me. If he stabbed me with those blades, I was dead.

Desperate, I flung a ball of Ice magic at him, but he just stood there and took it, letting the Ice hit and then crack off his makeshift metal armor. The iron bands were hard and thick enough to render my Ice power useless. I couldn't even get close enough to freeze him to death with my power, since I'd have to actually touch him to do that, something I couldn't do with all those damn spikes sticking out everywhere.

Pike kept laughing. In that moment, he looked and sounded exactly like his father, eerily so. I would have a whole set of fresh nightmares from this fight.

If I lived through it.

But I kept flinging my Ice magic at Pike, stalling for time to figure out how I could end him. Despite the fact that we were in a garden, Pike was completely wrapped up in his element. So how could I counter that?

I glanced at Lorelei, who was sprawled in the same position as before. No help there.

In between flinging balls of Ice at Pike, I scanned the rest of the garden, searching for some sort of inspiration in the pagoda and trees and flowers and rocks—

And I finally found it, glimmering oh-so-innocently in the moonlight.

Now I just had to set one final spider's trap for Pike.

I raised both hands, sending out another, stronger blast of magic. But instead of directing it at Pike, I aimed low this time. In an instant, three inches of elemental Ice anchored his boots to the ground.

He laughed again, leaned down, and started stabbing through the Ice with the two metal swords sticking out of his fists. "You think that's going to save you? Pathetic."

It didn't have to save me. It just had to buy me some time. Instead of answering, I turned and hobbled deeper into the garden, thumping up into the pagoda and then down the other side and out into one of the themed areas.

A loud *crack!* tore through the air as Pike blasted his way through the Ice around his feet.

Then his singsong voice echoed through the garden. "Oh, Gin . . ." he crooned. "Come out, come out, wherever you are . . ."

I rolled my eyes. He really needed to figure out a new game to play. The creepy psycho stalker act had gotten old a long time ago. I ducked around a patch of bonsai trees and hobbled forward. Besides, Pike shouldn't have been worried about losing track of me.

My blood trail was easy enough to follow in the moonlight.

Behind me, I heard the steady *scuff-scuff-scuff* of Pike's boots through the leaves, along with his crazy laughter. All the while, the metal encasing his body creaked, the iron bands protesting their grotesque shapes. I didn't look back. Instead, I focused all my energy on getting to the exact spot I wanted. I rounded another row of bonsai trees, looked over this part of the garden, and grinned.

Perfect.

I stepped forward, the ground shifting under my feet and making enough *clack-clack-clack*s to let Pike know exactly where I was. But it didn't much matter. I couldn't touch Pike with his metal armor, but he couldn't touch me now either. As I trudged forward, I pressed my hand against my side and fed a small stream of my Ice magic into my stab wound, replicating Lorelei's trick. I winced at the cold, biting sensation, but the wound froze over, stopping the blood loss—for now.

I let go of my power, staggered to a halt, and turned around.

Pike was about thirty feet behind me. He was so confident that he'd already beaten me that he was whistling a jaunty tune. Fool. He hadn't won anything but a cold, quick death, courtesy of the Spider.

He seemed surprised that I was standing upright instead of hiding in the shadows, but it didn't stop him from smirking at me again.

"What's wrong?" Pike crooned. "Too tired to keep running away?"

"Nah. Just catching my second wind."

He laughed again, but then he noticed the grin on my face, and his chuckles cut off into uneasy silence. "What are you up to?"

"Me? Nothing much. You're the one who fucked up, sugar, just by following me over here."

Pike scanned the landscape, looking at the bonsai and cherry trees and the hedge maze beyond them. He was probably searching for my friends, since they would find us sooner or later. But I didn't need them. Not for this.

When Pike didn't see any obvious threats, he started walking toward me again.

Come on, you bastard, I thought. *Come to Gin.*

Pike knew that something was up, but he couldn't figure out what. And in the end, he was too arrogant to really care. Fool.

He left the path behind and stepped into this section of the garden, stopping about five feet away from me. He was still holding on to his magic, the iron wrapped around his body making him look like some horrible abstract sculpture—a nightmarish metal monster come to life.

He was a monster, all right, inside and out, through and through to the core of his black, rotten heart. But unfortunately for him, I was the more clever monster here tonight.

"Tell me," I said, "what did your mysterious contact, the one who's been such a fount of knowledge, say about my magic?"

Pike shrugged. "She said that you were a very strong elemental. One of the most powerful she'd ever seen. Apparently, you killing Mab and then Madeline Monroe only reinforced her opinion. But I told her that I could handle you. After all, metal is everywhere, and that's my element, my specialty."

"Very true. And you are very clever with it. Even I have to admit that your makeshift armor is pretty snazzy."

Pike puffed up at my compliment, but I was about to pop the overinflated balloon of his ego.

"But I'm clever too—clever enough to *win*."

"And why would you think that when I'm so close to killing you?"

I smiled, but it was a cold, heartless expression. "Because you're in *my* killing fields now, bitch."

I spread my arms out wide, gesturing at the landscape around us. The one that seemed so benign, so innocent, so harmless. It was anything but. Because there were different kinds of gardens besides those with pretty trees and flowers.

Like the rock garden we were standing in.

White, gray, and black stones stretched out all around us, arranged in elaborate floral patterns. A small stone platform perched at the edge of the garden, offering visitors a better view of the patterns.

Of course, I'd ruined the pretty designs by hobbling out into the center of them, dripping blood everywhere, and sending loose rocks skittering sideways with my slow, clumsy feet. And now I was going to ruin Raymond Pike with all the lovely stones around me.

He finally realized what I was up to and let out a loud, vicious curse, even as he surged forward to try to stab me to death. But this time, I was the one who waved my hand and stopped him dead in his tracks.

Rocks exploded all around him, as though he were standing in the middle of a minefield.

Despite all the metal wrapped around his body, Pike instinctively ducked. He started forward again, and I sent out another wave of Stone magic, making more of the rocks explode and then using my power to force all the bits and pieces right back at him until he was standing in the middle of a stone tornado. Shrapnel zipped through the air, pelting his body, the jagged fragments small enough to slide through the gaps in his makeshift armor but still plenty sharp enough to tear through his clothes and rip into his skin.

"What's the matter, Ray?" I called out above the din. "Don't like someone using your own tricks against you? It's not a metal box filled with nails, but I think it's pretty damn effective, don't you?"

Pike was too busy ducking shrapnel to answer. But he realized that he couldn't endure my stone bombs forever, and he reached down, peeled one of the spikes off his arm, and threw it at me.

I ducked, but the motion sent a hot rush of pain shooting through my injured side, making me double over and lose my grip on my Stone magic. Pike used the opportunity to surge forward and slam his body into mine.

I landed on my back—hard—my head snapping against the ground. I had to work hard to blink the spots out of my eyes.

Pike loomed over me, that smug smirk stretching across his face again. "Now what are you going to do?"

One of the metal bands around his arms snaked down his hand and latched onto my throat, forming a circle there—one that slowly started to tighten.

More of Pike's metal magic blasted over me, cold, hard, and unyielding, the sensation eerily similar to my own Stone power, even though he was killing me with it.

Pike put his knees on my chest, cutting off even more of my air. I kicked and flailed and thrashed, but he was stronger and heavier, and I couldn't buck him off. My hands clenched, digging through the stone shards that littered the ground like crushed bones. I searched and searched through the stones, but I'd done too good a job, and nothing but fragments remained.

The white, gray, and black spots flickering in front of my eyes grew darker and darker. I was seconds away from blacking out. The end would be quick after that.

Desperate, I threw my hand out to the side, making an Ice dagger, which I slammed into Pike's chest. But the Ice shattered against his metal armor. He chuckled, amused by my pitiful attempts to hurt him, but he relaxed his concentration on his magic, just for a moment. I pushed back with my own power and managed to hook my fingers underneath the metal band around my throat.

"What do you think you're doing?" Pike asked. "That's not going to help you."

I didn't bother answering him. I was too busy coating the metal band with all the Ice magic I could bring to bear.

"Enough of this," Pike growled. "I'll choke you to death with my bare hands if I have to."

He reached forward to do just that, but I let loose with another blast of Ice magic, combining it with my Stone power and focusing them both on breaking the metal ring around my neck. There weren't enough stones left for me to kill Pike, but maybe I didn't have to use my element to end him.

Maybe all I had to use was *his*.

The iron didn't want to bend, much less break, but the extreme temperature swing of my Ice coating it and then being cracked away was enough to get the metal to creak and groan around my neck. With one hand, I slapped away Pike's grasping, choking fingers as best I could. With the other, I kept hold of the band around my neck, freezing and shattering my Ice and Stone magic on it over and over again.

But I couldn't hold off Pike forever, and he managed to dig his thumbs into my windpipe, right above where the metal was wrapped around my throat. He pressed down as hard as he could, putting all his weight into choking me to death.

I kept hammering at the metal band with my magic. That was all I could do.

And finally, *at last*, it was enough.

The iron gave up, and the metal squealed as it finally cracked open and fell away from my throat. A metal shard broke off in my hand and threatened to fly away, but I tightened my grip on it, using my Ice magic to freeze it to the spider rune scar in my palm before it could skitter out of range.

Then I snapped my hand up and slammed the metal into Pike's throat.

I got the angle just right, and the shard sank deep into the tender flesh of his neck above his makeshift armor. I helped it along, driving it through his muscles and tendons, twisting it in as deep as it would go.

Pike choked out a scream and arched back. I managed to bring my knee up and get my foot in between us. Gritting my teeth against the pain in my side, I kicked the bastard off me.

For a moment, I lay there panting, sucking down all the sweet, sweet air I could. Then I rolled over and gingerly pushed myself up into a seated position. The Ice that I'd used to seal my stab wound had cracked away during our fight, and blood streamed out of the deep gash again.

Pike had managed to get back up onto his knees, blood dripping out of his neck and spattering onto the crushed stones.

"Bless your heart. You're going to die in another minute, two tops," I said, my voice hoarse and raspy from where he'd bruised my throat. "Just like your father. His own mace was the end of him. And you? You're choking to death on the precious metal that you love so fucking much."

Pike looked at me, clutching at the broken shard in his windpipe. He didn't try to yank it out, but I must have nicked his carotid artery, given the dark color and copious amounts of blood that were pouring out of the wound. He could leave the metal in there as long as he wanted, and it still wouldn't save him. Nothing would do that now.

But that didn't mean he still wasn't going to try.

Pike sent another surge of magic blasting over his body, and all the iron bands detached themselves, crawled up his arms and chest, and clamped around his throat. He was tightening the metal around his own neck to try to cut off the blood loss.

And it was *working*.

The blood slowed to a trickle, then stopped altogether. Pike gave me an evil look and stretched his hand out toward me, ready for another round.

"Oh, come on," I muttered. "You have *got* to be kidding me."

Pike gurgled some unintelligible curse and dragged himself a little closer to me.

I shook my head, reached for my Ice magic again, and created a dagger with it. Maybe Pike was more zombie than I'd given him credit for. Either way, if I had to kill him again, so be it. And I'd keep right on killing him until he was good and dead.

"Seriously, sugar, just give it up and die already—"

Crack!

A black, bloody hole appeared in the middle of Pike's forehead.

He blinked, and his head lolled to one side, as he looked at his killer. He focused on her a moment, anger and bitterness flashing in his eyes, and then he toppled over to the ground.

I waited, still holding on to my Ice dagger, but Pike didn't move or stir. Blood gushed out of his head wound, mixing with the stone shards, and slowly, the bands of metal around his body relaxed and dropped away, the iron *clank*ing to the ground all around him. That's when I knew that he was finally dead.

I looked to my right.

Lorelei stood at the edge of the rock garden, dusting the shattered remains of her elemental Ice gun off her hands. She walked over to Pike and stared down at him, her mouth a determined slash. Then she grabbed another Ice gun from one of her holsters and shot him in the head again, just to make sure. She tossed the remains of that gun away, grabbed a third one, and repeated the process.

I approved of her thoroughness. She didn't want him coming back to life any more than I did.

Finally, when the sharp retorts of the shots had faded away, Lorelei dusted the Ice off her hands a final time.

"I had him, you know," I rasped.

"Sorry to steal your thunder. But I waited a long time for that."

"And how does it feel?"

Lorelei looked down at Pike's body, her hands clenched into fists, her face tight with grim satisfaction. But slowly, her hands relaxed, and her features smoothed out, her bitter emotions melting into weary relief, mixed with more than a little pain.

"Finished."

She stared at her dead brother a moment longer, then turned and left him behind.

* 31 *

"Gin! Gin! Gin!"

Owen's, Finn's, and Bria's voices rose above the hedge maze, floating through the branches and creating strange echoes in the night.

"Over here!" I rasped, the effort searing my bruised throat.

The three of them ran into the Japanese garden. I was still sitting in the middle of the ruined rocks, too tired to move, so they hurried over to me.

Jo-Jo was with them, and she quickly sank down onto her knees beside me, her clear eyes sweeping over my body and focusing on the gash in my side, which was still leaking blood. She shook her head, making her white-blond curls dance around her head before settling back into place.

"That's a nasty wound," she said. "You're lucky he didn't slice right through your kidney."

"What can I say?" I drawled. "I always seem to bring out the best in people."

Jo-Jo laughed, but relief echoed in her chuckles.

"Anyway, I lived, and he didn't, and that's all that really matters."

Owen threaded his fingers through mine. "I'll second that," he murmured.

I grinned, and he leaned over and kissed me, despite what a bruised, bloody mess I was.

Jo-Jo reached for her Air magic, and the pins-and-needles of her power started tugging at my skin, stitching everything back together that Raymond Pike had torn apart. Owen held my hand while she healed me.

Finn and Bria went over to make sure that Pike was dead. The metal elemental lay where he had fallen in the middle of the shattered stone garden, his sightless eyes glaring up at the moon and stars, as if he were wondering how he had wound up in such a sorry state. He really should have known better. Bloody was how things always ended in Ashland.

Especially when the Spider was involved.

While Jo-Jo worked on me, Xavier entered the garden, along with Silvio and Sophia. Corbin shuffled along behind them, looking even more beaten-up and bedraggled than ever before, urged on by the Ice gun Mallory kept poking into his back. Lorelei walked alongside her grandmother, telling her everything that had happened.

Xavier and Sophia made sure that I was okay, then went over to where Finn and Bria were still examining Pike's body. Jo-Jo finished healing me, but I still felt a little wobbly on my feet, so Owen put his arm around my waist and helped me over to Lorelei. Silvio joined us.

Mallory pushed Corbin down onto his knees in a patch of leaves. A surly expression twisted his face as he glared up at the petite, elderly dwarf.

Lorelei nodded at me as I came to stand beside her. I nodded back.

Then she looked at Corbin. "Start talking. Or I'll let Gin ask the questions. I doubt that she'll ask as nicely as I will."

I arched an eyebrow. "Getting me to do your dirty work again?"

A faint grin curved her lips. "I thought you wouldn't mind in this case."

I pretended to think about it. "You're right. I don't mind. Although you'll have to let me go get one of my silverstone knives. If I use the ceramic ones you gave me, the blade will probably break off while I'm cutting through something vital—"

"All right! All right!" Corbin yelled. "I'll tell you what you want to know. Just keep Blanco away from me."

"Talk. Now," Lorelei hissed. "Before I change my mind."

For the next ten minutes, Corbin spilled his guts about how Pike had approached him in a Southtown bar about a week ago and told him all about his plans to terrorize Lorelei. Naturally, Pike had offered Corbin enough money to make it worth his while to report all of Lorelei's plans and movements back to her half brother. Betrayal, greed, double crosses. It was all pretty standard stuff. But there was one thing that still bothered me.

"And what about Pike's source?" I asked. "The one who told him where to find Lorelei in the first place?"

Corbin gave me another surly look.

I took a step forward.

"I don't know! Okay? I don't know. Pike never told me how he found Lorelei. Just that someone tipped him off. He never told me who it was."

Unfortunately, his panicked words rang with truth. Besides, Pike hadn't struck me as the kind of guy to share important info with his minions.

Lorelei looked at me. "Are you satisfied?"

"I'm good. I didn't really expect him to know anyway."

"All right, then. Questioning's over."

Lorelei snapped up her last elemental Ice gun and shot Corbin in the head.

Crack!

The shot echoed through the gardens, even as Corbin toppled over to the ground—dead.

I stared at Silvio. "And you think *my* managerial style needs improvement."

The vampire shrugged his lean shoulders, then gave Lorelei an admiring look. "Actually, it was a rather quick and effective solution to deal with a spy like Corbin."

"Yeah," Lorelei sniped. "That's me. Quick and effective."

"You're going to have to be," Bria chimed in, walking over and waving her phone. "Someone's reported hearing several gunshots near the gardens. A patrol car is on its way to check things out."

"Which means that we need to move. Clear the vans off the road, get rid of the bodies, and vamoose like this never happened." Finn quirked his eyebrows at me. "Unless you two ladies want to hang around and explain things to the cops?"

I looked at Lorelei, who shook her head.

"No," she said. "I'll have enough headaches finding a replacement for Corbin. Besides, this was a . . . personal matter. I'd rather keep it that way."

Her gaze drifted over to Pike's body, and her mouth twisted. Lorelei might have said that things were finished, but they weren't. Not for her. Not now, maybe not ever. Something I could relate to all too well. Perhaps we should start our own sleep-deprivation club. Nightmares Anonymous of Ashland. Heh.

Finn nodded. "All righty, then. Xavier, Bria, Owen, Silvio. You're with me." He went over, grabbed Sophia's hand, and gave her a low, gallant bow. "Naturally, I will leave the bodies to your discretion, my lady."

Finn smooched a kiss to Sophia's hand, making her laugh, reach out, and rumple his hair. He grinned, then hurried after the others. Sophia drew a tape measure out of the pocket of her black coveralls, bent down, and measured Corbin's body, before going over and doing the same thing to Pike's. Jo-Jo trailed behind her sister, along with Mallory.

Lorelei started to follow her grandmother, but I called out to her.

"One more thing."

"What?"

I stabbed my finger toward Pike. "There aren't any more like him around, are there? No more Pike brothers or sisters or aunts or uncles? Nobody who's going to wonder what happened to cousin Ray-Ray and come to Ashland looking for revenge? Because I don't need to start another blood feud. I have enough problems right now."

My voice was light, but it was a legitimate concern. My past experience with Madeline had taught me that you never knew when another relative of a dead enemy was going to pop up, come to town, and try to screw you over every which way she could.

Lorelei chuckled, then shook her head. "It was just Raymond. Trust me. This is done. You don't have to worry about anyone else."

"Good," I drawled. "One near-death experience a month is plenty for me."

Lorelei laughed again, but the sound faded away all too quickly. She stared at me, emotions flashing in her eyes. After a moment, she nodded at me. I nodded back.

I didn't know if we would ever truly be friends, but we weren't enemies anymore. And that made me happier than I'd thought it would.

Lorelei and I walked over to where Sophia was still crouched down, measuring Pike's body. In the distance, a police siren wailed. Bria and Xavier would stall the cops as long as they could, but Finn was right. We needed to leave.

"Sophia?" I asked. "Are you going to haul the bodies back to the vans?"

"Nah."

"Then what are you going to do with them?" Lorelei asked.

The Goth dwarf glanced over at Corbin, then back

down at Pike. A grin split her face, and her black eyes brightened. Sophia rasped out a single word.

"Fertilizer."

Sophia found a shovel in one of the maintenance sheds and quickly buried Pike and Corbin close to the pagoda. She'd just finished when voices started drifting through the hedge maze, indicating that the cops were here. Silvio had already texted me to say that Finn and the others had moved the vans and sedans off the road and out of sight. Once Sophia was done, the rest of us left the garden and went our separate ways.

The next day, life was pretty much back to normal—or as normal and nonviolent as it ever truly got in Ashland.

And it stayed that way over the next week. A story ran in the newspaper about a mysterious disturbance at the botanical gardens and someone vandalizing one of the rock gardens, but the cops attributed it to mischief-making kids, and that was the extent of the news coverage.

No one seemed to be missing Raymond Pike. Silvio scoured the news outlets in West Virginia, but there wasn't so much as a whisper about Pike disappearing. It looked like Lorelei was right, and he was the end of the line. I hoped so. Although I kept thinking about what he'd said to me in the garden, about his source being a coldhearted woman. Something about his specific words chimed a warning bell in the back of my mind, although I couldn't figure out why.

"Well, well, well," Finn drawled. "Lookie here on the society page. Mallory has made a sizable donation to the botanical gardens to help clean up all the recent vandalism, along with another anonymous donor." He snapped his newspaper down and stared over the top of the pages at me, his green eyes sharp and accusing. "You wouldn't happen to know who that is, would you, Gin?"

"I thought the gardens might need some more fertilizer." I paused. "Other than what Sophia provided."

Finn sighed. "First you offer that bounty for Pike's whereabouts. Then you pay those giants to double-cross him. And now you're handing out charitable donations. If you keep giving away our money at this rate, there won't be any of it left!"

"What's this 'our money' nonsense? It's *my* money. I'm the one who earned it. I'm the one who bled for it."

Finn ignored me and elbowed Silvio in the side. "Tell her I'm right. After all, she has to pay your salary too."

The vampire shook his head. "Oh, I don't think there's any need to worry about Gin's finances. Not given how healthy business has been at the restaurant over the past few weeks. Just look at everyone piled in here today."

The restaurant was as crowded as ever. Most of the folks were just here to chow down on a hot plate of barbecue, but more than a few underworld types were in the mix too. Apparently, eating at the Pork Pit was one of the ways to show your support for me, the new head honcho. At least that's what Silvio kept claiming. Maybe I should start selling T-shirts with my spider rune and the words *Team Gin* on them. Heh.

Finn finished his lunch and left to go meet some new client. Thirty minutes later, the bell over the front door chimed, announcing the arrival of two customers I could have done without: Dimitri Barkov and Luiz Ramos.

I still hadn't settled their business dispute, and the two of them were getting antsy. Silvio had invited them to come to the Pork Pit so we could decide things once and for all.

It was three o'clock on the dot when they stepped up to the front door, both trying to enter at the same time. They ended up getting stuck in a logjam, glaring at each other, neither one willing to give an inch, not even so they could get inside. I grinned. This might be more amusing than I'd thought.

Sophia, who was wiping down one of the tables, went over, grabbed hold of their arms, and yanked them through the doorway. Dimitri and Luiz both stumbled forward before righting themselves. They started to glare at Sophia, but she crossed her arms over the black figure of Death that decorated her bright pink T-shirt and stared them down, daring them to give her a dirty look.

Dimitri and Luiz both swallowed and turned away. They were smart enough not to want to mess with the Goth dwarf, especially when she was eyeing their heads like she wanted to crack them together and leave them both addle-brained puddles on the floor.

The two mobsters smoothed down their ties and headed over to where I was sitting behind the cash register, reading *For Your Eyes Only* by Ian Fleming for my spy literature course over at Ashland Community College.

"Fellas," I drawled. "What's up?"

"It's time you made a decision, Blanco," Dimitri said, snapping up to his full height. The motion made the black toupee perched on top of his head wobble dangerously, as though it was about to fall off.

"Yeah," Luiz chimed in. "You've kept us waiting long enough. If Mab were still running things—"

"If Mab were still running things, she would have killed you both and taken the coin laundries for herself," I drawled again. "Actually, now that I think about it, that option is looking better and better all the time. Maybe then I could enjoy some peace and quiet, instead of having the two of you constantly whining at me."

Their cheeks flushed with anger, but they bit back their harsh words.

"Just tell us what you've decided," Dimitri ground out through clenched teeth. "Please."

I set the book aside and laced my fingers together. "I've considered both your proposals. And I've decided that neither one of you is getting the laundries."

Their mouths dropped open.

"What?" Luiz screeched, drawing the attention of the other customers.

I arched my eyebrows, and he realized his mistake. His voice was quieter but still full of anger as he spoke again.

"You can't do that!" he hissed.

"Sure I can. After all, you two geniuses came to me to mediate your little dispute," I said. "Besides, if you really wanted the coin laundries, then you should have made the winning bid."

Dimitri's eyes narrowed. "Someone outbid us for the laundries? Who?"

I pointed at a woman finishing her lunch at the far end of the counter. "Her."

Jade Jamison dabbed at her lips with a white paper napkin, then gave Dimitri and Luiz a cheery wave and a saucy wink before going back to her cheeseburger, onion rings, and strawberry milkshake.

"Her? But all she does is run hookers and hire out people to clean houses!" Dimitri sputtered. "In the *suburbs*!"

The way he said *suburbs*, you would have thought it was one of the worst places in all of Ashland. He might have been right about that.

"True," I said. "But she also happened to top both your bids by ten percent. So Lorelei has decided to sell the coin laundries to her. It's just business. I told Lorelei that you would understand. Right?"

Dimitri and Luiz looked at me, then at each other, the wheels spinning in their hamster brains. The idiots were actually thinking about teaming up to try to take me down again.

So I reached over, picked up a wayward butter knife lying on the counter, and started twirling it around and around in my hand, making sure that the utensil caught the light and reflected it back into their faces.

"Right?" I asked a second time, my voice much colder than before.

Luiz was the first to back down. "Oh, yeah," he said, holding his hands up and backing away from the cash register. "Like you said, it's just business. A winning bid is a winning bid. Right, Dimitri?"

The Russian was far more reluctant, but a few more spins of the butter knife convinced him. "Yeah. Right."

That didn't stop them from giving me sour looks as they whirled around, huffed and puffed their way out of the storefront, and skedaddled down the street and out of sight. They were pissed—pissed enough to make another run at me sometime soon—but I'd be ready for them.

And next time, I wouldn't be as nice as I had been today.

I tossed the butter knife into a bin of dirty dishes.

Jade Jamison finished her meal, then slid off her stool and sidled over to me. "Thanks again for backing my play for the laundries. I appreciate it. And thank Lorelei for me too."

"You're the one with a million bucks to spend. If you want to invest in some coin laundries, who am I to keep a rising entrepreneur down?"

Jade grinned. She slapped a hundred-dollar bill on the counter, refused any change, then sashayed out of the restaurant. I put the extra money in the tip jar for the staff to split. I liked her style.

Silvio watched Jade leave, then turned back to me. "Finally," he murmured. "I can mark *something* off your to-do list."

"My to-do what now?"

He turned his tablet around to me, scrolling through screen after screen after screen. "You've got meetings the rest of the week. I hope you didn't think that Dimitri and Luiz were the only bosses who wanted some of your time and attention."

My eyes glazed over just looking at all the lists on his tablet. "But why so many of them? And why now? A week ago, everyone was dragging their heels about actually involving me in any of their dealings."

"They heard what you did for Lorelei."

I frowned. "What do they think I did for her? We didn't exactly broadcast our garden party with Pike."

"I might have casually spread the word around that Pike was trying to muscle in on some of Lorelei's territory—and everyone else's in Ashland."

"And?"

A sly grin creased his features. "And that you took care of it as the big boss."

I groaned. "So now what? I'm a hero to the underworld too?"

Silvio's grin widened. "Something like that. After all, good public relations is the first step to winning hearts and minds . . . and loyalty."

I groaned louder. Silvio chuckled, enjoying my misery. I shot him a dark look, but that only made him chuckle harder. But he quickly went back to work. He was too much of a professional, and he had too much to do, according to him, to keep harping on how I just kept digging myself in deeper and deeper with the Ashland underworld.

While Silvio typed away on his tablet, setting up meetings between the other bosses and me, I looked out over the restaurant, scanning the crush of customers as they came and went and chowed down on their barbecue.

Raymond Pike might be dead, but he'd left a loose thread behind: whoever had given him all that information about me, Lorelei, and everything else going on in Ashland.

I wondered if Pike's friend, the one who'd known so much about me, was worried that she hadn't heard from him in a week now. Or maybe she'd already realized that he wasn't ever coming back.

This person seemed to be connected to the Ashland grapevine, so it wasn't out of the realm of possibility that she had heard the whispers about me dealing with Pike. I wondered if she had spies in town—spies who could be in my restaurant at this very second.

But it didn't much matter. She wasn't going to make an appearance today, and I didn't have any way to start tracking her down, not a name, not a rune, nothing but Pike's smug mentions of how powerful she was. So she would stay in the shadows—for now.

Whoever the mystery woman was, if she wanted to come to Ashland and take me on, she was more than welcome to step into my parlor.

Then I would show her what coldhearted *really* looked like.

❊ 32 ❊

Despite Silvio's protests that we should squeeze in at least one more meeting, I departed work early, leaving the restaurant in Sophia's and Catalina's capable hands. But I didn't go home. Instead, I went to the other place I'd been visiting a lot recently.

The cemetery.

Most people would have thought it morbid, but I actually enjoyed driving out to Blue Ridge Cemetery, walking the winding paths, and admiring the tombstones. It was calm and quiet and just about the only place where I could be by myself these days, without worrying about someone trying to kill me.

So I parked my car, got out, and meandered along the paths, staring at the fading flowers, stuffed animals, and other ornaments that marked the tombstones of loved ones. A faint breeze gusted through the cemetery, making the last of the autumn leaves spiral down to the ground, covering up the green grass like jagged red, orange, and yellow jewels. It was a pretty scene, and I breathed in, enjoying the crisp chill in the air. It wouldn't be long now before fall slipped into winter and flakes of snow replaced the leaves. I just wondered how many new enemies the changing season would bring with it.

I headed over to Fletcher's grave and did a careful scan of the cemetery, just to be sure that my peace and quiet wouldn't be disturbed by some idiot who thought he was tougher and stronger than I was. Most of the time, the cemetery was deserted, especially this late in the day, when the sun was setting over the mountains and the landscape would soon be cloaked in darkness.

But I wasn't alone today. Another figure stood at a grave partway up the hill.

Lorelei.

She was about halfway between my Gin Blanco tombstone and the one that marked the final resting place of Genevieve Snow, my childhood self. That was where her mother's grave was. I didn't know how Mallory had managed it, but she'd gotten Lily Rose buried here all those years ago.

Lorelei looked at me, waved, and turned back to the tombstone. I waved back, then went about my own business. Even though we'd arranged to meet here, away from prying eyes, neither one of us wanted to talk right now. We were both too busy thinking about the ghosts of our past and how they'd come back to haunt us over the past several days.

I crouched down next to Fletcher's gravesite, setting a small jar of his barbecue sauce on top of the tombstone.

I'd made it fresh earlier in the day, and it was my own little way of honoring him. Every time I came back, the jar that I'd left the time before was gone. I didn't know what happened to all that barbecue sauce, and I didn't really want to. Maybe it was stupid, but I liked to think that it went to Fletcher, wherever he was.

I stayed there for several minutes, just soaking up the quiet and the sense that Fletcher was watching over me. Then I stood and looked up the hill. Lorelei must have sensed me staring, because she turned around again. She laid a bouquet of white lilies and red roses on top of her mother's grave, then stuck her hands into the pockets of her blue leather jacket and walked down the hill toward me.

We met in the middle.

"Lorelei."

"Gin."

We looked at each other, then at the graves we'd come to visit. Lorelei grinned when she spotted the jar sitting on top of Fletcher's tombstone, but she didn't comment on it.

I didn't ask Lorelei how she was doing, but she didn't seem as tense as before and certainly not as hostile toward me. Good. I needed more allies in the underworld, and I wanted her to be one of them. But time would tell whether that would actually happen.

"I'm glad you agreed to meet me here," Lorelei said.

"I like it here. It's a good place to think."

"Yeah." She stared toward her mother's tombstone a moment longer, then focused on me again. "I have some information for you."

"What sort of information?"

Lorelei hesitated, then reached into the pocket of her jacket and drew out a folded piece of paper. "I found this among Raymond's effects. Your sister, Bria, brought them to me yesterday."

"I know. She told me that she and Xavier cleaned out Pike's penthouse."

Management at the Peach Blossom had finally realized that he wasn't coming back and had called the cops. Bria had arranged it so that she and Xavier caught the case and could bury it just like we had buried Pike.

"Bria thought that I might want his stuff, and I went through everything, just in case he had set something else in motion that I didn't know about. Some plan to be executed in case he disappeared or died or both."

Worry flooded through me. "Had he?"

She shook her head. "Not that I've been able to uncover. Seems he was too confident that he would be able to kill me. But he'd been writing to someone, and they had sent him a letter back. I thought it was a little weird, since most folks just text or email now. But Raymond liked to be old-fashioned that way, just like our father. I remember him writing letters too."

Lorelei handed me the folded sheet of paper. I opened it and read the short note:

Mr. Pike,
    Glad to hear that things are progressing on schedule in Ashland. Please keep me apprised of your situation. Happy hunting.

No signature was scrawled across the paper, but a rune had been stamped onto the bottom of the letter: a heart made of jagged icicles fitted together like the pieces of a jigsaw puzzle.

The letter said nothing important, nothing that gave me any clue about who had written it, although I was willing to bet that it was the woman Pike had referred to in the gardens. But a cold chill crawled up my spine all the same, as though someone had just walked over one of my graves. Because I'd seen that rune before, and I knew exactly where.

On a file in Fletcher's office.

One of the hidden folders that I'd pulled out from a trick drawer in the bottom of his desk. The only one that had been secreted away in that particular spot, as if he hadn't wanted anyone to find it, not even me. Ever.

Lorelei stared at me. "You know something about it."

I shook my head. "Not exactly. But the rune . . . it might be a lead. I have a feeling that I'll find out more about it sooner or later."

Definitely sooner, since Fletcher had kept a file on this person, whoever she was.

I held up the letter. "Can I keep this?"

"Sure. It's a copy."

I tucked it into my back jeans pocket. "Thanks. And I have something for you too."

I reached into another pocket and held out my hand. A red-rose-and-thorn pin sparkled in the center of my palm, right on top of my spider rune scar.

Lorelei blinked. She recognized the pin as one she'd been wearing at the cabin all those years ago. Her hand trembled a bit as she reached out, carefully plucked the pin out of my hand, and traced her fingers over it. The motions made the diamonds in her rose-and-thorn rune ring glimmer. The ring matched the pin almost exactly.

"Where did you get this?" she whispered, running her fingers over it. "I thought I'd lost them all in the woods that day."

"Apparently, Fletcher found one of them. It was in his house. I thought you might like it back."

Her lips curved up, but her smile was sad. "My mother gave me a set of these pins for my fourteenth birthday, a few weeks before she died. That's why I chose it as my rune."

Tears glistened in her eyes, but she blinked them back and slid the pin through the bottom of her braid, admiring the way it shimmered in the fading sunlight.

When she looked at me again, her eyes were clear. Another gust of wind swept through the cemetery, stirring up the leaves and swirling them through the air between us.

"You know, I never did thank you for what you did for me that day in the woods," Lorelei said. "And everything that you've done over the past several days, including this."

I shrugged. "It's what I do. It's what Fletcher taught me to do, even if I didn't realize it way back then."

She smiled, her expression warmer than I'd ever seen it before. "Well, I'm glad that he did."

I smiled back at her. "Yeah. Me too."

* * *

Lorelei and I said our good-byes, and then I got into my car and drove home to Fletcher's house. It was full-on dark now, but instead of taking a shower and going to bed, I grabbed a glass and a bottle of gin from the kitchen. I had a feeling I was going to need them. Then I headed back to the old man's office, flipped on the light, put down the glass and the bottle, and grabbed the hidden file, the one with the icicle heart rune on it.

I laid the file flat on Fletcher's desk, staring at the rune he'd drawn on the tab. Maybe it was my imagination, but the rune seemed darker than the ones on the other files, as if he'd sat in this very seat and traced and retraced it onto the folder. Curiouser and curiouser. What bothered him about this person more than all the other dangerous people he'd spied on over the years?

Time to find out.

I drew in a breath and opened the file, expecting . . . well, I wasn't quite sure what I was expecting. Maybe another blast from the past, like Raymond Pike. Somebody related to some job Fletcher and I had done way back when. But it was just like any other file in the office. A detached recitation of facts about a certain individual.

I didn't see her name listed anywhere right off the bat, so I leaned back in the chair and started reading through all the information.

She was a wealthy Ice elemental from a prominent, old-money family in Ashland—the Shaws. I frowned. I'd never heard of that family before, and I didn't remember

Fletcher ever mentioning them. That was strange—very strange—especially since Fletcher knew everyone who was anyone in Ashland, no matter how legitimate or crooked they were.

So I kept going through the file, reading and absorbing all the information. And there was a lot of it. Whoever the Ice elemental was, Fletcher had spent more time monitoring her than anyone else, even Mab. I wondered what it was about her that had interested, and concerned, him so much.

In many ways, she was exactly like Mab—wealthy, powerful, ruthless—but apparently without the Fire elemental's driving need to make everyone aware of exactly how deadly she was.

This woman . . . she was like *me*.

Or, at least, how I used to be before I'd inadvertently outed myself as the Spider by killing Mab. Someone who spent her time in the shadows and struck out at her enemies before they even realized what was happening. That was enough to make a cold ball of worry form in the pit of my stomach.

Then I came to the final thing in the file, a picture.

She looked to be in her fifties, a timeless beauty with blond hair and blue eyes that were so pale they bordered on gray. Fletcher must have been doing surveillance on her, because the photograph looked to have been taken from quite a distance, as though he hadn't wanted to risk getting any closer to her. But she wasn't happy with the person she was staring at. Her mouth was set in a firm frown, and her eyes almost seemed to be glowing, as though she were getting ready to reach for her Ice magic and use it to freeze the person she was sitting with.

I stared at the photo, then slowly turned it over, knowing—or at least hoping—that something would be written on the back.

Oh, there was something written on the back, all right. Just a few sentences that took me only a few seconds to read, but they were more shocking than anything I'd found in Fletcher's office—*ever*.

Once again, I sucked in a breath. Because once again, I'd been completely wrong. I'd thought that Raymond Pike had been after me when Lorelei was his real target all along. And once again, I'd thought that whoever had sent him to Ashland had been targeting me.

But this wasn't about me at all.

It was about *Finn*.

With shaking hands, I read the note again. And then again, just to be sure that I wasn't dreaming the words. But I wasn't, even though I really wished that I was.

Her name is Deirdre Shaw, Fletcher's handwriting spelled out. *She is a very powerful Ice elemental who will do whatever it takes to get what she wants. She is not to be trusted, under any circumstances.*

And she is Finn's mother.

That was it—that was all the note said—but it was more than enough to rock my world to its foundation.

I sat back in my seat, my eyes wide, staring at the photo. Fletcher had always told me that he was a widower, that his wife died when Finn was just a baby. Jo-Jo, Sophia, Finn—none of them had ever mentioned Fletcher's supposed wife, Finn's mother, except in passing, and

I'd always assumed that it was because she'd died many years ago.

But according to Fletcher's file, she was very much alive. And, from what Raymond Pike had said, she was extremely interested in the goings-on in Ashland. Deirdre Shaw . . . she must have been the person Lorelei had done business with. She must have somehow recognized Lorelei during their dealings together and then sicced Pike on her. But why? How would Pike killing Lorelei benefit her? What was she up to?

And how much was it going to affect Finn?

The questions swirled around and around in my mind, but there were no answers, and certainly nothing that would help me figure out how to tell Finn about this. Or even *if* I should tell him about this.

I would always be haunted—and somewhat trapped— by my past, both as Genevieve Snow and as the Spider. The people I'd killed, the ones who'd tried to kill me, and all the hurt, damage, and fallout from that. I didn't want that for Finn. *Any* of it. And I especially didn't want him to be dragged down some dark, ugly road involving his own mother. It would only end in heartache for him.

But once again, Fletcher had left me with a mystery to solve and a dangerous enemy to deal with. The old man wasn't around anymore to look out for Finn, but I was. And I would protect my foster brother from this as long and as best as I could.

I sat back in my chair, considering my options. Then I reached out, poured myself a glass of gin, and downed the whole thing in one gulp. The liquor slid down my throat, then flared to life, burning in the pit of my stomach. But it was nothing compared with the determination roaring through me to get to the bottom of this.

I pulled the file on Deirdre Shaw closer, and I read through the information again.

The Spider had work to do—and secrets to dig up.

Turn the page for a sneak peek at the
next book in the Elemental Assassin series

bitter bite

by Jennifer Estep

Coming soon from Pocket Books

Digging up a grave was hard, dirty work.

Good thing that hard, dirty work was one of my specialties. Although this was a bit of a role reversal. As the assassin the Spider, I'm usually putting people into graves instead of uncovering them.

But here I was in Blue Ridge Cemetery, just after ten o'clock on this cold November night. Flurries drifted down from the clouds that blanketed the sky, the small flakes dancing on the gusty breeze like delicate, crystalline fairies. Every once in a while, the wind would whip up into a howling frenzy, pelting me in the back with swarms of snow and spattering the icy flakes against my chilled cheeks.

I ignored the latest wave of flurries stinging my face and continued digging, just like I'd been doing for the last hour. The only good thing about driving the shovel into the frozen earth was that the repetitive motions of scooping out the dirt and tossing it onto a pile kept me warm and limber, instead of cold and stiff like the tombstones surrounding me.

Despite the snow, I still had plenty of light to see by, thanks to the old-fashioned iron streetlamps spaced along the access roads throughout the cemetery. One of the lamps stood about twenty feet away from where I was digging, its golden glow highlighting the grave marker in front of me, making the carved name stand out like black blood against the gray stone.

Deirdre Shaw.

The mother of my foster brother, Finnegan Lane. An Ice elemental. And a potentially dangerous enemy.

A week ago, I'd found a file that Fletcher Lane—Finn's dad, and my assassin mentor—had hidden in his office. A file that claimed that Deirdre was powerful, deceitful, and treacherous—and not nearly as dead as everyone thought she was. So I'd come here tonight to find out whether she was truly six feet under. I was hoping she was dead and rotting in her grave, but I wasn't willing to bet on it.

Too many things from my own past had come back to haunt me for me to leave something this important to chance.

Thunk.

My shovel hit something hard and metal. I stopped and breathed in, hoping to smell the stench of decades-old decay. But the cold, crisp scent of the snow mixed with the rich, dark earth, creating a pleasant perfume. No decay, no death, and most likely, no body.

I quickly cleared off the rest of the dirt, revealing the top of the casket. A rune had been carved into the lid—

jagged icicles fitted together to form a heart. My stomach knotted up with tension. Fletcher had inked that same rune onto Deirdre Shaw's file. This was definitely the right grave.

I was already standing in the pit that I'd dug, and I scraped away a few more chunks of earth so that I could crouch down beside the top half of the casket. The metal lid was locked, but that was easy enough to fix. I set down my shovel, pulled off my black gloves and held up my hands, and reached for my Ice magic. The matching scars embedded deep in my palms—each one a small circle surrounded by eight thin rays—pulsed with the cold, silver light of my power. My spider runes, the symbols for patience.

When I had generated enough magic, I reached down, wrapped my hands around the casket lid locks, and blasted them with my Ice power. After coating the locks with two inches of elemental Ice, I sent out another surge of power, cracking away the cold crystals. At the same time, I reached for my Stone magic, hardening my skin. Under my magical assault, the locks shattered, and my Stone-hardened skin kept the flying bits of metal from cutting my hands. I dusted away the remains of the locks and the elemental Ice, took hold of the casket lid, dug my feet into the dirt, and lifted it.

The lid was heavier than I'd thought it would be, and the metal didn't want to open, not after all the years spent peacefully resting in the ground. It creaked and groaned in protest, but I managed to shove the lid up a couple of inches. I grabbed my shovel and slid it into the small opening I'd created, using it as a lever to lift up the lid the rest of the way.

Dirt rained down all around me, mixing with the snowflakes, and I wrinkled my nose to hold back a sneeze. I wedged the length of the shovel in between the lid and the edge of the casket, so that it would stay open. Then I wiped the sweat off my forehead, put my hands on my knees to catch my breath, and looked down.

Just as I expected, snow-white silk lined the inside of the casket, with a small square matching pillow positioned at the very top, where a person's head would rest. But something decidedly unexpected was situated next to the pillow, nestled in the middle of the pristine fabric.

A box.

It was about the size of a small suitcase and made out of silverstone, a sturdy metal that also had the unique property of absorbing and storing magic. The box's gray surface gleamed like a freshly minted coin, and it looked as clean and untouched as the rest of the white silk.

I frowned. I'd expected the casket to be completely empty. Or for there to be a decaying body inside; if I had been extremely lucky, Deirdre Shaw would have been in there, dead after all.

So why was there a box in it instead? And who had put it here?

I kept staring at the box, more and more knots forming in the pit of my stomach and then slowly tightening together. I'd recently gone up against Raymond Pike, a metal elemental who had enjoyed planting bombs before I'd helped plant him in some botanical gardens. Raymond had received a letter with Deirdre Shaw's rune stamped on it, and had bragged that the two of them were business associates—and that she was the most coldhearted person he'd ever met. I wondered if he'd booby-trapped the box in Deirdre's casket as some sort of favor to her, to blow up anyone who might come investigate whether she was truly dead.

So I reached out, using my Stone magic to listen to all the rocks in the ground around the casket. But the rocks only grumbled about the cold, the snow, and how I'd disturbed their final resting place. No other emotional vibrations resonated through them, which meant that no one had been near the casket in years.

I crouched down and brushed away the dirt that had fallen on top of the box when I opened the casket lid. No magic emanated from the silverstone box, although a rune had been carved into the top of it—the same small circle and eight thin rays that were branded into both of my palms.

My spider rune.

"Fletcher," I whispered, my breath frosting the air.

The old man had planted the box here for me to find. No doubt about it. He was the only one who seemed to know that Deirdre Shaw wasn't actually dead. More important, Fletcher had known *me*. He had realized that if Deirdre ever made an appearance back in Ashland, back in Finn's life, I would find his file on her and come to her grave to determine whether she was dead and buried.

Once again the old man had left me with clues to find from beyond his own grave, which was located a hundred feet away. For whatever reason, he and Deirdre hadn't been buried side by side. Something I hadn't really thought too much about until just tonight. I wondered why Fletcher hadn't buried the supposedly dead mother of his son next to his own cemetery plot. Something must have happened between him and Deirdre—something bad.

I opened up the bottom half of the casket and ran my fingers all around the silk, just in case something else had been left behind. But there was nothing else. So I hooked my hands under the box and lifted it out of its silken cocoon. It was surprisingly heavy, as though Fletcher had packed it full of information. The weight made me even more curious about what might be inside—

"Did you hear something, Don?"

I froze, hoping that I'd only imagined the high, feminine voice.

"Yep, I sure did, Ethel," a deeper, masculine voice answered back.

No such luck.

Still holding the box, I stood on my tiptoes and peered over the lip of the grave. A man and a woman stood about forty feet away, both of them dwarves, given their five-foot heights and stocky, muscular frames. I hadn't heard a car roll into the cemetery, so the two of them must have parked somewhere nearby and walked in like I had. They were both bundled up in black clothes and weren't carrying flashlights, which meant that they didn't want to be seen. Shovels were propped up on their shoulders, the metal scoops shimmering like liquid silver underneath the glow of the streetlamps. There was only one reason for the two of them to be skulking around the cemetery this late at night.

My mouth twisted with disgust. Grave robbers. One of the lowest forms of scum, even among the plethora of criminals who called Ashland home.

They must have sensed my stare, or perhaps noticed the massive pile of dirt that I'd dug up, because they both turned and looked right at me.

"Hey!" the woman, Ethel, called out. "Someone else is here!"

The two dwarves raced in my direction. I cursed, put the box on the ground next to the tombstone, dug my fingers into the grass, and scrambled up and out of the grave. I'd just staggered to my feet when the two dwarves stopped in front of me, their shovels now held out in front of them like lances.

Ethel glared at me, her blue eyes narrowing to slits. "What do you think you're doing here? This here is *our* cemetery. Nobody else's."

"Aw, now, don't be like that, Ethel," her companion said. "Look on the bright side. At least she did the hard work of digging up this grave for us already. Looks like she found something good too."

He stabbed his shovel at the silverstone box. My hands tightened into fists. No way were they getting their grubby hands on that. Not when it might hold more clues about Deirdre Shaw—where she might be, and why everyone thought that she was dead, including Finn, her own son.

Don grinned, his bright red nose and bushy white beard making him look like Santa Claus. With her rosy cheeks and short, curly white hair, Ethel was the perfect counterpart. If Santa and Mrs. Claus were low-down, no-good grave robbers.

"Why, we should thank her, Ethel," Don drawled. "Before we kill her, of course."

Ethel nodded. "You're right, hon. You always are."

The two dwarves tightened their grips on their shovels and stepped toward me, but I held my ground, my gray eyes as cold and hard as the snow-dusted tombstones.

"Before the two of you do something you won't live to regret, you should know that that box is *mine*," I said. "Walk away now, don't come back, and I'll forget that I ever saw you here tonight."

"And who do you think you are, giving us orders?" Ethel snapped.

"Gin Blanco. That's who."

I didn't say my name to brag. Not really. But I was the head of the Ashland underworld now, which meant that they should know exactly who I was—and especially what I was capable of doing to them.

Ethel rolled her eyes. "You must really be desperate to claim to be *her*. Then again, dead women will say anything to keep on breathing, won't they, Don?"

The other dwarf nodded. "Yep."

I ground my teeth together. For some reason, low-life criminals had no trouble tracking me down at the Pork Pit, my barbecue restaurant, and no qualms whatsoever about trying to kill me there. But whenever I was away from the restaurant, got into a bad situation, and tried to warn people about who I really was, nobody ever seemed to believe me. Irony's way of screwing me over time and time again, and laughing at me all the while.

"Besides," Don continued, "even if you really were Gin Blanco, it wouldn't matter. Everyone knows that she's the big boss in name only. It won't be long until someone kills her and takes her place."

I had to give it to him: he was right. The other bosses were still plotting against me, and many of the city's criminals were waiting to see how my underworld reign played out—or how short-lived it might be—before they officially took sides. Still, it was kind of sad when even the local grave robbers didn't respect you.

I opened my mouth to tell them what idiots they were being, but Don kept on talking.

"Enough chitchat. It's freezing out here, and we need to get to work, which means that your time is up. But since you found that box for us, I'll offer you a deal. Turn around, and I'll whack you upside the back of the head." Don swung his shovel in a vicious arc. "You won't even know what hit you. I'll even plant you in that grave, so you get some kind of proper burial."

I palmed the silverstone knife hidden up my right sleeve and flashed it at them. "As charming as your offer is, I'm going to have to decline."

Ethel glared at me. "So that's how it is, then?"

"That's how it *always* is with me."

The two dwarves looked at each other, then raised their shovels and charged at me. I reached for my Stone magic, hardening my body again, then surged forward to meet them.

I sidestepped Ethel and got close enough to Don to slice my blade across his chest, but he was wearing so many puffy layers that it was like cutting into a marshmallow. I slashed through his down vest, and tiny white feathers exploded in my face, momentarily blinding me and making me sneeze. Don yelped in surprise and staggered back. I sneezed again and went after him—

Whack!

A shovel slammed into my shoulder, spinning me around. But since I was still holding on to my Stone magic, the shovel bounced off my body instead of cracking all the bones in my arm.

I blinked away the last of the feathers to find Ethel glaring at me again.

"Look at that gray glow to her eyes," she huffed. "She's a Stone elemental. We'll have to beat her to death to put her down for good."

Don brightened, his blue eyes twinkling in his face and adding to the Santa Claus illusion. "Why, it'll be just like our honeymoon all over again," he crooned. "Remember robbing that cemetery up in Cloudburst Falls, honey?"

The couple smiled and stared dreamily into each other's eyes for a moment before coming at me again. Well, at least they still did things together.

Instead of trying to saw through all their winter clothes and their tough muscles underneath, I reached for my magic, raised my hand, and sent a spray of Ice daggers shooting out at the two of them. Ethel threw herself down onto the ground, ducking out of the way of my chilly blast, but Don wasn't so smart, and several long, sharp bits of Ice punched into his chest. Given how strong dwarves were, he grunted, more surprised than seriously injured, but he did lose his grip on his shovel, which tumbled to the ground.

I dropped my knife, darted forward, and snatched up his shovel, since it was the better weapon in this instance. Then I drew back my arms and slammed the shovel into his head as hard as I could, as though his skull was a baseball that I was trying to hit way out past center field.

Thwack.

Don stared at me, wobbling on his feet, his eyes spinning around and around in their sockets. His dwarven musculature might be exceptionally tough and thick, but a cold, metal shovel upside the head was more than enough to put a dent in that bowling ball of a skull. Still, it was just a dent, and he didn't go down, so I hit him again.

Thwack.

And then again and again, until the bones in his skull and face cracked, and blood started gushing down his head, face, and neck. A glassy sheen coated Don's eyes, and he toppled over, more and more of his blood soaking into the frozen ground.

"Don!" Ethel wailed, realizing that he wasn't ever going to get back up. "Don!"

She tightened her grip on her shovel, scrambled back up onto her feet, and charged at me again. "You bitch!" she screamed. "I'll kill you for this!"

Ethel stopped right in front of me and raised her shovel over her head, trying to build up enough momentum to smash through my Stone magic with one deathblow. But in doing so, she left herself completely open. It was easy enough for me to palm another knife, surge forward, and bury the blade in her throat.

Ethel's eyes bulged wide, and blood bubbled up out of her lips. She coughed, the warm drops of her blood stinging my cheeks like the snowflakes had earlier. I yanked my knife out of her throat, doing even more damage, but Ethel wasn't ready to give up just yet. She staggered forward and raised her shovel even higher, still trying to gather herself for that one deadly strike.

Too late.

The shovel slipped from her hands, and her body sagged and pitched forward. She landed facedown in the mound of loose earth that I'd dug up, as though it were a giant pillow she was merely plopping down on. Well, I supposed that was one way to take a dirt nap.

While I caught my breath, I watched and waited. More and more blood poured out from the couple's wounds, but Don and Ethel didn't move or stir. They were as dead as the rest of the folks here were.

When I was sure that they were gone, I retrieved my first knife from the ground, wiped Ethel's blood off the second one, and tucked both of my weapons back up my sleeves. I looked and listened, but the night was still and quiet again. No one was coming to investigate. The cemetery was located off by itself on one of the many mountain ridges that cut through Ashland, and I doubted that the sounds of our fight had been loud enough to attract any attention. Still, I needed to do something with the bodies. I didn't want anyone to know that I had been here tonight, much less whose grave I had been digging up.

I looked at the dwarves' bodies, then down at the open casket.

Don was right. I'd gone to all the trouble to unearth Deirdre Shaw's grave. She wasn't in her casket, so somebody might as well get some use out of it.

I grinned.

And it might as well be me.